I0744270

### Advance Praise for Klara's Journey

*"K.S. Wright nicely contrasts Klara's personal revelations and experiences with the rising conflicts and challenges of her world. Her encounter with demons, rituals, and matters of her own heart ("I don't believe I'm capable of even knowing what love is.") makes for a satisfying contrast between high-octane adventure and psychological development as Klara moves into positions of power she'd never imagined, both personally and as a member of society."*
—MIDWEST BOOK REVIEW

*"Libraries and readers seeking stories that represent the intersection of fantasy, history, romance, and psychological growth will welcome the opportunity to follow Klara on her life-changing journey through a world in flux."*
—MIDWEST BOOK REVIEW

*"In her debut novel, Wright does a masterful job of portraying Klara's journey. The Klara that the reader first meets is guarded and cut off from emotion. After she joins the Keltoi, she begins to open her heart to the possibilities of family and love, though her growing trust proves to be dangerous. Wright also ably develops the rough-hewn Keltoi into distinctive, enjoyable characters. Wright has created an enthralling new series lead, so here's hoping Klara hangs on until the second book."*
–KIRKUS REVIEW

*"A woman's striking metamorphosis and pain drive this compelling debut."*
–KIRKUS REVIEW

*"… a satisfying milieu of discovery and unexpected twists of plot to keep the romance elusive and fresh and the action spirited …"*
— D. DONOVAN, EDITOR,
DONOVAN'S LITERARY SERVICES

# Klara's Journey

Hart & Hind Publishing Company
PO Box 52
Viola, ID 83872
www.hartandhindpc.com

Copyright © 2023 by K. S. Wright.
Map by Chelsea Feenery
Cover and interior design by Damonza

All rights reserved. No part of this book may be reproduced by any mechanical or electronic means, including information storage and retrieval systems, without written permission of the publisher.

Thank you for purchasing an authorized edition of this book. Hart & Hind Publishing Company supports copyright. In 2019, half of all full-time authors earned less than $12,488 annually. Reproducing, scanning, and distributing any part of this book without permission is illegal and further depresses the already low wages received by most authors. Copyright enables Hart & Hind Publishing Company to continue publishing books for every reader. By complying with copyright laws, you are supporting writers, fueling creativity, promoting free speech, encouraging diverse voices, and working to create a vibrant culture.

The text of this book is set in 11-point Adobe Garamond Pro

This is a work of fiction. All characters and events portrayed in this novel are either products of the author's imagination or are used fictitiously. Any similarity to real persons, living or dead, is purely coincidental and not intended by the author.

Library of Congress Control Number: 2022934015

ISBN: 978-1-957910-00-0
EBOOK ISBN: 978-1-957910-01-7

First Edition 2023

Printed in the United States of America

*For my grandmothers,*
*who read everything I write even when it isn't very good.*

# TABLE OF CONTENTS

# KLARA'S JOURNEY

### ✦ THE KENETLON SAGAS ✦
### BOOK 1

## K. S. WRIGHT

# PROLOGUE

TANDING ATOP THE terrace, Waywyrd inhaled deeply, the sea-salted breeze penetrating his lungs. Detecting no sign of his sister, he let out a contented sigh, reveling in the thought of passing a solitary evening. He filled a wine goblet and sank into his favorite chair, absent-mindedly swirling the crimson liquid in his hand, its aroma a sweet assault on his olfactory senses. The view was magnificent, blues that were nearly blinding, the thin division between sea and sky becoming more pronounced as the sun prepared to set.

Hidden from view by the shrub-lined cliffs, the stone-built cottage offered privacy that was unmatched by the other villagers' homes. Whenever he spent time on land, this sea-side cottage was the perfect place to do it. The terrace offered stunning views of the Black Sea. The dazzling splendor of the sunsets was eclipsed only by the majestic ferocity of the storms. He liked nothing better than when the wind whipped up white-capped waves and the surf crashed on the rocks below. Sipping his wine, Waywyrd relished the heavy flavor, rolling it on his tongue.

An evening breeze caused the branches overhanging his secluded home to rustle and sway. Looking across the sea revealed still waters. No wind at all. Annoyed, Waywyrd felt traces of magic in the air. Damn that woman, he thought, out to ruin an otherwise lovely evening.

In the space of a heartbeat, a whirlwind appeared on the veranda, twisting in furious gyre. It dissolved, sending leaves and branches skittering across the flagstones as Pendrwyrd unfurled herself, standing as tall as the staff in her hand. Waywyrd shook his head. The ease with which that woman appeared out of thin air was uncanny, and he did not appreciate the fact that she was standing before him now, blocking the view. With a reluctant sigh, he put down his goblet.

"I've found her!" Pendrwyrd exclaimed. "Unfortunately, I can't get close to her. You'll have to do it."

Waywyrd looked doubtfully at his sister. "You've found her before. And lost her again. And why in the blazes should I have to do it? It's your task."

"The problem is her occupation," Pendrwyrd said, shooting a meaningful glance at the decanter of wine. "Klara's a whore. No respectable woman can openly talk with her without arousing suspicion; they're busy killing men, not bedding them."

"The occupation seems quite appropriate," Waywyrd mused as he filled another goblet and offered it to his sister. "After all, Abnoba offered herself as a prostitute. Besides, you've never been a respectable sort of woman."

Pendrwyrd took the wine and glared at her brother. She was the better wizard and well he knew it. They had matching scars on their faces and gray streaks in their hair as evidence of the first time he truly made her angry. He was eight, she was ten. As an adult he was smart enough not to press her too far.

"Alright," Waywyrd said. "You always were bossy."

"Only because you always drag your bloody feet whenever there's work to do," she snapped.

"Are you sure she's the one?" Waywyrd asked, still hoping to avoid the job. "Could it not be her daughter?"

Pendrwyrd slumped into a chair beside her brother, still holding her staff in the crook of her arm. "She hasn't got a daughter."

"Given her occupation it seems it would just be a matter of time," Waywyrd said.

"No," Pendrwyrd said, "she's too smart for that. I've seen her gathering pennyroyal and it wasn't a small quantity either. There was enough there to keep an entire village from getting pregnant."

"If she won't produce a child, why on earth are we wasting our time with her?" Waywyrd asked. It was one thing to go chasing across nations. It was quite another to go chase across nations for no reason.

"She'll accept a Kelto," Pendrwyrd said with a wry smile. "One came through not long after Lughnasad. He was a tinker who claimed he'd only spend one night in the village. He ended up staying three nights and her employer had a good portion of his silver before he left." She chuckled at that.

Then becoming serious Pendrwyrd added, "The last of the line of Duir are gathered together in Olbia. It's drawing unwanted attention; they cannot remain there. We must send for Nuallan and bring him to meet the others. Ice will be forming on the Danube soon so there isn't much time. They can make preparations for the journey over the winter and set out in the spring with the thaw."

"Ice has never been a problem for me," Waywyrd reminded his sister. "And I don't see why we need Nuallan. He's not King now, never has been, and never will be."

"Nuallan is old and won't relish traveling in the cold regardless of your mastery over water," Pendrwyrd said. "However, he's still loyal to Clan Duir. With him present you'll be more likely to get the others to agree to the expedition. For decades Nuallan has longed to see Thorn claim the Kingship. He's known Thorn since he was a child and will be able to prod him in ways you can't."

"If what you say about Klara is true, she doesn't seem a likely candidate," Waywyrd said. "Nuallan certainly isn't. Thorn left his old life behind long ago, and I thought Ffearn and Karn were—"

Pendrwyrd cut him off. "They are the last of the line of Duir. It will be one of them and it will be her. The *Book of Woe* clearly states:

'THE LAST OF THE ABNOBA'S LINE, THE KENETLO DO ADORE,
INSTALLED AS DRUIDESS, THE LINE OF KINGS SHE DOTH RESTORE.
AS ONE OF ABNOBA'S PROTECTED, SHE DOES EARN HER KEEP,
TO SEE THE RISE AND FALL OF KINGS, LIKE ABNOBA SHE
WILL WEEP.
ELAH DESIRES HER, AND LIKE ABNOBA SHE WILL KILL,
FOR, TO SAVE HER OWN DAUGHTER THERE IS NONE SHE WILL
NOT STILL.'"

Waywyrd was not convinced. "What even makes you think the time is now? How many prophecies are there? Three? Four? One says the line of Duir will be restored, another says kingship will be transferred to Clan Nuin." In the fading light Waywyrd produced a scroll.

Pendrwyrd rolled her eyes. "Your reliance on scrolls is disheartening. You should have learned to memorize the important bits by now."

"I keep them around because you refuse to acknowledge what's actually written on them, choosing to make things up as you go along instead," Waywyrd said.

Smoothing the scroll's parchment, he laid it on the table and set his wine goblet on the farther end to hold it in place. Squinting against the dim light, he read the first prophecy:

> "'Thorn of Oak takes Ash as sons,
> Goddess flees on Ashen mare;
> Sacred three grow as one,
> To Ash, Oak, and Thorn an heir.'"

"That isn't much to go on," Waywyrd said.

"It's enough," Pendrwyrd insisted.

Waywyrd ignored her and continued with the second prophecy:

> "'Draugr fight draugrs
> In a battle both lost and won,
> Oak falls ere he greets a son.
> As father of Thorn's heirs,
> Ash rises to take its place,
> Becoming King of the Kenetlo race.'"

"This is equally ambiguous," Waywyrd said.

"It's clear enough to me that there will be an heir to Clan Duir, but that kingship will be transferred to Clan Nuin." Pendrwyrd replied.

"Or," Waywyrd countered, "Thorn won't produce heirs and Brawn becomes King anyway. That certainly seems more likely. And Thorn's father fell in battle before Thorn was born, so it might not be a reference to Thorn's child at all, but to Thorn himself because he's already named his nephews as his heirs. Brawn stood against Thorn in the last election and two of the clans still support him whereas Thorn has lost the support he once had, so we needn't bother ourselves."

"There are other prophecies," Pendrwyrd reminded him.

"Oh yes," Waywyrd agreed eagerly. "There is this one:

> 'FOR HIS SINS ELAH MUST ATONE,
> BUT HE CANNOT BE KILLED BY ONE,
> WHO IS MAID, MOTHER, OR CRONE.'

"Which makes me wonder why you've got us looking for a woman? It seems a man is necessary to do this job," Waywyrd said.

"It's in the *Book of Woe*," Pendrwyrd replied with a sigh. "I just recited the relevant passage for you. A daughter of Abnoba's line will do the killing."

Waywyrd frowned and signed heavily. "The *Book of Woe* speaks of a woman who produces a daughter, but the prophecy regarding the battle of the draugrs speaks of a son."

Pointing an accusing finger at Pendrwyrd, he continued, "And you tell me Klara is capable of avoiding pregnancy altogether, so she will produce neither son nor daughter. The final prophecy says Elah will not fall at the hands of a woman, which means we don't need her at all; we should be looking for a man. My point is they can't all be right. Then there is the prophecy demons stand by: what was the name of the woman who wrote that?"

"Beatrice Nutter," Pendrwyrd replied.

"Nutter is right!" Waywyrd exclaimed. "The woman was barking mad! Have you read that thing? It says:

> 'THE KING TAKES A LOVER WHEN BROTHERS ARE LOVERS AND
> LOVERS OF THE KING'S LOVER; AND THE KING'S LOVER LOVES A
> BROTHER. WHEN THE LOVER OF BROTHERS IS THE KING'S LOVER
> AND NEITHER MAID NOR MOTHER SHE BECOMES DEFENDER OF
> MAIDS AND AVENGER OF MOTHERS. THEN THE KING'S LOVER, AS

THE LOVER OF BROTHERS BECOMES A MOTHER OF BROTHERS. AND WHEN THE KING'S LOVER BECOMES A MOTHER OF BROTHERS, THE KING BECOMES FATHER OF A DAUGHTER. BROTHER, OH BROTHER!'

Waywyrd finished, breathless. "If that woman is even half as accurate as you claim she is, we happen to be short a pair of brothers. Or multiple pairs of brothers as the case may be. We have nephews, uncles, and cousins, but no brothers."

Pendrwyrd dismissed his comments with a wave of her goblet. "We'll just have to make do with what we have."

"Prophecies don't work that way!" Waywyrd shouted. "All the pieces must be in place."

"You're deliberately being contrary," Pendrwyrd said. She drained her goblet and set it on the table with a deliberate thunk. "I'm going to establish a residence in the Urals not far from the village where Klara resides so I can keep an eye on her this winter. You need to collect Nuallan and deposit him with the others in Olbia. They must be on the road before the full Ash Moon. Once they are under way, you must get her to agree to join them."

"This is mad," Waywyrd said. "Nothing here makes a lick of sense; you have nothing to go on."

"Woman's intuition," Pendrwyrd said. "I find it to be highly accurate."

"Yours or the Nutter's?" Waywyrd chided.

"Both," Pendrwyrd said, then she slipped into a flutter of leaves and vanished.

# CHAPTER 1

# A STRANGER

K LARA'S EYES FLUTTERED, admitting nothing but blackness. The grass stuffing of her pallet had long since been squashed flat, offering no comfort at all. Now, her hip and shoulder ached from being pressed against the ground. Abandoning thoughts of sleep, she rose, intending to hunt before the alehouse opened for business.

Today was the Vernal Equinox. Everyone in the surrounding villages was celebrating, so the alehouse had been full the past two nights. Serik had not purchased enough supplies to make it through the holiday and the last of the mutton was put into a stew yesterday. If there was to be meat with the meal tonight, she would have to kill it. Collecting her bow and slinging her quiver across her back, she slipped out the back door and disappeared into the forest.

The alehouse had a reputation for serving the finest meals around. It had another equally well-known reputation for ignoring the local magistrate's ban on prostitution. Those two factors combined meant Serik did considerable business. Klara cooked the meals and served the men, with food or on her back, it mattered little. And while Serik's business made him a wealthy man, he did not share his riches. Unable to afford either horse or house, she was at the mercy of men like Serik and expected to earn her keep.

Worn thin by years of use, Klara's dress did little by way of keeping the breeze out and her in. Catching her golden braids in its grasp, the wind set them to bobbing at her back. Shivering against the chill, she made her way deeper into the forest. Upon reaching a creek, she climbed into a tree that afforded a good view of the stream and waited patiently as the forest awoke. Something was bound to water here.

The time needed to pull an arrow from her quiver, nock it, and then draw her bow might mean the difference between meat on the table or beans for supper. In anticipation of game, she pulled an arrow from her quiver and held it nocked at the ready.

As the forest came to life, birds began their morning songs. The gray dawn gave way to golden clouds with pale pink hues and finally hints of blue. Below her the brush began to rustle. A roe deer cautiously approached the stream. Klara drew her bow and waited. The deer had only presented her its hindquarters, which was a poor shot. After it finished drinking, it turned and stood quartered away from her. She loosed her arrow, which sunk deep into the animal's lungs. The deer jumped, ran thirty paces, and collapsed.

Climbing down from the tree, Klara went to collect her game. The deer was a doe. She pulled her knife from its sheaf, split the doe's belly open, fished her hands into the body cavity far enough to cut the wind pipe, and extracted the steaming innards as one jiggly mass. Lying amongst the offal were twin fawns.

"Absent gods," Klara said, rolling the gut pile away from her. "That arrow claimed three lives, not one."

This early in the year the bucks had yet to regrow their antlers so it was difficult to tell the sexes apart. Given a choice, she would have preferred not to shoot a doe. Cursing Serik for not purchasing more meat, she slung the field-dressed carcass over her shoulders and made her way back to the alehouse.

Built in a clearing alongside the road, the alehouse was a ramshackle two-room structure. Serik's house was nearly as large as the tavern, but much better kept. Both buildings were stone and timber construction with heavily thatched roofs. During the day, the alehouse doors were flung open to let the light in and the smoke out. Two oblong tables, each flanked by a pair of benches, filled the room. Another bench lined the front wall. In the center of the building, planks lay across casks of wine and ale. This formed a long bar that not only served to separate the alehouse's patrons from the hearth where she cooked, but kept drunkards from falling into the fire. There was no doubt in her mind that all those seats would be full this evening.

After hanging the deer out back, she went to wash up. Unfastening her belt, she shrugged the threadbare dress off her shoulders, revealing the ample curves the men so greatly desired, if only for a night. Long ago, she chose comfort over fashion, eschewing the fitted tunics and breeches sported by the bands of warrior maidens. Instead she wore the plain, baggy dress, belted at the waist, favored among women who had given up warrior life and settled down.

Klara dampened a corner of her dress and washed the blood from her hands and neck. Golden braids bobbed in the sunlight as she worked the cloth over the back of her head, taking care to make sure no blood was in her hair. When her skin was scrubbed pink, she pinned the braids so they encircled her head like a wreath. Most Skolts preferred wearing their hair loose, but long hair was bothersome, so she kept hers up and out of the way while she cooked and served.

Owning a single dress left her with a dilemma, either she washed it now or wore it all day, crusty and blood-stained. The men cared little about her cleanliness or attire; they preferred her bare. In truth, she preferred nudity herself, though not when it encouraged groping hands. After rinsing out the dress, she hung it on the line to dry in the morning sun and went inside to cook wearing naught but what the Goddess had gifted her.

Inside the smoky room, Klara made bread and cut up winter vegetables to be roasted with the venison, courtesy of this morning's hunt. With the bread on to bake and the meat and vegetables roasting, she put the damp dress back on. There was no need to give the men frequenting the tavern any more encouragement than the ale already provided.

Soon the room became boisterous, full of redheaded bachelors lacking nearby kin and eager to celebrate the holiday. Klara served food and beer while skillfully dodging the hands of men as she made her rounds of the room. Her curves were too great a temptation for them, which was not helped by the fact that the thin cloth of her dress left little to the imagination.

Toward the middle of the evening the tall, dark-haired foreigner, entered the alehouse, dashing her hopes that his absence in the intervening nights was an indication that he was just passing through the area. He was dressed entirely in blue and carried a walking stick with him, though she detected no sign of a limp. A nasty scar ran down the side of his face ending in gray streaks of hair at both ends, temple and beard. Despite the gray in his hair, he appeared to be in the prime of life. His tunic was plain, giving him a dull, unobtrusive appearance. But, given the quality of the garment, even without appliqués or embroidery, she knew he was no pauper.

When he had dined at the alehouse before, he held himself apart, refusing to interact with the Skolts. She had felt him watching her the previous nights, too, but he never asked for the pleasure of her company and left as soon as his meal was finished. That was odd. Most men who took a meal lingered to talk. Klara felt certain she needed to keep an eye on him.

Approaching his table, Klara asked, "What'll you be having tonight?"

"Ale and supper," the stranger replied. Before he could speak further, the man sitting opposite him reached out and squeezed her bottom. Swatting his hands away, she slipped behind the bar to dish up the food.

Klara returned with a platter and placed the food before him. "I saw you in here before but you didn't stay long. If you're still here that means you aren't just traveling through."

"I'm visiting my sister." The stranger tore off a bit of crusty bread and gave his meal an appreciative glance. "I didn't think you'd remember me. We never spoke more than a moment or two."

"With those streaks of gray in your hair and beard, you'd be hard to forget," Klara said. "And you didn't try grabbing my bottom. That's worthy of notice right there. This is the third meal you've taken here in a fortnight. Either your sister isn't much of a cook or you're looking for other entertainment."

The stranger laughed. "Cooking has never rated high on my sister's list of priorities."

Well, that was hardly unusual. Fighting and horse breeding generally ranked higher than domestic responsibilities. Rather than rebuke him, she said, "If you're to be frequenting the place, I'd best know your name."

"I go by Waywyrd," the man replied.

One of the regulars, Erasyl, pulled her into his lap, cutting short her conversation. His red beard tickled her cheek as he whispered in her ear, "I've got silver in my pocket that says you can make me a happy man."

"Erasyl, it doesn't take much to make you happy," Klara said, much to the delight of the other men, who roared with laughter.

The laughter continued as she led him past the bar. Erasyl fumbled in his purse for the proper coinage and passed it to Serik whose bulky biceps flexed as he received the payment. Serik's gray eyes flashed like flint against a striker. He did not mind how the men used her, so long as they refrained from misusing her. Bruised and battered, her valued dropped. A quiet man, Serik seldom needed words to get his point across.

Satisfied that Erasyl had received the unspoken warning, Klara pulled aside the goat-skin curtain covering the entry way of a small room partitioned off by the hearth. It was where she slept and where she serviced the clientele with silver enough to purchase her sex. Serik took most of the money, but she was given a roof over her head and afforded some manner of protection. Not a quarter of an hour later, her task complete, she resumed her duties in the tavern while Erasyl returned to his seat, a broad grin on his peasant face.

Pitcher in hand, Klara made the rounds of the room again and asked Waywyrd if he wanted more ale, but he declined. Having finished his meal, he paid and left. His gaze lingered on her before passing through the door. It was odd behavior and a little unnerving.

The tavern had emptied and Klara was sweeping up when Waywyrd returned, floating in on a cool breeze, and ordered another ale. She felt him watching her as she cleaned and Serik counted the money in the cashbox.

Once she had finished and put the broom away, she went to sit opposite him. "Not many men sit in an empty tavern."

"I was hoping we could talk privately," Waywyrd said.

"We can do anything you want privately," Klara replied. "But it all costs money."

"Really, I'd just like to talk," Waywyrd insisted.

At that moment Serik shouted across the room. "Klara, be sure he leaves. I don't want any trouble like we had before. And make sure he pays." Then Serik disappeared out the back door, heading for home.

Waywyrd sighed and reached for his purse. "How much?"

Klara told him and he reluctantly parted with the silver. She rose, intending to lead him to the room in back.

"That's not necessary," Waywyrd said, "here is fine." Puzzled, Klara wondered just what this man was after, but consented to sit opposite him again.

"My sister sent me for you," Waywyrd began.

Klara cut him off with a sharp wave of her hand. "If that's what you're after the price is double. Threesomes, foursomes, and moresomes all cost extra." This would be her first brother-sister combo and there was no way she was going to do it for the regular price.

Waywyrd coughed and cleared his throat, looking uncomfortable. "We are seeking a cook, not a whore."

"Oh," Klara said, her hands dropping to the table. "I just thought…" She paused, and then added forcefully, "You still have to pay. Serik won't believe you just wanted to talk."

"That's fine, keep the money," Waywyrd said, seeming somewhat relieved. "A party of Keltoi will pass this way around Beltene. They are traveling to their homeland in the Abnoba Mountains and need someone who can cook and hunt. My sister says you're capable of both. If you've been the one preparing my meals, I can vouch for your cooking."

Beltene was still moons away. The Skoloti did not celebrate Belenus or observe his holy days. The only thing they worshiped was their horses. Why not wait to hire a cook until they were ready to travel? She shook her head. They likely expected more from a hired cook than just cooking.

"So you want me to cook and hunt," Klara scoffed. "And at every village we pass through I get hired out as a whore; makes for a handy way to finance your journey. I'd still have to endure as much feasting, fighting, and fornicating as I do here, plus I'd be sleeping rough and dog-tired after a long day of walking."

"I do not expect that will be the case," Waywyrd said. "They are looking for someone to sign on as an equal in the company, not as a whore. You would share in the cooking, hunting, and other chores just as the other members of the party will. It seemed prudent to take on another member since there are already six in the party and seven is a luckier number."

"And there would be no sex?" Klara asked, looking for confirmation.

"Not unless you want it," Waywyrd said. "Then I expect there would be a number in the party who'd be happy to oblige." He was trying to hide a smile and failing miserably.

"How do I know this isn't a trap?" Klara asked. "You could be making the whole story up just to get me to leave here with you. What's your role in all of this?"

"You have no way of knowing if this is entrapment," Waywyrd agreed. "But you won't be riding off with me tonight. If you are agreeable, they'll meet you here. As for my role, I am a wizard enlisted to aid them in their journey, rather unwillingly, I might add."

"A wizard seems to be a far-fetched claim," Klara said. She had seen plenty of road-side charlatans in her time at the alehouse and was never impressed.

Waywyrd held up his flagon, which still held a small measure of ale and blew across its base. The ale froze and frost crept up the flagon's side. Then he turned it upside down. Not a drop of liquid fell from the lip. Righting the flagon, Waywyrd snapped his fingers. The ale was liquid again and all that remained of the frost was dew-like droplets running down the flagon's sides and dripping onto the table.

Klara took the flagon from him and considered the ale in silence. She took a sip, then wiped her hand across her mouth. "Well, I suppose it wouldn't hurt to meet them."

Waywyrd smiled, moved the walking stick to the crook of his arm, and proffered his hand. She took it and shook, feeling callouses on his rough skin. Then she walked him to the door. The man was utterly mad. Was there really was a party destined for the Abnoba Mountains looking for a cook? That seemed almost as unfathomable as his claim to be a wizard. Still, the trick with the ale was impressive and traveling to the Goddess's home was bound to be more interesting than working for Serik.

## CHAPTER 2

# MEETING THE KELTOI

RINKLING HER NOSE against the reek of unwashed men and stale beer, Klara knelt in the hot, dusty tavern, wishing she could be anywhere else. A quarter-season had passed since Waywyrd came to her with his offer, but there had been no sign of him since. Or the party of travelers he mentioned. That annoyed her and she was mad at herself for giving in to false hope.

Pausing, she wiped sweat from her brow with the back of her arm, then plunged her wet hands back into the soapy water. With the men working in the fields or busy with new foals, the days were slow at the alehouse. Serik had gone into Zlatoust for supplies, leaving her to tend the bar and scrub it down as best she could.

The only patron in the room was Arman, a dirty old man with an even dirtier mind. She felt him staring at her bottom, as she, on hands and knees, scrubbed the worn wooden bench that lined the front wall. A crusty mess, left by a patron unable to hold his drink, had gone unnoticed the night before. One of many such messes she cleaned up during her time at the alehouse.

"How 'bout it, Love?" Arman pleaded. Klara did not need to look at him to know he still sat at the bar, a post he had occupied for the better part of the morning, nursing his beer.

"Arman, I already told you I can't leave the room unattended." Then for good measure, she added, "I'd be fired." This was not his first attempt to get her to take him to the little room in back where she serviced the clientele when Serik was there to keep watch over the bar.

"Who said anything 'bout leavin' the room? There's no one 'ere, is there?" Arman remonstrated. "And you wouldn't want me tellin' Serik that you was to turn down a payin' customer, now would ya?"

Klara scrubbed at the mess a couple more times. The last of it finally came loose and she wiped the bench clean. Exasperated, she relented, "Take your trousers off and get up on the table." As Arman moved to do so, she waved to him. "No, not that one; it's got a leg that needs mending. Use the other one."

She hated servicing Arman, he was old and wrinkly. What was left of his hair was white and stuck out from his head. He was missing teeth and his breath stank. Still, she needed the money.

The sight of Arman's scrawny frame laying across the table, trousers around his ankles, evoked pity and revulsion in equal measure. He was as stiff as he was likely to get so she hitched up her skirt and climbed on top. She was already hot and sweaty from scrubbing the benches. Since Arman always insisted she do all the work, she would be drenched in sweat before he was finished. As she worked him, the table began to gently thud against the floor. That was likely the reason she did not hear the party of strangers arrive.

Arman had loosened the top of her dress so he could watch her bosom bounce. As the strangers entered the alehouse, they were afforded a view of her supple, round breasts set aflight by the rhythmic motions she employed.

The party comprised six Keltoi. It was unusual to have Keltoi in these parts, but who was she to question them? After all, prostitution was illegal and here she was caught in the act. For their part, the Keltoi had mixed reactions to the situation. She read disgust on some faces; others simply gawked.

The newcomers appeared to be travel-weary souls, wearing plain, practical tunics over their trousers, the clothing lacking the embroidery and appliqués common to Skolt dress. However, a pair of younger Keltoi took more care in their adornment. Unlike the others, their tunics were shorter and embroidered at the collar with silver thread. One wore blue, the other wore green. That pair might have money and she intended to earn a goodly portion of it before they left.

Her voice husky from exertion, she announced to the company, "It'll be a minute more, then I can take your orders. I expect it'll be ales all around."

"I'll have what he's having." The dark-haired, blue-clad Kelto stepped forward and nodded toward Arman, still prostrate beneath her on the table. The Kelto's bristly beard suggested it was stubble from yesterday's shave. A slight natural wave weaved through his black hair which fell just below his collar, giving it the appearance of being often tussled and seldom combed.

Stepping forward, his green-clad companion said, "Make that a double!" He was the only brunette in the party and the only one with green eyes. Thin braids on either side of his head kept his hair away from his face, the rest of his hair he wore loose. He was free of a beard, but his moustache needed trimming. The pair had easy smiles, suggesting affable natures. Klara liked them immediately.

"Do we pay now or later for the show?" the blue-clad Kelto quipped. His companion was near to laughing, but in the background the other Keltoi were averting their eyes.

"I cannot complete with them watching," Arman bellowed, his cheeks as ruddy as the beets she served for supper last night.

Sizing up the situation, Klara addressed the pair of young Keltoi, "Gentlemen, it appears there isn't going to be a show, but if you'll kindly wait outside, I'll be with you as soon as I finish here."

Once the room was empty and the door closed, Arman issued a satisfied grunt, signaling that he had ejaculated. He pulled up his trousers and reclaimed his seat at the bar. Klara let her skirt down and tucked her breasts back into her dress. Outside she heard raised voices and paused, her hand resting on the door.

"I won't have…that, as a member of my company!" This came from a strong, firm voice. It was the voice of one who was used to speaking his mind, likely the leader of the group.

"You said I was to choose the seventh member of the company, and I have. You must trust me on this." Klara was surprised to recognize Waywyrd's voice. He had not entered the alehouse with the others and she wondered if wizard's intuition had encouraged him to remain outside. Now, she feared her actions may have jeopardized any chance to join the expedition he told her about.

The first voice spoke again, "This is what happens when a wizard decides to get involved. Did you not look at him? The man has seen too many winters to be of any use to this company."

"I did not send you here for the man," Waywyrd snapped. "I sent you for the woman!"

At hearing that, Klara put on a smile and opened the door. As the Keltoi filed passed her, re-entering the dimly lit tavern, she noticed that the party was quite tall; it appeared that all of them were as tall as she was, or taller.

"Since we're here, we might as well have a decent meal," a balding Kelto said as he pulled out a bench and sat himself at one of the tables. Being dressed entirely in black, he made an imposing figure. A rim of collar-length, bushy black hair encircled his balding crown, blending with his beard. He was fit but carried more pounds around the middle than his companions. There was no doubt in her mind that he could end a fight. She hoped he was not the quarrelsome type given to starting them.

"And a round of ale," the pair of younger Keltoi said in unison as they joined their balding companion.

The company's leader grudgingly dug in his purse for the proper coinage and paid for the meal. Klara hastened to serve the ale and prepare the food. While standing at the bar, filling a platter with a traditional plowman's lunch, she felt the eyes of the younger Keltoi upon her. Their attention followed her as she moved about the room. In her line of work she had few Keltoi, but those who visited her were more considerate than other foreigners in bed. Truth be told, they were better than most Skolts, always paying generously for their dalliances.

Arman pulled her thoughts back to the present. "I'll have another," he said as he placed his coppers on the counter.

"Aren't you forgetting something?" Klara asked and tapped the bar next to his coins.

"I shou'd no' have to pay," Arman protested. "I was interrupted."

Klara looked him squarely in the eye. "You do have to pay, interruptions or no."

Arman grunted and put the rest of the money on the counter. Klara swiped it up and took it to the cashbox, pocketed her share, and brought him the ale. Then she gathered up the platter and carried it to the table where Waywyrd and the company of Keltoi sat.

With a playful light in his eye, the young dark-haired Kelto winked at her as she set the tray on the table and eagerly reached for his share of the meal. His companions attacked the platter with equal gusto. Now that food was set before them, Waywyrd called her to his side and banged his staff against the floor to garner their attention.

"Gentlemen," Waywyrd said, "I'd like to introduce Klara. She is an excellent cook and possesses many of the qualities needed for a long journey." The announcement was greeted by skepticism by all but the two young Keltoi. Then Waywyrd turned to her. "Klara, I'd like you to meet Thorn, leader of the company."

The Kelto he indicated was dark and brooding. Long black locks fell to his shoulders. His beard was neatly trimmed, a distinction that set him apart from his companions. She admired his well-muscled chest and arms. The gray tunic he wore was clean, but worn and peppered with singes. From this she surmised that he labored as a blacksmith. The manner in which he held himself indicated that he clearly knew his own mind and did not often look to the opinions of others. On his belt was a dagger which appeared to be of fine quality. His eyes, dark and piercing, were sizing her up, just has she had done to him. At last he said, "Have you any skill with weapons?"

Klara held his gaze. "I'm fair with a bow. But I find it better not to get into positions where I'd need to use it in the first place."

Thorn nodded, but whether it was in affirmation she did not know. There was something in the way his eyes followed her that left her feeling uneasy. Not lust but something just as intense, as if he were trying to see more than just her skin.

Waywyrd continued the introductions, gesturing around the table. "The balding fellow in black is Ruis, our guard. Next to him is Bardus, who has some medical training. This is Nuallan, and those two," he said, pointing at the pair of young Keltoi whose mouths were full of food, "are Ffearn and Karn."

"Which is which?" Klara asked.

"It don't really matter because they're never seen apart," Bardus said as he swiped another hard-boiled egg from the platter.

The dark-haired, blue-clad Kelto quaffed his ale, put down the empty flagon, and rose to address her. "I am Karn, and I believe we have a bit of business to discuss away from this lot." Because he was taller than his companions, like Skolt men, Klara needed to look up in order to meet his gaze. He winked, flashed her a playful smile and reached to take her arm.

"Sit down, you fool," Thorn bellowed. "We have real business to discuss." Karn glowered at the elder Kelto, but wordless sat.

Once Karn was seated, Thorn said, "We travel to Kenetlon, our homeland; the way is long and perilous. The principal city, Duirness, was laid to waste by war. The city and the surrounding lands were overrun by demons and many of the people fled. For years the city and its mines have lain abandoned. We are simple tradesmen who intend to resettle our ancestral lands. Waywyrd insisted we take on a seventh member of the company for luck. It seems this is where you come in. If you cannot fend for yourself in the wilds, you should not join us. You told me you were good with a bow. Can you ride?"

"Aye, I can ride," Klara replied. It was an unnecessary question. All Skolts rode.

From the direction of Ffearn and Karn, she heard snickers. Under their breath one of them said, "We saw how well she rode when we walked in," but she did not know which one owned the remark.

Anger flared in her cheeks and she turned on Waywyrd. "I'm not signing up to be their comfort-wench. When you came to me you said I'd not be a whore. You said there would be some cooking and they would need the use of my bow. You said I'd be an equal in the party. That's why I agreed, to get away from this godforsaken life."

"Calm down, calm down." Waywyrd's attempts to soothe her failed. Klara swiped his flagon from the table and tossed the contents in his face. Dumbfounded and a bit dismayed, she stepped back. He had enjoyed the splash.

Thorn stood. "There will be no sex." His voice was firm; however, he was not looking at her or Waywyrd. He was staring at Karn and Ffearn, who appeared somewhat uncomfortable under his gaze.

"Unless I decide I want it," Klara said, returning the empty flagon to the table.

"What?" Thorn exclaimed, turning in her direction.

Klara leaned around Waywyrd to look at Thorn. He seemed shocked by the notion that she might be willing to engage in the act at all, but it was her trade and she had to earn a living somehow. What did he expect from a whore?

"Unless I decide I want it," she repeated. "I'll not be your whore, but neither will I play the role of the Holy Virgin. I'm not saying there will be sex, but if there is, it will be on my terms."

Waywyrd cleared his throat and wiped the ale from his eyes, which gleamed with the unmistakable light of mischief. "Now that's settled. This journey will be most amusing for me and very good for you. You should sign the contract and bring us another round so we can imbibe while you gather your belongings. It appears my flagon has been emptied for me."

From the look on Thorn's face, it clearly was not settled, but both he and Klara let it be. She refilled their flagons while Nuallan unfolded the thin leather contract. Judging from the head of gray hair, stiff and wiry as his beard, he was at least a decade older than his companions.

Nuallan squinted at the leather, then at her, before speaking. "Your mount, food, and any other necessary items will be provided by the company during the journey in exchange for an equal share in the work. In addition, you will receive one-seventh of the profits, if there are any, which is unlikely. If you satisfactorily complete your duties, at the end of the journey you will be given an opportunity to buy the horse outright."

It seemed agreeable to Klara, so she carved her mark into the bit of leather next to the title "Luck Bringer." In all her life, she never had enough money to own a horse. If she plied her trade in the villages they passed through and was able to keep the whole of her profits, she might be able to afford the horse at the end. It looked like her luck was about to change for the better.

Nuallan gathered up the leather and folded it. Placing it in a pocket he said, "Now that everything is in order we can be on our way. Run along and fetch your things."

"Everything is not in order," Klara said, devising an impromptu test for her new employer. "You still owe the house for the second round and I need to clean up this mess." She had charged them amply at the onset, so additional coinage was unnecessary. She just wanted to know what measure of a man Thorn was.

In an imposing gesture, Thorn stepped toward her and pulled the purse from his belt. "You are a member of my company; what concern of yours are the affairs of the alehouse now?"

Klara held out her hand to accept the coins. Evidently, he was an honest one. "I see no reason to start a journey knowing the locals will be hunting you down as common thieves. Ruthless vigilantes patrol these parts. Serik hires them owing to his inability to take his complaints to the local magistrate. Illegally running a house of ill-repute leaves him without recourse for petty theft or other injustices."

"And I quite agree," Waywyrd added, leaning on his staff, looking amused and still quite soggy. "Better if we don't draw attention to ourselves."

Thorn shot a quick glance at Waywyrd but held his tongue. Leaving them to drink, she gathered up the dishes, washed them, wiped down the tables, and tidied the kitchen. Then she swept under their table and returned the broom to its place. Having restored the alehouse to order, she poured Arman another beer.

Her tasks complete, Klara stepped behind the goat-skin curtain to gather her belongings while her new employer and his company headed outside. Undergarments were items she typically eschewed, but she took a moment to don her drawers and bandeau. Since she owned so little, it only took a moment to collect her possessions before returning to the bar. It was empty, save for Arman.

Klara paused, hand on the door, and looked at Arman over her shoulder. "Watch the alehouse for me until Serik gets back." Then as an after-thought she added, "And tell him I quit."

## CHAPTER 3
# THE JOURNEY BEGINS

KLARA JOINED THE company of Keltoi outside in the summer sun. Most of them already sat upon their mounts. Bardus stood in the alehouse's yard flanked by a palomino mare and a buckskin gelding. His mane, tied at the nape of his neck, was as thick and black as the buckskin's. A hint of a smile was visible beneath his beard as he passed her the reins of the sturdy but scruffy-looking gelding.

She scratched the gelding's neck, drinking in his earthy scent while Bardus checked one of the mare's hooves. Skolts were horse-people and though she had never been wealthy enough to own a horse, she felt a kinship with the beasts. Content at having made the buckskin's acquaintance, she put her silver comb and brush in the saddlebag along with her coin purse and a small bundle of herbs. After tying her quiver to the saddle, she slung her bow across her back and mounted.

"Where's the rest of your gear?" Bardus asked, gentleness in his voice as he dropped the mare's hoof. From the handling of his mount, she suspected his medical knowledge might extend to treating beasts as well. It was a trait she admired.

"This is all I have," Klara said, kicking her heels and sending the gelding trotting to catch up with the rest of the company. All that she owned could be worn on her body or held in her hand. She lacked even a bedroll. The blanket she used each night was property of Serik, so must be left behind.

A slight breeze tickled the leaves of the deciduous trees and caused the smaller boughs of the evergreens to dip and sway. Dotted among the trees were clearings where farmers tried eking out a living or the occasional cabin of a woodsman. Traveling was easy because the road was in good repair and wide enough to ride two abreast. Each bend in the road offered new sights and her heart grew lighter the farther from the alehouse she got.

When she had her fill of taking in the landscape, she turned her attention to her companions, trying to pick up bits of conversation. It seemed they talked all the time but never of anything of consequence. They had not mentioned the Abnoba Mountains once and that was where Waywyrd originally claimed they were going. Was Waywyrd off in the head? Or was there was something they were not telling her? Both options seemed equally likely.

As she listened, Klara occasionally heard bits about mines and forges, or long-forgotten great halls, and a place called Silver Fountains. She had little interest in those things—her part was simply "Luck Bringer." It was an odd title to put on a contract but a far better title than local whore. So long as they made no more demands on her than cooking and hunting, she did not care where they went or what they called her.

Her traveling companions were a merry bunch who passed jokes among themselves and often broke into song. They knew an endless array of songs, most of which were of questionable taste. Thorn and Waywyrd rode at the head of the column either in silence or earnest conversation, but never, it seemed, engaging in the idle chit-chat and constant banter of their companions. Bringing up the rear, she observed the company, intending to decipher what manner of man each Kelto was and learn the pecking order they had established among themselves.

Bardus was kind and gentle, inasmuch as Keltoi can be, often laughing at his companions' jokes or telling his own. When it came to their bawdy songs, Bardus had the best voice among them. The entire company was outfitted with swords and daggers, though she doubted either Bardus or Nuallan were the kind to have ever used one.

Nuallan had the look and feel of an accountant about him. The brown tunic and matching trousers he wore gave him an appearance that seemed as bland as his personality. Yet, she sensed that under that ordinary affect there was shrewdness. Judging from their meeting at the alehouse, he obviously handled the contracts and probably the finances of the company.

Next in the column were Ffearn and Karn. Those two seemed more like a single unit, sharing an intimate camaraderie that suggested they were brothers. They were close in age and appearance, though Ffearn seemed to be the younger of the two. After the pair completed an overly long recitation of a very dirty poem, she decided they were the jesters of the group but suspected there was more to them than that. They got along with the rest of the company, all of whom were older than they, though their companions tolerated their antics with the occasional mild irritation one might expect of older dogs tolerating a passel of puppies.

Like her, Karn wore a bow slung across his back and a quiver of arrows tied to his saddle. Sitting his horse like it was part of him, he was at greater ease in his saddle than his companions. Riding well was a skill Skolts admired and one which Keltoi seldom excelled at.

Leading a string of three heavily laden pack horses was Ruis. In addition to its other burdens, one of the horses carried three long spears with hafts of ash, though the tips were safely bound in leather. Which of the Keltoi were spear-bearers? Occasionally, Ruis tossed a remark back to the company that followed but did not fully take part in their constant conversation. He seemed to be a bit more serious that the rest, so whether his absence from the conversation was by accident or design, she could not guess.

Losing interest in her companions and their songs, Klara returned to examining her surroundings. Seeing the tunnels of a rabbit warren on the bank above the road, she reined in her horse. The others continued, their song becoming softer as the words drifted back to her on the wind. She unslung her bow and nocked an arrow. Her steed was well-trained and stood still while the sounds of her companions and their horses receded. Soon one rabbit, and then another, peeked out of their holes. Still she waited. By the time the first rabbit was fully out of its burrow and nibbling the grass on the verge, three more appeared.

Klara drew her bow, aimed, and waited to exhale. As she did, she released the arrow. Her aim was true. The rabbit issued one short scream before it expired. The arrow had pierced it through its heart and lungs, pinning it to the ground. She dismounted and was collecting her kill when her companions came charging around the bend, swords drawn.

Seeing there was no fight, they reined in their horses and sheathed their swords. Ruis looked down at her and shouted, "What in the Goddess's name were you doing, lass? You scared us near to death."

Klara held up the rabbit and said, "Getting dinner." She smiled up at Ruis with mischief in her eye. "There's no need to be scared. It's just a wee rabbit. As you can see, I've protected you."

Ruis laughed heartily. "Aye, I'll fear no more rabbits so long as you're about." Then he looked about the company and said, "Come on, lads, let's get turned around and pointed the right direction."

Waywyrd and Thorn hung back as the others made their way down the road. Klara tied the rabbit to her saddle and mounted her steed. They fell in step beside her, knees nearly brushing owing to the narrowness of the road.

"That was a foolhardy thing you did," Thorn said, looking forward and not at her.

"I don't see how? Everyone needs to eat and one rabbit won't feed us all," Klara said, irritation prickling her spine.

Waywyrd admonished her, "You are not on your own here. There is the rest of the company to think of. You gave us a fright." The tone was kind but firm.

"I can fend for myself," Klara said, her irritation growing.

"I take it you are used to traveling alone," Thorn said. Despite all her efforts, she remained unable to read this man's emotions and that vexed her. Inability to discern someone's intent was a dangerous shortcoming in her line of work.

"When you are with a group," Waywyrd said, "especially a heavily armed, impetuous group, you must think how your actions will cause them to act, or react. This time there was no danger, but in the future that might not be so."

"So you're telling me I can't hunt," Klara said incredulously. "I thought that was why you hired me."

"No," Waywyrd said. "We're telling you that you must think. There will be time for hunting. But hunting must be done at designated times. We do not want you to do anything that will bring attention to the company on the road."

"Nor do we want horses or men injured racing down the road to save you from a rabbit," Thorn added. Then he encouraged his horse into a trot and resumed his place at the head of the column. Waywyrd stayed behind with her.

"You should know that Kenetlo do not customarily eat rabbit," Waywyrd said as he fidgeted with his staff. "They consider the animal sacred. To them it's a sign of abundance and fertility. Generally, rabbits are only eaten when no other game is available."

Klara sighed and slumped in her saddle. "I'm not doing very well as it comes to making good impressions."

"I think you've made a better impression than you realize," Waywyrd said, "especially with Karn and Ffearn." Klara glared at him, assuming he was referring to the incident at the alehouse.

Waywyrd hastened to add, "That's not what I mean." He took a breath and continued, "You've proven you can handle Thorn, a lot better than they can for that matter. You got him to sit back down and wait for you at the alehouse, no one expected him to do that. And you've just proven yourself with a bow. A rabbit is not an easy target, as you know."

"It was standing still," Klara replied.

Waywyrd winked at her. "They don't know that."

"And why would Ffearn and Karn care how I handle Thorn?" Klara asked.

"Thorn is their uncle," Waywyrd said, "and they admire him greatly. I don't think either of them has ever stood up to him the way you did." This confirmed Klara's notion that the two younger Keltoi were brothers.

"What I don't understand," Klara said, "is why you chose me to join a company of Keltoi heading off into the wilds."

"You were chosen because you're good with men," Waywyrd said. Klara drew in breath, preparing to give him another tongue-lashing, but he hastily continued. "In your line of work you are used to tough customers and all manner of situations. You've learned to think on your feet and stand your ground. You impressively managed Thorn twice today and that's a feat not easily accomplished. He will need you before the end and hopefully will learn to trust you along the way." As Waywyrd said that, they rode into a small clearing with a stream, rushing cold and clear along the far edge.

"I reckon we have about an hour's worth of light left," Thorn said as he dismounted. "This is a good place to make camp."

Ruis dismounted and led his horse toward Klara. Upon reaching her, he said, "Well, Luck Bringer, technically it's my turn to cook, but seeing as y'er a member of the company now, it occurs to me you ain't never once had kitchen duty. Since dinner is tied to yer saddle and I'm a Kelto frightened of such monstrous creatures, it seems to me that you should be the one to prepare the beast." He turned and walked off without saying another word.

Since she was hired to cook, she may as well start now, though she failed to see how that made her lucky. After unsaddling her horse, she placed the saddle under a nearby tree, hung the bridle from one branch and the saddle blanket over another to let it air out. Then she led her mount over to Bardus at the picket line.

"Do you have any brushes or curry combs?" Klara asked.

Bardus looked up from where he was depositing a saddle and said, "Afraid not, lass."

Klara attached her horse to the line, picked up a pine cone and used it to give her horse a good scratching. It was not very effective, but it managed to loosen his shaggy winter coat, causing scents of horse and pine to fill her nostrils. It was a pleasant combination.

Bardus eyed her admirably. "I wish the lads would look after their mounts like that."

"It seems like the least I could do since he did all the walking today," Klara said. "Well trained too; he never flinched when I shot the rabbit or when you came charging back down the road at us."

After a little more scratching, Klara patted her horse's neck. "I can't stay to help. I've been assigned to cook."

"Oh, thank the blessed Goddess," Bardus exclaimed. "It was Ruis's turn tonight, but he has yet to turn out anything fit to eat." Then he took her hand, bowed and kissed it. "You are a welcome addition to the company indeed." Klara laughed and went to dress the rabbit.

Around her, everything in camp fell into place without anyone issuing commands. Clearly, these men had been traveling together long enough to develop a routine. Ffearn and Karn gathered firewood, Ruis fetched water, Bardus looked after the horses, and Nuallan arranged camp and inventoried their supplies. Thorn brooded and Waywyrd did whatever wizards do, which at that moment seemed like not very much at all.

Once the rabbit was cleaned and her hands washed, Klara returned to camp and asked after the cooking supplies. Nuallan pointed to a set of panniers placed near the fire where a cauldron of water was already warming. She placed the rabbit in an iron oven and dug through the packs. The company had little by way of food stuffs, no herbs at all, and only salt for seasoning. She found a sack of vegetables: carrots and onions, and another sack of dried peas. Before adding the vegetables to the cauldron of now boiling water, she ladled some into the communal drinking horn, added some of the herbs from her saddlebag, and set it aside to seep. This concoction she sipped as she cooked.

After finding some lard, she put a spoonful in the oven that contained the rabbit. Taking the rabbit in hand, she put the oven over the coals to melt the lard while she de-boned the rabbit and cut it into chunks. After browning the rabbit she dumped it into the cauldron with the vegetables and mixed it well.

As she set about mixing flour and lard to make dumplings, she gained an audience. Karn, Ffearn, and Ruis sat on a log across from her, looking expectant.

She shook her head. "It will be a while yet."

"That's alright," Karn said, a dreamy look in his eyes. "I just like the way it smells."

"Been eating your own cooking long?" Klara asked as she waved away the smoke.

"Ever since the full Ash moon," Karn replied, leaning forward and sniffing appreciatively.

Ffearn added, "It's not our cooking that's the problem. Ruis's cooking has nearly killed us on more than one occasion."

"Pity that," Klara quipped and drained the contents of the drinking horn.

"It's true," Ffearn said. "I thought I was done for the last time he cooked. It's a wonder I pulled through. Good thing you're here to do the cooking now. It'll be a worry off my mind not to fear poisoning from Ruis's food."

"I wouldn't lay your worries to rest just yet," Klara said with a sparkle in her eye. "I'm just cooking tonight because Ruis was afraid to touch the rabbit. I expect he'll still be doing his share of the cooking, us being equals in the company and all."

"Say it isn't so!" Ffearn said, clutching at his chest in mock horror.

Ruis smiled at her for a long time. At last he said, "I think you'll do just fine here, lass." Then he rose and went to join Nuallan, Thorn, and Waywyrd, who were deep in conversation by the picket line.

After supper had been eaten and the dishes washed, the Keltoi gathered around the fire. Someone produced a skin of wine. Sampling the wine each time it made its rounds, Klara watched the fire crackle, sending sparks skyward as if they too could reside among the stars. At length Bardus began to sing, soft and low.

> "Gone the sun,
> Our day is done,
> Grant us rest,
> Let us be blessed.
> We'll sleep soon,
> Beneath the moon.
> By Goddess light,
> Keep us safe tonight."

The words swam in her ears. Was this an enchantment? Or was the wine stronger than she first suspected? One by one the Keltoi rose and went to where they laid their bedrolls. After a time Klara realized that she and the brothers were the only ones still sitting at the fire.

"It's time we put this out," Ffearn said. "It might attract unsavory characters while the company sleeps."

"Aye, I suppose you're right," Klara said. As she rose, Ffearn busied himself sprinkling water on the coals to quiet the fire. Turning her back on him, she headed toward the tree where she laid her saddle. She would spend the night sleeping atop a sweaty horse blanket, but she had experienced far worse when living on her own.

Having freed herself of the constricting bandeau, she considered the best way to use her saddle as a pillow. Without a sound Karn appeared out of the darkness, blanket in hand. She knew he was eager to get under her skirt, so she gave him a hard look and waited for him to speak.

He held the blanket awkwardly before him. "I have the first watch, so I thought you might like to use my blanket. Bardus said you didn't have one."

"In exchange for what?" Klara asked, her tone sharp. "I use the blanket now and when your watch is over you join me under it, is that the idea?"

"In exchange for nothing," Karn said, looking hurt. "I have first watch, Ffearn has second watch. Ffearn and I will trade his blanket when he takes over the watch. It will only work tonight because every night a different pair is on watch. I just thought I'd offer." He started to walk away.

Klara called after him, "Wait, Karn." He stopped and looked back at her. "I'm sorry. I made assumptions I shouldn't have. Force of habit, I guess. If it wouldn't put you out greatly, I would like to use your blanket."

Karn smiled and handed her the blanket, but the smile did not reach his eyes. Wordlessly he walked back into the night.

Warm under the woolen blanket, the words of Bardus's song swirled in Klara's mind with visions of firelight and Kenetlo faces. It was not long before she was drinking in the sweetness of sleep that comes after a long day.

# Chapter 4

## Unexpected Bedfellows

After fastening herself back into her bandeau, Klara shook out Karn's blanket and rolled it up so that he could attach it to his saddle. Surveying the camp in the bright morning light, she saw Thorn sitting on a rock in the distance, seemingly deep in thought. Aside from him and Ffearn, who was on watch, the rest of the company still slept. She took the silver comb and brush out of the saddlebag and laid them in her lap. Then she set about unraveling her braids and brushing her long, blonde hair.

Freed from its braids, the hair fell to her waist. She had always thought long hair was a nuisance but could not bear to cut her locks. As a child she had learned to braid and found many ways to secure her hair so that it was out of the way. This morning, she divided her hair into four equal parts and braided each section. She was feeling the top of her head, trying to decipher where each end should be tucked and pinned, when Ffearn walked up.

"You're not a blonde as I first thought," he said. "Your hair is truly the color of gold."

Klara smiled at him. "It takes a good deal of work to fashion raw gold into something beautiful. The task is made more difficult because I can't see the back of my head."

"Then you're in luck, because I am a jeweler," Ffearn replied. "Perhaps I can be of assistance. What is it you need done?"

Holding the ends of two braids in each hand, Klara said, "The ends of the right go under the left and the ends of the left go under the right and they need pinned in place well enough to last through a long day of riding."

"I think I can manage that," he said.

Klara dropped her braids and gathered the hair pins from the lap of her dress and handed them to him. Ffearn stepped behind her, first taking up one braid, then another, until all four of them were fastened in place. When he finished, he whispered, "The effect is truly magnificent."

"You shouldn't tease," Klara said as she turned to face him.

Ffearn's eyes were intense and admiring. "I do not tease," he said earnestly. "Your hair resembles fine ropes of gold and it shimmers like the setting sun on tranquil seas. I do not think I have seen anything so stunning in all of the great halls I've ever chanced to be in."

Klara could not imagine seeing her hair in the same light Ffearn did. To her, it was just hair. "I think lack of sleep has addled your brain," she said holding the bedroll toward him. "As it happens, I am in possession of a bedroll and know that yours is currently occupied. Perhaps you should get some sleep while you still can. With me and Thorn awake, you don't need to stand watch any longer."

"An excellent suggestion," Ffearn said, grabbing the blanket and heading off to bed down beside the lump she supposed was Karn.

Calls of fowl emanated from the forest, filling the chilly morning air. At the clearing's edge, thin rays of pale sunlight filtered through the verdant canopy providing a welcome invitation to explore. Since the company still slept, now was a good time to hunt. Collecting her bow and quiver, Klara headed in the direction of the fowl. She had not gotten far when Thorn's voice stopped her.

"Where do you think you're going?" He had abandoned his rock and was walking toward her.

Klara frowned. "To get supper." She had been hired as cook and huntress. If Thorn refused to allow her hunt, then why was she here?

"You shoot one of those birds and the whole forest will come to life." Gesturing toward her dozing companions, he added, "And then all these sleeping men will wake and rush for their swords, giving us a repeat of what happened yesterday." Klara raised her eyebrows at him, but he continued, "Before the next moon we will leave the mountains behind and begin crossing the Ufa Plateau. You and my nephews will be given time to hunt then."

"And what are we supposed to eat in the meantime?" Klara asked.

"Pottage," Thorn said. Then he turned and ambled back in the direction of his rock.

A bit dismayed, Klara returned the bow and quiver to the place by her saddle. Beans, peas, and lentils made bland fare when the only seasoning available was salt. She scuffed her foot somewhat petulantly in the pine duff. Upon noticing that Bardus was awake and busy tending the horses, her mood brightened. Kicking though the leaf litter and duff, she sought another pine cone. Succeeding in her quest, she stooped to collect her treasure, and then hurried toward the picket line intent on doing good.

Under her ministrations, the buckskin's shaggy yellow winter coat loosened itself and began to fall. When she finished, his coat looked little better, but the steed appeared a lot happier. She led him to the stream to drink and let him graze as she watched the camp come to life.

Horses snorted and stamped as her companions emerged from their bedrolls and stretched. Soon camp was a bustle of activity. Klara kept expecting someone to light a fire so she could get breakfast going. No fire or food ever materialized and she feared kindling a fire might have been her duty.

When the Keltoi began saddling their horses, she followed her companions' lead. Before they departed, Ruis walked among them passing out dried fruit and nuts for breakfast. The meal was eaten in the saddle.

Sunlight laid in dappled mosaics on the road. Ferns grew thick and heavy in the shadows. In damp streambeds, dew-covered moss glittered like emeralds alongside bubbling brooks. Regrettably, the group was just as merry on the road as they were the day before. The forest's secrets are only revealed to those who keep quiet. She felt keen eyes watching from the shadows, but the creatures refused to show themselves.

As the day wore on, they passed farmers and merchants traveling on business but had seen no warrior bands. In the afternoon, Waywyrd left his place at Thorn's side and came to ride beside her. This action prompted the Keltoi to at last include her in their conversation.

Ffearn shouted over his shoulder, "Do you not find Waywyrd oddly dressed for a wizard?"

Klara called back, "I never much considered it; he's the only actual wizard I've ever met. In truth, I didn't know there were other wizards." In her time at the alehouse she had met plenty of roadside charlatans, fustilarians, and conjurers of cheap tricks. She still suspected Waywyrd might be counted among their number.

"Aye, there are," Karn replied. "But they are, well, more wizardly, taken to wearing long robes and pointy hats."

"Long robes are difficult to ride in," Waywyrd said. "Just ask Klara how easy it is to manage in that dress. I'm sure she'd give you an earful. And despite the Skoloti tradition of wearing them, I've never liked hats, pointy or otherwise."

Every time Klara saw Waywyrd he was dressed as he was now, in a dark blue tunic and breeches of the same color. The hemlock staff he carried had been split by lightning and twisted at the top. As far as she was aware, he carried no weapons, nor had she ever seen him with one. The main distinction that set him apart from other men in a crowd was a streak of silver hair, which started at his temple. A lightning-like scar erupted from the silver patch and raced down the side of his face ending in another silver streak in his beard; otherwise his hair and beard were black.

"It's just that he looks like any other man," goaded Ffearn.

"If you was asked to pick a wizard out of a crowd of men, I don't think anyone would pick him," added Karn.

"In fact, we're not even sure he is a wizard," Ffearn said.

The playful banter continued for the better part of the afternoon, most of it at Waywyrd's expense. Birds chirruped and the horses tossed their heads, jingling their tack as if they too were enjoying the merry atmosphere. Eventually, Waywyrd's patience ran thin. The frown that started as a small furrow on his brow had grown until it encompassed all his facial features.

"The whole point of looking like everyone else is so I can come and go as I please without anyone realizing that I am a wizard," Waywyrd snapped.

Then, having his fill of ludicrous conversation, he rode to the head of the column, apparently desiring to be surrounded by more enlightened minds.

They made camp that night near a river that coursed its way over large rocks, alternatively running swift and white in some places and collecting in deep, still pools at others. Since she did not have kitchen duty, Klara helped Bardus with the horses. As she led them in turns to the river to drink, she felt its natural pull, as if it longed to draw her near.

While she and Bardus stood at the river with her buckskin and another of the mounts, she asked, "Do they have names?"

"The horses?" Bardus asked. "Some of them do. The saddle horses anyway. The pack horses and your mount are recent additions. If they had names, they're lost now. We never bothered to ask what they were when we purchased them."

Klara's horse stood, ears erect and alert. She turned to the gelding and stroked his powerful neck. "Then I shall call you Constant, for that's what you've been."

Once all the horses were set on the picket line, Klara stole away from the company and headed up river. A little over a quarter mile from the camp, she came upon a large pool surrounded by mossy rocks. She slipped out of her clothes then sat atop them while un-doing her braids, taking care not to lose any of the hair pins.

In the fading light, she sat nude with her hair loose about her. In time, the draw of the water became too great and she waded into the pool. When the water reached her thighs, she stopped and looked down at her reflection. Her skin was silky white, stretched over broad, well-curved hips, which rose to a stout, capable waist. She had never been one of those thin, willowy girls who lacked muscle. She ran as fast as most men and her arms and shoulders showed a hint of muscle and the suggestion of biceps, which she owed to the daily task of chopping wood. As for her chest, there was only one way to describe it: buxom.

Sensing that she was being watched, she waded farther into the pool. Once her feet no longer touched the bottom, she dove down, letting the water surround her. When she surfaced, she let the current carry her as she floated about the pool, her hair fanning out behind her, giving the effect of a halo. She figured either Ffearn or Karn was watching but cared little. The water felt too good to let either of them prevent her from enjoying it.

Eventually, it was time to return to camp. She scrubbed herself down with her palms and splashed water on her face, wrung out her hair, and waded ashore where she quickly dressed. When she arrived back at camp, Ruis was already ladling out bowls full of beans and passing around a sack of dried biscuits.

As she headed for the fire to collect her food, Thorn approached and asked, "Where were you?"

"I was bathing," Klara said. Her stomached rumbled. Goose pimples covered her flesh. Being damp and chilled, she was eager for the warmth of the fire and to fill her belly with a hot meal.

"You should not go off alone without telling someone," Thorn said. He seemed overly concerned for her welfare, though she could not fathom why. And the way he looked at her was unnerving, as if he saw something within her that everyone else missed. However, she was not about to be mothered by a man she barely knew.

"I wasn't alone," Klara said, mischief in her tone.

Anger flashed in Thorn's eyes. "Who was with you?"

Klara leveled her gaze at him. "I've yet to find a forest that didn't have some creature nearby to keep watch." Without waiting for a response she turned and headed toward Ruis and the fire, intent on collecting her supper, winking in the direction of Ffearn and Karn as she passed.

Ruis's meal lived up to all the expectations she had been given, which is to say, it was horrible. She took a bite of the dried biscuit and then laid it aside to give to Constant later. He would enjoy it far more than she did.

The beans were spectacularly terrible; she had no idea how he managed it. There was no seasoning save the charcoal from those bits that burned and crusted to the sides and bottom. Some of the beans were little more than mush, others were still hard and dry. Those combined with the crusty charcoal bits made her eternally grateful that he only cooked every seventh night. Then she watched in solidarity, knowing that washing was too good for any pot that created such a meal, as Ruis, by way of cleaning, turned the cauldron over in the coals and let the fire finish the work it started.

After dinner, Klara brought out her comb and brush and began working on the wet tangle of her hair, hoping it might dry a little by the fire.

Behind a thin curtain of flame, Nuallan coughed and shifted himself to a more comfortable position, then spoke, "If you do not mind my asking, lass, it seems to me that a silver comb and brush are strange implements to bring on a journey such as this. You might have made better use of them by trading them for material wealth."

Klara looked at the brush in her hand as if she just discovered it was there. "They were my mother's. It's all I have of her."

Nuallan's tone softened. "I am sorry to hear that. Did she pass recently?"

"No," Klara said, staring into the fire. "When I was twelve." Over the past two days Klara realized Waywyrd had told them nothing about her beforehand. Not even her gender, because when they arrived they assumed Waywyrd sent them to meet Arman, not her.

"So, you were raised by your father then?" Nuallan asked, bringing her attention back to the circle of men seated at the fire.

"No," Klara said. "My da died in a carting accident when I was very young. I have no memories of him. After I lost my mum, I was an orphan and had to make my own way in the world. I've been on my own ever since."

Leaning forward, elbows on his knees, interest evident, Bardus ventured, "And you had no relations to take you in?"

"Even if I had relations, unless they were strongly connected to the sisterhood, it's unlikely they would take me," she said. "My mum was burned by the Disciples of Elah. To this day I don't know why. Those who become orphans in such a way are often left to fend for themselves."

"These people burn women, leaving their children orphaned?" Bardus asked, disbelief evident by his furrowed brow.

"They burn women with their children," Klara corrected as she worked at a knot in her hair. "I wasn't home at the time, otherwise they would have burned me alongside her."

Nuallan slapped his thigh, becoming animated. "Then Waywyrd was right to pick you. You must've had a bit of luck on your side to have escaped the flames." He meant it kindly, but it did not sit well with Klara.

"Luck had nothing to do with it," she snapped, dropping the brush in her lap. "Our landlord was Parthian scum. He came over and said a snake had been at his eggs. He was too big to crawl under the coop and kill it himself. He told my mum he'd pay me a copper if I'd do it. When I reached his place the only snake he had to show me was the one in his trousers. When he'd finished and turned me loose, I saw the smoke rising from our place. I hid in the hedge as the Disciples of Elah finished burning my mum in the yard. Once the coals died down and everyone left, I went inside and put what I could carry in a sack. After that I headed into the forest so they wouldn't find and burn me, too."

An uncomfortable silence filled the circle of men as the magnitude of her words settled over the company. Klara looked at the fire without really seeing it. Angry tears stung her eyes and threatened to roll down her cheeks. She hoped her companions thought it was just a reaction to the smoke and not a product of her own weakness.

After a pause she continued, "Disciples of Elah never take anything from the house because they believe it's tainted. We were poor; there are not many trades a woman can undertake with a child at her side. My mum took in washing and mending, but that was barely enough to pay the rent. These were the only things of any value. Mum said they'd been a gift from my da."

In the distance lightning flashed, followed by a rumble of thunder that rolled across the sky. Thorn broke the stillness that had descended on their circle by announcing, "Get the tents out, we may have rain."

As the men moved to follow his orders, he placed a hand on her shoulder. Staring up at him, she held his gaze, seeing her own pain and weakness reflected in his eyes. After a pause, he said, "In our lands the penalty for such a crime is death. I hope the man who violated you met the justice he deserved."

"In Skoloti the punishment is to lose a part of his manhood," Klara replied. "Though, I didn't stay around long enough to learn if he ever met with a blade."

"Being an orphan is no easy task," Thorn said, his eyes heavy with grief. In that moment she felt like she had glimpsed a window into his soul. Lightning flashed again and she saw tears in his eyes. She thought he was going to say more, but after a brief pause Thorn sighed, removed his hand, and returned to his stolid, unreadable self.

Klara watched the lightning flicker a few more times, then gathered up her saddle and other belongings and put them under the tarp with the rest of the company's gear. With nothing more to do, she returned to the fire and resumed brushing her hair. As the first patter of rain began to fall, she considered how she was going to pass the night. She had noticed a large spruce tree on the edge of the clearing when they rode in. That might keep her dry, but she doubted she could find it again in the dark. Lost in contemplation, listening to fire hiss as the rain drops landed on the coals, she was surprised when someone touched her elbow.

It was Ffearn, his voice gently coaxing, "Come away from the fire and out of the rain."

"I was just considering finding my way up to that spruce tree," Klara said.

"You've got no blanket," Ffearn said. "Come sleep with Karn and me. You'll be warmer and dryer."

Recounting her mother's death and how she had been violated left her emotionally exhausted. She was not interested in servicing anyone tonight, regardless of how much they might be willing to pay. "Ffearn, I'm really not up to—"

Ffearn must have read her mind because he never let her finish the sentence. "Just sleep, nothing more."

Wordlessly, she allowed herself to be led away from the fire. A new flash of lightning illuminated the clearing, which had been transformed into a village of five small tents. Karn was still awake and waiting for them when she pushed aside the flap and entered. The three of them laid huddled together under the blankets. Ffearn had taken the middle, lying between her and Karn, facing his brother.

Karn rose up on an elbow. Looking at Klara over his brother, he asked, "How did you know I was watching you at the river?"

"I didn't," Klara said. "I just suspected. Anytime women are naked, men will find means to watch."

Ffearn snorted out a laugh and Karn lay back down. Pressing her back against Ffearn's, Klara felt his warmth against her. The lightning flashed outside and the thunder rolled, but inside the little tent she felt safe from life's torrents and was lulled to sleep by the sounds of her companions' breathing.

ɕ

When Klara awoke, she had the tent to herself. Her bandeau had become twisted and uncomfortable as she slept. Inside the privacy of the tent, she straightened and re-laced it. Having gotten herself back in order, she emerged into the morning light. The rain stopped at some point in the night, but the grass was still wet. Carefully, she pulled the blankets out of the tent and shook them out. Around her, others were emerging from their tents and doing the same. She was pleased to see that Nuallan had a fire going and was preparing a hot breakfast.

She approached him, carrying her saddlebag, and asked, "I noticed you've got no herbs for flavor. Would you mind if I added some of mine to the drinking horn this morning?"

"Bitter or sweet, anything would improve our morning draught," he replied as he passed her the horn.

She was grateful that he did not ask which herb she possessed. Leaving the tea to seep, she joined Bardus and helped tend the horses.

"We'll be making a slow start this morning," Bardus said. "We can't pack the tents away until they dry, or they'll mold. But it'll give the horses time to graze."

They took the horses down to the river to drink, then ran a new picket line so they had access to fresh grass. By the time they finished with the horses, breakfast was ready. Klara and Bardus joined Waywyrd at the fire and she gratefully accepted the drinking horn as it was passed to her. In addition to the herbs, Nuallan had sweetened the brew with a good measure of honey, which warmed her as she drank.

Waywyrd sat opposite her, stroking his beard. "I see you've passed the night."

"And quite comfortably, too," Klara replied. She took another drink, keenly aware that she needed to make sure she got enough pennyroyal in her system to prevent pregnancy. She was taking no chances after her encounter with Arman back at the alehouse.

Waywyrd harrumphed, then queried her, "And where have your tent-mates gone off too this morning?"

"Don't know," Klara said. She took another drink before passing the horn back to Waywyrd.

They sat in silence a moment watching Nuallan stir a large cauldron of porridge. She turned when the jovial pair of young Keltoi entered the clearing. Ffearn and Karn had wet hair and seemed to be in unusually high spirits. They wore their white undershirts loose over their trousers and were swinging their tunics as they swaggered her direction. Clean, they made more of an impression on her and in their ease she noted that both cut a fine figure.

"I see you're not the only one to sneak off for a bath," Waywyrd said, gesturing toward Ffearn and Karn with his staff.

This time, Nuallan harrumphed. There was an obvious note of disapproval in the grunt and a sour expression on his face. From across the fire, she registered the hint of a grimace cross Ruis's brow, too. Odd, cleanliness should not invite such disdain.

The brothers joined her at the fire, one settling on either side of her. The pair of them smelled fresh and clean. Obviously they had procured soap from somewhere. Karn was freshly shaven. Ffearn had trimmed his moustache and taken the braids out of his hair.

Karn winked at her as he accepted the drinking horn, but it was Ffearn who spoke first. "Seeing as twice now you have enjoyed the warmth of our blankets, we were wondering if we might trouble you for the use of your comb?"

Klara smiled. "That seems like a fair trade." It was a far better offer than she expected him to make. The offer she anticipated required the use of more pennyroyal. Her supply was limited and on the road there was little opportunity to gather more.

The brush and comb were passed back and forth between them as they braided their hair. Karn and Ffearn both put braids at the side of their face, but where Ffearn left his to hang long, Karn pulled his back and fastened them behind his head. Since he had the shortest hair of the trio, the braids just barely met.

Once their hands were free of their hair, each gratefully accepted a steaming bowl of porridge. Thorn looked the three of them over. Klara thought she sensed disapproval in his countenance, but he said nothing. She was glad that she was getting better at reading his mood but confused by the apparent disapproval of cleanliness.

Ruis looked at her appraisingly and asked, "Have you any skill with a blade, lass?"

"I've never used one outside of a kitchen," Klara answered honestly. She had a rough knife that she used for everything from hunting to cooking, though butchering a carcass might as well be kitchen work.

"That may be something we have to remedy," Ruis said, "but not today."

After the overnight rain, the day turned warm and it was not long before the tents were dry. The party folded them up and stored them away, then saddled their horses and made for the road.

The next few days passed much as the others had. She became accustomed to the rhythms of the road and the ways of the Kenetlo. As the days blended together, Klara found comfort in the pattern her life took on. She found pleasure in working with the horses. Evenings were passed companionably around the fire before turning in for the night. The nights she passed with her back pressed to Ffearn's, falling asleep to the sounds of her tent mates' breathing. It was evident from the disapproving looks Nuallan and Thorn gave her that they were not pleased with her sleeping arrangements, but nothing was ever said.

CHAPTER 5

# COMMON THIEVES

T was Thorn's habit to break the day into two parts. The company rode out early in the morning, stopping briefly to water themselves and the horses at midday, then rode on again until he decided it was time to make camp. Today the heat was blistering. At midday they lingered under the canopy of trees that lined the creek, enjoying a respite from the sunbaked, dusty trail. The horses milled about, impatiently swishing at flies with their tails.

While waiting for Constant to finish drinking, Klara scanned the road behind them. How far they had traveled?

A lone rider descending the hills caught her attention. Shielding her eyes from the sun, she surveyed the trail looking for other travelers, but saw none. From her time at the alehouse, she knew people seldom traveled alone. A knot in her gut told her to be wary. As she watched, the rider disappeared behind a screen of brush. How many other travelers were concealed by the foliage? The area was ripe for an ambush.

Turning her attention to the Keltoi, she scanned their faces for signs of unease. They appeared unbothered by the rider. Most of the company reclined against trees, just as reluctant to return to the trail as the horses. Waywyrd had plopped down in the middle of the stream and was only visible from the neck up. Karn and Ffearn sat in the shade, rolling a pair of dice between them. They were the only ones engaged in the game. That was odd. Whenever dice were produced a crowd of men generally gathered. Having worked in many public houses, she had learned most of the games travelers brought to the taverns. Intent on joining the game, she headed their direction.

As she neared, Nuallan said, "I would go no further, lass. You get into a game with them and they'll have your shirt."

Klara stopped, surprised, and looked at Nuallan.

Karn rolled the dice again. "I wouldn't mind having her shirt."

Leaning forward to examine the dice, Ffearn said, "I'd wager for her skirt. Do you think we'd have her bare in two rounds or three?"

"That dress she's wrapped in is the only clothes she's got." Karn swiped up the dice and rolled again. "One round and she'll be riding in naught but her drawers."

Nuallan called to them, "Oh, go on with ye!" Then to Klara he said, "You see here, none of us will play with them."

"That's because they're bloody cheats," Ruis said from where he sat, back against a tree.

"And they have some secret language between them," Bardus interjected, without so much as raising his head from where he laid sprawled in the grass. "They always know the other's bet. It's impossible to win if you start a game with them."

Ffearn and Karn's heads snapped up. "We do not cheat!" they said in unison.

"We are highly skilled professionals," Ffearn said.

"Who can recognize opportunities when we see them," Karn added.

Frowning as he walked by, Thorn said, "Put those damned dice away and mount up."

Around the clearing everyone rose, dusted themselves off, and headed for their mounts.

"I take it Thorn does not approve of their gambling," Klara said.

"It's not a matter of approving or disapproving," Nuallan said. "They bring in a lot of money for the company, but he worries they might get reckless. Disputes over gambling winnings are common and Thorn prefers to avoid brushes with the law and the locals whenever possible. Thankfully, the lads have learned not to draw too much attention to themselves at the dice tables." Then he, too, turned toward his mount, leaving Klara to do the same.

As they rode, the uneasy feeling in her stomach persisted. Whenever they passed clearings or outcroppings that afforded a view of the road behind her, she looked for the lone rider. Most of the time she only saw an empty landscape, though she occasionally got a glimpse of the other traveler. The distance between them was still great, but the horseman was narrowing the gap.

Upon reaching a clearing, Thorn reigned in his horse and said, "It's time to make camp. The horses are hot and need time to graze. This spot will do for the night."

"I don't think we should camp here," Klara said, shifting in her saddle. The rest of the party was shocked; none of them had directly challenged Thorn.

Thorn turned on her. "And why not?"

Klara was quick with her reason and leaned forward in the saddle as she gave it. "There is a rider behind us. I've been tracking his progress since midday. It's hard to tell at a distance, but he might be one of the bounty hunters Serik hires and he's moving fast. I doubt he would ride at that speed unless tracking some quarry."

"You should have told me sooner." Thorn's brow furrowed into a frown.

"When I first spotted him, he was in plain sight. I assumed everyone was aware of the rider behind us," Klara said. Then she added, pointing ahead of them, "If we can make it to that overlook before nightfall, we should be afforded a view of him when he passes through here. If I can get a good look at him, I might be able to identify him. I've seen a lot of men pass through the alehouse."

Thorn called to the company, "Water yourselves and the horses, then we ride."

When they reached the overlook Klara indicated, Thorn sent the rest of the company ahead with instructions to find a suitable camp, but not light a fire. Thorn, Klara, and Waywyrd tethered their horses in the trees, out of sight of the approaching rider. Then they walked to the edge and lay on their bellies, waiting.

An evening breeze wafted up from the valleys below, causing the smaller branches to dip and sway. The sun rode low, threatening to set and extinguish its light before the rider entered the clearing they had just vacated. When he finally arrived, Klara saw a fresh-faced youth, little more than a boy, who had visited the tavern on occasion. She had suggested he look for other employment. It seems the lad failed to heed her advice. He dismounted and looked around the clearing, examining their footprints. Then he dusted his hat against his trousers, mounted his horse and returned the way he came.

The grit and gravel of the outcrop grated against the larger rocks as Thorn shifted his weight and addressed Waywyrd. "What do you make of that?"

"I'd say he was a scout and not too far behind us," Waywyrd replied.

"That is my thinking as well," Thorn said. "The question is, who's he with and why?"

"I think," Waywyrd said, "those questions will best answered if you ask Klara."

Fearing she already knew the answer, Klara kept scanning the road for signs of movement. In time, the scout returned with two other riders and began to make camp. She knew them: they collected bounties rather than find honest employment in the trades. Farther down the road a cart rolled into view.

"Slavers," Klara said, pointing at a cart. She counted half a dozen slaves yoked like oxen to a wagon. They were driven by two men liberally applying their whips. Three more men rode as guards behind the cart. She turned to face Thorn and Waywyrd, both of whom were giving her expectant looks. "Those are the bounty hunters Serik hires. He's not the only one who hires them, but I don't like the coincidence."

Waywyrd spoke, waving his staff at the scene unfolding below. "With any luck they are not tracking us, but I would guess that whoever they're looking for used our tracks to hide their passage at some point. Still, we should be on our guard. If there is a thief about, I'm sure he'd have no qualms about availing himself of one of our horses during the night."

The three of them crept back from the ledge, mounted their horses and headed in the direction of the rapidly setting sun, trusting their mounts to find the camp the others prepared ahead of them.

Arriving in camp, Ruis handed Klara some jerky and a dried biscuit. Not much of a meal, but it would do. Tired, she passed her horse to Bardus and made her way to where Ffearn and Karn had stretched their bedrolls. They asked about what she saw and she recounted the incident while she and Ffearn put their hair in long braids to keep it from tangling in the night.

When she lay down, she realized that she was not on the outside with her back to Ffearn as she usually slept, but was between them. She briefly wondered if this change had been contrived before drifting off to sleep.

Klara woke and gazed into Ffearn's sleeping face, Karn spooning her as he slept. Finding the change agreeable, Klara closed her eyes again, enjoying their warmth and the sounds of their breathing.

Karn stirred beside her. His arm was around her waist and he pulled her to him. Nuzzling the hair at the back of her neck, he whispered, "You must lie still and be very quiet."

Klara was tempted to protest, but the comment carried no hint of lust. Curious, she obliged him. Taking his arm from her waist, he reached out and gently tugged Ffearn's moustache. Ffearn's nose wrinkled, but he did not rouse. A few moments later Karn tugged his brother's moustache again. This time Ffearn's eyes fluttered and he woke.

"Morning," Ffearn said sleepily. "I see you're feeling chipper."

"It's a grand day to be a Kelto," Karn said.

"Every day's a grand day to be a Kelto, you feeble-minded dotard," Ffearn said.

Klara was taken by the intimacy of the moment as the brothers exchanged their greetings. The movement of their blankets did not go unnoticed by the rest of the company.

"Out of bed you lot," Ruis called. "Check yer blades, they may see action today."

The trio sat up and stretched. After issuing a jaw wrenching yawn, Klara asked, "Why would there be a fight today? Was there trouble from the thief last night?"

"Nah, no trouble at all, lass" Ruis replied from where he sat by the fire sharpening a dagger, "and that's worrisome. I made a tempting pile of our food stuff last night, hoping to catch a thief, and caught none so much as a mouse. And yon slavers are heading the wrong direction to be taking their wares to market. They're still looking to add to their stocks. Bounties or no, they may be pursuing us."

Nuallan shook his head and grunted as he walked past the trio.

"You know," Klara said to her bedfellows, "I get the feeling Nuallan doesn't entirely approve of our sleeping arrangements."

Ffearn and Karn chuckled, then sobered and prepared themselves for the day.

As the company descended from the heights of the mountains, the conifers she was used to seeing gave way to a more open deciduous forest. Sunlight lay dappled on the road and birdsong filled the air. Wind swirling through the verdant canopy conjured images of rushing water. The area was filled with more birds and small rodents than she had seen on previous days. Then she realized the men were not singing. She had become accustomed to the Keltoi singing and scaring off everything for miles. The sight of so much game left her longing to hunt.

Two fat fowl were pecking at the twigs on the forest floor off to her right. Her mouth watered at the thought of them roasted over a fire, skins golden and crispy, fat dripping on the coals. But, if she shot either of the birds, Thorn would have her hide. The tension running through the company was almost palpable. Instead, she looked longingly at the plump birds, nostrils flaring at the imagined scent of roasted game hen smothered in gravy.

A little before midday Thorn led them off the road and began doubling back. Upon reaching a part of the forest where the brush was so thick they were unable to see the road, Thorn called the company to a halt and had them dismount. As she watered the horses, Klara watched Thorn, Ruis, and his nephews gather in a clump, heads together, taking in hushed tones. Then the group dispersed, heading into the forest.

Bardus and Nuallan quieted their horses, so she led Constant and the string of pack horses over to them. Bardus took the lead of pack horses from her saying, "Now we wait. Thorn and the lads will have their quarry before long. But if something goes wrong, you take your horse and go. We'll make sure nothing gets left behind."

Time passed slowly as she, Bardus, Nuallan, and Waywyrd waited with the horses. She impatiently watched a bumble bee crawl across Constant's neck. Should she flick it off? Or would that result in one or both of them getting stung?

Her thoughts were interrupted by the sound of approaching hooves. As near as she could tell, it was a lone rider. The thud of the horse's hooves drew closer and then there was an explosion of sound in the undergrowth that set off a cacophony of scolding squirrels. A skirmish ensued somewhere on the road out of sight.

Klara longed to take her bow and creep through the trees to see the outcome. Bardus made her wait until Thorn called for them. Emerging from the brush, she saw the scout kneeling on the ground between Ffearn and Karn, each of whom had a hand on him as Thorn questioned him. The sandy-haired youth wore an insolent expression. It was clear they were not getting answers.

Klara listened as Thorn continued his questions.

"Who are you tracking?" Thorn asked.

The boy said nothing.

Thorn tried, "Who are the men you are with?"

Still the lad said nothing.

Thorn gestured to the others. "This is the whole of our company. As you can see, whoever you are looking for is not with us." Then he squatted in front of the lad. "But if you tell me who you are looking for, perhaps I can give you some answers. I may have seen him on the road and not known he was a wanted man."

The lad's nostrils flared, trying to keep himself from openly gasping for breath after the scuffle, which had clearly left him winded. He fixed Thorn with a gaze sharp as flint. Still, he said nothing.

Standing, Thorn nodded to Ruis, who walked over to the boy, took hold of his head and said, "Perhaps he hasn't got a tongue?" Ruis was not gentle as he forced the boy's mouth open and looked inside. "There's one in there, right enough. But that's something I can alter."

The boy gave no response and his eyes remained hard and cold.

"Stand him up," Ruis said.

Karn and Ffearn pulled the boy to his feet. Once he was standing Ruis punched him in the stomach.

The boy doubled over, then stood erect and spat in Ruis's face. "I ain't tellin' you nothin'."

Klara realized he was stalling. The other riders must not be very far behind him. Balling his hand into a fist, Ruis prepared to deliver another blow.

"Ruis, stop," Klara said, stepping forward.

Ruis turned toward her. "Sorry you have to see this, lass, but we need information."

Gesturing toward the boy, she said, "He's not going to tell you anything. You roughed him up and still he says nothing. He won't talk for you, but I bet I can get information out of him."

Ruis looked at her confused, so she added, "Give me a quarter of an hour with him and you'll know everything we need to know; half an hour and you'll have his whole life story."

"You really think you can get anything out of him?" Ruis asked, letting his fist relax.

"I do," Klara said. It was evident by the way the boy's eyes followed her, and not Ruis, that she had the better chance at actually getting information.

"Alright," Ruis said. "Have a go at him."

Klara looked at Ffearn and Karn and said, "Strip him." Turning to Bardus, she said, "Get a rope."

Klara instructed them to lay him face up in the middle of a sunny spot on the road. Then she directed them to use the ropes to tether his arm to young trees on either side of the track. Once he was secured, the naked boy laid helpless in the sun. Klara shimmied out of her drawers and handed them to Ruis. A look of surprise crossed his face as he accepted the garment. Then she walked over to the boy, who had already changed his strategy and was talking plenty. Mostly, cursing Ffearn and Karn.

The boy struggled against the rope, shouting, "Untie me you surly flea-bitten arse bandits. Damnable cock-knockers. You craven bunch of sods."

Klara walked over to the boy, who gulped hard and ceased his cursing. All his pluck vanished as he commenced whimpering.

"Oh please," he pleaded, "If you're a witch as well as whore don't do anything unnatural to me."

Klara knelt beside him, speaking in a calm and reassuring voice, "You know who I am, don't you?" The boy nodded in agreement, so she continued. "I've seen you at the alehouse, but you've never had money enough to afford me. Would you like to try me now, free of charge?"

"Yes." The lad gulped. His eyes flitted toward the party of Keltoi, fear and excitement plainly written on his face.

Klara bushed the lad's hair out of his eyes, bringing his attention back to her. "I promise that if you do as I ask, they won't harm you."

The boy sighed and a little of the tension left his shoulders.

Cocking her head, she asked, "Have you ever been with a woman?"

"Yes," the boy replied.

"Good," Klara said. "Then you will have some idea of how this works."

Klara spat in her hand and grabbed his penis, which was instantly erect. Quick as lightning, she straddled him. After a few strokes his eyes rolled back in his head and she knew he was ready to be questioned.

Raising herself so that she was nearly off him, she said, "If you want more, you have to talk. I ask questions, you answer them. The more you talk, the more I do this," and lowered herself on to him again. He sighed as she did so, pleasure and anxiety both showing on his face. "Do you understand?" she asked.

"Yes, ma'am," the boy replied.

"Good, then we can begin," Klara said. "Who are you tracking?"

The boy found it difficult to talk with Klara astride him, but he managed, "We're trackin' a party of Keltoi, a wizard, and a whore. I think I've found them."

"Why are you tracking us?" Klara asked, as she continued to gently rock her hips.

"We was paid to bring you to justice," the boy croaked.

"We've broken no law; who paid you and why?" Klara demanded.

The boy did not answer. She raised herself up and waited.

"Hey, why'd you stop movin'?" he asked.

"You didn't answer the question," she replied, her breast dangling in his face.

The boy lifted his head to look her in the eyes. Beads of sweat forming on his brow trickled down to his temples. "Murad handles the business arrangements. He said Serik hired us to find you."

"Me?" Klara asked, resuming her motions. "Why?"

The boy was eager to perform now. In a rush he said, "We're supposed to take you back to Serik, the others we'll sell at the slave market in Olbia. Murad said Serik hired him 'cause some Keltoi stole everything he had out o' his cashbox. There was a witness, an old man. The old man said the Keltoi came in, ate a bunch of food, drank a bunch of ale, but didn't pay and took all the money. The old man said you ran off with them, but not without having sex with all of them on the table before his very eyes."

Klara sat back hard. "Arman."

"No, don't stop," the boy pleaded, straining against the ropes, attempting to continue thrusting beneath her.

"Arman lied," she said. There was no way she was going back to Serik. Not under these circumstances. Not ever.

"Okay, Arman lied," the boy said as he bucked and writhed beneath her. "Can you keep movin'?"

"You got any money?" Klara asked.

"Some," the boy replied. "But…you said this was free!"

"Karn, did you find any money in his purse?" Klara asked. The boy was straining under her, trying to raise his hips. She grasped him tightly with her thighs to minimize his movements.

Karn stood some distance away, arms crossed. "He wasn't carrying a purse. Least ways we didn't find one when we stripped him."

"It's in my saddlebag," the boy shouted. Then he pleaded, "Please, my balls is achin'."

Ffearn collected the saddlebag and rifled through its contents. He found and held up the coin purse saying, "There isn't much here."

"Is there enough for a pair of boots?" Klara asked, still trying to keep the boy from thrusting and finishing the act before a bargain was struck.

"Might be," Ffearn replied.

Turning her attention to the boy prostrate beneath her, she said, "Questioning was free. I have my answers now. If you want more, I get all the money in your purse."

The boy hastily nodded in agreement.

"Okay, lad, you have a deal," Klara said.

"Yes, yes, yes," the boy stammered as the action resumed.

It was only a matter of moments before he was finished. Klara stood and Ffearn tossed her the coin purse. Then she walked over to Ruis to collect her drawers.

"Yer interrogation techniques are…" Ruis paused searching for the right word. "Effective," he said as he held out the garment.

She took her drawers from Ruis's outstretched hand and shimmied into them, then unsheathed her blade, saying, "I'm going to send Serik a message."

Ruis raised an eyebrow as he eyed the blade. It was thick with nicks and notches from quartering game. The rough handle had been mended more than once, and presently was wrapped in leather because it had begun to separate. Still, the blade was sharp and that was all that mattered.

She returned to the boy and knelt beside him. He whined as she drew the blade across his chest, deep enough to cut, but not scar. The others crowded around and watched as the blackthorn rune, a symbol of negation, welled with blood.

Klara stood and addressed the lad. "Arman lied. I want you to remember that. If any money was stolen, Arman stole it. If you want to collect money for the capture of a thief, go catch Arman. And I assure you he'll be easier to haul in than we will." Klara looked around at the startled faces of the company. "Leave him tied here. It'll slow them down because they'll have to untie him and it's likely he won't be able to ride for a few days."

"I don't see how carving on his chest is going to keep him off a horse," Ruis said.

"It's not his chest he needs to worry about," Klara said, "it's his wee penis."

"It's not wee," the whimpering boy protested.

Klara gave him no more than a passing glance and continued, gesturing skyward, "The sun is full overhead here and the trees farther from the road. He'll be badly burned; the thing will probably blister."

"Mount up," Thorn shouted. "We need to keep moving."

Back in the saddle, Thorn had them gallop until the horses were lathered. They stopped only briefly to let the horses drink, then resumed travel, keeping the horses at brisk trot. Klara assumed that he intended to distance themselves from the riders behind them. The faster pace was a welcome distraction. The countryside slipped by quickly, which kept her mind occupied. It also prevented conversation.

She felt sheepish about her actions, but her life was in danger. Sex was the most effective way of gathering information. She had no intention of returning to the alehouse and if she were taken back as a slave she would have more to worry about than outwitting the Disciples of Elah.

After a couple of hours at a sustained trot, Klara bounced out of her bandeau. She was still contained within her dress, but there was no longer any support and she was starting to get tender. Had she been alone, she would have stopped and readjusted herself. In the company of these men she refused to mention the predicament, fearing they might view it as a form of weakness or an inconvenience that slowed them down. The miles pounded painfully on, the edges of the trusses beating against her soft flesh with every step the horse took. She felt bruises blooming along her ribcage and gritted her teeth, determined to endure the torment. Day faded into night, bringing out swarms of mosquitos, thick as storm clouds, drawn by the sweat of men and horses, needling her exposed skin and adding to the agony.

When the light finally gave out, Thorn let them slow to a walk but, after so much abuse, even the motion of the horse walking was painful. Watching the stars through the openings of the trees, she felt dizzy and lacked the fortitude to swat at the insects eagerly making a meal of her. Finally, they entered a clearing and Thorn let them make camp.

Klara rode Constant to the picket line and gingerly eased herself out of the saddle. She attached him to the line and hung his bridle over her shoulder while uncinching the saddle's straps. As she pulled the saddle over his back, it settled on her chest and she stifled a cry. The noise caught Bardus's attention.

"Having trouble tonight, lass?" he asked from somewhere near her, but hidden from view by horses and the dark of night.

"No," Klara grunted as she carried the saddle away from the picket line.

Unconvinced, Bardus appeared out of the shadows, took the saddle from her, and placed it with the others. Once his back was turned, she headed for the trees, arms held tightly across her chest to prevent anything from moving.

"No, you don't," Bardus said as he hurried after her. "Come here so I can have a look at you."

Klara turned, still clutching her chest. "I'm fine, just tired is all."

Bardus grasped her wrists and pulled her arms away from her body, enabling him to look at her in the moonlight. "You are not fine," he said. "You are bloody. Do you mind telling me how you came to be injured?"

"Sorry, Bardus," Klara stammered, scenting the copper tang of blood rising from her breasts. "I didn't know I was bleeding."

Disbelief was evident on his face. "But you knew you were hurt?"

"I was sore," Klara said. "I'm sure it'll be fine in the morning."

"I won't know that until I see what kind of damage you've done," Bardus said. "I'll get a candle lit so I can examine you. While I'm doing that, you can get out of that dress."

When he headed for his pack, Klara turned and continued toward the trees, hoping to evade further examination. She was nearing the edge of the clearing when Bardus shouted, "Get back here and take that dress off or I'll have the lads drag you down here and do it for you!"

Klara stopped in her tracks. Ahead of her Karn and Ffearn were gathering firewood. Their heads snapped up, their hair radiating silver halos in the moonlight. The whole camp had heard him. Slowly, she turned and started back his direction. She was not the only one to answer his call. By the time she reached him, so had Ffearn, Karn, Thorn, and Waywyrd.

"What seems to be the trouble?" Thorn asked.

"She's injured." Bardus grabbed her by the wrist and led her to the fire.

"I'm not," Klara said, trying to free herself of Bardus's grip.

"You're bloody, that means you are." Bardus released her and pointed toward a log. "Now, out of that dress so I can have a look at you. And sit there until I get my kit."

"It's not necessary," Klara insisted.

Putting a hand on her shoulder, Bardus pushed her onto the log. "I'll have these lads hold you down so I can cut that dress off of you if I must."

At that Klara relented, unbuckled her belt and slipped out of her dress.

The top fell away revealing her swollen and tender breasts. Bardus handed the candle to Ffearn and raised her left breast revealing the bruising underneath. The skin was rubbed raw and had begun to bleed. He raised her arm and found the puncture wound from the wooden trusses in her bandeau, which hung uselessly around her waist. The trusses, now exposed, had poked through the fabric and her skin.

Thorn's face showed no expression, but she sensed concern in his voice. "How did this happen?"

"Trotting," Klara replied sheepishly.

Taking Waywyrd with him, Thorn turned and walked off.

With the assistance of Ffearn and Karn, who fetched medical supplies and held candles, Bardus began to clean and dress her wounds. As he did he asked, "Now, suppose you tell me more about how this happened than just trotting."

"My bandeau was loose," Klara said. "I've been sleeping in it, so the laces stretched a bit. And I've not been tightening it in the mornings because there really isn't any privacy to do that sort of thing. I didn't want to encourage anyone… I mean… Well, I wasn't looking for work. Then today, when we were trotting for so long, it loosened even more and I bounced out."

"Why didn't you tell us you needed to stop?" Karn asked, holding the candle's flickering flame a tad to near her nipple.

Klara was crestfallen. "I knew Thorn wanted to keep going. I didn't want to be the reason you were held back."

"So rather than ask us to stop for a short while, you put two holes in your carcass, rubbed your skin off, and bloodied your clothes?" Bardus asked.

"That about sums it up," Klara said, shamefaced. Unable to meet their eyes, she stared at the dirt, hoping Ffearn and Karn would find something to do other than hover over her.

"Lads, fetch her a blanket," Bardus said. When they had gone, he looked at her and said, "You've had sex in front of this entire company twice now and that hasn't bothered you a bit, but you won't tighten your bandeau in front of the two you've been bedding with for the last quarter moon?"

"Whoring is different, Bardus," Klara replied. "It's work. It's not something I think about. It's like mending a shirt or butchering chickens. Anyone can do those things and not feel awkward. I didn't want to encourage Ffearn and Karn is all. I joined your company to get away from whoring. I can do it if I must, I'd just rather not."

They sat in silence for a moment, then Bardus said, "You will take your bandeau off every night and you will put it back on and lace it properly every morning. Those lads have likely seen as many naked bodies as you have; they'll not be shocked at the sight of you dressing or undressing."

When Karn returned, Bardus had finished bandaging her. Karn handed her the blanket and a knee-length tunic with Skolt-style fleece trimmings at the cuffs and hem. She had never seen him wear it. Nor had she seen any of her companions dress in the traditional Skoloti style.

"I know it won't do for the day, but you can sleep in it tonight." Then pointing to his pack, Karn added, "I've got soap in here somewhere. Your dress needs washing."

Klara wrapped herself in the blanket but did not don Karn's tunic. Then she gathered up her clothes and made her way across camp, Karn trailing her.

At the stream Klara said, "You don't need to stay with me, I can manage. And I don't need your tunic; I'll put the dress back on once it's dry."

Karn looked at her confused. "It might not be dry until morning, and even then might still be damp."

"I've stood watch before," Klara said, "I can wait for it to dry." Then she dropped to her knees and began soaking the dress, scrunching it in both hands to ensure it was thoroughly wet.

"Why won't you wear the tunic?" Karn asked, dropping to his knees beside her. Klara heard a hint of desperation in his voice.

Harsh, angry words erupted from her. "I don't like to be indebted to people." Refusing to make eye contact, she focused on scrubbing her dress in the creek. She did not want to be beholden to anyone, least of all someone who might call in the debt at some point in the future.

Instead of replying in kind, Karn reached out and touched her arm. "There's no debt to be paid. You have a need I can fulfill. It's like taking turns with the cooking or sharing the watch."

"Those things are different," Klara said, but there was little conviction in her voice.

Karn reached up and brushed an errant hair from her face. "No," he said, "They are the same." They looked into each other's eyes, but neither spoke. Eventually, Karn took the soap from his pack and handed it to her. Then he rose and left, leaving his tunic behind.

After scrubbing her dress and under things the best she could in the dark, Klara hung them over branches to dry. She donned Karn's tunic, wrapping it snuggly around her and belting it in place. Then she gathered up the blanket and returned to camp. Ffearn and Karn insisted she sleep in the middle for warmth. Sleep consumed her instantly.

## CHAPTER 6

# HIGH ROLLERS

THORN ROUSED HER at dawn. Circles so dark they might have been made with charcoal ringed his eyes. Clearly he was as exhausted as Klara felt. In the gray light, she saw Bardus sitting beside a small cooking fire adding herbs to the drinking horn. Stiffness had settled in her muscles overnight. Now, her aching body protested, unwilling to move.

"Come," Thorn said, gently shaking her shoulder with his heavily calloused hand. "Bardus is waiting. He wants to look at your wounds now that there is some light."

Klara crawled from the bedroll, joints popping in protest, and was followed by her bedmates. The trio made their way to where Bardus sat at the fire.

"I see you found something to wear," Bardus said, shifting his attention from the herbs in his kit to a nearby pile of wood, from which he chose a pitchy piece and added it to the fire. "However, I'll be needing you to take it off." Then looking at Ffearn and Karn, he added, "Lads, fetch her a blanket so she doesn't have to sit bare while I examine her."

Stiffness in her limbs slowed her movements as she removed Karn's tunic and handed it to him. Then she wrapped the blanket about her waist before sitting on a log near the fire. Bardus unwound the bandages while the entire camp watched.

As Bardus prodded the hole under her right arm, Ruis walked up with an armful of firewood and whistled. "Would you look at that?"

"That's a real beauty, that is," Nuallan said, as he squinted at her in the dim light.

"I'd never of put a bandeau on the list of things you'd need to defend yerself from," Ruis said, "but it's done a right nasty job there, hasn't it?"

"Wait 'til you see underneath," Ffearn added. "Took the skin right off."

Raising her breast, Bardus took a good look while the rest of the camp continued to ooh and ah at her injuries. Seeing every one of them staring at her bosom, Klara announced rather sarcastically, "I'm so pleased that everyone cares so greatly about my health."

"You'd best get used to it, lass," Bardus said as he focused his attention on the underside of her other breast. "Comparing battle wounds is a long Kenetlo tradition."

"But we weren't in battle," Klara said.

"We weren't," Ffearn said. "But from the looks of it, you were."

"Can you sit a horse?" Thorn asked, his eyes soft with concern.

"Aye," Klara said irritably. Why did Thorn become mawkish at the thought of her in pain?

"Good," Thorn said. Then to Ffearn and Karn, he added, "Go collect her things."

"My saddlebag," Klara called to the pair of Keltoi, "bring it here and not to the picket line. I need my herbs." Klara noticed that Bardus watched with interest as she sprinkled some of the pennyroyal into the drinking horn.

"I believe I've seen that herb before," Bardus said, unrolling a fresh bandage.

"Aye," Klara answered. "It's quite common." Skoloti women were permitted free access to pennyroyal, but the Disciples of Elah and their converts sought to ban the practice of consuming the herb. She did not know if the Kenetlo approved of using herbs to prevent pregnancy and figured now was not the time to find out.

After Bardus finished bandaging her, Ffearn and Karn helped her dress by the fire, taking care to make sure the bandeau's laces were tight. Her dress was still damp, but she would manage. The days had been hot, so she expected it to dry quickly now that the sun was up.

The company rode out early and remained quiet on the road. There was no singing, but the Keltoi did a good deal of talking among themselves. She was grateful that Thorn let the horses walk; though, as tightly as Bardus had her bandaged and Ffearn and Karn had her cinched, nothing was going to move even if they kept the horses at a trot. At the head of the column Thorn and Waywyrd were talking earnestly and at times appeared to be locked in an impassioned disagreement.

Whenever chance afforded them a view, Thorn searched the road behind them. Klara often looked behind her too, but never saw any sign of the bounty hunters. Ahead of her, Ffearn and Karn were hatching some plan. She heard them mention the town of Ufa several times and got the impression they were up to no good.

During the morning ride, her mind wandered as she contemplated the journey. Waywyrd had told her they were destined for the Abnoba Mountains, but Thorn said they traveled to Kenetlon and mentioned a city named Duirness. During their rides, she had overheard them mention a place called Silver Fountains, too. She had no idea how far away these places were or how long it would take them to get there, hoping only that they were beyond the slavers' reach.

Since she only cooked one day out of seven, if she were to be of any value to them, the Keltoi must expect to be on the road for several moons. The longer the better. Cooking for these Keltoi was easy work and she hoped to leave her life as a whore far, far behind. She had no idea how she would support herself when they arrived, but there was time to figure that out later, provided Thorn did not sever her contract in Ufa for being fool enough not to tighten her bandeau in the mornings. After a while, Waywyrd left his place beside Thorn and came to ride beside her. Grateful for his company, she smiled as he approached.

"You've made quite an impression on Thorn," Waywyrd said as his dun fell instep beside her and Constant.

Klara sighed regretfully. "I expected as much. It seems I'm to be nothing but trouble."

"Quite the contrary," Waywyrd said, "Thorn was impressed that you traveled without complaint with such wounds and still had the vigor to protest when we arrived at camp. Although, he would have preferred it if you stopped them and took care of the problem at the outset."

Shaking her head, Klara considered how to explain her reluctance to ask for what seemed like a reasonable accommodation in hindsight. "I've been nothing my whole life," Klara said. "I often feel like I need prove myself because no one has ever believed in me. That's why I didn't want to stop; I thought it would be seen as weakness."

"They say," Waywyrd mused as he adjusted his grip on his staff, "that when no one believes in a god, the god ceases to exist. You say no one has ever believed in you and yet, here you are. I'd say that means you are mightier than the gods." He paused to look at her, swaying slightly in his saddle. "You should not doubt yourself; there is strength in you that you have not tapped yet."

Changing the subject, Waywyrd asked, "So aside from riding at a brisk trot, how are you enjoying your time among the Kenetlo?"

"In truth, I don't much think of them as Kenetlo," Klara said. "They are all quite tall, as far as Kenetlo go. The only one shorter than me is Nuallan."

"Actually, that's not true," Waywyrd corrected as he again fiddled with his staff, "Ruis and Bardus are shorter than you, also. The difference is that you are poorly shod whereas they have sturdy boots with thick soles for traveling and heels to accommodate their stirrups. You should purchase a pair when you get a chance. But, as you say, the company is quite tall. Karn is the tallest Kelto on record. Ffearn and Thorn are not far behind him. Karn's height has proved advantageous to the company in the past and it will do so again."

"How do you mean?" Klara asked, curiosity clearly getting the better of her.

"Well, as tall as he is, he can, and I'm told often does, pass for a Skolt," Waywyrd said. "I see you and Karn get along admirably. It's a good thing, too. The pair of you will need to get along today."

Klara looked at him quizzically, brow furrowing into a question. "Why's that?"

"At midday we will split the company," Waywyrd said. "Karn will change and the two of you will travel into Ufa ahead of us under the guise of a married couple. The rest of the company will follow in stages later."

"Are you mad?" Klara exclaimed. She had no interest in playing wife to anyone. If she had, she would have joined one of the bands of warrior maids and gone off in search of a conquest.

"No, not at all," Wayward replied, ignoring her indignation. "Our pursuers are still behind us and will spread word that a bounty is being offered for a company containing six bedraggled Keltoi, a wanton prostitute, and a wizard. However, no one is looking for a married couple, a minor lord traveling with his entourage, and a merchant with his servant. The hard part was getting Thorn to agree to be my servant."

"And you think breaking the group up will allow us to pass unnoticed?" Klara asked, still uncomfortable with the idea.

"Oh yes," Waywyrd said. "Each group will bring one of the pack horses with them, which will help allay suspicion as well. And we must make sure that we don't all end up at the same inn. There are two inns in Ufa. You and Karn will stay at the farther one and stable your horses there."

"But why must I play the role of wife?" Klara asked. "And wouldn't Ffearn make a better Skolt? His green eyes and brown hair would be less noticeable among the reds and blonds of the Skoloti."

"Well, given your attire we can't very well pass you off as a warrior," Waywyrd said.

Waywyrd was right. Killing a man in battle was a Skoloti prerequisite for marriage. Klara found staying alive on normal days difficult enough. Lacking the desire to deliberately ride into bands of foreigners to kill or be killed, she never joined any of the warrior bands and therefore lacked any of garb commonly worn by warrior maids.

"Since they're looking for a whore," Waywyrd continued, "sending you on as you are is out of the question. And we can't very well keep you in company with a bunch of Keltoi. Besides, Ffearn is terrible with horses and Karn is already quite good at playing the role of a farmer, so a farmwife you must be."

Klara had to admit that even though Ffearn might look the part, Skoloti was horse culture. His poor riding and lack of horse knowledge would draw far more attention than Karn's dark hair.

When they stopped to water the horses at midday, Karn went up stream to wash and change. He returned wearing the tunic he lent her the night before. Under the tunic, he wore his breeches tucked into his boots as Skolts do. Because Skolts wear their hair loose, he had unfastened his braids, letting his hair fall about his face. Klara easily pictured him behind a plow in this guise and saw at once that he would pass for a Skolt. The only alteration to her costume she could make was to her hair, which she now wore loose in the tradition of farmwives.

The group gathered in the shade along the stream as Thorn laid out their plan. "Karn, you and Klara will ride out first. Ffearn, your group will follow later in the afternoon. Waywyrd and I will arrive sometime late in the night."

When it came time for Klara and Karn to depart, the brothers gave each other a rousing embrace. They clasped each other's arms, and with a smile too big and far too much mischief in his eyes, Karn said, "Until tonight then."

"Tonight," Ffearn confirmed. Then patting his brother's face he said, "Get on with ye."

Karn mounted up and took the lead of a sorrel pack horse. Traveling the road in the afternoon heat, the pair looked more or less like a married couple on their way to visit distant relations. As they rode out of sight of the rest of the company Klara asked, "What was that all about?"

"What was what all about?" Karn replied looking more than a little confused.

"You and Ffearn," Klara said, eager to know precisely what sort of mischief she needed to head off, or avoid if possible. "I get the feeling you have something planned for Ufa. What is it?"

Karn's brown eyes sparkled and a board grin lit his face. "I'll not tell you a thing."

"Why not?" Klara asked, somewhat perturbed.

"You'll have to torture it out of me," Karn said, eyes still full of mirth. "I hear you are quite convincing when it comes to questioning a feller. I have it on good authority that you can get a man to spill his secrets in just a quarter of an hour. I've heard your interrogation techniques were—what was the word? Effective," he added with a wink, "though, I think it will take a good deal more than a quarter of an hour to learn my secrets."

"I'm afraid you're out of luck then," Klara said, doing her best to keep a stony expression on her face. "I never work without an audience."

"Truly?" he asked, eyes wide with amazement.

"It seems you may never know." Klara smiled at his gullibility and shook her head. Men were always eager to believe a titillating tale. Changing the subject, she said, "Your horse is a magnificent beast."

Beside her, Karn's horse arched his neck and shook his mane, seeming to have perked up at the praise. The gelding was black save for a white star, well put together, and sound of lung and limb. Intelligent, too, and well trained.

"That he is." Karn patted the beast's neck. "Nearly cost me my life, though."

"How's that?" Klara prompted, curious.

"I was working as a farrier out of Uncle Thorn's blacksmith shop," Karn said. "A man wanted him shod, which I did. But he said it was poorly done and refused to pay, so I refused to return the horse. He and his friends caught me in the street one night and beat me badly. I was greatly outnumbered. If Thorn and Ruis hadn't come looking for me, I might have been killed. Thorn ran them off, but they called the magistrate and accused me of horse-thieving. Thankfully, Uncle Thorn is known for honest dealings. The magistrate examined the horse's shoes and judged the work acceptable. That made him mad and he bellowed quite a bit. I suggested a round of dice. If he won, he wouldn't have to pay. If I won, I got the horse. He was quite pompous and wanted to save face in front of his friends, so he agreed. Of course, I won. I've named him Night."

Klara and Karn conversed amiably as they passed the miles. Karn's good-natured temperament put her at ease and she found herself laughing at many of his jokes. Upon reaching Ufa, they agreed to stop at the inn and stable their horses before making purchases in the village. Spending money was an extravagance Klara was seldom afforded and she was nearly giddy as they walked down the dusty lane, dodging squalling children and squawking chickens, headed for the cobbler.

As Klara sat on a bench outside the man's home, the cobbler measured her foot and promised the boots the following day. From there, they went to the weaver for fabric to mend her bandeau. Tired of being encumbered by her skirt, she longed for the freedom trousers afforded her companions. For that she chose a piece of gray wool. The last stop was the smith where she purchased a needle and Karn bought a silver clip. Only two small coppers remained in her purse once her purchases were complete. Klara shrugged as she peered into her purse; poverty was her usual state.

Shopping complete, they wove their way through the village, back to the inn. Eager to make their purchases, they had stabled the horses, not bothering to examine their lodgings before setting out. The building was small and owing to the heat the fire was out, casting the dining hall in darkness. Standing just inside the doorway, Klara let her eyes adjust to the dim light. A warm glow came from a doorway to the back. The clatter of pots and savory aromas told her that was the kitchen.

A child popped its head out of the room that must serve as the living quarters for the family and pointed at another opening, saying, "Guest room is that one."

The communal guest room was empty save for them. Precious little light peeked in under the eaves through the crack where the wattle and daub walls met the thatched roof. There was a pallet in each of the room's four corners and the rushes were fresh underfoot. Klara appreciated that, hoping it meant the straw for bedding was also changed regularly and free of lice.

Karn dropped his saddlebag on the pallet he had selected as their bed, saying, "Wait here while I look for Ffearn. I'll return soon so we can maintain the pretense of being married by supping together."

Already laying out her fabric and contemplating which project to begin first, mending the bandeau or cutting pieces for trousers, she absent-mindedly waved him away. Opting to begin with the bandeau, she went in search of the innkeeper to borrow the woman's shears. Having returned to her room, Klara disrobed and began the project.

She had chosen a heavy fabric to recover the trusses. However, mending the bandeau was only the first step in solving the problem. She needed a way to prevent it from slipping, even if it became loose. The obvious answer was a strap. From the remaining fabric, she cut two wide straps which she intended to fasten to the breast of the bandeau, then run over her shoulders, to the opposite shoulder blade. Then she sat cross-legged on the pallet and began to sew.

Karn returned, bounding through the door without knocking. In his excitement he failed to notice that Klara sat bare-chested before him, bandeau in her lap.

"Ffearn managed to arrange a game for tonight," he said. "There's quite a buzz in town about the Kenetlo Lord who's going to lose all his money." Flopping down on the ox hide beside her and putting his hands behind his head, he looked toward the rafters and mused, "It's a shame we can't arrange things together like we usually do. I may end up having to get soused tonight." As he turned to face her, he realized that she was absent a shirt.

Eyeing her carefully, he asked, "Were you deliberately waiting for me like this?"

"I wasn't waiting for you at all," Klara said. Holding up her sewing, she added, "I was mending my bandeau." She was not sure how he managed it, but he looked relieved and disappointed at the same time.

"Well, then," he said, "will you need me to help you back into that thing or will you be going to dinner bare?"

Klara smirked at him as she laid aside the needle and thread. Standing, she gingerly held her breasts, "I'll be needing a bit of help if you can manage it."

When she had dressed, they went to the dining hall and enjoyed the hearty food produced from the innkeeper's well-stocked kitchen. After dinner they checked on the horses, which also seemed to be enjoying the comforts of civilization. Klara was restless. Neither she nor Karn were used to being idle. But she did not want to risk walking through town again since they had a bounty on their heads.

Looking for diversion, they searched the stable until they found a brush and curry comb. After all three horses were brushed, they stood back to admire their work. Karn draped his arm around her shoulders and Klara leaned into him, enjoying how his musky scent mingled with the scents of fresh straw and horses.

"It's time I got to the game," Karn said, "but I'll see you back to the room first."

In their room, Karn said, "Don't bother waiting up. There's no way of knowing how long I'll be, but I expect it'll be late. And I'm sorry you can't come. It'd be fun to have you there, but women generally don't frequent the dice tables and Waywyrd doesn't want us to draw unwanted attention."

"Karn, I'm a whore," Klara said. "I happen to know the only women inside a tavern are the entertainment."

Skolt women were pragmatic. Their disdain for prostitution was over-ruled by the knowledge that the trade kept many of the young, uncut men from preying on their daughters. Since the trade was plied at taverns, Skolt women avoided alehouses, save to reclaim an errant husband. Accompanying Karn to the game would be as good as announcing her profession to the town.

"Besides," she added. "I have no intention of waiting up when there is a bed in my presence." The ox hide she sat upon had been thrown over a pallet of fresh straw and she had enjoyed its softness as she sewed. Now, she was looking forward to a comfortable night's sleep.

After he left, Klara sewed a bit more. When the last of the light died out, she contemplated her sleeping options. At the alehouse she generally just wrapped the blanket around herself and slept nude. On the road with these Keltoi she had been sleeping in her dress but hated the way it tangled around her legs. She was vulnerable while she slept and anyone might pay for use of one of the other pallets. In the end she decided to sleep bare, hoping they might be the only travelers at the inn tonight. When Karn returned she would borrow his tunic for the remainder of the night.

Near midnight, Karn woke her by stumbling around the room. He barely managed to get out of his boots before crawling into bed.

"I thin' I came ou' okay," he slurred. "S'up to Ffearn now. He's still mos'ly sober, so it should come out alrigh'. I wish I'd talked to the servin' wench ahead o' time. I'm goin' have a bloody-awful headache in the mornin'."

"How would talking to the local whore have helped that?" Klara asked as she made room for him under the blanket.

"The girls water-down our ales. They taste like piss that way, but we can match the 'thers drink for drink withou' gettin' wasted. They don' notice we aren't drinkin' and we still have our wits."

Karn slid his arms around her as he spoke. "Hey," he said, startled. "You're bare again."

"I've no other clothes," Klara reminded him. "I was hoping to borrow your tunic."

"Righ'," Karn slurred. He attempted to unbuckle his belt, but his fingers refused to cooperate. Klara moved his hands aside and did it for him. Pushing the tunic over his shoulders revealed a thick, dark, mass of chest hair. Klara longed to run her fingers through it but restrained herself as Karn finished removing his tunic and handed it to her. Rather than let Karn spoon her as he so often did, she rolled to face him and found him already asleep.

Klara woke before Karn and watched the shadows dance across his chest as the sunlight filtered through the cracks under the eaves. Still drowsy, she ran her fingers through his chest hair, feeling the curvature and firmness of his pecs. She had always liked chest hair. Of all the silly laws magistrates passed, she saw no reason why one prohibiting hairless men from going about shirtless did not exist. Karn, however, she would gladly have shirtless anytime. Then she admired the tone of his biceps as she trailed her hand down his arm.

Karn woke and playfully pulled her to him. "I see you find Kelto-flesh agreeable to you."

"Why would I not?" Klara asked.

"Most Skolt women don't care for Keltoi and Elb maids are even more particular." he said. "Though, I don't much fancy Elb maids either, so I guess it matters little."

Klara sat up and commenced pulling loose straw from her hair. "Did you sleep well?"

"I did," he said, sitting up. "But I've got a splitting headache and need to piss. And I'm eager to see if Ffearn won, lost, or ended up jailed, so we'd best get moving."

They dined heartily at breakfast knowing they would not see sausage and eggs again for a long while. After that, they collected Klara's boots from the cobbler and Karn inquired after the game. From the scraps of conversation she heard, it sounded as if the cobbler was one of the participants. As it was told, the Kenetlo Lord won back all the money he lost earlier in the night and had all of them nearly broke before hitting another losing streak.

Klara waited until they were on the road before she queried Karn. A summer breeze was toying with her hair. "Was Ffearn playing with his own money or the company's?"

"Both," Karn said. "Why?"

"Well, if he lost all the money, then won't that make it difficult for the journey ahead?" she asked. Granted, her position with the company was simply part-time cook and huntress, but she liked knowing her skill with a bow was not their sole source of sustenance.

"He didn't lose it all," Karn said. "I have some of it, and I came out ahead last night. Besides, I'd bet he came out ahead as well."

"Didn't the man just say he hit a losing streak at the end?" Klara asked.

"That's how we run the game," Karn said. "We take turns winning a bunch. Then we lose a little back so the locals don't get suspicious and run us out of town. The important thing is Ffearn's already long gone with their coin and not jailed as a high roller, especially if he were to be caught with our weighted set of dice on him." The scheme was more intricate than she had realized and she considered the ingenuity of it a credit to them.

When the party of Keltoi ahead of them stopped at midday, they waited for Klara and Karn to catch up to them. The brothers, gleefully reunited, embraced and went off to compare winnings. As they did, Bardus made Klara strip and examined her injuries. He had purchased a salve from the apothecary and applied it liberally before binding her again. As she was dressing, Ffearn and Karn came over and announced that they doubled their money the night before. Nuallan looked pleased as he accepted the fistfuls of coins.

Ruis pushed himself up from the rock he had been sitting on and said, "Let's be on our way."

"Shouldn't we wait for Thorn and Waywyrd?" Klara asked.

Ruis seemed unconcerned as he replied, "They'll catch us up." Then he turned and headed for the horses, expecting the others to follow suit. Soon, the company was back on the road.

With both of the brothers present, the night's game was relived in all its detail. Particular attention was given to how Karn's drunkenness nearly cost them the game at one point. Karn accepted the ribbing from his companions, pointing out that he came out ahead in the end. Eventually, the conversation turned away from the game as the brothers recited the new limericks they learned for the rest of the company.

"At one point," Ffearn said, "A feller named Kurt stood to toast us saying:

> 'HERE'S TO THE BREEZES,
> THAT BLOWS THROUGH THE TREES-ES,
> AND LIFTS THE GIRLS' SKIRTS ABOVE THEIR KNEES-ES
> THAT SHOWS US THEIR RIGGIN'
> THAT SQUEEZES AND PLEASES
> AND SPREADS DISEASES
> BY JEEZ-ES!'"

This was met by hearty cheers and applause from the rest of the company.

Not to be outdone, Karn added, "My particular favorite was:

> 'OL' DONN FARMER SAT IN THE CORNER,
> COURTING A STRUMPET, SAYS I.
> HE SLIPPED HER THE TONGUE,
> AND TICKLED HER BUM,
> SAYING, 'NONE IS AS NAUGHTY AS I.'"

And so the afternoon's ride proved pleasant as the Keltoi were again a merry bunch. The singing resumed, along with jokes and chatter.

# Chapter 7

# A Contest of Skill

HEN RUIS CALLED the party to halt and make camp for the night, Thorn and Waywyrd still had not caught up with them. This worried Klara and she said as much.

Laughing off her concerns, Ruis said, "Lass, I expect Thorn's absence has more to do with avoiding my cooking than any trouble on the road."

Klara had to admit, if she were given an opportunity to miss one of Ruis's meals, she would have taken it, too. When she finished helping Bardus water the horses and had all of them set on the picket line, she turned toward Ffearn and Karn, intending to join them by the fire.

Bardus called to her, "Hold on a moment, lass."

Klara headed back to him, expecting that he was going to have her disrobe again. Instead, he produced a brush and curry comb from one of the panniers. Holding them out to her, he said, "I thought Constant might enjoy these a bit more than pine cones."

"Bardus, I can't accept these," Klara said. Gifts often came with the expectation of reciprocity. Generally, the only ones she accepted were those that appeared unbidden and anonymously as she slept.

"They're not for you," Bardus assured her. "I talked Thorn into letting me use some of the company's money to buy them. He wasn't too happy about it, but I told him they'd be used on all the horses. In the presence of your beast, the rest of ours look mighty raggedy."

It was true. Klara managed to brush out Constant's entire winter coat. Now he looked sleek and healthy. It probably helped that he was getting extra feed too, since she had been slipping him most of the dried biscuits that came her way.

"Anyway," Bardus said, nodding toward the panniers, "I wanted to show you where they were. I'll be keeping them in the panniers with the tents and other camp supplies."

Klara smiled at him. "Thank you. Shall we break them in now?"

"I've already done that," Bardus said. "I brushed Thunder in the stables last night. But the other horses could use a good brushing."

Thunder was Ffearn's dapple gray gelding. Klara furrowed her brow in confusion. "Why were you brushing Thunder and not your own horse?"

"Well, it wouldn't do for a high and mighty Kenetlo Lord to be seen brushing his own horse, now would it?" he said with a wink. "Especially not when he's paying someone to do it for him while he's off gambling."

"Is the whole company in league with Ffearn and Karn's ruse with the dice?" Klara wondered aloud.

"That we are," Bardus said. "It's how most of our money comes in, so we have to make sure nothing seems amiss. The lot of us are tradesmen without fortune to pay for our quest, though not as poorly off as Nuallan would have you believe. Thorn was the finest swordsmith in Olbia. He taught Ffearn the finer work necessary for the hilts and pommels. The lad has a talent for such things and soon the nobility sought him out for their jewel work. A fair bit of money changed hands when Thorn sold his shop. We pooled most of our money at the outset, and the lads keep us in coin as we go. It's not a lot, but it pays for the occasional hot meal and a night at an inn now and again."

Bardus chuckled and scratched his beard. "Well, that goes for everyone except Karn. Since he has to play the part of a traveling farmer, he sleeps in the stables and eats from the stores in our packs to keep folks from suspecting he's with our company. He was right happy yesterday when Thorn told him he'd get to room with you and not bed with the horses."

"Well," Klara said, "that explains why he was so eager to get out of bed and down to breakfast."

"Had intentions of detaining him in bed, did you?" Bardus teased. "Lot of good that will do you."

"No," Klara replied. "I've just never seen anyone so excited over eggs and sausage." Then she added, "How about we brush your mare?" Bardus happily agreed.

The scents of dinner wafted over to them as they brushed Honey, Bardus's palomino mare. It was not a pleasant smell. That was encouraging. It assured her Thorn and Waywyrd were fine. More than fine actually, because they were avoiding Ruis's cooking, whereas in a very short while she would be handed a bowl full of ruined beans.

⁂

Upon waking, Klara found she had the blankets to herself. There was no sign of Ffearn or Karn anywhere in camp. Where had they gone off to? Wrapping herself in their blankets, she went to sit by the fire and continue the work she began on her bandeau the previous day. Nuallan was fixing porridge for breakfast. He was in a foul mood, grumbling as he banged the dishes and rattled the pot.

Bardus relinquished his watch and joined her at the fire. "I'm plumb tuckered out."

Bardus sighed, ignoring Nuallan's scowl as he accepted a steaming bowl of porridge. "After breakfast I'm going to sleep for a bit, but I want a look at your wounds again sometime today. It's important that they don't go putrid."

"Not expecting Thorn and Waywyrd soon then?" Klara asked.

"Not until at least midday," Bardus said. "And that's if they set out by noon yesterday. If they were delayed in town, we may not see them until tonight."

Well, that gave her more time to sew and for her tender breasts to recover. However, given a choice between sewing and hunting, her preference was hunting.

"You were on watch when Ffearn and Karn left camp this morning," Klara said. "Do you know where they've gone?"

"The lads like to go off alone together," Bardus replied, "always have. They'll be along when they're ready, which shouldn't be too much longer now. They won't want to upset Thorn by not being in camp when he gets here. Now, let me get some rest and I'll come look after you in a bit."

Bardus had not given her an answer, but she did not question him further. They might have been hunting, or scouting, or simply sneaked off for a bath, at which point she would have liked the opportunity to join them because they had the soap. Behind her, Ruis snored loudly. That only left Nuallan for company, and he was not much by way of company this morning. By the time Ruis finally woke, her fingers had grown tired.

"So you've given up clothes all together and have decided to go 'round in yer blankets, have ye?" Ruis teased as he accepted his porridge from Nuallan.

"Well, I cannot mend the bandeau if I'm wearing it," she replied. Klara showed him how she had covered the trusses and reinforced the sides, as well as the designs for the straps.

Ruis gave the contraption a disapproving look. "I cannot fathom wearing such a thing, nor why women do it."

A change in the wind sent smoke her way. Klara coughed and sputtered attempting to wave the smoke away as she answered. "If your testicles were as big as my bosom, would you want them free and flopping when you rode a horse, or would you rather have them tucked up somewhere safe?"

"I take your point," Ruis said between mouthfuls of porridge. "Still, it don't look comfortable."

"It isn't," Klara said. "If you've nothing better to do, help me mark where the straps should be fastened. I can't do it by myself."

"Get one of the lads to help you," Ruis said, still shoveling in his breakfast.

"They've gone off somewhere," Klara replied, "and I want to finish this today, if I can."

Ruis's mood darkened. At last he relented, "Fine, I'll help you." He quickly consumed the final spoonful and handed the bowl back to Nuallan.

She was healed enough get into the bandeau herself. Once she was laced in, she instructed Ruis to pull the straps tight across her back and to use a piece of charcoal to mark where they touched. Klara thanked him, worked her way out of the bandeau, and began sewing along the lines.

Ruis collected something from his pack before resuming his seat. Holding a dagger out for her to see, he said, "I picked this up in Ufa. It ain't much, but it's better than the butcher knife you've got. Once you're healed up, I'll show you how to defend yerself with it. Mind you don't go using it in the kitchen, though." Winking, he laid the dagger beside her.

Picking up the blade, Klara unsheathed it. It was old, double edged, made of bronze, and amazingly sharp. It had decorative wavy lines on the guard and pommel. The ash handle was worn smooth by use.

"I'll have to remember that," she said, giving Ruis a solemn look. "One should not carve men and roasts with the same knife."

"You sure you don't carry a bit of demon in yer blood?" Ruis threw back at her. "There's more sass in you than any woman I've ever met."

"Given the way you smell, I reckon I might be the only woman you've ever met." Breaking into a broad grin, Klara realized she liked Ruis. He never wanted anything more from her than a hot meal. It was easier accepting gifts knowing that nothing was expected in return. Picking up her sewing, she resumed her work.

The vocal jabs they were shooting at each other across the fire woke Bardus, who consented to join them. As Bardus sat, Ruis asked, "The lads been gone long?"

"Aye," Bardus issued in response. It was clear something was on their minds. After passing the drinking horn around and consuming the last of the liquid, Bardus said, "Can I interrupt your work long enough to get a look at you?"

Klara was grateful for an excuse to lay the project aside.

After examining, Bardus said, "Your wounds are healing well enough. Wear your bandeau as little as possible. The less time you spend in it, the faster you'll heal."

While Bardus was re-wrapping her bandages, Ruis asked, "How long before she's fit for weapons training?"

Bardus surprised her by saying, "You can start today, provided neither of you get too rough. As long as she's bandaged properly there's little concern about dirt getting in the wounds. Mind, though, I don't want you knocking her around to the point that you re-open them." This greatly pleased them both.

Nuallan harrumphed as a means of announcing Ffearn and Karn's return. Each of them carried a pair of forest grouse and were leaving a trail of feathers behind them. It was clear they were pleased with themselves and that the outing had done them good. As they rid themselves of the game and joined her at the fire, Klara noticed they had bathed again. Karn's hair was freshly braided and adorned with the silver clip he purchased in Ufa. Ffearn's moustache was trimmed and silver beads were woven into it as well, causing the ends to droop under the weight.

Klara was just opening her mouth to compliment Ffearn when Karn declared, "You're bare again!"

"What do you mean again?" Ffearn asked, a slight accusatory note in his voice.

"For the last two days, she's been bare every time I've come upon her," Karn said, feigning alarm.

Klara looked at them and said, "I'll tell you two what I told Ruis this morning. I cannot mend the bandeau if I'm wearing it. Besides, Bardus forbade me to wear the thing at night anyway."

This exchange lightened the mood considerably. Bardus and Ruis went to gather firewood while Ffearn and Karn brushed their horses. Only she and Nuallan remained at the fire and he was still grumpy. Why bathing and hunting put the company in such a foul mood perplexed her. So far, she and the pair of brothers were the only ones to indulge in a bath. Maybe Kenetlo viewed bathing the same way they viewed eating rabbit—something generally to be avoided.

Early in the afternoon, Klara announced that the bandeau was complete. She managed to get into it all by herself and was satisfied with the design.

"That's quite the contraption you have there," Ffearn said. "I don't see how a chap would get you out of it."

"That's the point," Klara replied. "I don't want anything coming out of it."

Ffearn came closer to admire her handiwork, saying, "I've fleeced a maid or two of their bandeaus before, but never have I seen the likes of this." He slid a finger under the strap at her shoulder and felt strength of the fabric.

Looking down to admire her work, she said, "I think it will hold up no matter what Thorn asks of me now." Then looking at Ffearn she added, "I meant to compliment you on your moustache earlier. I quite like it."

Ffearn slipped an arm around her and pulled her close, whispering playfully, "Karn told me you're fond of Kelto-flesh."

"Do the pair of you have no secrets?" Klara exclaimed, pushing him away so she could don her dress.

"None," Ffearn said with a twinkle in his eye. "Now, let's go see what the rest of the camp is up to."

At seeing her dressed, Ruis insisted they use their time to teach her to defend herself. Ruis made her face off against Ffearn and Karn using sticks, walking her through several defensive postures. She was an eager student, but such things take time, and she needed a lot of practice. After she was knocked to the ground several times, Bardus called a halt to the exercises citing concerns about re-opening her wounds.

As Ffearn helped her up, Ruis said, "Not to worry, lass; you just weren't meant to handle a blade."

Klara spun on her heels and immediately challenged him. "Not meant to handle a blade? Ever notice how you handle one? It's utterly disgraceful."

"Now, lass, them's fightin' words," Ruis replied.

"They were meant to be," Klara said as she squared her shoulders. "I challenge you to a contest of skill with a blade." Everyone instantly stopped, waiting to see what would happen next and if they might need to restrain Klara.

Ruis began to loosen his muscles as he prepared for her charge, saying, "I'll best you in any contest, then I'll paddle yer backside if need be."

"So, you're accepting my challenge," Klara said, seeking verbal confirmation.

"Aye," Ruis said, "whenever you're ready." His hand already rested on the hilt of the dagger he wore at his waist.

"You just hold on a minute there, lass," Bardus said. "Ruis served as a spearman under King Thorgal's rule and has enjoyed plenty of training in the craft of war since. I'll not have you damaging yourself for no reason."

Klara shot him a disdainful glance. She had no intention of damaging herself. And—she would not lose.

Ruis relaxed as Klara turned and walked away, presumably thinking she had backed down. She headed Nuallan's direction and snatched up the grouse. Then she returned to where Ruis and the others were standing.

"First one to properly butcher two birds and have them cut up as fryers will be the victor," Klara said with a triumphant look in her eye. "That is my challenge."

"That was not the challenge," Ruis exclaimed aghast.

"I said," Klara reminded him, "a contest of skill with a blade. You happen to use a blade when butchering hens, though I've been told not to use the same blade as the one reserved for butchering men."

A wave of surprise and laughter went through the company. Around her the group began to goad Ruis. In producing the grouse she had beaten him already. There was nothing for it but to go along. Amid the cheers and jeers, Nuallan called time for them to begin.

Klara made quick work of her birds, deftly plucking and cutting them into frying pieces. She had even gone so far as to begin rolling them in flour and seasoning them with salt before Ruis finished. When Ruis finally did finish with his birds, the pieces were oddly misshapen, but at least they were usable. Klara was declared the victor and received several slaps on the back for having outwitted the elder Kelto.

The contest had just concluded when Thorn rode into camp leading the remaining pack horse. "I see you are all in high spirits," he said as he dismounted. Handing the lead of the pack horse to Bardus, he added, "I have only been gone a day. What could possibly be the cause for such celebration?"

Ffearn said, "Klara just defeated Ruis in a contest of skill with a blade."

Thorn looked her over. "This is a tale I must hear, but first let me see to these horses." It was the same look he had given her back at the alehouse. Like he was trying to see something inside her. Something she did not think was there.

When Thorn returned to the fire ring, Klara asked, "Will Waywyrd come later tonight?"

"No," Thorn replied. "He had other business to attend to, but he said he would join our company again when we reach Yar Chally."

This news dampened her spirits. She was not fully a part of the company of Keltoi, feeling separated because of her gender and her ethnicity. She would miss Waywyrd's companionship on the road since the Keltoi seldom included her in their conversations.

As Nuallan cooked supper, the company recounted how Klara challenged Ruis and beat him with both blade and wit. When they concluded their tale, Ruis asked, "What of the slavers? Do they still pursue us?"

"That is what held me up," Thorn said. "They arrived as I was preparing to depart. I lingered to see what news might be gathered. It seems our Luck Bringer has convinced them to look elsewhere. As Klara predicted, the boy was badly burned and rode face up in the cart under a blanket as they came into town. He has no intention of rejoining them on the road and has reconsidered his profession. The men claim she is a witch and her powers combined with that of the wizard are too great for any mortal to capture."

The party was astounded at the news and began chattering among themselves. Ruis quieted them by continuing his questions, "So, have they given up their pursuit?"

"Not entirely," Thorn said. "Because no one in town saw our party arrive, let alone depart, they assume we must have parted ways. The local constable told them about the Kenetlo Lord at the game last night. They decided Ffearn could not have been with our company, given his high manners and fine dress."

This put the party at ease. Klara realized Ffearn must have a change of clothes to disguise himself just as Karn did because she had yet to see him in anything that qualified as 'fine dress.' Nor had she seen him use anything that came close to resembling manners. She wondered how the full process of their ruse played out.

"However," Thorn said, "there were some religious zealots in town, Disciples of Elah. They were very interested in capturing the prostitute and the wizard, claiming they needed to atone for their sins. Fortunately, they headed back the way we came, thinking we must have left the trail before entering town. We should start early in the morning to put as much distance between us and them as possible."

A chill ran down Klara's spine. Much of her life had been spent avoiding the Disciples. Now they were seeking her again. When it came down to it, she greatly preferred the company of horse-eating demons over that of the Disciples, especially with their Holy Virgin nonsense.

At last supper was ready. Nuallan had fried the grouse until it was dark and crispy. Using the scrapings, he made a thick gravy which he ladled over the top of the dried biscuits. The party ate eagerly, having been left a little hungry after being present for Ruis's cooking the night before. Klara saved the biscuits for last, letting the gravy moisten them enough to be edible. Constant would have to go without his snack tonight.

As they ate, Klara voiced the questions that had been nagging at her since joining the company. "Waywyrd said you were headed for the Abnoba Mountains, but when I signed on, Thorn, you mentioned Kenetlon and the city of Duirness. Later, I overheard Nuallan mention a placed called Silver Fountains. Which is it?"

"They are one and the same," Ffearn said through a mouthful of grouse.

"You are quick with words," Thorn said, setting his bowl in his lap. "I do not recall mentioning either more than once, and I never heard Waywyrd speak of the Abnoba Mountains."

"I lived on my own as a child," Klara replied, wiping her greasy fingers on her dress. "I had to be quick or I would be dead. If someone mentions where you might steal a bit of meat or some grain, they won't tell you twice and will deny they told you once."

"I suppose that is true enough," Thorn said. "But to answer your question, it is as Ffearn said. They are one and the same. Kenetlon is our county, Duirndunum is our ancestral lands and Duirness was the principal city within Duirndunum. Silver Fountains is an abandoned mine outside the city. The Abnoba Mountains are the mountains that surround Duirness. It will be many moons before we set eyes on Kenetlon and longer still to see Duirndunum."

Klara knew only that the Abnoba Mountains were named after the Goddess herself. It was rumored that she made her home there. The closest Skoloti came to worshiping anything was their horses, often scoffing at the notion of gods and goddesses. While she felt a kinship with the horses, something deep within her had always led her to worship Abnoba. Yet, Abnoba was the goddess of the Kenetlo and this group of Keltoi seldom mentioned her. Which was something more to wonder about.

After dinner, Klara borrowed the soap and went upstream to bathe. The pool she found was small, not quite waist deep. The forest around her smelled of rich, moist earth, oak, and moss. To her, the scents of the earth were nearly as intoxicating as the wine the Keltoi passed around the fire on occasion.

The soap and water stung as she washed around her injuries, but it felt good to be clean again. The night was dark with a waning moon overhead. She preferred the silky coolness of moonlight over the scorching brightness of the sun. Stars speckled the sky giving off cold and distant light. By this time, she knew that Thorn worried when she was alone, so she did not tarry, but having finished washing, she dressed and returned to camp.

When she arrived in camp, the elder Keltoi were awaiting her. Now that she was back, they took a turn washing in the pool upstream, leaving her, Ffearn, Karn, and Thorn to mind the fire. Evidently, washing was not taboo. If not washing, then what had darkened their moods earlier?

The trio sat in companionable silence, passing the brush and comb between them as Ffearn and Klara put their hair in the long braids they wore at night. At length Klara asked, "How did you kill the grouse?"

The pair of them looked surprised and a little guilty. "We snared them," Karn said. "Why?"

"There were no holes in the carcass where an arrow would have pierced them," Klara said. Sensing their unease she asked, "Is something wrong?"

"No," Karn said, brushing aside her concern. "It's just that no one has ever questioned how we take game."

"They might not have noticed," Klara said. "Ruis certainly wouldn't have; food is foreign to him. I doubt he knows what meat is supposed to look like. I assumed you took them with your bow and just now realized there were no entry or exit holes. I didn't know you had string for a snare." At that Ffearn and Karn looked visibly relieved.

When Ruis, Bardus, and Nuallan returned, Thorn took his turn, walking alone into the woods. Klara watched him go. If he wanted a bath, he could have gone with the others. Why wait and go alone?

Those who had just bathed sat around the fire, half-heartedly attempting to dry themselves. Yawning, Klara stood and went to bed down. Her bed mates did not join her until their uncle had returned, flanking her with their warm bodies.

As she lay there, she asked, "What does the third packhorse carry?" When they were traveling, she was so busy cooking, tending horses, or thinking of other things, that she had not considered the question. Now that they had a whole day of leisure, all kinds of questions came to mind.

They looked at her perplexed, so Klara continued, "The horse Karn and I brought into town had the food and cooking supplies. The horse that went with you, Ffearn, has the tents, ax, spears, Bardus's medical supplies and things for the horses. What does the third horse carry?"

"Oh," Ffearn said, "That's our cloaks and furs. It's too hot to be wearing those all summer. It was cheaper to buy a horse to carry them than it would have been to sell them and buy new ones come winter."

Klara sat straight up. "You mean to tell that all this time I've been sharing your blankets because otherwise I thought I'd freeze and you've got an entire packhorse laden with furs! I could have been snug, and warm, and dry, and sleeping by myself!"

"Well, you can't blame me for trying," Karn said, as he too, sat up.

"Oh aye, I can!" Klara exclaimed turning on him.

"But as you can see," Ffearn said, mischief in his eyes, "We have behaved admirably this entire time. So, clearly there was no ill intent."

"I do not think 'admirable' is the word I would have chosen," Klara replied, swiveling to face him.

"You know," Ffearn said, "you should consider it a great honor to lie between us for we cannot bear to be separated."

"It's true," Karn said. "We have vowed never to be parted and here you are betwixt us. It doesn't seem right somehow."

"Not right at all," Ffearn agreed. And with that the brothers reached to embrace each other crushing her between them in a bear hug.

"Ouch!" Klara laughed. "Stop it! Let me go!" They did not stop and the three of them, locked in embrace, fell backwards onto their bedding.

"Worse than a bunch of bairns," Nuallan scoffed and rose from the fire, heading for his own beadroll.

"Aye," Bardus agreed from where he sat, stirring the coals, "we might have to paddle the lot of them and send them to separate bedrolls."

Ffearn's face lit up. He let go of Klara and sat up, announcing, "Oh, aye, spank me!"

Karn, now sitting, was a second behind him. "Aye, you must spank me, too."

Klara laughed at the absurdity of their comments, which only served to encourage them. "Well, I have no desire to be spanked or share your blankets any longer." She rose, intending to head for the paniers containing the cloaks and furs with the objective of finding something suitable to bed in.

Karn clasped his arms about her waist, pulling her back down. "Oh, no. If Bardus spanks one, he must spank us all! You included. In fact, I think you should be spanked twice."

Looking self-satisfied and about to bust with laughter, Ffearn reached for Karn's shoulder and proclaimed, "And after the spankings, the feral sex!"

Thorn stood and said, "I said at the outset that there would be no sex." Then with a hint of something forgotten and far away he added, "If they behave like children, perhaps we should treat them as such. Come Bardus, sing them off to sleep."

Bardus's voice rang deep and true from where he sat by the fire:

"SOFTLY FADES THE LIGHT OF DAY,
AS OUR CAMPFIRE DIES AWAY,
IN HIS HEART EACH KELTO MUST ASK,
HAVE WE DONE AS THE GODDESS ASKS?

"HAVE WE HELD OUR OATHS TIGHT?
HAS THE GODDESS'S LAW BEEN OUR GUIDE?
BLESS OUR LORD AND BLESS OUR LAND,
LET US EVER HAVE WORK AT HAND.

"WE HAVE HELD OUR OATHS TIGHT,
GUILTLESS WE CAN SLEEP TONIGHT.
FAITHFUL LADY, THIS YOU SHOULD KNOW,
EVER WILL WE SERVE YOU SO."

The three of them settled back to listen to the sound of Bardus's voice and stared into the star filled sky. Snug under the blanket, pressed between these two brothers, Klara could think of no other place on earth she would rather be, and it was with that thought that she fell asleep.

# CHAPTER 8
# WOLVES ON WATCH

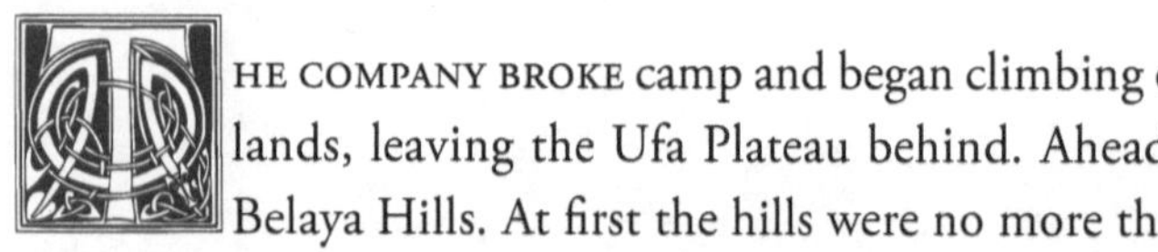

THE COMPANY BROKE camp and began climbing out of the bottom lands, leaving the Ufa Plateau behind. Ahead of them lay the Belaya Hills. At first the hills were no more than gently sloping mounds, beyond which the terrain became steeper. The air was fresher on the breeze, filled with the scents of pine and fir wafting down from the hills. Soon they left the deciduous forest behind and began seeing evergreens again. Being in the presence of towering evergreens was comforting, though Klara had never liked spruce, finding them a most disagreeable and unfriendly tree.

Constant snorted, interrupting her musings about trees. Scanning the brush, she caught sight of a wolf. The tawny animal moved like a shadow among the thick trunks. It was odd seeing one so near the road. Wolves were intelligent and prone to staying away from humans. It was not unheard of for one to kill a farmer's sheep or fatted calf, but for the most part they enjoyed their own company and avoided men.

The animal looked long and lank, but what confused Klara was that it looked at all. She was certain the wolf was staring at her. The gleam of its golden eyes met hers, holding her gaze for the few moments it took for the horses to pass. A small shiver ran up her spine. Under normal circumstances all she expected to see of a wolf was its hind-end as it hastened from the approaching noise.

Klara took a moment to contemplate the animal's boldness. Perhaps it was a bitch staying near enough to keep an eye on a den full of pups? If the creature were nursing, that might explain why it was so thin, but she saw no sign of the pendulous teats that marked a nursing bitch. Or perhaps it was very old and unable to hunt? This time of year the forest was bursting with game; chicks had hatched, rabbits had kindled, and deer had fawned, so most predators were fat and happy, not thin and lean.

As her mind wandered through the interconnectedness of the forest, following the invisible strands that ensnared all living things in nature's intricate web, movement in the shadows again caught her eye. It was another lean wolf. This one was black, ears alert, eyes gleaming with intelligence and curiosity. Its thick ruff laid flat along the ridge of its spine, telling her it was no threat. At least, not yet. It might be the other animal's mate. The first wolf was long behind them, or so she hoped. They were far enough from the first wolf that both of them were not standing watch over the den. And there should not be a second den. Even if there were a pack in the area, only one bitch produced a litter each year.

It was almost time for their midday break. Klara assumed Thorn would stop as soon as they came across a stream suitable for drinking. She felt uncomfortable about dismounting and having the company become disorganized while wolves were about. The horses sensed them, too. Their ears were cocked, their eyes wide, and their nostrils flared, trying to catch the scent. Remembering the scolding she got over not reporting her sighting of the horseman on the road, she decided to tell Thorn about the wolves.

Klara caught a few sidelong glances as she rode to the head of the column and fell in step with Thorn and his mount. Sensing that he already had something on his mind, she did not speak immediately, but rode quietly beside him. Perhaps he had seen the wolves, too.

Thorn, lost in thought, was shocked to find her riding beside him. He startled, causing his already nervous horse to crow-hop.

"What were you thinking about?" she asked as soon as Thorn's sturdy black mount had settled back into step beside her.

"My nephews," Thorn said. "I'm quite fond of them. You spend a good deal of time in their company and have a rather unconventional bedding arrangement. Are you fond of them also?"

Klara tried to read his mood, but he was his usual, stoic self. "I enjoy their company and they are friendly enough," she said. "They often play the part of the jester, but they must be fine tradesmen or possess some wisdom they don't show. Otherwise, the others would not treat them with such respect." There was more to them, she knew, but had yet to make out what it was.

"You are astute in your observations," Thorn said, giving her one of his penetrating glances.

"Actually, it's my observations I came to talk to you about," Klara said. "I've spotted two wolves now and neither was behaving as a wolf ought. Until I'm sure they have lost interest in either us or the horses it would be unwise to stop."

"Are you certain of this?" Thorn asked.

"I'm certain that I saw two wolves," Klara replied, not sure how best to explain. "The rest is just a feeling. The horses are uneasy, too. See how they watch the trees more than the road." Klara gestured toward Constant and Anvil, whose ears were cocked, alert for threats. Anvil was Thorn's gelding. She had laughed when he had told her that like an anvil, the beast was sturdy enough to take a beating and just as black.

Thorn's dark eyes held her gaze as if he were searching for truth in something other than her words. "Well, Luck Bringer," he said at last, "you have served us well before. I will heed your advice and continue riding. Do you think I should inform the others?"

"No," Klara said. "If you tell them, they'll be nervous, which will only feed the horses' fear. If one were to bolt, that might end badly. Better if you say nothing. I know the wolves are watching us, but I don't know why. I hope that if we continue through their territory they'll let us pass unmolested."

"That seems reasonable," Thorn said as he scratched his beard. "Tell me if you sense any change, good or ill. The men and horses will want to stop for water soon."

"I will," Klara promised. Then she returned to her place at the rear of the column, gaining more than a few inquisitive glances on the way back. As they rode through the afternoon, Klara again spotted the black wolf and another, better fed, tawny one. Each time, they looked with interest at the company as it passed.

Leaving his brother's side, Karn came to ride beside her. "Would your conversation with Thorn have anything to do with why we haven't stopped yet?"

"Aye," Klara replied. "We're being shadowed by at least three wolves. I didn't think it wise to stop."

Karn patted his horse's neck. "That's why Night's so jittery. I wondered what had gotten into him." Then Karn also turned his eyes to the trees.

Riding in silence, she remained alert for signs of wolves. What she saw next startled her even more. Over Karn's shoulder, a silver fir rune was carved into the trunk of a mature pine. Just two paces from the trail, a sapling had been bent over and pinned under a stag's antlers, arranged tines down. Anyone riding by might assume they were sheds.

Neither Karn nor any of her companions noticed, but Klara had lived among demons and knew to heed the warning. The rune indicated a message; the trapped sapling indicated a need for protection. Demons had traveled this way, but who was the message intended for?

Life among demons taught her to be alert; it also taught her to keep quiet. Keeping the observation to herself, she mulled over the possibilities. It was a reasonable explanation for the wolves, and one that meant no threat to them. However, the very real possibility that they needed to protect themselves from something must be communicated. Leaving Karn at her post at the rear of the column, Klara immediately rode forward to speak with Thorn again. By now the men and horses were both parched and wanted to stop.

"I've seen a third wolf," Klara said as she reined Constant back to match Thorn's pace. "Everyone is thirsty and we cannot travel through the night. It would be prudent to find a camp we can defend if it becomes necessary."

Thorn agreed.

Choosing not to tell him about the message, Klara remained with Thorn, looking for an appropriate camp. In time, they came upon a bend in the river. Centuries of water coursing downhill had undercut the stone wall it flowed against. She saw several of these formations earlier in the day, tell-tale signs of where the water had been and a testament to how fast it flowed. Sometimes these hollow places were along the river, other times far from it. The one she spotted now was nearer the river.

Pointing to it, Klara said, "We could camp there?"

Thorn agreed. Their back would be protected by the rock, with the river deflecting a frontal attack. There were tracts of land on either side to watch, but it was better than being wholly exposed. Debris and driftwood littered the ground, showing just how far the water rose during the heavy spring runoff. That was fortuitous because they needed ample fuel to keep the fire going tonight. Thorn called the company to halt. Before everyone could scatter, tending to their camp chores, he called them together.

"We will double the watch tonight," Thorn said. "Klara has informed me that we are being followed by a pack of wolves. I want an archer on each watch. That means you will take first watch with me, Klara. Ffearn and Karn will have the second watch."

As Thorn spoke, one of the tawny wolves showed itself in full view of the company and sat on its haunches, surveying the camp. Its pink tongue lolled out the side of its mouth, panting as if it were a dog. Worse, it showed no indication that it intended to leave. Evidently the day's journey had not caused it to lose interest. Everyone stared at the animal and its brazen behavior.

At sight of the wolf, Thorn shook his head and added, "It appears it's going to be a long night."

The men gathered driftwood, stacking it in two large piles on opposite sides of the camp. Before night fell they would kindle the bonfires in an effort to discourage the wolves from getting too close. As the horses were unburdened and watered, the two other wolves joined their companion, looking long and hard at the group before loping off.

As Klara stood watching the animals go, Ruis walked up behind her and clapped her on the shoulder, saying, "I'd sleep better tonight if I knew yer bow was as deadly to them wolves as it is to rabbits."

"I'd sleep better if I had that assurance, too" Klara replied, fingering the weapon she wore slung across her back. "I've never killed a wolf before. Deer are my usual prey."

"There's a first time for everything, lass," Ruis said, then he headed toward the fire, carrying the three spears usually left with their supplies. When he reached the fire he handed a spear to Thorn and another to Ffearn.

Soon the coarse rasp of the whetstones running along blades filled the camp as the trio began sharpening their weapons.

Long after the Keltoi had wrapped themselves in their bedrolls, Klara and Thorn sat quietly, taking turns feeding the fires. Thorn held his spear at his side, Klara's bow laid across her lap. A thin sliver of a crescent moon hung in the sky above them. In the distance a wolf howled, a lost and forlorn echo that caused Klara to shiver.

"Don't you think it's a sad and lonesome sound?" she asked, more to herself than of Thorn.

"Aye," Thorn said, still staring at where the firelight danced upon the water's surface. "There were many times when I thought that were I not a man, I too would be capable of such sounds." Shaking himself from his memories he turned and addressed her. "You have keen eyes and notice much. How is it you see what my companions and I overlook?"

"Learning to discern small changes and read the undercurrents of a situation was necessary for my survival, I suppose," she said, watching the moon as if it might reveal the secrets of the night to her. "I was on my own at twelve, often hiding in the forest. But there were times when hunger or want of company pushed me down to farmsteads or into villages. Unlike beasts, men often say one thing when they mean another and behave in ways contrary to their intentions. These wolves are not behaving right, that is plain to see, so we can defend ourselves from it. Men would behave as you expect then change suddenly to get what they want. I've had much practice reading the hearts and minds of men. After that, knowing the mind of a beast isn't so difficult. I lived amongst demons for a time also and they are little more than beast themselves."

Klara thought of her time among the demons. Asmodaios, the Chief Demon, took her in when she was fourteen. At the time he was running with a pack of Ke'let hunting down Disciples of Elah who strayed into the northern lands. One of the Disciples offered her work as a cook; she was starving so she accepted. When he got her to their camp he took to beating her instead. She tried escaping, but he caught her and she ended up taking a blade to her thigh. Bleeding and unable to run, Klara lay with her hands and feet bound, listening while the Disciples discussed her fate. That was when Asmodaios struck the camp. Afterwards, the demon permitted her to live among them and their wolves while her wound healed.

Klara touched the place on her thigh where the scar was. As they sat shoulder to shoulder, staring into the night, Thorn, too, seemed consumed by memories. Their fingers brushed and intertwined. Not the fullness of holding hands, just the last two fingers on each side. It was a gesture of connectedness more than anything.

"Given your skill with a bow and knack for surveillance, why not seek employment as an interpreter or escort for merchants along the trade routes?" Thorn asked, without breaking his stare over the water or his contact with her hand.

"Lack of skill wasn't the problem," Klara answered soberly. "It was my gender. Most traders who travel the Volga and Ural are foreigners who will not hire women as guards or escorts. Goths will, but if you hire on with a Gothic vessel you risk becoming cargo yourself. Since I had no desire to be a warrior, I tried my hand at other trades: milkmaid, kitchen maid, but none of them worked out. I'm good with horses and hired on as a drover once. But there I quickly learned that which is not given freely can be taken by force. Since it seemed I must endure the sex of men regardless of occupation, I decided I might as well be paid for the trouble."

Thorn turned to her. She saw the same far away sadness in his eyes she had seen when she recounted the death of her mother. He released her fingers and raised his hand to her arm. "You will not find such treatment here. Among my people, and in our land, male and female are equals." His eyes appeared liquid but, as always, he fought the tears back.

"They once said the same of Skoloti, too," Klara replied. "But we have been overrun with foreigners from the south who do not hold the same opinion. Now every woman must be trained as a warrior before she is wed, so that she can defend herself and her daughters."

Thorn let his arm fall back to his side as they resumed their watch. The three wolves returned, eyes glinting in the firelight, coming near, but not too near, the flames. Moving deliberately, so as not to startle the pack, Thorn and Klara gained their feet and held their weapons ready.

The black wolf sat on his haunches and raised his head as the last of the moon slipped over the ledge behind them. He let out a long eerie howl, causing the horses to snort and stamp. Behind them, the slumbering men startled into wakefulness, scuttling toward their weapons. But the wolves never moved toward the camp. She was grateful to relinquish her turn on watch and, though she did not think it possible on this night, she slept.

Klara sat bolt upright. A scream awakened her, but from whence it came she knew not. The sound roused the other Keltoi also. She saw Ffearn and Karn, standing tense between the fires, their weapons in their hands. As she sat, a second scream filled the night, grating across her nerves. Ruis was on his feet, spear in hand, making as if he were preparing for war. The horses stamped nervously.

Thorn came to her, knelt, and grabbed her shoulders. "What do you make of that?"

"I don't know," Klara answered bewildered. "The sound was piercing, but distant. It could be the scream of another traveler along the road or the scream of prey succumbing in the night magnified by our own imaginations. I can't tell."

Still grasping her by the shoulders, Thorn looked deep into her eyes. She saw firelight dancing in his, illuminating his fear. "Demons," he demanded. "You said you lived among them. Could this be demons?"

Klara recalled the message on the road. Were the demons in need of protection? Or were they were offering it? The bigger question looming in her mind was protection from what? Rubbing her temples, she paused before answering. What might her companions know of demon breeds and cultures?

Klara shook her head. "The Charontes are hammer wielders who work in the mines and forges, not generally given to night raids," she said. "The Ke'lets are hunters. If Ke'let are hunting in the area, that might explain the wolves, but we've nothing to fear from demons."

Releasing her arms, Thorn said, "I wouldn't be too sure of that." Then he stood and went to add wood to the fire.

No one slept for the rest of the night.

⚘

Eager to put the wolves and night screams behind them, Thorn had the company ride out as soon as it was light. He asked Klara to send word up the line of Keltoi if anything was amiss and Klara promised she would.

Remaining vigilant, Klara searched the shadows for wolves or anything else that might bring harm to the company. There was no sign of the wolves that morning and she hoped they had either satisfied their curiosity or decided the company of Keltoi was too much trouble to eat and moved on to tastier game.

Over the course of the morning, the road narrowed considerably, becoming little more than a winding track. On the trail, the ten horses strung out single file. Longing to be at the head of the column to watch for a threat, Klara ended up being grateful for her position at the rear. A couple hours into the ride she saw the same message as the day before. This time, the rune was fresh. Quickly slipping off her horse, Klara freed the sapling and kicked the antlers so the tines were pointed up, then mounted again, and proceeded to follow her companions.

By freeing the sapling and turning the tines up, she indicated that they did not need or want protection. While grateful for the offer, if that was indeed what it was, given the reactions of her companions last night she assumed that if demons walked into camp it would end poorly. And if the message was a request for protection, this company of Keltoi was unlikely to offer it. Thankfully, no one noticed her brief detour from the path and the party stopped at midday as usual. The horses, once watered, chomped hungrily at the grass.

The company continued unhindered through the afternoon, the path making its way upward, guiding them between rolling peaks. Upon reaching the apex of their ascent, Klara took in the view. The trees thinned at the lower elevations. At first she thought she saw the shores of a lake, but before her spread a vast expanse of grassland that looked as though it were a purple sea. In the distance, a thin line separated the steppe from the blue horizon of the sky. Marveling at the sight, she knew it was too distant for them to reach the ocean of purple by nightfall. They camped in the forest again that night, but she was eager to see the grasslands.

CHAPTER 9

# DISAGREEMENTS AND A BLOODY NUISANCE

KLARA'S EYES FLUTTERED, admitting the morning light. She squinted, confused, and closed them again. After wiping the sleep from her eyes with a reluctant hand, she reopened them and was greeted, not by the sight of Ffearn's sleeping face but by his boots. Karn was still asleep, his arms wrapped warmly around her, but Ffearn was obviously awake and standing over her. Twisting her neck, her eyes traveled up the length of his body, to meet his gaze.

"It's about time you woke," Ffearn snapped, a morose and sullen expression was painted across his face.

Klara extricated herself from Karn's grip and rose, asking, "Are we riding out early?"

Looking down his nose at her, Ffearn issued a clipped, "No."

Klara yawned and wrapped her arms about herself as defense against the morning chill. "Breakfast can't be ready?"

"No," Ffearn grunted, his frame a silhouette against the morning sky.

"Then why should I be up?" Klara asked. It was one thing to be awakened rudely, it was quite another to be awakened rudely for no reason.

Ffearn did not answer. Instead he stormed off and sat by the fire.

Klara shook Karn, saying, "Get up, it's your turn to cook. Ffearn's in a foul mood; go make breakfast."

Karn, roused from slumber, put a cauldron of water on to heat while Klara shook out and rolled up the bedrolls. When she finished, she noticed the pair of them had walked some distance from camp and were sharing terse words. They were far enough away that the conversation was inaudible. She suspected that was out of consideration for those who were still sleeping.

Preferring not to know what the argument was about, Klara opted to avoid them. She assumed it had more to do with lack of sleep and the general level of exhaustion than any actual slight or offense. Leaving them to it, she began taking the horses for water. Bardus woke as she bustled about and joined her. When they finished, breakfast was ready and the brothers were in a better, though not altogether chipper, mood.

"Looks like someone woke up on the wrong side of the bedroll this morning," Ruis said, picking up on the tension between the brothers, as he too, arrived at the fire ring in search of sustenance.

"Precisely," Ffearn spat. He looked as if he would just as soon throw his porridge at Karn as eat it. Karn did his best to ignore the remark.

Ruis sat beside Klara and waved his spoon at her in a slightly accusatory manner. "Ya know, them two have been right chipper since you joined us. Did you forget to sleep with them last night?"

"I slept where I always have," she said as she accepted a bowl of porridge. "He was in a foul mood when I woke up."

"By he, which do you mean?" Ruis asked.

"Ffearn," Klara said. "He was so out of sorts that I woke Karn and sent him to make breakfast. The two of them had words this morning."

Ruis blinked at her in surprise. Ffearn and Karn were inseparable. Clearly, he was having a hard time believing they had argued.

When they rode out, Ffearn and Karn were jostling to bring up the rear—the place usually reserved for her. As the road continued its way down the hillside, it widened again and was able to accommodate them riding two abreast; however, Ffearn and Karn lagged behind. They were often so far behind that she sometimes lost sight of them altogether. By evening though, they had resolved their differences and re-joined the company as their usual merry selves.

That night in camp, as Karn cooked, Ruis made Klara practice dagger technique with Ffearn. Ruis ran her through the defensive postures again, teaching her to block Ffearn's attacks. She was improving but still spent a good deal of time on the ground after her legs were knocked out from under her. She was certain Ffearn was being rougher than necessary and suspected it was a holdover from this morning's foul mood.

Lying face down in the dirt, Klara tried to catch her breath. "Ouch," she hollered as Ffearn's boot connected with her ribs. Then his knee landed in the center of her back, painfully pinning her to the spot. She raised her shoulder blades in pain, trying to extricate herself. Her head jerked as Ffearn grabbed her hair and yanked it back, exposing her neck, which he jabbed with the stick he had chosen as a practice weapon.

"Absent gods," Klara exclaimed. "You don't need to kick me while I'm down. Just pinning me would suffice."

Ffearn released her hair and shoved her face in the dirt as he got up. "Why should I be gentle with you? Your enemies aren't going to stand around asking 'please' and 'thank you'."

Klara rolled to her side before rising, catching a glint of fire in Ffearn's eyes. He was still mad. All the merriment earlier was just pretense. But mad about what?

"Ffearn, that's enough," Bardus called. "You keep on like that and you'll reopen her wounds."

Grateful that Bardus had halted the exercise, Klara rose and dusted herself off before heading to the fire. After dinner the company settled by the fire to talk and sing. Though the days had been hot, the nights were still chilly. Klara got out the gray fabric she bought in Ufa, cut the pieces she needed to make a pair of trousers and began to sew.

"Seems all you do is sew. Not the kind of activity we usually see 'round our fire," Ruis said as he rotated to toast his backside.

Klara held his gaze. "I work magic in these stitches. It foretells the future and is how I manage my work as Luck Bringer. That boy wasn't far off when he said I was a witch."

Ruis looked at her with something akin to awe. It was the kind of look one reserved for a wizard. "Really?"

"No, not really," she said. "I'm hoping to rid myself of this blasted skirt." As she said it, she knew that she left herself wide open for ribbing from Ffearn and Karn, but none came. That was odd of itself. It was unlike them to pass up an opportunity for ridicule. She continued, "I'd like to be able to ride in trousers as you do. They're a lot easier to move about in than a dress."

The fire snapped and popped, sending sparks skyward as Bardus added more wood. "And what do you plan to do with the skirt once you're dressed as a man?" he asked.

"I'll cut a length off the bottom and hem it to make a tunic. That way I can pass myself off as a warrior maid working as an escort. The excess I'll tear into strips for bandages and rags," Klara said, stretching her ribcage, which was still sore from Ffearn's beating. "This dress has seen a lot of use so that bit of cloth doesn't warrant saving."

"You needn't tear it, lass," Bardus said with a knowing glance. "If you need rags, come see me, I have plenty in my kit." Thankfully, Klara noted, the comment was lost on the rest of the company. Being men, they overlooked the need for a store of rags.

"Bardus's right," Thorn said. "That dress may come in handy in the future. We may need to disguise you at some point as we've done with Karn. You two did well posing as farmers last time."

If she kept the dress instead of converting it into a tunic, that posed a problem. The fabric she purchased was barely enough to make trousers and she lacked the funds to buy another piece. However, it was not a problem she could solve tonight. Because the watch was doubled when the wolves were following them, it was already her turn again. She needed to sleep now if she were to have any hope of keeping her eyes open and remaining alert in the dark of night.

On the nights she had second watch, she slept outside Ffearn. That way, when Thorn woke her, she was able to slip from the blankets without disturbing Ffearn and Karn. Tonight, as she woke, she followed Thorn's gaze as he stared down at the sleeping faces of his nephews. They appeared peaceful in their repose, though; each had grasped the other's hand as they slept. Not the kind of hand holding where fingers were interlaced, it was how you clasped your opponent's hand when arm wrestling. She shrugged. Given their moods earlier today, for all she knew, they might be arm wrestling in their sleep.

Klara felt Thorn watching her as she walked to a rise above camp. Was her placement in the watch deliberate? Her order in the cooking rotation occurred by happenstance, compliments of Ruis and the rabbit. By the time Thorn announced her place in the rotation for night watch, she had already established a pattern of bedding with Ffearn and Karn. As their uncle, perhaps he wished to see for himself the manner in which they shared blankets. After all, he had announced there would be no sex. The thought of it was enough to keep her mind occupied as she stood watch.

As they sat eating breakfast, Thorn said, "Since it is my turn to cook, perhaps Ffearn, Karn, or Klara will provide us some meat. We can make camp early so they can hunt and give the horses an opportunity for more grazing."

From where he sat at the fire, Ruis said, "Aye, I'd dearly love some meat. After eating beans for so long, I don't much fancy them anymore."

Bardus picked up a stick and playfully poked his friend in the ribs. "Beans aren't so bad, so long as you aren't the one cooking them." Smiles spread across the faces of the assembled company. Ruis was a good sport, and there was no denying the truth in Bardus's words.

The thought of meat lifted the entire company's spirits and they were a merry lot when they rode out that morning. As they descended the mountain, the forest changed from being a mix of conifers to becoming a stand of widely spaced oak trees which rose to great heights. They were magnificent to look at and Klara craned her neck to examine the canopy. The top-most branches were so high she was unable to see which animals lived there. Large leaves littered the ground, as did evidence of where squirrels and other rodents dug under them looking for last year's stash of acorns.

To Klara it did not seem like a forest at all. The trees were so widely spaced and the area between them so open that it felt more like she was riding between the stone columns of the temples and official buildings she had once seen. The difference being, these trees were far more magnificent than anything a man might craft out of stone and she felt more reverent in their presence.

When they made camp that afternoon, they were nearly out of the trees altogether, though there were a few standing here and there, like sentinels surveying the land. Not being accustomed to open spaces, Klara chose to hunt back the way they came, working herself deeper into the forest. Karn and Ffearn hunted in the opposite direction, further into the grasslands.

At first Klara thought she was doing little more than taking her bow for a walk. With so much open space surrounding her, she felt certain any prey would see her coming and quickly disappear. Still, she might as well enjoy her time out of the saddle and the leisurely stroll under the oaks.

About a mile from camp, the bleat of goats carried to her on the wind and she thrilled to the hunt. Her heart raced, preparing for the challenge of stalking her prey in such open country. Crouching, she made her way in the direction of the bleats. Cresting a small rise, she saw the herd.

A group of kids frolicked not far from her. She focused on a young, strutting billy. Taking her time, she nocked an arrow and drew her bow, patiently waiting while the little billy kicked, hopped, pranced, and butted his comrades. She loosed her arrow the moment he stilled, the thrum of her bowstring was quickly followed by a meaty thunk. The force of the arrow dropped the little goat. Desperate to follow the herd as they crested the rise and disappeared, the billy jumped to its feet, it ran a short way and then collapsed again, flopping like a landed trout.

Upon reaching the goat, she cut its throat, letting it bleed out. The billy had broken the shaft of her arrow with its thrashing, the jagged end protruding from its side. She was not happy about that. After splitting its belly open, she fished out the jiggly mass of innards, taking care not to cut herself on the arrowhead still lodged in the goat's side. With the body cavity empty, she pushed the broken arrow all the way though. The salvaged arrowhead could be used to make another arrow in the future.

After field dressing the goat, she wiped her hands on the dry grass in an attempt to remove the blood. Then she squatted behind a tree to relieve herself and saw the crimson stain of blood on her thighs. At first she thought the blood had come from her hands, then realized her bleeding had started. This left her more than a little irritated. Her cycle was quite literally a bloody nuisance under the best of conditions, and on the road among a company of Keltoi was not the best of conditions. It seems that she needed to visit Bardus and his store of rags sooner rather than later. Slinging the goat over her shoulders, she headed back to camp.

"Praise the return of a successful huntress," Thorn called as she approached.

Klara looked up and saw the Kelto smiling and waving her direction. Neither Ffearn nor Karn were in camp. Had their hunt been successful, too? If they had brought down something large and needed to track it, they might not be back until after dark.

Dropping her kill beside Thorn, she said, "I need to see Bardus. Then I'll butcher this."

"That will be fine," Thorn said. "I am not ready to start cooking yet. Not knowing what we might be feasting on left me unable to make meal preparations ahead of time. It seems tonight it will be roast kid." His smile was almost as big as Ruis's.

After taking care of her personal needs, she returned and found the rest of camp had been busy in her absence. Thorn was surrounded by Nuallan and Ruis, the trio busy assembling a spit on which to roast the goat.

At her approach, Nuallan announced almost gleefully, "Since you are doing the cooking tomorrow, we did a little fishing while you were away. We have a nice mess of fish on a stringer down at the creek and were hoping you would fry them up for breakfast."

Klara allowed that she would fry the fish. The Keltoi practically purred like a litter of kittens. Then she dragged the goat away from camp, chopped off its head and skinned it. Pausing from her work to bat away the flies, she saw Ffearn and Karn returning with a pair of fowl. Meal options had just improved considerably.

While Thorn cooked supper, Klara worked on her trousers. She had never been much for sewing, but all the practice she was getting lately made her fingers quick and nimble. The two pieces were already connected from waist to crotch. Now she needed to finish the legs and put in the hems. Tiring of the project, she laid her work aside and turned to Ffearn and Karn saying, "If you'll pluck those birds for me, I'll brown them tonight so the meat will keep better in the heat."

Karn smiled and patted his brother's shoulder. "We'd be happy to. It'll give us something to do while waiting for supper." She was glad to see them getting along again. What had gotten into them before?

As they cleaned the fowl, Klara put the iron oven in the coals to heat and added a spoonful of lard. When they returned and passed the birds to her, she deboned them, cut the meat into chunks, seasoned them with salt, and commenced browning.

Giving her a confused look, Ruis asked, "You so unsatisfied with Thorn's cooking that you've decided to fry them fowl for yerself?"

"I'm sure Thorn's cooking will be fine," Klara said. "I'm browning these birds now to get a head start on the cooking I have to do tomorrow."

"Oh," Ruis said as he scratched himself, "I didn't know you could do that."

Leaning forward, Ruis watched with interest as Klara pulled the oven off the coals in order to let the greasy mess congeal. Klara smiled to herself. His sudden interest in cooking was likely born out of a fear that she might challenge him to some other contest of skill.

They ate the roast goat, tearing hot strips of meat right off the bone, the juice dribbling down their chins. Soon, all that was left was a pile of bones. After dinner she and Thorn did the dishes and packed away the cooking supplies in companionable silence. She had long felt comfortable amongst Karn and Ffearn, but for the first time she truly felt like she was a part of the company and that they all fit together somehow.

Afterward, Klara pulled the unfinished trousers on under her skirt and was pleased with the fit at the waist. Eager to get started on the legs, she walked across camp and called out, "Ffearn, can you help me?" As she said this she began to raise her skirt.

Karn nudged his brother with his elbow and winked. "If it's help under your skirt you need, I'd be the one better suited for that."

"Is that so?" Klara said. "Well, I just might take you both at the same time; how does that suit you?" The brothers looked mildly shocked, mildly amused, and mildly pleased all at the same time. It was a look she recognized. In her time as a whore she saw it on many men's faces when they learned she did things their wives refused.

Smiling at the pair of them, she directed their attention to her pant legs. "Mark where the hem should go. It needs to be a pinky length from my foot. One of you measure, the other can mark. Just punch a hole in the fabric with your knife."

"I don't think Ruis would consider that an approved use of a dagger," Karn said.

"Just get on with it," Klara replied, "or I'll show you where you can stick your dagger."

They obliged her. Klara returned to the circle around the campfire and began to sew as the Keltoi conversed around her. Soon, Karn and Ffearn announced it was time to put the fire out. Karn had first watch and Ffearn was eager for sleep. Klara fell asleep with her back pressed against Ffearn's and woke with Karn spooning her. The watch changed, as had her bedfellows, silent as a thief in the night.

For breakfast, Klara collected the mess of fish and began frying them. She saved the grease from browning the fowl the night before and used it to make gravy. If the morning light and birdsong were not enough to wake the slumbering Keltoi, the smells emanating from the campfire certainly were.

Ffearn, still on night watch, was the first to make his way to where she cooked. Klara handed him the drinking horn filled with honeyed water and a bowl containing a hot fish fresh from the pan and two biscuits over which she ladled gravy.

Ffearn looked greedily at the bowl and said, "I take back every mean thing I've ever said about you."

"I was unaware you've been saying mean things," Klara said, the ladle poised dangerously in her hand. She might crack him on the head if she did not like the answer.

Ffearn looked abashed. "I might have said a harsh word or two to Karn on the topic. But I see now that I was mistaken."

She wanted to quiz him further, but he was already fully engrossed, licking gravy from his fingers. Had the argument been about her? And if so, what had she done to anger Ffearn? She shrugged. Whatever it was, he seemed over it now.

It was not long before the rest of the company joined them. Klara dished up bowls of food as the drinking horn made its way around the fire. There was much grunting, slurping, and burping as the Keltoi enjoyed the biscuits and gravy and fresh fish.

Ruis broke the silence, though there was nothing silent about their food consumption. "If we catch a mess of fish every night before you cook, will you make us a breakfast such as this?"

"No," Klara replied as she forked over another fish, "for that I also need fowl or some other meat. It's the grease that makes the gravy." Ruis looked disappointed so she added, "But if you catch the fish, I will fry them."

At that, Ruis brightened and turned to Thorn. "Ya know, that wizard sure knew his business. I canna' fathom why folks don't think to bring a woman with them on all their journeys."

"Even if they did think of it, you're unlikely to find one who would come," Nuallan said as he pulled the backbone from his fish. "Most women do not care for journeys, especially after their babes arrive. We ought to count ourselves lucky to have found Klara at all."

That comment prompted Bardus and Thorn to exchange glances. Had Bardus told Thorn she was menstruating? Certainly he must have. As leader of the company Thorn needed to know if anyone smelled of blood and might be attracting predators, especially after their run in with the wolves.

With full bellies, the Keltoi were a cheerful lot as they rode in the summer sun. Klara marveled at the expanse of grassland surrounding her. When they were saddling the horses, Thorn had told her this was the northern end of the Transvolga Plain and beyond the river was the Veiluga Lowlands, adding that they will be traveling through steppes for a considerable time. Were it not for the road, she would be completely lost and might wander for days without discovering a single discernable landmark.

The abundance of grass proved too tempting for Constant, who grabbed mouthfuls whenever the party paused. At midday, Klara unbridled Constant and removed the bit.

Seeing her at work, Bardus said, "You do that and you'll have less control over his head."

"I know," Klara said as her fingers worked at the stiff buckles. "Constant just finds the grass so tempting. I don't want to interfere with his eating. If he refuses to mind this afternoon, I can always reattach it."

Constant gave her no problems and looked especially satisfied with life as she attached him to the picket line when they made camp that night. Clearly, he was at home on the steppes. Klara wished she felt the same way. The openness unnerved her, as did the ceaseless wind that had been with them throughout the day, although, the uneasy feeling might be partly due to being forced to hide bloody rags in her saddlebag. Leaving Constant in Bardus's care, she went to cook.

Wasting no time, Klara immediately focused all her attention on making bread. It might not be the best bread, but it was bound to be better than dried biscuits. When she finished kneading, she placed two loaves side by side in the iron oven to rise. Then she used the fowl to make a stew. Feeling secure in her seasoning, she let everything cook while she walked over to Bardus, who was still tending to the horses.

"Sorry I abandoned Constant like that," Klara said. "I just wanted to make sure I had enough time to make bread."

"We're going to have bread?" Bardus asked, nearly dropping the lead of the sorrel pack horse in his excitement.

"Aye," Klara said, happy to see someone appreciated the effort. "It's rising now. I need to put it on the coals soon, though. I just wanted to apologize."

"There is no need to apologize; you do more with your horse than any of the rest of them, lass." Then making shooing motions with his hands he added, "Now back to the fire with you and don't you dare burn that bread."

At the fire ring, Klara rotated the oven and scraped up a bunch of coals to put on the lid. She stirred the stew again, tasting it to make sure it was not bland. To her taste, she was satisfied. Given what they usually ate, it probably mattered little if she seasoned the food or not. Leaving the stew to simmer and the bread to bake, she headed for the stream.

The stream was wide and shallow, providing mostly muddy pools. She walked quite a ways before coming across a couple likely rocks to sit upon while washing out the rags she secreted away earlier. The water was far from clean; she shrugged, knowing the rags might never be completely clean again anyway.

Before beginning the task, Klara stripped, allowing her dress to fall to the ground. The sun felt good on her skin. Wadding into the water, she figured that if she must wash, she might as well wash herself in the process.

Seating herself on one of the rocks, she began the repetitive process of rinsing and scrubbing her rags.

As she scrubbed, self-loathing seethed from her. She hated being a woman. She hated her bleeding. She hated the fear that gripped her when she was not bleeding. She abhorred the thought of being with child. She hated men for wanting her sex. She used pennyroyal, lots of it, to prevent pregnancy—sometimes taking double doses just to be sure, just to be safe. The best part of her situation among the Keltoi was that they did not expect sex. No sex meant not worrying about pregnancy; no pregnancy meant she still had her freedom.

She was so engrossed in her task and her thoughts that she failed to see Ffearn and Karn approaching through the grass until Karn, clearly worried, exclaimed, "Are you injured?"

Startled she looked up. "No, I'm fine."

"But the rock and those bandages are covered in blood," Karn protested as he strode through the tall grass.

"Some blood, aye, but mostly mud. The water is not the cleanest," Klara said, slapping the rag against the rock and continuing to scrub. "Is it not possible to find some privacy? I came here to be alone."

"We'll not leave you here injured," Karn said as he slid down the bank to the streambed, followed closely by his brother.

"I'm not injured," Klara said obstinately. "It is the blood of my cycle!"

Ffearn immediately began backing away, revulsion evident on his face.

Klara rounded on him, "Aye, go. You wouldn't want to be seen near a woman showing the weakness common to her sex. Sure, you like my cooking and having my warm body in your bed, having fun at my expense when I'm forced to disrobe before you, but to look upon the very thing that makes me woman you cannot bear. Do you think I cannot see the look of revulsion on your face? And know that I would have it, too, if I had been born a man and not an accursed woman."

As Ffearn continued backing away, he tripped on a large tuft of grass and fell. She flung the rag at him. Stunned by the exchange, Karn did not to press her further. Instead, he retreated the same direction as his brother. When she finished washing the remaining rags, she went searching for the one she had thrown at Ffearn, but was unable to find it.

Sighing, she said, "Just my luck, it's been dragged off by some rodent." Thankfully, Bardus gave her plenty so there was no need to ask for more. She gathered up her things, dressed, and headed back to camp.

With darkness upon them, the men made their way to the fire expecting to be fed. After passing out dishes of stew, Klara asked Nuallan to hold a dish rag for her. As she lifted the lid of the oven Ruis asked, "What's in that?"

"Bread," Klara replied, her attention focused on the hot iron in her hands.

"It looks like a butt," Karn exclaimed, craning his neck to see inside.

Ffearn leaned over his brother's shoulder to look, too. "Couldn't be a butt, not hairy enough."

"Out of my way," Klara said as she removed the bread from the oven and placed it in Nuallan's waiting hands. In all fairness it did look like a butt. But she knew what would happen when the two oblong loaves expanded to fill the round oven leaving a vertical line between them, so unlike her Keltoi companions she was not shocked at the sight of the loaves.

Nuallan turned the hot bread over in his hands. "All be, I would not have believed it, but it does look like a butt. Anyone up for a nice, warm piece of arse?" The entire company laughed.

After they ate, the men assumed their usual repose by the fire. Klara, Ffearn, and Karn avoided one another, a fact that was not lost on the rest of the company and dampened the mood of the camp. After the dishes were washed and put away, Klara opted to take a walk rather than sit around the campfire.

The moon was new, so the night was especially dark. Taking Constant with her for companionship, she relied on his sharp ears to catch the sounds of any potential threat. If need be, he could bear her safely back to camp. Constant was pleased with the change in routine and she petted his neck while letting him graze.

Stiff wind buffeted her, whipping her skirt around her legs. In the distance heat lightning illuminated the far off mountain ranges as if it were a beacon calling her to them. Beside her, Constant stood still, ears alert, as if he too were contemplating the land beyond the mountains. Bardus's song carried to her on the wind. Tonight he was singing a mournful lament, every bit as melancholy as her current mood.

"OUR HEARTS BELONG TO THE KING OF THE SILVER THRONE,
AND THE MOUNTAINS, WITH HEART OF STONE.
WE FLED AWAY,
DARED NOT TO STAY,
AS DEMON FORCES, RIPPED FLESH FROM BONE.

"THE KINGS' LINE ENDED, IN DEATH THEY SLEEP,
LYING SILENT, WHILE WIDOW AND ORPHANS WEEP.
WE FLED AWAY,
DARED NOT TO STAY,
THERE WERE NONE LEFT, DEFENDING THE KEEP.

"EACH NOBLE CLAN, AT WAR WITH THE OTHER,
AND OUR LINEAGE TORN ASUNDER.
WE FLED AWAY,
DARED NOT TO STAY,
AND OUR FAIR CITY, FALLEN TO PLUNDER.

"NOW A PEOPLE, LACKING HEARTH OR HOME,
LONG WE'VE WANDERED, STILL WE ROAM.
OUR RACE IS SCATTERED,
THE KINGS' LINE SHATTERED,
THERE IS NONE LEFT TO CLAIM THE THRONE.

"WE FLED AWAY,
DARED NOT TO STAY,
GODDESS FORGIVE US, IS ALL THAT WE PRAY."

The words ate at her soul. She stood silently in the dark for a long time after his singing ended. It was late when she returned to camp, though Thorn was still awake. Was he waiting for her to return? Unable to bring herself to lie beside Ffearn after their exchange earlier in the day, she crawled under the blanket beside Karn.

❧

Klara again woke to the sight of Ffearn's boots as he looked down at her and Karn in the pale morning light.

"Sleep well?" Ffearn spat.

"What is your problem?" Klara demanded as she brushed her hair out of her eyes.

The exchange woke Karn, who appeared stricken to find Klara in his arms. She caught the look and turned on him, "That repulsive, am I?"

She attempted to rise, but Karn grabbed her by the arm. "Wait, both of you!" Rising he let go of her arm and gestured toward the expanse of grass, "Over there, away from the camp."

Ffearn went willingly, but Klara headed the opposite direction. Karn grabbed her arm again, and, holding it firmly, marched her out onto the windy steppes. Once they were a considerable distance from camp, Karn began, "Ffearn, I'm sorry. I made you a promise and I failed to keep it. That is not Klara's fault and the anger you direct at her is misplaced. It's me you should be angry with."

"Were it not for her, your oath would not have been broken," Ffearn said. His jaw was clenched and so were his fists.

"That may be," Karn replied, "but it was not her doing. Klara does not know of the oath we have taken, nor could she."

Just what in the Goddess's name was going on? Her head swiveled between the pair of bothers. Each of their faces contained hurt and sadness.

Karn turned to Klara. "You must understand that Ffearn and I have shared a bed since we were babes in arms. Ever have we awoke to see the face of the other."

"I understand nothing," Klara said, freeing herself from Karn's grip. "You still share a bed, but what's that to me?"

Karn tried to explain, holding his palms helplessly before him, "When you sleep next to Ffearn, you sleep backs together, so that when Ffearn and I wake, each other's face is still the first thing we see. When you sleep betwixt us, it is the same, only we see your face as well. But when you sleep to my left, in my sleep I roll to embrace you, turning my back on Ffearn."

"This doesn't make a lick of sense," Klara said, exasperated, trying to hold errant hairs out of her face as the wind whipped it in all directions. "We're all in the same bed; it matters little who faces which direction."

"It matters," Ffearn said, clearly perturbed. The veins in his neck had begun pulsing with anger.

"If you wish to share our blankets, you must either sleep next to Ffearn or between us. If you sleep to my left again, we will have to ask you to bed elsewhere," Karn said.

Klara threw up her hands. "Absent gods! Have the pair of you lost your minds?"

"No," Ffearn sneered, "But you're about to lose your blankets."

"Stop it," Karn said, stepping between them. "Can the pair of you not see that I care for you both?"

This stopped Klara cold. Karn said he cared for her, yet she was supposed to sleep alongside Ffearn. Had one of them won, or lost, the right to sleep next to her in a round of dice? Was she being passed off as some possession? The concept of it addled her brain. The pair of them continued talking but the words made little sense.

"I'm not a possession," she said, turned, and walked toward the fire.

The morose atmosphere followed her back to camp. As she saddled Constant and made ready for the day's ride, Ruis tried lightening her mood by asking, "You three had a bit of a lovers' quarrel this morning, eh?"

Klara did not look up from her work cinching the saddle's straps. "It can't have been a lovers' quarrel; we've not had sex."

"How am I to know? Maybe that's what the argument was about," Ruis chided. He meant well, but Klara glared at him nonetheless.

Their ride over the next few days followed the same pattern that developed thus far. They took turns at cooking and the watch. She helped Bardus with the horses. When they had a bit of free time in the evenings, Ruis ran her through the defensive moves with her dagger. That was about the only time she interacted with the pair of brothers and their avoidance of each other provided her plenty of time to work on her breeches.

Each night she dutifully slept next to Ffearn. More than once she considered digging in the pack of furs to see if there was anything there that might make suitable bedding. Unfortunately, everything in that pack was someone's personal property, not communal camp gear, and that stayed her hand.

For their part, Ffearn and Karn seemed perfectly pleased with the world, joking and laughing with each other as they always had. Klara, though, was not herself. The wind constantly beat at her body and the wide expanse of the grasslands made her nervous. They had not spoken of their sleeping arrangement since they argued and neither had made any advances toward her, sexual or otherwise. Still, she thought of the exchange often. She did not understand the situation and she was not a person given to trusting things she did not understand.

# CHAPTER 10
## SHE'S NOT OUR WHORE

XCITED, KLARA DRESSED in her trousers for the first time. Since she lacked a shirt, she still wore the dress to keep her top covered and wondered how to manage in both dress and breeches. After a moment's pause, she took the hem of her skirt and tied it about her waist. She figured she looked ridiculous, but riding would be easier without the extra fabric dangling around her legs and that was the goal.

"You need to let your skirt down and try to look respectable," Thorn said as he carried a pannier to the picket line.

Klara looked hard at the Kelto. "Why?" she demanded. If Thorn was going to refuse to let her wear trousers he should have told her before she went to the trouble of sewing a pair. The wool might have been put into a skirt and skirts were easier to sew.

"We've crossed into Mordovia and will reach the town of Yar Chally today," he said, hefting the panniers over the back of one of the pack horses. "There is no way we can pass you off as a man, so breeches are out of the question. Mordvin women are not permitted to be warriors as Skoloti women are."

"Then it's a good thing I'm no Mordva," Klara replied and headed for the picket line. Having men constantly telling her what to do was irritating. Now she was in a country where men believed that was their right.

Thorn bristled. "As leader of this company, it's my job to see my nephews safely returned to Kenetlon. I am not going to let you jeopardize that." He cinched down the pannier and came after her, demanding, "Put that skirt down."

Klara rounded on him, her brown eyes lit with an internal flame. "I'm tired of being told what to do and where to sleep. And I'm not going to let you dictate how I dress. Skolts trade with Mordvins. Skoloti traders and warriors cross the line all the time."

Thorn stood so close that she felt the heat of his breath and the flush of his anger. "You are just a whore. You have never been to Mordovia. You know nothing of the world."

Klara slapped him, hard. The red imprint of her hand marred his cheek. Anger burned in her chest. She knew plenty. Skoloti traders took their husbands with them because the Mordvins refused to barter with women. Skolt women might not visit the taverns, but their husbands secretly frequented the places, as did Parthians, Mordvins, Kenetlo, and Goths. All of them brought news of the world.

Thorn stood unwavering before her, their eyes locked. The pair stood silent for a moment. Something in his eyes shifted and changed. The look was subtle, less challenging. She raised her hand to slap him again, using anger to mask the pain his words had inflicted. He caught her by the wrist before she made contact and held her arm suspended mid-swing.

At length Thorn said, "My nephews," he paused, "having you in their blankets, nothing will come of it. If you are looking to better yourself, you best look elsewhere."

He released her wrist and she let it fall to her side. Did he really think she was trying to seduce them? It was an appalling accusation.

"I'm not looking for a husband and have no intention of marrying anyone," Klara said, incredulous. Surely she had made her thoughts on the matter clear long before now.

"Good," Thorn replied, "Because neither do they. Now, let your skirt down so we can go. And you might reconsider your bedding arrangements."

Just where was she supposed to bed? Cowering under her saddle blanket by the fire? She lacked a bedroll and Thorn knew that.

Despite her row with Thorn, news of the town had the men excited, especially Karn and Ffearn who planned a dice game during the morning ride. Their banter carried back to Klara. She was still grumpy over having to change out of her trousers and furious that after all this time Thorn still saw her as nothing more than a whore. And what did he mean by looking to better herself? She had already bettered herself by simply leaving the alehouse.

In an attempt to force Thorn from her mind, she turned her attention to the conversations of her companions. Ahead of her Ffearn and Karn were talking, their horses' heads bobbing in time with their steps.

"You do a good job of playing the poor, dumb farmer," Ffearn said. "But you need to lay off the drink. We could have brought in lot more money last time."

"There were extenuating circumstances," Karn said, shifting himself in the saddle.

"Aye," Ffearn agreed. "Those circumstances were that you were completely soused. You missed several signals that might have changed how the rounds played out."

"The circumstances to which I refer," Karn said, pointing an accusing finger as his brother, "was that I was busy playing the role of a married farmer, so I didn't have an opportunity to cozy up to the serving girl. That meant that I ended up drinking twice the ale you did."

"That's precisely the problem," Ffearn said. "You got pickled, cockered, stewed, sloshed, smashed."

"And just how was I supposed to not get drunk and still match you and every other man at the table drink for drink?" Karn asked, incredulity dripping from his voice.

"By getting friendly with the serving girl, just like I did, just like we always do," Ffearn replied, as if this explained everything.

"And how am I supposed to do that when the whole tavern saw me ride into town with my wife?" Karn demanded, clearly irritated.

Ffearn continued to goad his brother, "It shouldn't matter one way or the other if you're married. It didn't stop the other men at the table from giving the girl's bottom a nice squeeze. I'm sure Klara can back me up on this. Go on, ask her."

Karn called over his shoulder to Klara, "Do you get many married men?"

"More married than not," Klara replied, irritated at being included in their squabble. She patted Constant's neck; at least he was never disagreeable. When she looked up, both of them had turned in their saddles and were looking at her expectantly.

"You're joking, right?" Karn asked. "You're just siding with Ffearn for the fun of it."

"No," Klara replied. "Married men often want things their wives refuse. Or their wives refuse them altogether, so they come see me. Though the way some of them smell, I cannot say I blame their wives."

"See," Ffearn said, looking smug. "You should listen to me more often, because I am older and therefore wiser than you."

"You're the older one?" Klara asked, surprised. "All this time I thought you were younger than Karn."

"Nay, there you are mistaken," Ffearn announced haughtily. "I get to play the Kenetlo Lord because I am the older, wiser, more mature part of this scheme. Karn has to play the traveling farmer because he is younger, and therefore dumber, than I am."

Klara rolled her eyes. She was beginning to regret signing on with the company and wondered if she and Constant might be able to simply disappear one night.

"May the Goddess strike you down for your lies," Karn exclaimed. "We were born on the same bloody day!"

"Ah," Ffearn said, "but I was born before you, therefore I am the older and wiser amongst us."

"You're twins," Klara said. That explained a lot. The pair was unusually close, even for brothers. Why else would two grown men share a bed and spend nearly all their waking hours together?

"Actually, we're not," Karn replied, again turning in his saddle to look at her over his shoulder.

"But we didn't know that until we were thirteen," Ffearn added.

Their comments left her addled. "Absent gods, how can that be?" she asked.

"It's Uncle Thorn's fault," Karn said.

"Aye, it was he who rode into Hallstatt and shattered our world," Ffearn said. "As I recall, Karn cried when Uncle Thorn told him."

"I did not cry," Karn said, pointing an accusatory finger at his brother. "You cried."

Ffearn adamantly objected, "I would do no such thing."

Klara's head swiveled back and forth between the brothers. Even their horses were irritated by the bickering. She watched as Ffearn and Karn's mounts tried adjusting to the constant movement in their saddles, the pair gesticulating wildly, punctuating their points.

"As I recall," Thorn shouted from the head of the column, pausing for effect, "both of you cried."

This exchange left Klara even more confused than before. She took a moment to gather her thoughts before offering a carefully worded question. "If you are brothers and born on the same day, how are you not twins?"

"That's because technically we aren't brothers," Ffearn said.

Klara leaned forward in her saddle, skeptical of their story, but interested nonetheless. "But you were born on the same day and you thought you were twins until you were thirteen, when Thorn told you otherwise?"

"Precisely," Ffearn said.

Nuallan looked back and saw the completely stymied expression on her face. "Lads, don't keep leading her on," he said, coming to her aid. "Tell her how it is."

"We're cousins!" Karn announced gleefully.

Ffearn began, "Our mothers were twins and our fathers are brothers, though they are not twins."

Karn continued, "Our fathers were much older than our mothers. They didn't have much in common with our mothers and often spent time apart, so we didn't see them much."

Ffearn picked up the tale, "Since we were born on the same day, for convenience the household had our mothers share a room in our grandfather's hall. Our mothers raised us as siblings, and since they were twin sisters, and we knew our fathers were brothers, we assumed we were brothers as well."

Karn interjected, "We shared a cradle when we were but babes in arms, and when we outgrew the cradle, they gave us but one bed. We've been together our whole lives."

Now, Ffearn continued, "When we trained as warriors, we became sword brothers and that is a bond deeper than kinship. There have been few days in our lives where we have not awoke to see the face of the other."

Then Karn continued, "And despite what Uncle Thorn says, we'll always consider ourselves brothers."

Klara was not entirely sure she caught all that and looked to Nuallan for confirmation. He nodded in her direction and seemed to indicate that what they said was truth. Given this, perhaps their insistence on where she bedded had nothing to do with winning or losing a bet. Aside from Karn's occasional jocularity, neither made any serious attempts to employ her services. And Karn had mentioned an oath. Did sword brothers swear an oath to each other? Or was their oath something done privately, like becoming blood brothers?

When they stopped at midday, Klara and the pair of brothers, or cousins, or whatever they were, were back on easy terms. Ffearn, Karn, Ruis, and Bardus all immediately stripped to the waist and headed for the water to wash and trim their beards in preparation of playing their part in the ruse with the dice game. Klara, who had been washing every night as of late, did not join them, nor did Thorn or Nuallan. She watched as those two conferred some distance from the rowdy bunch of Keltoi.

Freshly washed and shirtless, the pair of Keltoi headed to the packs strapped on their horses. She admired their chests from afar. Would Thorn send her ahead with Karn again? She liked the idea of having another opportunity to see his Kelto-flesh up close.

As she wondered this, Thorn announced, "Nuallan and I have decided against having a game tonight." Ffearn and Karn began to protest, but Thorn held up his hands to stop them.

"Waywyrd said he would meet us in Yar Chally with news necessary for our journey," Thorn said. "Also, we have reason to believe the town might not be overly friendly toward foreigners. If we need to leave quickly, I want to make sure the entire company is together."

Ffearn and Karn were obviously disappointed, and Klara realized she was, too.

When they reached the town late that afternoon many heads turned, giving disapproving stares to the company of Keltoi who brought a lone Skolt woman with them. Stopping at the first inn they came to, Thorn ducked through the low hung door and went inside to inquire about a room. Reemerging, Thorn said the innkeeper flatly refused, stating he would not let rooms to mixed companies.

The Keltoi mounted up and rode to the opposite end of the little town, stopping before the only other inn. This time Klara followed Thorn and Nuallan inside, knowing Thorn tended to be direct and that was not always the best way to handle men.

Once inside, Thorn stated, "I need a room for a party of seven if you have one, or multiple rooms if necessary as beds allow."

The innkeeper, a squat little man with graying hair, squinted at Thorn in a way that made Klara suspect his eyesight was poor. "We are not the kind of establishment that will let rooms to a bunch of foreigners to go on grunting through the night as they pass their whore between them."

"Klara is not a whore," Thorn began obstinately.

Klara knew Thorn was going to continue and that whatever came out of his mouth next would not result in the party being given a room. From over his shoulder, she quickly interjected, "I'm the cook."

The innkeeper squinted at her. "Cook you say? Just what is a Skolt woman doing cooking for a bunch of Keltoi on the road? And if you ain't a whore, why aren't you in breeches like your warmongering sisters?" he asked, not altogether convinced.

Klara gave Thorn a pointed look then softened her features before addressing the innkeeper. "My husband died in a carting accident," Klara said. She was not a good liar and hoped the innkeeper's poor sight kept him from seeing the lie on her face. "I had no money for travel and cannot live on my own here in Mordovia. I'm working my way back to Gelonus to live with my kin."

The innkeeper was quick to contradict her. "No Mordva man would take a Skolt to wife."

"My husband was a Skolt. We were traders," Klara replied, placing a hand on her hip and using her other to gesture toward him. "I'm sure you know Skoloti women seldom stay at home and often travel. My team broke their legs in the accident and had to be put down, and then I was robbed while trying to find someone to mend the cart."

Stroking his chin, the innkeeper pondered her tale. At last he said, "I'm not sure I believe you, but it does seem a likely tale. I'll not let you a room on the chance it's not true, but I'll let you stable your horses and sleep in the barn on the chance that it is true. Mind, though, that you sleep separate."

"Thank you," Thorn said. "How much for the stable and a hot meal?"

The innkeeper looked at Thorn and grinned. "And what would you be needing with my wife's cooking, when you have a cook of your own?"

Thorn turned an icy gaze on the man. "Even cooks deserve an afternoon off now and again."

"Well," the innkeeper said, "This ain't her afternoon off, now is it?"

Thorn and Nuallan settled the bill. The party stabled the horses and found some fresh straw to bed down in later. Once the horses were tended to, the company scattered. Thorn and Nuallan went in search of Waywyrd. Ffearn and Karn disappeared in the direction of a tavern. Ruis mysteriously disappeared as well, leaving her and Bardus with the horses.

"Come on, Bardus," Klara said. "It seems I'll be cooking tonight and I don't much fancy beans. Let's find the market and see if we can't purchase something better."

Bardus readily agreed.

In the market, Moksha and Skoloti tongues mixed in her ears. The sight of a Skolt and a Kelto walking together caught more than a few side-long glances. It was evident that Bardus felt uneasy. As a whore, Klara was used to such treatment. They managed to find a merchant willing to sell them a chunk of pork and another who offered root vegetables: onions, turnips, parsnips, and carrots. There was little in the way of fresh produce, but she was able to pick up some greens and radishes along with a basket of strawberries. Klara insisted Bardus buy more honey and a few other kitchen staples.

When they returned, she built a fire behind the stable and began sorting out their foodstuffs. While waiting for the Keltoi to return, she put a cauldron of honeyed-water on to heat and made pastries filled with chopped strawberries coated in honey. After frying the confections, she cleaned out the oven in order to make the now infamous butt-bread. From time to time the innkeeper or his wife stuck their heads out the back door, checking to see that she was still cooking and not up to some Skoloti mischief.

Thorn and Nuallan returned, absent Waywyrd, and joined her at the fire. Thorn dipped the drinking horn in the cauldron and passed it between them before addressing her and Bardus. "Waywyrd has not arrived yet," Thorn said settling himself on the ground before the fire.

"But when he arrives he'll know where to find us," Nuallan added, joining Thorn on the ground. "The entire town is abuzz about you, lass."

"Aye, it seems I should have let you and Karn ride ahead, or at least let you wear your breeches," Thorn said. "They're not accustomed to seeing a woman in the company of men. Why, I'm not sure. Do Skoloti warriors travel this way?" Apparently he had forgotten his claim this morning that she knew nothing of the world.

"Our warriors go where there's trouble," Klara said, as she kneaded the bread. "The Mordvins generally do not cause trouble, but they shelter the Parthian scum who do. Warrior bands are often entirely comprised of women. Traders travel in mixed companies, but those are generally married couples."

As the Keltoi conversed, Klara put the bread on to bake, then chopped vegetables and seasoned the meat. Bardus told Thorn and Nuallan about the disapproving stares he and Klara experienced while they were at the market. Nuallan inquired about the cost of the meal and fetched the company's cashbox to reimburse them.

Laying the coppers in her palm, Nuallan said, "You do not use your own money to feed us."

The innkeeper thrust his head out the back door again. Bardus nodded in the little man's direction. "Been doing that all afternoon, he has."

"Is that so?" Thorn said, scratching his beard.

"Aye," Klara said, putting the coppers in her purse. "I've made sure to be at the fire the entire time. But something doesn't sit right."

"You're right about that," Ruis said, walking up and joining the group at the fire. "There ain't hardly any women to been seen in town. All shut up in their houses, I imagine. Seems like they're expecting trouble."

The Keltoi sat in contemplative silence, passing the drinking horn between them. After a while Thorn asked, "Did you see the lads head into a tavern?"

"Aye," Ruis said, "And they were looking entirely too happy about the prospect."

"I was afraid of that," Thorn said. "They better not have arranged a game. We may need them here tonight."

"You want me to go fetch them?" Ruis asked.

"No," Thorn said resignedly and adjusted his position to something more comfortable. "I think that might only make matters worse. If we keep altogether, the town will suspect we are plotting something."

Now that the bread was on to bake, Klara browned the roast, adding garlic, vegetables, and some water before setting the oven over the coals. Thorn watched her work.

When she settled back in her seat, Thorn said, "At least it looks like we will eat well, even if it'll be out here around the fire and not inside."

Propping himself up on an elbow, Bardus said, "From the smells that keep coming from the inn every time they open that back door, I'd wager we'll be eating the better meal." Then he leaned back, evidently intent on napping. Soon soft snores from Ruis and Nuallan indicated that they had joined Bardus in blissful slumber.

Thorn shifted and looked uncomfortable. "Klara, I want to apologize for what I said this morning. I care deeply for my nephews and will see no harm come to them. But I was wrong and should have let you wear your breeches. I was also wrong in calling you a whore—I ought not have done that. I am sorry I hurt you."

Klara was not about to admit she had been hurt; instead she asked, "What did you mean by saying if I were looking to better myself, I best look elsewhere?"

Thorn's eyes glistened with the barest hint that they might become liquid. "Marrying above your station." Thorn sighed and ran his fingers through his hair as if he were searching for words he could not bear to speak. "My nephews are not likely to marry. They seem to need no more companionship than each other. I—" Thorn stopped himself, as if reconsidering what he was going to say. "I'm sure others would take greater comfort in your company."

"I have no intention of marrying anyone," Klara said. "I sleep where I do because those are the only blankets that have been offered." Thorn nodded, turning an uncomfortable gaze to the fire. The pair sat in awkward silence as afternoon rolled into evening.

The sun had set, sending copper and violet streaks across the sky, when Ffearn and Karn finally returned. It was evident from their swaggers and the way they smelled that they had an ale, or two or three.

"Seems the town can't get enough of our whore," Ffearn said as he flopped down by the fire.

"You didn't tell them she was a whore, did you?" Thorn demanded. Was his harsh tone now supposed to be reparation for his gaffe this morning?

"Of course not," Karn said, joining his brother. "We insisted she was our cook, just like we'd been told. But they were mighty interested."

"You wouldn't believe the prices we were offered for a piece of her arse," Ffearn said, using a stick to poke at the fire. "More than we could make in this bloody town playing a game of dice, that's for sure. I'll have to start considering myself a rich man every time I bed beside her."

"Watch what you say," Thorn snapped. "You didn't arrange a game tonight, did you?"

"No," Karn said, sounding defensive. "You told us not to. We played a little this afternoon and won just enough to cover our ale. Besides, men's tongues are freer when they've got dice in their hands."

"Well, did you learn anything useful from your afternoon at the tavern?" Thorn asked, clearly perturbed by their indifference to the collective welfare of the company.

"Only that there isn't a whore in the whole town," Ffearn said. "Not even so much as an alewife to serve us. It was all done by men. These Mordvins don't seem to allow their women much freedom. It's certainly not Skoloti."

Klara pulled the oven off the coals in order to let the roast rest while she sliced the radishes and tossed them and the greens with vinegar and oil. That complete, she sliced the bread and began dishing up their bowls and passing them around. The men happily tucked into their meal.

The innkeeper appeared at the door again. This time he came over to where they sat around the fire. "The missus wants to know if there'd be anything you need from the kitchen?" he asked.

It was obvious that he was not there to offer assistance, but to judge whether Klara might pass as a hired cook. Thankfully, the smells emanating from tonight's dinner were particularly tantalizing. It helped that she had picked up a few more seasonings and kitchen staples in the market.

"No," Thorn said balancing the food in his lap. "Our cook seems to have purchased everything she needed at the market."

The innkeeper leaned forward, sniffing the air like a hound trying to scent its prey. "And if I might ask, what is it you're dining on tonight?"

"Roast pork," Ruis said, stabbing a piece of meat with his knife and raising it appreciatively to his mouth.

"And roasted veg," Karn added, spearing a turnip.

"And greens," followed Ffearn, eyeing them gratefully.

"And fresh bread," Nuallan said, raising a slice to his nose, inhaling its earthy aroma with a contented sigh.

"Oh, and what were those things I watched you make earlier? The ones with the strawberries?" Bardus asked, waving his knife her direction.

Klara fetched the stack of pastries from under a rag and offered one to the innkeeper. "Strawberry pastries," she said, holding the platter before her. "I thought they'd go well after dinner when the company sat about relaxing with their skin of mead."

The innkeeper took a timid bite. Juice spurted from the pastry, dribbling down his chin, the explosion of flavor evident in his eyes. "Oh, quite nice," he said, wiping juice from his beard. "Are you sure you don't want to leave this lot and live a respectable life here? Me and my missus could use a new cook."

Klara did her best to look kindly at the man as she said, "I do live a respectable life and I am eager to get on to my kin in Gelonus."

"Oh well," he said, "just mind you all sleep separate. We don't tolerate immoral behavior in Yar Chally." Then he went back inside to see to his own dinner and Klara reclaimed her seat at the fire.

"You made pastries," Ffearn and Karn said in unison, the food that had been garnering their rapt attention now forgotten in their laps.

Karn continued dreamily, "I've not had sweets in ages."

"It's amazing the things you can accomplish when you're not drinking and gambling," Klara teased and passed the pastries their way.

After dinner Karn helped Klara wash the dishes and store the cooking gear away. She stood a moment surveying the scene before her. If the way to a man's heart is through his stomach, that saying must be doubly true for Keltoi. The men were contentedly stretched before the fire, each purring like an over-fed cat.

As she stood in the shadows, Karn walked up behind her and slipped his arm around her waist. He held her close and whispered, "I am glad you're no longer mad at me. Will you sleep in the middle and let me hold you tonight?"

Klara leaned back, pressing herself against him, enveloped by his scent. "Not tonight," she whispered back. "I expect the innkeeper will return to check on us more than once."

Karn sighed. "You're probably right." They parted and walked back to the fire to join the rest of the company.

Once everyone was seated around the fire, Thorn said, "I think we ought to leave early tomorrow."

"What about Waywyrd?" Klara asked. The farther they traveled, the more quarrelsome these Keltoi got. She missed Waywyrd's pleasant company.

"I do not think it would be wise to wait for him," Thorn said.

"Aye, I agree," Ruis said. "The wizard will find us."

"I also think we should set a watch," Thorn added. "We may be in town, but I sense trouble and do not want to be caught off guard." The rest of the group murmured their assent.

They put out the fire and went into the stable to bed down. Fresh straw was thrown into two of the empty stalls, giving off a clean scent that mingled invitingly with the smell of horses. The Keltoi not on watch would sleep in one stall, Klara in the other. The mound of straw beckoned to her and she longed to ease her weary body into the softness it offered.

"Here you are, deluxe accommodation and the whole stall to yourself," Karn said, opening the stall's door.

The innkeeper walked up behind them. "No, you don't. She ain't sleeping down here with you lot."

"Then where am I supposed to sleep?" Klara asked, turning to face the little man.

The innkeeper's chest puffed up like a fat fowl. "In the house with my missus and me."

"No," Karn protested. "We'll not be parted."

"Is that how it is?" the innkeeper said, squinting at Karn. "Perhaps this young Kelto arranged your husband's carting accident, eh?"

"That is not how it is," Karn said, his voice raised and an angry flush rising in his cheeks. "I've heard the comments of the men down at the tavern and I will not let her sleep anywhere save surrounded by an armed detail, which we happen to be."

The innkeeper scratched at his chin. "Heard them, have you? They're a filthy lot, demanding access to our women. Well, we don't take to the mixing of bloodlines here either. Do you intend to take her to wife?"

By this time they had caught the attention of the other Keltoi. Thankfully, Karn remembered their ruse and was able play along. "No," he said, "She is our cook and we will see her safely on to Gelonus."

Thorn approached, carrying a mound of cloth in his hands, and fortunately managed to keep his head. "My nephew is young and brash. He seeks only to defend the lady's honor. You cannot fault him for that. He and his cousin were at the tavern earlier today. The men there offered them payment in exchange for a night with our cook. I think it would be prudent to have her bed near those who would defend her if it comes to that. We will leave early in the morning and trouble you no more."

The innkeeper considered for a moment. "Then put her in the hayloft. That way at least she'll be in a separate room. And I'd keep an eye on your nephew; I'm not mistaken about what I saw in that young Kelto's eye."

The way he squinted, Klara doubted he saw much of anything, objects or intent. Still, she climbed the ladder and settled herself among the loose hay. She would have preferred to have a blanket but knew she would pass the night warmly enough if she burrowed herself into the hay the way she did when wandering the countryside as a child. It was not long before she heard footsteps on the ladder and Karn's frame appeared in the loft.

"The innkeeper has gone," he said, kneeling before her.

"Karn, you shouldn't be here," Klara said. "It'll only cause trouble in the end."

"I'll not be staying with you this night," Karn said, and as he did he draped something around her shoulders. "If you cannot share my blanket, at least you can pass the night wrapped in my cloak."

"Thank you, Karn," she said, reaching up to touch the heavy woolen cloth.

Karn turned to leave. As he climbed down the ladder he paused and said, "Klara, I don't care what Bardus says, you'd best sleep in your bandeau tonight. We may need to leave in a hurry."

While drifting off to sleep, she again heard footsteps on the ladder and sat up. By the stature of the Kelto who darkened the doorway she thought Karn had returned. But it was Thorn who coughed to announce himself. He was carrying a bundle in his hands and held the cloth toward her.

"My cloak," Thorn said. "I meant to give it to you earlier, but the innkeeper arrived. Anyway, you can use it, so you need not bed..." his sentence trailed off.

"Thank you, Thorn," Klara replied. "But Karn just lent me his cloak. I don't need yours."

Thorn sighed and made his way back down the ladder.

Klara nestled into the hay, pulling the cloak snug about her. It smelled faintly of Karn and that gave her comfort as she drifted off to sleep. She had not slept long before waking to the flicker of torch light and the angry shouts of drunken men. Scrambling to her feet, she looked down to where the Keltoi bedded. Relief swept over her when she saw that none of them slept, but all of them were on their feet, swords and spears in hand.

"Send out the whore," a man called from the yard.

"We have no whore," Thorn shouted, "just a cook and we do not hire her out."

Klara crawled to the window and looked out. The men had formed a mob in the yard and were not likely to change their minds and go home. No matter what happened, this was going to end badly. From her vantage point in the loft, she counted ten men, mostly Parthian, but there might be more in the shadows or around back. From this spot she could even the odds, if only she had her bow. Returning to the ladder, she quickly climbed down.

"What are you doing? Stay up there!" Karn shouted.

"I need my bow," Klara said. "I have a good view of the yard. I can reduce their numbers if it comes to a fight." She grabbed her bow and quiver and ascended the ladder just as quickly as she had descended it.

"Wait, I'm coming with you," Karn called after her. He grabbed his recurve and followed close on her heels.

The crowd of men was clearly agitated. A man holding a torch shouted, "Skoloti bitch, I bet she ain't had an uncut man. Send her out so we can show her what it's like to take favor with a real man."

"Cut men make better lovers," Klara shouted from shadows as she peered out the loft window. "Go home and ask your wives. Surely, they can tell you."

Karn's eyes went wide. He grabbed her by the arm and pulled her back from the window. "What are you doing? You'll get us killed."

Pushing him away, Klara whispered, "Hush, I know what I'm doing." She had worked in taverns long enough to know how to fell a braggart.

The torch wielder turned to face the crowd. "Those bitches geld their men like they geld their horses. Not likely to get a cock-stand after abuse like that. What good is an impotent man?"

"Plenty good, if he learns to use his tongue," Klara shouted, keeping to the shadows. Her only hope was to shame him enough that his comrades saw him as a laughing stock. Then they would brawl among themselves and forget her. "You seem to do an adequate job at wagging yours and I'll bet it's bigger than what you got in your pants."

Some of the men sniggered. That was a good sign.

The torch wielder grabbed his crotch with his free hand and thrust his hips. "I'm as big as any stallion."

"Ho-ho," called the crowd, clearly appreciating his bluster as they slapped each other on their backs.

"Then perhaps we should send out a mare," Klara said. "I've heard of men who have such preferences."

From the back of the crowd a man guffawed. "Your mare seems more travel weary than most, Akos. Have you been riding her day and night?" The crowd erupted in laughter.

The torch wielder, Akos, was intent on working the crowd, fanning the flames of fury. He stormed through the mob, firelight dancing across his face, casting unnatural shadows. Reaching the heckler, he cuffed the man on the ear, choking off his laughter.

Waving the torch above his head, Akos shouted, "If the Skoloti are permitted to exist, soon all men will be cut. I ask you, why must a man face the cruel blade just because a women refuses to adhere to her godly duty to bear children?"

"Why must a woman bear children just because you're too cowardly to face the blade?" Klara shouted. Immediately, she knew she had over-reached. The crowd sobered, a hushed silence falling over the men. Tension built as the crowd of men began muttering amongst themselves.

Turning toward the stable, Akos raised the torch over his head bellowed, "Burn her out!" Then he hurled his torch toward the opening in the loft. Without thinking, Klara stepped from the shadow and let fly with an arrow. Akos fell to the ground before the torch reached the stable, an arrow protruding from his chest.

When the torch landed, Karn quickly scooped it up and stamped out the straw that already caught fire. They had no water with which to douse the flame, so he threw it in the direction of the trough. The torch landed on the edge and teetered before falling into the water, extinguishing itself.

The men gathered around their fallen comrade. "Murderers!" they shouted.

Klara sighed. Things had gone from bad to worse and it was her fault.

In the distance, Waywyrd's voice rang out, "Make way for the law!" Using his staff, he pushed the men back before dismounting. The men parted and began encouraging the town constable to arrest the Keltoi for everything from prostitution to murder.

Klara looked at Karn and said, "When we go down there, we best say it was the other way round. You shot him and I threw the torch."

Karn nodded in agreement.

They slipped back down the ladder. Klara unstrung her bow, hiding it and the quiver with her saddle. After the constable dispersed the men, Thorn opened the stable doors.

Klara threw her arms around Waywyrd. "Never have I been so glad to see you."

Waywyrd hugged her and patted her head. "Now, now, my dear, you're fine," he soothed. Klara thought his comment and behavior odd, but she played along.

Turning to the constable, Waywyrd said, "You see, it is as I say. My niece was in the stable all along. She sent word to me saying her husband died in a carting accident and that she took employment as a cook in order to travel to Gelonus to live with my wife and me. I decided to ride out to meet her. When I heard this mob shouting about a cook and a company of Keltoi, I knew it was her."

How had Waywyrd picked up on their story? She quickly realized he just told her how. The mob had been shouting about it for the better part of the evening.

"You're not Skoloti," the constable said, a note of accusation in his voice. "How do you come to be related to her?"

"I am her Uncle," Waywyrd replied. "My brother, misguided man that he was, married a Skolt and nothing but ill has come of it."

The constable snorted and stormed off. The innkeeper confirmed the story, stating that was the same explanation they had given when they arrived. Then the constable questioned Klara. She took him to see where the floor was scorched, claiming that was where she stamped out the embers.

"If I hadn't been quick, the whole place would have been engulfed and the innkeeper might have lost all his stores and possibly the horses besides," Klara said, playing on the man's Mordvin loyalties. "Akos's attempted arson might very well have bankrupted the poor innkeeper."

"The innkeeper says you were told to sleep apart, so what was that young Kelto doing in the hayloft with you?" the constable asked, letting go of the accusation of murder. Clearly he was hoping to make good on a prostitution charge, or at least fornication.

"I did sleep apart," Klara said. "I was woken by the shouts of men. I called to the Keltoi that I could see ten men in the yard; that's when Karn came up with his bow." This satisfied the constable, who seemed irritated to have been pulled from his bed by rabble-rousing foreigners and was eager to return to it.

"Come, Klara," Waywyrd said. "I've taken a room for us on the other side of town." He walked off, leading his horse and leaning heavily on his staff, using it as walking stick. Klara looked at him and then turned to look at Karn over her shoulder. Their eyes met, but neither could say anything without letting the constable know they were not wholly honest. Turning, she followed Waywyrd into the night.

Waywyrd had spared no expense and taken a private room with two straw-filled pallets and a curtain between them. "This will give you some privacy," Waywyrd said as he pulled the curtain into place. "Before retiring I'm going to barricade the door. I'll see you in the morning."

As she lay down, Klara realized she was still wearing Karn's cloak and wrapped it tightly around her. Uncertain of what would happen next and thinking anxiety might keep her awake, she eventually succumbed and slept.

## CHAPTER 11

# A WIZARD AND A WARDROBE

WHEN KLARA WOKE it was already midmorning. Through the gap in the curtain, she saw Waywyrd sitting on his bed sorting through his pack. She rubbed the sleep from her eyes and stared intently, hoping to catch a glimpse of any sort of magical objects that might be hidden inside. Unable to see anything, she quit spying on the wizard and pushed the curtain aside.

"It is about time you were up," Waywyrd said, dropping his pack in a heap at his feet. "We have much to do today, starting with getting you properly dressed."

"I am dressed," Klara said, picking straw from her hair, an unpleasant reminder of the previous night's activities.

"You can't go about looking like that," Waywyrd said. "It's no wonder the men of this village thought you a whore."

"I am a whore," Klara corrected bitterly, Ffearn's and Thorn's words still ringing in her ears. Thorn had apologized, but she still felt like she may never be rid of the epithet.

"Not anymore you're not," Waywyrd said. "You are my niece and you came to me for help. You will look respectable before we leave here today."

It was then, Klara realized, he might be speaking for the benefit of other ears. No doubt word of the escapade had already traveled through town.

Klara lowered her voice. "I've got breeches in my saddlebag, but in Mordovia I don't think it will help because I lack a tunic, so I'd have to travel bare chested. As far as clothes go, this is all I've got."

"Then we'll just have to buy you something new," Waywyrd said, his voice warm as fresh milk. He rose from his bed, offering her a hand. "There are a couple traders in town. They should have something that will suffice."

"I haven't got enough money," Klara replied, ignoring the proffered hand and straightening her dress, ashamed of her poverty. Until now, the only life she had ever endangered by her choice of occupation was her own. Now, she had put others at risk and had no means by which to rectify the situation.

"Well, I do," Waywyrd said. Klara began to protest, but he cut her off. "You do not have a choice in the matter, so you'd best come along and choose something you like, perhaps something suitable for a farmwife." He winked conspiratorially, indicating her part in the gambling ruse.

She allowed Waywyrd to lead her through the maze of dusty lanes until they reached the docks where a ferry brought those traveling to and from Kazan' across the river. There they found an establishment dealing in trade goods. A mound of cooking utensils in copper, iron, and bronze occupied one corner. Piles of fabric, everything from rough spun to felt, lined the wall. The trader folded his arms across his chest and looked down his nose at her, remarking to Waywyrd that he needed to keep her in line and teach her to be respectable.

Offering the shopkeeper a pained smile, Klara jabbed Waywyrd in the ribs with her elbow and refused to purchase anything there. As they wandered through the trade district, Klara looked for the Keltoi but saw no sign of them. She knew better than to ask in public.

At the next establishment, the trader also refused to speak with her, insisting on conversing only with Waywyrd as was the Mordvins' tradition. While the trader and Waywyrd talked, the man's wife dug through mounds of fabric and tutted over Klara with much "poor little lamb-ing." Klara was not fond of that either, but consented to be tutted over if it would get her back on the road.

Sorting through a hodge-podge assortment of clothing, Klara searched for something usable. Since she had a pair of gray breeches in her saddlebag, she wanted to purchase a tunic, rather than a dress. The shop did not have any of the fitted tunics popular among Skoloti warrior maids. Pulling a blue and green plaid jerkin from the pile, she held it up to examine it. There was little evidence of wear and it hit her on the hips, so it wouldn't get in the way as she rode. It was cut low, with a square, open collar. A shirt was necessary to keep her ample bosom from being on full display.

Pointing to a white shirt the trader's wife had just discarded, similar to the ones Ffearn and Karn wore under their tunics, Klara said, "I'll take this and that, if Waywyrd has enough for both."

"But those are men's garments, dear," the woman exclaimed.

"It's what I want," Klara said. "The jerkin and the shirt."

"Oh, no," the woman said. She pushed Klara out of the way and thrust her arms into the mound of clothing. "Try this."

The woman pulled a plain blue wrap-around skirt from a pile, then spun to the other stack, plunged in, and emerged with a woman's shift. "I know you Skolt maids tend to be a little… eccentric in your dress, but see how well the skirt matches the jerkin. It's much more respectable and the wrap is long enough to, umm. . ." The woman blushed. "Well, there's plenty of room to accommodate your girth when in the family way."

Klara fingered the fabric of the skirt. The weave was tight, with few imperfections, and it was a good match for the jerkin. No need to fear the chill of winter either, since there was enough fabric to wrap it around her twice before she tied its strings. With the shift covering her bosom beneath the jerkin, it was a sufficiently modest ensemble and would not attract attention in her role as a farmwife. But Klara knew exactly what she wanted.

"No, just the jerkin and the shirt," Klara said as she laid the skirt and shift aside. The trader and his wife appeared scandalized, both looking to Waywyrd for confirmation of the sale.

Waywyrd hemmed and hawed for a bit, then announced, "We'll take the lot."

The trader's wife broke into a broad grin. The trader himself was busy tallying the sale upon his fingers.

Waywyrd paid the man and said to Klara, "Seeing as we are in town, I expect you to dress as a young woman ought." Then he turned to the trader's wife, saying, "My good woman, could I trouble you to take her in back and have her dress." The woman's chest puffed with pride, as if she had just been appointed some important task, and marched Klara through a curtain that opened into their living quarters.

As Klara began to disrobe, the poor woman gasped in shock, pointing at the contraption she now called her bandeau. "Haven't you poor women got any proper clothing in Skoloti?"

"The reinforcement and straps are necessary to keep me held in when on the road," Klara said, "Otherwise, big as I am, they'll just bounce out."

"But your drawers are worn thin, little more than a rag and you're wearing men's boot sock," the woman exclaimed. "Don't worry, I'll see you properly dressed." Then she slipped back through the curtain and into the shop. Sighing, Klara sat, waiting to hear Waywyrd's edict on the matter, not entirely sure if the woman's concern was for her welfare or if she was just hoping for a larger sale.

Klara listened as the woman, flustered and unable to speak directly to Waywyrd stuttered, "Umm, sir, no." There was the shuffling of feet, then loud enough for Klara to hear clear in the other room, the woman said, "My good husband, the lass needs new garments for... err... support."

"Very well," Waywyrd said. "I shall pay for whatever is necessary."

When the woman returned she passed the garments to Klara, who laid them aside and took off her old bandeau in preparation of fitting the new one to her bosom.

"Oh my stars!" The woman gasped, pointing to the scars beneath her breast. "You poor little mouse. Did those filthy Keltoi beat you?"

"I wasn't beaten or abused," Klara said. "That's just what happens when you spend time on the road in a poorly designed bandeau."

Finally dressed, Klara emerged from the back room feeling a bit like a fatted calf on parade before the sacrificial slaughter. Every item she wore, from her stockings and drawers to the jerkin and skirt, were new. Or, at least, new to her.

Waywyrd nodded his approval and gestured toward the woman, who held Klara's old clothes. "Burn her rags," he said. "I believe she needs a fresh start."

"No," Klara said, snatching the bundle of clothing from the startled woman's arms. "I need my bandeau and my socks." There was no way she was going to be parted with the reinforced bandeau, not with plenty of time on horseback ahead of her.

Waywyrd sighed. "Fine, let her keep the socks and bandeau, but burn the rest." With their task complete, and purse much lighter, the Klara and Waywyrd took their leave.

Outside the shop, Klara tucked her new shirt under her arm, looked up at Waywyrd, and said, "Isn't this a bit excessive? It's more clothes than I've ever worn at any given time in my entire life."

Waywyrd smiled down at her. "You look lovely, my dear. And you'll attract far less attention now."

"I don't know how I'm going to repay you," Klara said, looking down at her new garments, self-consciously smoothing the skirt. "I don't come by much money. Never enough for nearly new trade goods anyway."

"You don't need to repay me, I didn't purchase them," Waywyrd said. Then taking her arm and heading back toward the inn, he added, "Now let's see about lunch; you didn't get breakfast."

Klara did not question him as he led the way across town, but she was utterly confused. Surely, he had paid for the clothing. She saw the coins exchange hands. Or maybe the clothes were stolen? Had he duped the trader with some sleight of hand or wizard's trick?

Back at the inn they dined on cheese, bread, and cold meat. Klara cocked her head and stared at Waywyrd as he chattered about how much she was going to enjoy living with him and his wife in Gelonus. He seemed truly excited to get back to the city, though until this point she had not known he was married.

After lunch they walked to the stable where she had killed the man the night before. The Keltoi had indeed left town, leaving her Constant and her tack. Her heart sank. Would she ever see Karn and Ffearn again? And why was Waywyrd actually taking her Gelonus?

As she saddled Constant, she overheard Waywyrd and the innkeeper talking. The innkeeper seemed impatient and eager to be rid them. After the events of last night, there was little wonder why.

"Will you and the young miss be heading out, sir?" the innkeeper asked, squinting up at Waywyrd.

"No, much too late in the day for that, I'm afraid," Waywyrd said shifting the staff to the crook of his arm. "I'm just taking my niece out for a ride. I'll move her horse down to the stable at the other end of town where my own is stabled. It seems we have much to discuss."

"Right you are there, sir," said the graying innkeeper, conspiratorially. "I seen the look that passed between her and that young Kelto when they were getting ready to bed down. You best warn her off Keltoi."

Waywyrd leaned in showing great interest in the little man's revelation and inquiring, "Which young Kelto would that be?"

"The dark one; the one what shot that man," the innkeeper replied.

"Oh my," Waywyrd said, feigning shock. "I will have to look into that." This left the innkeeper with a satisfied expression.

While Waywyrd and the innkeeper talked, Klara finished saddling Constant, managed to fetch her bow and quiver from its hiding place, wrap them in Karn's cloak, and fasten them to the saddle. When they arrived at the other stable, Waywyrd paid the stable boy a copper to saddle his horse while he took her bow up to their room. Klara noticed that Waywyrd had a new horse. What had become of the other one?

The breeze ruffled her hair as they rode out of town. She let Waywyrd set the pace, though they only followed the road a short distance before turning their horses into the grasslands. Soon she was completely lost. There were no discernable markers or landscapes in the grasslands and she had lost sight of both the road and the town.

Waywyrd turned in his saddle and said, "Now that we're alone, I think you might have some questions."

Questions tumbled out of Klara. "Why are we going to Gelonus? How will I get Karn his cloak? If you didn't buy these clothes, who did? And how will I pay them back? Are they stolen? If so, how did you do that? And why did the Keltoi leave me behind?"

When she paused for breath, Waywyrd asked, "Is that all?"

Klara nodded.

"Well, then," Waywyrd said, dismounting and letting his horse have its head to graze. "We are not going to Gelonus, but will travel that way for a short while. You can give him the cloak the next time you see him. Thorn paid for your clothes; you do not need to repay him. They left you because if they took you with them it would endanger their lives and your own."

Klara dismounted and slipped Constant's bridle off, letting him graze. "When will we see them again?" Klara asked, not knowing whether she felt hope or despair.

"I don't know," Waywyrd said. "In a few days, I expect."

Klara let out a sigh, the tension in her shoulders relaxing at the news. She had not known the prospect of not seeing them again weighed so heavily on her. "Why did Thorn buy the clothes? I cannot pay him back."

Waywyrd gave her a gentle smile. "Thorn bought them because it was essential for your survival and you do not need to pay him back. He saw it as an expense necessary to the company. Ffearn and Karn certainly won't mind because it'll give them an excuse to strike up another dice game. Besides, I think Thorn has become quite fond of you; the two of you have much in common."

Eyes cast down, hands fidgeting in the fabric of her skirt, Klara stood in silence, unsure if she should say more. After a long awkward pause, she said, "I have other questions."

"I thought you might," Waywyrd said. "Shall we sit?"

Under the bright summer sun, Klara sat beside Waywyrd, lost amongst the sea of grass, watching the horses graze and feeling their contentedness. She decided to start with a safe topic and work her way up to the more weighty ones. "What happened to your other horse?"

"I sold it," Waywyrd replied. "I much prefer traveling by water. I only use horses when I must travel on land. Duns are common and cheap. They can be readily bought and sold as necessity dictates."

They sat in silence for a while longer, before Klara gathered up the courage to ask her next question. "Why aren't you with your wife in Gelonus? You don't fit with the party of Keltoi or ply your trade in the taverns we pass. I'm not sure why you're here. There's far more money in sleight of hand than dice."

"I'm not some common conjurer of tavern tricks," Waywyrd snapped. He rose quite suddenly and began pacing. "I told you at the outset that I was enlisted to aid them in their journey, which is far more serious than you realize."

"I'm sorry," Klara said. "I meant no offense. I just don't know what it is you do. If we are simply traveling from one point to another, then we don't need much assistance and surely you'd rather be with your wife."

"If last night was any indication, then my assistance is something you most assuredly need," Waywyrd said. "And I'm not married. There isn't a maid on land who could tempt me."

Klara blinked at him. "What then, men?"

"I didn't say that," Waywyrd replied, running a hand through his hair. "I said no maid on land. I have a strong preference for mermaids."

Klara raised an eyebrow and gave him a disbelieving stare.

"Well, we all have our preferences," Waywyrd said. Pointing his staff at her, continued, "Now it's your turn to answer my questions. What really happened last night?"

Klara was confused. "It happened as you saw."

Not liking the look Waywyrd was giving her, she fidgeted with her skirt, looking everywhere except at him, lest he do something unnatural to her. And what good answer was there for why she had Karn's cloak? Or why she had refused Thorn's, especially now that he had purchased an entirely new wardrobe for her.

"Then why was it your arrow and not Karn's sticking out of the man's chest?" Waywyrd demanded.

"Oh," Klara said, understanding now. "I shot him and Karn threw the torch, but we figured that if I was to play the cook it would be better if we said it happened the other way around."

"That was certainly wise of you," Waywyrd said, giving her a penetrating look. "But that doesn't explain why the innkeeper says I need to warn you off Keltoi or what Karn was doing in the hayloft with you."

"The innkeeper just misunderstood," Klara said. "Karn meant that the party would not be separated, not the pair of us. He really came up to the hayloft only after I collected my bow."

Pulse racing and using bluster to cover her own muddled feelings on the matter, she added, "Besides, where I bed and with whom is nobody's business but my own."

Waywyrd hmmed sagely as she had heard wizards are wont to do.

## CHAPTER 12

# A KING AND HIS KIN

LARA WOKE EARLY, packed her things and was standing over Waywyrd shaking him, eager to be on the road. Waywyrd reluctantly opened one bleary eye and said, "You cannot wear trousers in town."

"Fine, I'll wear the bloody skirt. Let's just get moving." She slipped behind the curtain, hastily changed, and repacked. Then she sat impatiently drumming her fingers against her thigh. She hated to be idle and longed to be on the road. After what she thought was an interminable length of time, Waywyrd finally appeared, looking ready to travel.

"Don't you want breakfast?" he asked, staff in hand.

Klara shook her head, but Waywyrd took her by the elbow and steered her to the dining hall for toast and eggs anyway. She bolted down the meal and stared pleadingly at Waywyrd as he slowly savored every bite. Abandoning him, she went to ready the horses. She had them saddled and was pacing in the yard when Waywyrd finally appeared.

"If you ate any slower, you'd starve to death at your plate," Klara snapped as she handed him the reins to his mount.

"If you're going to do something, you should do it deliberately," Waywyrd replied, as he mounted. "Otherwise, there's no point in doing it at all."

"Which is precisely why I wanted to skip breakfast," Klara said as she swung into her saddle. The longer she sat in town, the greater the distance between her and the Keltoi became.

They let the horses walk, smiling and nodding at passing travelers to ensure reports of them being seen dallying along road to Gelonus would make it back to the village. When they stopped for the day, the sun was little more than a fiery glow on the horizon and the first stars were twinkling in the dusky eastern sky. Waywyrd anxiously looked both ways, but she saw no one in either direction. Then he peered across the river, scanning the opposite bank.

"Good," Waywyrd said, more to himself than to her. "We need to ford the river. Kazan' is on the other side. I thought it best to cross under cover of darkness."

"But don't we need to use a ferry?" Klara asked. When Waywyrd had told her they would take the road to Gelonus, staying on this side of the river, she had assumed they would cross at another ferry later on. The Kama River was wide and who knew how deep it was. She could swim, but how would she manage with her gear and a horse?

"I can adjust the river's flow," Waywyrd said. "That'll make crossing easier."

Giving him a disbelieving look, Klara followed Waywyrd to the riverbank where he dismounted and passed her his reins, saying, "Wait here until I call for you, then you must move with all haste. I cannot hold the flow back for long or it'll flood upstream."

Sweeping his staff back and forth before him, Waywyrd waded into the water, muttering to himself as he went. A swell rose just upriver from him and though Waywyrd was a full head below the waterline on the banks, the water in the channel never made it above his waist. Growing until it was more than twice as tall as the wizard, the swell towered above him, burbling with white capped waves at its crest.

"Now," Waywyrd shouted.

Klara rode into the river, its muddy bottom sucking at the horses' hooves. Constant was belly deep, the water tugging at the hem of her skirt and soaking her toes, when the dun shied. He tugged at the reins, white-eyed, nostrils flaring at the up-river water rising well above their heads. Despite her own fear, she coaxed him onward. The going got easier as they neared the middle, the hard packed clay and gravel bars supporting the horses' weight. Once she reached the far shore, and the horses were back on solid ground, she looked back. The swell burst, crashing down over Waywyrd.

"Waywyrd!" Klara screamed as he disappeared under a wall of water.

The river overflowed its bank, chasing her and the horses to higher ground. Then the surge was over, but there was no sign of Waywyrd. Jumping from the saddle, she ran to the river, chest pounding from fright. Wading knee-deep into the water, she looked downstream, hoping to catch sight of Waywyrd clinging to a log or branch, but saw nothing save the swirl of the current. Had he really been swept away?

From out of the dark, a flutter of bubbles raced up-river toward her. Absent gods, what was that? Backing away from the bubbles, she eagerly sought the safety of the shoreline. Before she reached it, the bubbles erupted in a splash and Waywyrd materialized before her, sopping wet and dripping.

Holding out a large wriggling, fish, Waywyrd smiled and said, "I've got supper."

Klara knocked the fish from his hands, which disappeared back into the river with a fearsome splash. "You scared me half to death and all you can think about is supper?"

"It would have been good eating," Waywyrd said. "Now I'll have to catch another."

Before he could make a dive for the water, Klara grabbed him by the tunic and pointed to the beach. "Get back on land," she said, "before you nearly drown again."

"Pfff," Waywyrd said, spouting water as she pushed him ashore. "You can't drown a water wizard."

Klara's muddy boots squelched as they walked up to the horses and made camp. The first order of business was lighting a fire and hanging her wet clothing by it to dry. Now that she was no longer terrified, she realized fish would have been nice for supper. Sighing, she donned dry clothes. Afterward, she dug in her pack for dried meat and nuts, which would constitute supper.

Waywyrd was blissfully sitting by the fire, his garments steaming as a muddy pool formed beneath him. Klara raised an eyebrow as she passed him his share of the meal. He seemed to enjoy the damp.

Looking at her with some trepidation as he accepted the food, he said, "I'm not going to have to bandage you now, am I?"

Klara shook her head and slipped a thumb under her jerkin, giving it a slight tug. "I'm wearing my reinforced bandeau, the one you said to burn. So long as I'm wearing it, nothing will budge." It was more than a little disconcerting that he was more concerned with the condition of her breasts than having nearly drowned her, the horses, and himself.

The following day, Klara had Waywyrd up and on the road so early that the sky was neither light enough to be called day nor dark enough to be called night. Now that she was dressed in her trousers, she insisted on keeping the horses moving at a brisk trot. Eager to overtake the Keltoi, she had refused to stop earlier to cook. Feeling irritable and anxious, she dug in their packs and divvyed up the jerky and dried fruit for supper.

As they prepared to bed down for the night, Klara asked, "Do you have any idea of when we'll catch up to the Keltoi?"

"We are moving in the same direction now," Waywyrd said, pulling the blanket snug around himself. "Aside from that, you know as much as I do."

Wrapping herself in Karn's cloak, Klara tried to sleep, but it eluded her. The wind rushing over the grass filled the night with a hollow, reedy sound. After considerable tossing and turning, she gave up on the notion of sleep and rose, pacing the camp, the wind buffeting her body as if it were deliberately trying to hinder her strides. Her nocturnal ambling woke Waywyrd.

"That won't help, you know," he said, his face lit by the stars and the dim glow of coals.

"I just feel out of sorts," Klara said, taking a seat near the remains of the fire and pulling the cloak tight about her.

"Tell me," Waywyrd said, shifting under his blanket, "Why are you so restless? What makes you so eager to push on and not enjoy the countryside?"

"The open country makes me feel uneasy, so does this ceaseless wind." Klara paused, staring at her hands, folded in her lap. When she spoke again it was little more than a whisper. "And I miss my friends."

"Friends?" Waywyrd asked.

"Aye," Klara said softly, raising her brown eyes to meet his gaze. "I've never had friends before. Among the Keltoi, for the first time, I feel like I belong somewhere. Even when Ruis teases me or Bardus makes me stand around bare, or Ffearn and Karn are being, well, Ffearn and Karn. It's hard to explain, but I feel like they are my people, even though I'm a Skolt and they are Kenetlo."

"And do you feel this way about Thorn, also?" Waywyrd probed from where he lay, now propped on an elbow.

"Yes and no," Klara answered. She was not trying to be contrary; she simply did not know how to explain what she felt.

This was not the first time Waywyrd had asked her about Thorn. Why? There was a pregnant pause, in which she felt Waywyrd staring at her, waiting for an answer.

Recalling the watch she and Thorn shared while the wolves harried their camp and how their fingers intertwined, she took a deep breath and pressed on. "Sometimes Thorn is so gruff and pensive. Other times I see such sadness in his eyes that it nearly breaks the very heart of me. I like him and know he cares for me because of the concern he shows when I go off alone. But that concern is often accompanied by anger and I don't know why. I know, too, that he carries some heavy burden that he will not share."

"You are quite perceptive," Waywyrd said. "Thorn has always been guarded with his emotions and, in time, I expect he will warm to you. But the road is long and now you must get some rest." Then he rolled over, pulling the blanket over his head, thereby ending the conversation.

"Out of bed," Klara demanded as she burrowed out of leaf litter and shook off Karn's cloak. It was already light and she chided herself for over sleeping as she rummaged in her saddlebag. "The sun is up and we should be on the road."

Waywyrd pulled his blanket back just far enough to expose his face and squinted at her. "The sun is not up," he snapped. "It's barely past gray. There is no reason to be traveling before the sky pinks." Maneuvering himself into a cross-legged position, he reached for his staff. "Honestly, there's no reason to be traveling before it's blue. I haven't had a hot meal in days because you insist on riding as long as it's light."

Equally agitated, Klara dropped a handful of dried fruit in his lap. "You can eat in the saddle." She longed to rejoin the Kenetlo, had no notion of how far ahead of her they were, and Waywyrd was only slowing her down.

Huffing loudly, Waywyrd gathered up the fruit and pocketed it to be eaten later. Then he prepared himself for the day's travels. Just two hours into their ride, they came upon the Keltoi camp. The company was just settling down to a breakfast of porridge. Spotting her, Karn and Ffearn shot from their seats and raced to meet her. Klara practically leapt off her horse and into their waiting arms.

"We'd nearly given you up," Karn said. "Thought the wizard might have stolen you away."

A rare smile graced Thorn's face as he said, "Now that you're here, and so early, we can break camp and get underway. There will be plenty of time to talk on the road."

"We most certainly cannot break camp," Waywyrd said as he slid from the saddle. "Klara has done three days riding in just two days. The horses are exhausted, as am I. I've not eaten a hot meal since we were back in Yar Chally." This drew surprised stares from the rest of the company.

"Was their trouble on the road to quicken your pace?" Thorn asked.

In kinder tone Waywyrd said, "No, someone was just eager to get back to her friends."

"I see," Thorn said. He turned and approached Klara. Having reached her, he took the sleeve of her shirt between his thumb and finger, feeling the cloth. "When I instructed Waywyrd to buy you something suitable to wear I did not expect to see you in a shirt and breeches."

Klara felt bashful, but held his gaze. "I have a skirt and woman's shift, also. I just felt riding would be easier in breeches, and it has been."

"Well, since we will not be riding today, I for one, would like to see you in your new skirt," Thorn said. It was kindly said, but she suspected it was an order.

"Aye, Thorn," she replied. "I'll see to my horse and change directly."

Taking Constant's reins, she led him down to the stream for water and then attached him to the picket line. The horse gratefully fell to grazing. She patted his neck and spoke softly, "At least you're happy to be back."

Karn walked up behind her, causing her to jump. "Don't mind Thorn, he's been out of sorts the last few days. I'm sure he was worried about you. I certainly was."

Klara tried to smile. "Well, I'm here now," she replied, apprehension in her voice.

Karn took her hand and pulled her behind the horses, out of sight of the company. "Aren't you happy to be back?"

"I was, I mean, I am," Klara stammered. She had not traveled this far just to become a kept woman and comfort wench. And for what? A new skirt? Had she really sold herself for so little?

She met Karn's eyes and words tumbled out of her, "I'm worried about Thorn. The clothes cost a lot of money, money I don't have. I'm not sure what he expects in return."

"He expects," Karn said, "that the next time we come to a village you won't draw the attention of so many men and end up shooting them out of barn windows. What did you think he would expect?"

Klara looked at him but could not put voice to her fears, though Karn read it plainly in her eyes. He pulled her to him and held her close, "Nay, Klara, he would not expect that."

As he held her, she began to cry. She had not openly cried for years and was ashamed to do it now but once the tears started she could not stop them. Karn held her for a long time as the tears slid silently down her cheeks.

When at last her crying stopped, he said, "If you won't wear the skirt for Thorn, will you wear it for me?"

Nodding her agreement, Klara snuffled and wiped her nose on the back of her sleeve. Then, because there were no trees to hide behind, Karn turned his back while waiting for her to change. When she was dressed, the pair of them walked toward the fire ring. With just grass and dried dung to burn, the fire was only used for cooking and was out now.

As Klara stepped clear of the horses, she drew stares from the rest of the party. Because she had exchanged her shirt for the woman's shift, there were tucks and gathers covering her bosom and sleeves, instead of the clean lines she sported earlier. The jerkin was cut so that it showed the length and curve of her waist and the skirt fell full from her hips.

"You look stunning," Ffearn said, his spoon held motionless midway to his mouth.

"Aye, I cannot see letting the lads knock you about dressed like that," Ruis added from his seat beside Ffearn.

Nuallan came up to her and patted her hand. "You are as lovely a sight as ever graced the Great Hall at Duirness."

Thorn rose and walked over to her, his dark eyes intense and admiring. "But do you like it?"

"Aye, I like it," Klara said, looking down and self-consciously smoothing the skirt. "Waywyrd had me choose it myself. But the price was dear, and I don't know how to repay you."

The softness returned to Thorn's eyes. "The contract states that the company will provide you with any necessary items while you travel with us. I found this to be necessary."

"Thank you, Thorn," was all Klara managed to say. They held each other's gaze overlong. Before it stretched into an awkward silence, Karn took her arm and led to the fire ring.

Ffearn handed her a bowl of porridge and the drinking horn, which she gratefully accepted. "When you've finished those, would you mind letting us use your brush and comb?" he asked. "We've been getting right scruffy looking without you here to remind us to braid our hair."

"You know," Waywyrd said, handing an empty bowl to Nuallan and shifting his staff to the crook of his arm, "it seems all your beards have been trimmed and you've been bathing regularly while I was away. Even the horses have been brushed. You are looking less like the ragtag band that started this journey and more and more like a king's escort."

That was true enough. Ffearn and Karn had taken to adorning themselves with silver. Nuallan always braided his beard, and now Bardus was sporting a well-manicured mustache. Even Ruis had trimmed his beard, though it was not as closely cropped as Thorn's.

"I do not think it a look we should be striving for," Thorn said, his voice rolled like thunder and a dark shadow crossed behind his eyes. "If we cannot be on our way, tell us what news there is of Kenetlon."

"Much of the news is sad, I am afraid," Waywyrd said, his eyes passing over every member of the company before settling on the pair of brothers.

"Ffearn and Karn, your grandfather has passed from the Earth. Ffearn, your father, Brawn, is now Lord of Clan Nuin."

Karn balled his hand into a fist and seated it firmly in his palm, the sharp slap of skin connecting reverberated through the air. The anger behind the action startled her. It was not the response she had expected. Karn's jaw was clenched, his brow furrowed into a furious frown.

"I'm not troubled by the death of that old gaffer," Karn said. "Has Brawn lifted our banishments?"

"He has not," Waywyrd replied, shifting uneasily. "And I'm sorry to report that after your mothers died, your fathers married their mistresses and named the children of those unions as their heirs."

Only now did Klara see loss and sadness register on Karn's and Ffearn's faces, though she suspected that was owing to their intact banishments, not their grandfather's death. She had assumed that they came from a wealthy house, but never did they give any indication that they were nobles or had been banished.

Waywyrd continued, "It may give you some peace to know that not all in the Alps of Norikum agree with what has happened. There are still those who do not look kindly toward an attempt to install illegitimate children as clan heirs. You lads were favored when you were young and many there still see Ffearn as the true successor to Clan Nuin as well as Clan Duir. They would like to see Ffearn stand for election and would follow him if you found means to return."

"You know I can't do that, Waywyrd," Ffearn said. "Thorn is my King. I follow him."

The shock of this statement barely had time to register before Thorn declared, "I am no one's king. What news of the other clans?"

Addressing Thorn, Waywyrd continued, "Your cousin Gaul is quite successfully running the iron mines and forges in Volkmer. There is calm in the lands of the Volkai and Gaul keeps regular patrols running along the border between his lands and Bevin's, though, I do not think he would support any attempt by you or Ffearn to claim the kingship. Bevin has squandered what was left of his father's wealth and the land of Bohmer is in shambles. The tin mines are producing poorly and he has trouble finding and retaining labor. The Charontes are leaving in droves."

"Likely headed for Silver Fountains." Thorn spat and rose as if to leave the circle.

"No, they're not," Waywyrd corrected, waving his staff at Thorn in a menacing manner. "In fact, the demons have been leaving the area and surrounding lands at a surprising rate. They have been gathering their forces and riding through the lands of Skoloti and Odryssa. There is something that draws their attention to the East."

"Well," Thorn said, "at least there is some good news." He turned and walked off, moodier than his usual self. Ffearn and Karn also rose without speaking and walked off together.

Klara looked at Waywyrd, hoping for an explanation of what just happened, but Waywyrd rose, stretched, and announced, "I think I'll go take a nap." Then he too walked off.

Feeling utterly bewildered and out of place, Klara looked around the fire ring at the few faces that remained. How was she to process talk of kings and nobles and banishments, all coming from a bloody damned wizard? Especially when the banished kings and nobles were the very men who had born witness as she plied her trade and shared her bed.

In a small voice, Klara asked, "Can someone please explain to me what all of that was about?"

None of them spoke. The silence dragged on. Then Bardus said, "Nuallan, you best do it. You were King Thorgal's cousin, and advisor; none would know better than you."

Klara looked at the Kelto expectantly.

Nuallan sighed. He gave Bardus a look she failed to understand, and snapped, "Will you lot never learn to use titles?"

Then Nuallan looked at Klara and cleared his throat before beginning. "Queen Boudika was expecting when King Thorgal died. It was still early yet, so none outside the household knew she was with child. Because of that, many claim the child in her belly was not heir to Clan Duir, but a bastard from another union. The Queen died in childbed. Fearing for Thorn's life, his grandfather, Lord Gwynn, claimed he was born still and gave him to a wet nurse who raised him in secret. Most Kenetlo refuse to believe Thorn is the rightful heir of Clan Duir and refuse to follow him as King, even though he was legally elected to the position."

"I'm confused," Klara said, shaking her head. "Not just about Thorn, but isn't kingship passed down and determined by lineage? Why would there be an election?"

"Many nations adhere to hereditary kingship," Nuallan said, with an obvious note of disdain. "Kenetlo do not, nor do Goths for that matter. Lineage of the clans is hereditary, but anyone may be nominated to lead. If the druids approve the nomination, an election is held."

Klara nodded that she understood, so Nuallan continued, "Anyway, as I was saying, Thorn was young when he abandoned his title. He's spent years living in the wilds. His sisters were six when King Thorgal died. Through a bit of treachery, they ended up being taken into Clan Nuin and lost to Clan Duir; otherwise I would have nominated one of them to stand for election. Thankfully, no one else can be named king while there is still debate over Thorn's claim to the title.

Pausing, Nuallan gestured across the fire toward Ruis and Bardus as he said, "And though it doesn't seem to matter to this lot, his title is still King and you should be addressing him as Your Majesty."

Her jaw dropped open in disbelief. She rose a hand to her chest where her heart was racing. A frown crossed her brow. Thorn, a king? And she needed to address him as 'Your Majesty?'

Ruis snorted. Bardus coughed. Both shifted uneasily in their seats.

"Tell her about the lads," Bardus said. "She should know it all."

Nuallan harrumphed. Obviously there was some disagreement among the company on this topic. Screwing up his face, Nuallan said, "When Ffearn was born many saw him as the successor to not just Clan Nuin but to Clan Duir as well. Thorn would support Ffearn's Kingship if he stood for election, but Ffearn rightly refuses to stand."

It was a lot to take in and Klara felt overwhelmed. Still, there was another question nagging at her. "Waywyrd said Ffearn and Karn were banished. Why?"

Sighing heavily, Nuallan pulled at his tunic. "That does complicate matters further. The lads were banished by their grandfather. As part of the banishment they lost all claims on Clan Nuin. But they were, and, if what Waywyrd says is true, still are favored by the people. The people would see Ffearn made king, but the noble houses will not and it becomes a legal matter. As for the why, the official proclamation cited too many scandals involving far too many serving girls."

"Why did no one tell me this?" Klara asked, eyes pleading as she scanned the faces of her companions.

"We did not know ye," Nuallan answered. "These are grave matters, not the kinds of things one tells a whore."

Klara was crestfallen. Unable to look them in the eye she turned her gaze to her hands instead. There were no words to express the sadness she felt. She thought they were her friends but realized that in the company of kings, she was just a whore. Rising, she too walked off to be alone with her thoughts.

In the open country of the steppes with nothing but grasslands surrounding her, Klara had to walk a considerable distance to find some privacy. She was a mile upstream before a bend in the brook and a few small hills blocked her view of the camp. Finally finding herself alone she sat and, for the second time today, cried. This time, though, she cried herself to sleep.

Klara woke to see Thorn's face as the Kelto gently shook her. Startled, she pushed herself away from him. Seeing her fright, he backed up, giving her space.

"I'm sorry, I did not mean to frighten you," Thorn said. "I came looking for you and saw the blue of your skirt flapping in the wind. I was afraid you had fallen or were injured."

"I'm fine," Klara replied, pushing her hair from her face as the sound the rushing wind filled her ears. Her mind was frantically whirring under the weight of the new information, trying to decide how or if to address Thorn. "I just came out here to be alone."

"Then I am sorry I disturbed you. I'll go," Thorn said and began to back away.

"No," Klara said. "Stay." Fidgeting uncomfortably, she brushed the grass from her hair and clothing. There were things she wanted to ask, but she feared the answers.

Lowering himself to the ground, Thorn sat beside her. It seemed he, too, had things he wanted to say, but neither knew where to begin, so they sat in silence. At length their hands found each other's and they allowed their last two fingers to clasp as they had done the night they stood watch together. It was only once that connection was made that they were able to find their voices.

"Why didn't you tell me you were a king?" Klara asked, looking across the steppes, not daring to meet his eyes.

"King of what?" Thorn said, using his heel to dig at a tuft of grass. "Of five misguided Keltoi, ten horses, and a woman whose beauty and tenderness tugs at my soul each time I look upon her?"

Klara turned to him. "I'm sorry, Thorn, I didn't mean, I just, …" She was unable to find any words that would suffice. Lots of men had called her beautiful. Why did this feel so different?

"There is nothing to be sorry for," Thorn said, staring across the vast expanse of grass. "We are not nobles, just the last of a noble house. The line of Duir ends with me. Nuallan would have me return and take a wife, but I have no intention of remaining in Kenetlon. I only go back now so that Ffearn and Karn may live among our people again. Their banishment is from the Clan Nuin, so I will grant them the land and title to Clan Duir. There isn't much hope the pair of them will produce heirs either."

Thorn sighed. "They will not tell me the true reason for their banishment, but I'd wager it has nothing to do with serving girls."

Looking down at their hands, Klara wondered if she should pull away. She had no business among kings, even a deposed one. Was that what had happened? It was all beyond her.

Turning to face her, Thorn said, "I expect you will be parting ways with our company now."

"I don't know," Klara said. "I suppose so. I know Nuallan will be pleased to be rid of me and the others too, I expect. It's amazing how much has changed since I rode into camp this morning."

Thorn took her hands in his. The grasp was gentle despite the roughness of his callouses and the firmness of his grip. "How can you think we would want you to leave?"

"Because I'm just a whore and you're all nobles," Klara said.

"You are not a whore," Thorn said. "You are our Luck Bringer and seventh member of our company. We are wandering vagabonds and cast-offs reaping the fruits of our own poor choices. You are the only honest member among us, as you were but a child when ill fate chanced upon you. It is you who should wish to be rid of us."

"How could I wish that?" Klara said. "Nuallan does not care for me, but you have taken me from a life I hated and given me opportunity to start afresh." Despite his gruffness, Thorn had always treated her fairly. And he had never laid a hand on her, not even the day she had slapped him.

"Then will you stay?" Thorn asked. Klara sensed a hunger in the question which came from somewhere deep within him. She recognized it as the same longing she felt when she had been parted from them. She needed these Keltoi, and, in a way she did not understand, she knew this was where she belonged.

"I will stay if you will have me," Klara said.

A smile warmed Thorn's face. "We would have you." Then he rose and pulled her to her feet. "Now, it is time we head back to camp; we do not want to be caught out here after dark."

When they returned, Nuallan approached her. "I think I need to apologize," he said. "I seem to have hurt your feelings and should not have said what I did. You are a member of the company and entitled to as much information as the rest of us."

Klara accepted his apology and went in search of Waywyrd. Having found him, she flopped down in the grass beside him and asked, "Have a good nap?"

"Yes," Waywyrd replied, scratching under his beard. "Did you?"

Surprised, Klara asked "How did you know I was napping?"

"I am a wizard, I know many things," Waywyrd replied, settling his staff on his lap.

"A tight-lipped wizard," she retorted, plucking at a blade of grass. "Why didn't you tell me I was going to be riding with kings?"

"Because you did not ask," he said. "Besides, if I had told you, you would have refused to join the company."

"Well, I'm asking now. Is there anything else I should know?" Klara asked. But he was right, she would have refused if she had known. In her experience, those with power were often unpleasant to deal with.

"Oh," Waywyrd said, "there are a good many things you should know. For instance you should know that the sky is blue and grass is green. You should also know that water is wet, rocks are hard, and the sun is hot. You'll also find it helpful to know which way is up."

Klara glared at him.

"You should also know that Ffearn and Karn are out looking for you. I expect they'll be pleased to see you have returned," Waywyrd said and waved his staff toward a pair of dark, ambling, humps on the horizon. It was Ffearn and Karn, silhouetted by the last rays of the sun.

Klara walked out to meet them and embraced them both. They were not themselves and seemed eager for the day to be over. She did not blame them. After dinner, there was no singing or talking by the fire. Instead the six Keltoi stood in a circle and began to chant:

"WHEREFORE NOW, THERE IS A KELTO TO DIE,
UNDER LIGHT OF MOON OR SUNNY SKY.
NONE ALIVE, NOR AMONG THE DEAD,
CAN EVER HOLD THEM AGAIN IN DREAD.
TO THE OTHERWORLD THEY NOW FARE,
THERE TO STAND AGED, WARN OUT WITH CARE.

"GONE TO FIND THE GODDESS'S SHRINE,
TO SEE IF SHE WILL TAKE THEE TO BE THINE.
AND IN THE MOURNFUL WONDER OF DEAD EYES,
PRAY THE GODDESS TAKE YOU NOT TO BE UNWISE.
OFFER THY LINEAGE AND PRAY THE GODDESS HATH FOUND,
THAT BY YOUR OATH YOU HAVE BEEN BOUND.

"CEASELESS WE ASK IN WHICH WAY THE JOURNEY LIES,
FOR THAT WHICH BRINGS SORROW ALSO MAKES US WISE.
AND INTO THE EARTH EACH SOUL MUST BE BOUND,
ENTERED IN THEIR TIME TO THE BURIAL MOUND.
AND SOMEWHERE UNDER STARLIGHT OR THE SUN
FROM THEIR KIN THIS LAST SONG IS SUNG."

Klara sat silent while they chanted, mesmerized by the unity of their voices as they made the mournful offering. Wordless, the circle broke and each Kelto headed for his beadroll. Klara sat wondering where to bed. She still had Karn's cloak, so could sleep alone if that was asked of her. Knowing that Ffearn was king or next in line to it and that he and Karn were of noble birth made her uncomfortable about their sleeping arrangements. Now she understood why Nuallan so obviously disapproved.

Karn returned to the fire ring holding a single finger to his lips indicating that she should remain silent. He led her to the bedroll where they undressed in silence and slipped under the blanket beside Ffearn. Having napped earlier, Klara was unable sleep, but the brothers, or cousins, or king and lord, or noble princes, or whatever they were, did. For a long while Klara listened to the sounds of their breathing and of the night, and eventually she too slept.

⁓

In the morning Karn nestled into Klara, burying his face in her hair. When she roused he held her close and whispered, "Be still."

By this time Klara knew what he wanted. They watched Ffearn's eyes to see whether he yet slumbered. Seeing no movement there, Karn reached out and tugged Ffearn's moustache. Ffearn's eyes fluttered as he woke and yawned.

"'Tis a grand day to be a Kelto, brother," Karn said and then exited the blankets and went to relieve himself.

Ffearn sat up and shouted at Karn's retreating back, "Why is it always a grand day to be a Kelto when she sleeps beside you and not when she sleeps beside me?"

Klara laughed at him. "I slept between you, and as it happens, I am still in bed with you."

"Hmmm," Ffearn mused, "So you are." Then he straddled her, pinning her down, and began tickling her face and neck with his moustache.

Klara shrieked with laughter. "Stop it! That tickles."

Ffearn paused. "I'll not stop 'til you cry uncle," he said and resumed his ministrations.

Helpless, with her arms pinned to the ground, Klara laughed. "You must stop or I'll wet myself!"

"Cry uncle," Ffearn said, "or better yet, don't cry uncle. Thorn's not much good at this kind of thing. I don't think he's ever tickled a maid with his beard."

Above her Klara saw Karn, hoping he had come to her aid. Instead he placed his hands where Ffearn's had been and straddled her as Ffearn made his exit.

"Now what's this I hear about crying uncle?" Karn said. "Are the two of us not enough to keep you satisfied? You need him, also?"

Karn began to tickle her with his scruff. Klara wiggled, laughed, and bucked, but could not unseat him. Thorn's face appeared above them and he tapped Karn on the shoulder.

Looking up, Karn said surprised, "Oh, Uncle."

"Precisely," Thorn said. "Let her up."

As Klara dressed and Ffearn and Karn rolled up the blankets, she overheard the comments of the rest of the company, who had already gathered at the fire.

"Are they always like this?" Waywyrd asked, leaning on his staff and watching them intently.

"Aye, the three companions," Bardus said. "Most times they're worse."

"It's like having a pack of hounds always underfoot," Nuallan quipped.

"Except," Ruis added, "As hounds go, that lot is twice as loud and half as useful."

"Oh my," Waywyrd said. "Have you considered separating them?"

"We threatened to paddle the lot of them one night and send them to separate bedrolls, but I think they rather liked the idea of being spanked," Bardus said.

"You can't change the order them three sleep in, either" Ruis added, "or they'll get moody and have a row."

"Oh, dear," Waywyrd said.

"You can tell what kind of day we will have based on the shape of the blankets," Nuallan said. "If she sleeps outside of Ffearn with their backs together, the day will run smoothly. If she sleeps outside of Karn with him spooning her, there will be stormy weather in the company. And if she sleeps between them, we're in for mischief. As you can see, today it'll be mischief."

Since they would be riding, Klara dressed in her breeches and the shirt and jerkin. After belting on her dagger, she sat down to breakfast.

Ruis eyed her approvingly. "Now there's a sight," he said. "If we encounter bandits or outlaws on the road they'll not know whether to run from you or to you."

"Good," Klara said as she accepted a steaming bowl of porridge. "While they stand there addled, I'll expect you to slay the lot."

Ruis clapped her on the shoulder. "I like a woman who knows how to give orders, especially one who looks both lovely and fierce at the same time."

"Did you notice that they match?" Bardus said, waving a spoon her direction.

"What in blazes are you talking about?" Ruis asked.

"Her and the lads," Bardus said. "Look here, have her stand between them." The trio did as instructed, all the while spooning porridge into their mouths. "See, Ffearn's tunic is green, Karn's is blue. Klara's jerkin is both blue and green, and they all wear the same color trousers; looks as if they are members of the same company and she commands them."

"We are a member of the same company," Ffearn said, slipping his arm through hers.

"And she does command us," Karn said, doing likewise.

"The trousers look better on her, though," Ruis said.

Laughter filled the circle of Keltoi.

After breakfast, the day's ride proved pleasant. Happy to be back among friends, Klara easily resumed the routines of life on the road. She hoped that what Thorn said was true—they were no more than wandering vagabonds. Though if his kingship was more than he let on, she might be in for more surprises farther down the road.

# Chapter 13
# Godly Killings

Now that the Keltoi were traveling along the Volga trade route, the road had improved considerably and the countryside was populated by small farmsteads and clusters of houses. No longer wandering days at a time without seeing anyone, the party frequently crossed paths with other travelers: Skoloti, Parthians, and, of course, Mordvins. They even saw two Gothic trading vessels floating on the river current, the gruff voices of the men at oars carrying to them over the water. Thanks to the improved conditions of the road, the company traveled easily for nearly a quarter moon and found themselves in high spirits just two days outside of the city of Kazan'. Everyone was looking forward to hot meals and soft beds by evening of the following day.

Since Waywyrd had rejoined them and there were eight in the company again, Klara had a riding companion when they rode two abreast; this morning it was Ruis. Around her, the Keltoi sang and laughed, or told dirty jokes and laughed, or recited naughty poems and laughed most of the morning.

When there was a break in the general commotion, Ruis turned to her and said, "You seem to get along well enough. You take yer turn at cooking and the watch. You run through your paces with the dagger when I set the lads up to face off against you, and you see to the horses, but why do you never join in the singing?"

"I don't know your songs," Klara said. "It seems you sing new songs every day, so I've yet to learn any of them. You have songs for good times and bad, songs for the road, and songs for around the campfire; there must be hundreds of them."

Ruis scratched his bald head as if deep in contemplation. "Well, if you don't know enough to sing our songs, do you know any of yer own?"

"Most of the songs I've learned are drinking songs, taught to me by the men who frequented the taverns where I've worked. I don't know any traveling songs," Klara said.

"Aye, a drinking song will do," Ruis said enthusiastically. "Let's hear it."

"Honestly, Ruis, I don't think…" Klara began to protest, but Ruis was calling for the attention of the rest of the company.

"Lads," Ruis said, "This lass ain't sung a single word since she joined us." This was met with mutters of disapproval. "She just informed me that's because she don't know the words to our songs. But she does, in fact, know how to sing and is going to grace our ears with a drinking song."

There were a number of hearty "Hear, hears."

Klara looked dolefully at Ruis.

"Come on, out with it," he demanded.

There was nothing for it. Klara patted Constant's neck for reassurance, then took a deep breath and began to sing.

"To the tavern we go a wandering,
With spirits low and mean,
And out we come a frolicking,
So fair to be seen.

"Wealth and increase unto you,
And your blessed ale too.
Goddess grant you a bonny barley crop this year,
Goddess grant you enough to make beer!

"Bless the Lord of this house,
And bless the Lady too,

Bless all the working servants,
Who out a reaping go.

"Wealth and increase unto you,
And your blessed ale too.
Goddess grant you a bonny barley crop this year,
Goddess grant you enough to make beer!"

This was greeted by cheers all around. The company made her repeat the song so they could learn it and add it to their repertory. During Klara's third recitation, she saw a plume of smoke rising in the westward sky.

The singing and jokes stopped as the Keltoi became serious. Tensions ran high; everyone was on alert for a potential threat. Many possibilities ran through her mind, but none of her companions were engaging in speculation, so she kept her thoughts to herself. Her initial hope was that whatever was burning might be far enough from the path to easily pass it by.

As they approached the plume, the acrid scent of smoke wafted to them on the wind and it became evident that its source was near the road. Thorn held up a hand, signaling the company to halt. The men loosened their swords, enabling them to draw quickly if necessary.

Waywyrd came to ride beside Klara. Looking at her, he said, "You need to move up to the middle of the column." Klara watched as the company rearranged itself and felt self-conscious about being the only one who needed told what to do.

Once they repositioned themselves, Klara saw that Thorn and Ruis headed the column. The string of horses was passed off to Nuallan, whom she was now riding beside. Ffearn and Karn brought up the rear. At once Klara saw this was a defensive positioning. Warriors fore and aft, women and children in the middle, she thought sarcastically. Thorn raised his hand again, this time waving it forward. The horses' tack jingled as the company began to move.

As quietly as eleven horses are able, they approached the homestead. A lone thatched roof cottage stood watch over a smoldering cross and pyre erected in the yard. The company halted and took in the scene. The nauseating smell of charred meat choked the yard. Seeing the remains of a woman and two children on the pyre, anger welled within Klara.

"Elah." Klara spat as she slid off her horse, heading for the cottage.

"Where do you think you're going?" Thorn called.

Klara shouted over her shoulder, "To see about a blanket." Then she ducked through the threshold of the little home, letting her eyes adjust to the light. Smoke permeated everything. It was obvious that this woman and her children were just as poor as she and her mother had been.

Smoke stung her eyes as she passed through the main living area and into what served as the bedroom. Two dirty blankets were spread across a pallet of straw in the corner. Pulling aside the blankets, she stripped the pallet of its bedding and kicked through the loose straw, immediately finding what she was looking for—the woman's coin purse.

Karn entered the room as she collected her prize. "I see you found the blankets," he said.

Klara looked up at him. "They're moth eaten, flea bitten, and probably lice ridden, so I'm going to pass." Then, holding up the coin purse she added, "But I found this."

Karn walked over to her and patted his own purse, saying, "You needn't rob the dead as long as I've got silver."

Klara understood his meaning. Stepping close to him, she pressed her body against his. Karn wrapped her in his arms. When his hands were resting on her back, she looked him in the eye and said, "You're saying you'll pay me for sex?" Though it was not a question and she already knew the answer.

"The thought had crossed my mind," Karn said, a frisky smile playing across his lips.

Klara raised a hand, tracing the collar of his tunic with the tip of her finger, following the line of it down his chest until her hand rested near his heart. In a silky voice, she crooned, "Sex was my job, but now I'm on holiday. There'll be no sex because I don't work when I'm on holiday."

"Technically, you are working," Karn said. "Thorn has you under contract."

How daft could a person actually be? Pushing him away, she said,

"Well, sex isn't in the contract." Then she brushed passed him, heading for the door.

"What if I got Nuallan to put it in the contract?" Karn called after her.

"No." Klara tossed her reply over her shoulder as she exited the cottage.

"You can't blame me for trying," Karn said as he too emerged from the little house, rubbing his smoke-irritated eyes.

"Oh, aye, I can," Klara said and mounted Constant with such force that the gelding seemed shocked. Anger seethed off her in waves.

Waywyrd looked her over and tested her mood by asking, "Didn't find any blankets?"

"No," Klara snapped.

Karn mounted his horse as well. The rest of the company had already gotten their fill of vulgarity by examining the pyre while she and Karn were inside. As the company stood disorganized in the yard, thundering hoof beats reached their ears and moments later a stream of warriors came galloping over the hill, quickly encircling them. Shrill war cries rang from the women as they closed ranks and drew their bows. The company of Keltoi was bunched together like sheep, their weapons drawn, but lacking enough room to fight.

A fierce woman in a blood stained tunic nudged her horse forward a few steps, her flaxen hair violently whipping in the wind. "I am Yalena, Fighting Bitch. You will give us the woman."

"No," Thorn said. "She is a member of my company and..." A resounding thump filled the air as Waywyrd smacked Thorn in the chest with his staff, abruptly cutting off his sentence. The force of the blow caused Thorn to stumble back a couple steps.

Klara kicked Constant in the ribs, hastily positioning herself between Thorn and the warriors. Reaching out, she laid her hand upon Thorn's head, gently pressing downward. The action shocked him enough that he blinked at her as he tried to catch his breath. Then Klara turned her attention to Yalena.

If she wished to be considered an equal, it was important to use a title when addressing these warriors. Straightening in her saddle, Klara said, "I am Klara, Luck Bringer, and this is my company."

Yalena scrunched up her face in disgust. "What would a sister be doing riding with a band of foreign men?"

Klara felt the tension and unease of the men and horses behind her, but knew she must not break eye contact with this woman. "I have been hired as huntress. What are you sisters doing so far from Skoloti?"

Yalena nodded toward a pair of women who rode double. "We tracked the filth who abducted Milica Battle Mare's daughter. We saved the girl and killed four Disciples." War cries erupted from the group of women, rejoicing in their triumph. When the whoops subsided, Yalena continued, "We saw the fire when we passed and have only returned to bury the dead, but cannot afford linger. Most of the Disciples escaped our blades and outran our arrows." Nodding toward the pyre she asked, "Will you help us inter this sister and her children?"

"Aye," Klara replied. Turning in her saddle, she waved for the company to put their weapons away.

Thorn grabbed her arm as she dismounted. "We should not tarry here if there are bandits about."

Klara leaned into the pressure on her arm, whispering hot words in his ear. "Do not give them cause to think I'm a captive. They will gladly kill you and escort me back to Skoloti."

Thorn released his grip. The warriors were already busy extinguishing the remains of the fire. The Keltoi began scraping away the turf to prepare the ground for digging.

The woman and her children were laid in a shallow grave, though there were no rocks to heap upon them to keep the carrion eaters at bay. Had the sisterhood buried her mother after she fled? Klara had never returned to find out.

As they left the farmstead, Waywyrd chose to ride beside Klara. Thankfully, he was smart enough to know when to remain silent. The afternoon and the memories it conjured left her feeling out of sorts. After a while, Klara pulled out the coin purse she collected from the house and opened it, disappointed by the contents. There was little reason to expect it contained very much, but if this was the whole of the woman's savings Klara felt sorry for her. There must have been more in the house, probably hidden under the hearth stone, which she would have checked if Karn had not been pestering her.

Waywyrd tested the waters, "You find that in the house?"

"Aye," Klara said. "It's not a blanket, but there might be enough to buy a blanket when we reach Kazan'."

"It sounded as if you and Karn had words," Waywyrd pressed.

"He said I didn't need to rob the dead, because he's willing to pay me for sex," Klara said. She was still sore about the offer.

A mildly amused look crossed Waywyrd's face. "I take it you informed him otherwise."

Klara smiled at him, remembering a common joke. "Do you know what they call women who won't have sex?"

Caught off guard by the sudden change in demeanor, Waywyrd said, "No, I don't."

"Wives!" Klara burst into laughter.

Waywyrd chuckled as well. Klara continued, "I've been bedding with Karn and Ffearn for over a moon and have yet to service either of them. I had clients at the alehouse who complained their wives made them go a fortnight or more without sex. I often wondered how that could be done; now I know."

Waywyrd adjusted his grip on the staff, a wry smile on his face. "So now that you've seen the error of your ways, any plans to rectify that situation in the future?"

"None," Klara said, feeling the weight of the afternoon dissipate.

Knowing there was no immediate danger about, the men resumed their chatter. Though they had not spoken since their exchange at the cottage, Klara was grateful when they finally reached a place to camp and she had an excuse to get farther away from Karn. It was her turn to cook and that kept her occupied.

Since Thorn had not given her any time to hunt, beans were featured on the menu again tonight. Beans are not an exciting meal, but she was a better cook than any of her companions. After putting the cauldron on the fire to boil, she added the beans, some diced carrots and onions, a big spoonful of lard, and some salt. That was the easy part. All she needed to do now was to stir the pot occasionally to keep them from burning and giving a repeat of one Ruis's performances.

While the beans boiled, Klara turned her attention to making bread. By her standards, the bread was far from impressive, but her butt bread had become a favorite among the company. When she finished kneading, she placed two loaves side by side in the iron oven to rise and went down to the stream to wash her hands. Across the clearing, Thorn, Waywyrd, and Ruis were locked in an impassioned discussion, one she was not about to join.

As the sun set, the Keltoi made their way to the fire expecting to be fed. After they ate and washed up, the men assumed their usual repose by the fire.

Ruis asked, loud enough to cut the chatter, "Klara, today you said Elah killed that family, and before you said it was Elah that killed yer mother. Can you tell us more about who's doing these killings?"

Klara sighed. This was not a topic she wanted to discuss. From across the fire Thorn shot Ruis an angry glare. Was he trying to spare her from having to recount painful memories?

"It's just that if this Elah person is a danger to us, we best know what we're up against," Ruis said, returning Thorn's gaze.

Ruis was right. Clearly the Disciples were here. Painful as it might be, she needed to tell them who was responsible for the killings.

Klara nodded, then began, "The Disciples of Elah are foreign men who worship Elah and a woman they call the Holy Virgin. They try converting others to their cause but don't seem to have much success. Skoloti have no gods and no interest in worshiping one. Most other people are already committed to their own gods and goddesses. In addition to seeking converts, the Disciples kill prostitutes, women who have children out of wedlock, and sometimes women who are rumored to be fornicators. If there is a band in the area, having me in your presence can put you at risk."

This caught Thorn's attention and his head snapped up. Previously, he had been trying to appear disinterested; now he leaned forward, intent on the conversation.

"If we are at risk, then I'd like to know more about them," Ruis said. "How do they operate?"

"When the Disciples hear of a woman who is considered immoral or impure, they gather, remove her from her home, and either stone or burn her as we saw earlier today," Klara said. Her chest tightened at the memories and she felt the sting of impending tears. The wind changed, sending smoke her direction. She paused, attempting to wave it away. It did little good and she reconsidered. Smoke stinging her eyes was a plausible excuse for tears.

Klara continued, "The distinctive mark of an Elah killing is the cross erected in the yard. They never rob their victims or loot the house. Anything the victim touched is considered impure. If you get there before the neighbors start getting nosey, you can usually find a coin purse, as I did today, and sometimes the odd piece of silver. I've never heard of them attacking an armed company, or even men at all for that matter. When a married woman is targeted, they burn her when her husband is away. If something goes wrong and the husband tries to stop them, the Disciples kill him, too. I guess they figured they didn't get all riled up for nothing."

Balancing his dagger on his knee, Ruis continued to query her, "You said his disciples do the killing, but who is Elah and are we likely to run into him?" Klara suspected the dagger would be sharpened before the night was out.

"Seeing as he is a god, no, you aren't likely to meet him. The last person to meet Elah was the Holy Virgin," Klara said.

"So you're telling us them folks is a bunch of religious rabble intent on murder," Ruis said, still fiddling with his dagger.

"That is the gist of it," Klara said. "The good news is, they are mostly cowards, killing unarmed women and children. But with me in your company it's best to take care what you say when others are around."

Thorn asked, "Is there any more you can tell us about Elah, or the Holy Virgin, that might help us understand the minds of his disciples?" He, too, had his dagger out, now.

"Well, the Holy Virgin isn't actually a virgin and they're pretty touchy about that," Klara said, wondering if everyone intended to sharpen their blades tonight. She planned to leave them to it. The excitement of the day had left her exhausted and all she wanted was a bed.

Screams echoed in the distance. Her companions shivered, though it was a warm night and they were sitting around the fire. The somber tones of wolves howling carried to them on the wind. A ripple of unease ran though the horses on the picket line. All the Keltoi were fingering their daggers now.

Looking at Klara, Thorn asked, "Ke'lets?"

"Aye," Klara confirmed, a sad and lonesome feeling welling within her. "They're hunting."

Thorn rose. Klara saw fear in his eyes, though he managed to contain it.

"Get your weapons; we'll double the watch tonight," Thorn said. The company was quick to follow his command.

Reaching out and taking Thorn by the arm, Klara directed his attention back to her. "Not us," she said. "They're hunting the Disciples. Those who burned that family will likely find justice tonight."

Thorn collected his whet stone and settled back in his seat. The others followed his lead. With everyone seated, Thorn prompted, "Please, continue your story."

"According to the Disciples, Elah came to earth and found a woman so pure and holy that he impregnated her by magic so she'd always be a virgin," Klara said. "That's the part they get touchy about. Everyone knows the Divine like sex, lots of it, making a magical sexless pregnancy unlikely. If the girl was with child, it involved sex. Worse, the girl was only thirteen, which makes their god a pedophile."

The constant rasps of blade sliding across stone was disquieting. Klara took a breath to settle her nerves and continued, "Her parents quickly married her to a mortal man. Although it's said, her husband didn't touch her until after the child was born and she was of age. She ended up having a son, which she named Messias. For the most part, she lived a normal life with her husband and had other children by him. When Messias reached manhood he was arrested for inciting rebellion, blaspheming the local religions, and engaging in heresy. The punishment was death, but, the Disciples claim Elah is a necromancer who revived his son after he had lain in a tomb for three days. The Ke'lets actively oppose Elah and work to bring his Disciples to their own form of justice."

Ffearn looked completely bewildered. "The Holy Virgin isn't a virgin, but a woman raped as a child. They worship a God who produced a bastard by killing women who also have bastards? And this dead son had been made undead. That doesn't make any sense at all."

Karn was shaking his head. "I am greatly confused."

Clearing his throat, Waywyrd said, "So are the Disciples of Elah. The important thing to know is they are zealots and zealots can be dangerous."

Thorn looked at Waywyrd. "What know you of this matter?"

"For the most part," Waywyrd replied, "it is as Klara said. They attack the weak and innocent in defense of something indefensible. It's not just prostitutes they kill; herbalists, healers, and midwives are also targeted. The Disciples believe that illness is an outward sign of deeper sins and that purification comes through suffering. A woman who gives a neighbor blackberry bark to cure a bit of stomach upset is burned just as readily as one who had a child out of wedlock. This puts them at odds with the other religions of the area. It doesn't endear them to the Divine either; the council of the gods has punished Elah before and refused to intervene when a mob convinced their rulers to kill his son. Most people refuse to worship a necromancing pedophile, so converts are few. However, if they've made any converts, it may be dangerous to venture into some of the towns. They do not like seeing single women in the company of men; though, that is not unique to the Disciples of Elah."

The mood of the company was somber as they extinguished the fire and headed for their bedrolls. Klara was not looking forward to this moment. The first time she bedded between the pair of Keltoi she awoke to find Karn wrapped around her, spooning her as they slept, and he had done this often since. Tonight Karn had first watch and Ffearn second watch. After his comments earlier today, Klara did not relish the prospect of having Karn join her under the blankets after she was already asleep.

When Klara reached the spot where the trio had decided to throw their bedrolls, she was grateful to find that Ffearn and Karn agreed to trade a blanket, leaving her the other one, as they had done her first night with the company. She was less pleased to learn they traded places in the rotation, leaving her to bed down near Karn now.

Klara lay awake looking at the cold light of the stars overhead. She knew by his breathing that Karn was not asleep either. Rolling to his side and propping himself on an elbow, he said, "Klara, I want to apologize for today. What I said was meant in jest; I didn't mean to offend."

Klara rolled to face him. "Are you saying you don't want to have sex with me?"

"No, it's not that." Struggling for words Karn continued, "I'd be glad to bed you, if you'd let me. It's just that I wouldn't expect you to do it for pay."

"So you want me to service you for free?" Klara asked, protectively pulling the blanket to her chin.

"No." Karn was shaking his head. "This is coming out all wrong. What I am trying to say is that I don't think of you as a whore that I could pay for pleasure as I wanted it. You're a member of the company and I'd like to think we're friends. I'd not do anything you didn't want."

His words found their mark and Klara began to feel less anxious about bedding beside him. Had it really just been a misunderstanding? She sighed deeply.

"I'm sorry too, Karn," she said. "I didn't enjoy my job as a whore and have longed to get away from it. I hated the sex, always have."

"Did you never find pleasure in it?" Karn asked.

"There is no pleasure in being beaten and forced," Klara said. "Many men felt guilty about visiting me and not being satisfied with their wives, so with them it was a thing quickly done, like washing a shirt or butchering a hen. Some are better than others, but the goal is to be done with it and collect my coins, so I can get back to serving ale or whatever needed doing. It's not a thing I'd do if given a choice."

"And do you feel the same when I hold you?" Karn asked.

Klara recalled the memory of Karn's arm around her waist that night in Yar Chally. He reeked of lust, but also offered protection and comfort. He had lent her his tunic and later his cloak, never asking for anything in return. And there was something else, a feeling, not as strong as with Thorn, but just an indecipherable.

"No, it feels different," she replied. "When you hold me as we sleep I know that is all you will do, so I can rest easy."

"Then may I hold you now?" Karn asked. Klara agreed and fell asleep with her head buried in Karn's chest.

## CHAPTER 14

# FIGHTS OVER GAMBLING WINNINGS

K LARA AWOKE TO find Karn gone and Ffearn in his place, snoring softly. Rising quietly so as not to disturb the slumbering Kelto, she saw Thorn and Waywyrd, already awake and engaged in conversation. Looking about her, she spotted Karn, who was little more than a dark smudge nestled against a tree, and walked over to him.

Taking the blanket from her shoulders, she placed it around his and said, "Go, sleep now, while you can. I'm up now, as are Thorn and Waywyrd." Karn thanked her and headed for the lump on the ground that was Ffearn.

The sun crept over the horizon, the day turning as bright and fair as Klara's mood. She took the horses down for water then dug the curry comb out of the panniers and set to work on Constant's coat. The scent of his warm flesh wafted up to her with every stroke. After just a few passes, she thought his eyes actually rolled into his head. By the time she finished brushing him—if it could be called that, for the silly horse seemed to think it was some erotic pleasure—he had been lulled to sleep. Swatting him on the rump, she woke him and commenced saddling her mount.

When they rode out, Waywyrd made the mistake of riding alongside Klara. This prompted Ffearn and Karn to engage in a fair bit of teasing at his expense. Karn began by saying, "As a wizard he's supposed to know the meaning of life, and well, everything."

"It's because wizards are always engaged in deep thought," Ffearn added.

Waywyrd ignored them.

Hoping to get a rise from him, Klara joined in the fun. "The last time I asked him if there was anything I needed to know he told me the sky was blue and grass was green. If that is the extent of his knowledge, I'm not much impressed."

"Well, Waywyrd," Karn said, turning in his saddle, "Now would be a good time to astound us by saying something profound."

They waited expectantly as Waywyrd, lost in thought, mumbled to himself. They had given up on him, thinking he had no intention of answering any of their queries when he said, "Fifty-four."

Ffearn nearly choked on his laughter. "That's the most profound thing you can come up with?"

Waywyrd looked at him with a puzzled expression. "What was the question?"

The three of them laughed at him. Realizing they were unlikely to get a rise out of him this morning, Ffearn and Karn turned their attention elsewhere and began discussing things among themselves. Beside her, Waywyrd swayed like a drunkard in his saddle. This amused her. Was he as uncomfortable as he looked?

In time, Waywyrd put aside his thoughts and turned his attention to Klara. "I see you and Karn have gotten over your disagreement. It's a good thing too; the pair of you need to get along today."

"Why is that?" Klara asked as she patted Constant's neck.

"At midday we will split the company again," Waywyrd said. "Karn will change and the two of you will travel into Kazan' ahead of us under the guise of a married couple. The rest of the company will follow later."

Klara narrowed her eyes, giving the wizard a stern look.

"Well, don't blame me," Waywyrd said. "It was your idea. Just yesterday you said you'd been playing wife to him for the better part of the journey. Thorn and I just thought you could use a little more practice at it."

When they stopped to water the horses, the company headed for the stream to wash up and generally make themselves more presentable. While the men were at the river, Klara switched outfits. She even put on the other bandeau and stockings before donning her skirt, figuring that if she was to play the role of a Skolt woman she might as well do it properly. Then she laughed, remembering that she was a Skolt, and freed her hair of its braids.

Klara had not seen Ffearn in his other outfit yet. When she turned to face the men at the river, she was taken by how dashing he looked. He had weaved the silver beads into the ends of his moustache again and changed his green tunic for one of gray, the fabric shining like silver in the afternoon sun. Embroidered across his chest was a silver chalice with cool blue water spilling over the edge and falling to the ground where it met oak leaves, which twisted up to encircle the cup as a wreath.

Ffearn was in the process of putting on his cloak when Klara approached him. Mesmerized by the crest, she reached out to touch his chest, feeling the fineness of the stitches under her fingers. Eventually, she pulled her gaze from it and met his eyes.

Ffearn took her hand in his, saying, "It's the crest of the Clan Duir, the King's Crest. Thorn gave it to me. I only wear it when we need to gamble, and sometimes not even then. It is a hard thing to wear, knowing it will never really be mine." Pausing, he added, "You best go, I see your husband awaits."

Klara was momentarily confused, then realized he meant Karn. She stood at Karn's side as Thorn laid out their plan. "This is a big town with multiple inns. Make sure we don't all end up at the same one. Karn, choose one for you and Klara near midtown. Ffearn, I want you down at the docks so you can leave early without drawing attention to your departure. Waywyrd and I will come late and fit in as we can."

"Klara, Karn, after the display yesterday, try not to bicker when you're in town. You're supposed to be married, you know," Waywyrd said, leaning on his staff. The proclamation drew puzzled stares from the rest of the company. He looked around at the company and then back at Klara and Karn. "Never mind, argue all you want, you are supposed to be married after all." And with that they were sent on their way.

It was mid-afternoon when they reached Kazan'. Klara and Karn stopped at the market, where she purchased a bedroll before searching for an inn. The first one said they were full, but the second one still had room and was able to stable their horses. The accommodation was small and stuffy, tucked in a corner of the hayloft.

"Sorry about the smell," the young maid said as she passed Klara a pitcher of fresh water. "With this being the first market of the season, town is overflowing with Gothic traders and fuller than usual. We've got no beds left. This is normally the stable hands' room. They'll be sleeping with the stock tonight to ward against thieves."

Klara smiled at the girl. "This will do fine." The child slipped out the curtained door, the ox hide softly swishing back into place behind her.

Klara set the pitcher on the floor and fished in her pack for a rag. Then, using water from the pitcher, she wet the rag and washed her face. Leaning forward, she ran the damp rag across the back of her neck, but it did little to cool her. Karn sat on the pallet that served as the bed, his back against the wall.

Dropping the rag on the floor beside the pitcher, Klara turned to face him. "You know, this afternoon I forgot I was a Skolt."

Karn looked at her, surprised. "How could you forget a thing like that? And what did you think you were?"

"Silly, I know," Klara said. "Thorn may not know this, but he purchased more than just my outerwear. The trader's wife insisted on all new under things. Waywyrd bought everything she suggested. As we were getting ready by the river, I thought to myself, 'If I'm to play the part of a farmwife, I may as well do it properly and wear them all.' Then I laughed at myself."

"You still haven't told me what you thought you were," Karn reminded her, leaning forward, eager to hear the answer.

"I thought I was a Kelta," Klara said. "What else? I guess I've been riding with you for so long that I forgot I was a Skolt."

"Kenetlo are like that," Karn said with a grin. "You spend much time amongst us and you'll lose all sense of manners and decency, too."

"Then perhaps I was a Kelta all along and never knew it, for I've never had any manners or decency to begin with." Klara laughed. Then more seriously she said, "It's bloody hot in here. Why don't we go outside and see what amusement there is."

While walking around town, Karn floated the idea of a dice game with a few of the merchants finding little interest. One of the shops was a silversmith. Among his goods was a set of silver hair combs decorated with the endless knot, which the smith must have taken in trade. They admired the craftsmanship but neither had money to spend on silver. As they continued their walk, they saw Ffearn and the rest of the company ride through town.

Klara knew Karn was eager to meet with his brother and choose a venue for the game. Taking her arm, Karn led her back to the inn. After supper she went to their room and he went in search of Ffearn.

When Karn returned, he said, "Ffearn's arranged a game at a rough looking tavern on the outskirts of town. Still, we should bring in a good haul because eight men are going to play and two of them are the wealthy merchants I talked to earlier. Now all I have to do is wait 'til game time."

"And what did you intend to do to pass the time?" Klara asked.

"I planned to lie on that bed and not do a thing," Karn said as he mopped sweat from his brow. "Did you have plans?"

Klara shook her head. "None specifically."

"But generally," Karn probed.

"It was nothing, just foolishness," Klara said and bit the corner of her lip in a playful manner. It was awfully hot and it would be good to get out of her clothes.

Looking at her, Karn said emphatically, "I am always up for foolishness. Tell me what it is and if I can, I will oblige."

Klara could not resist him, nor did she want to. "I was just thinking what a shame it is that no one will ever see all the garments Thorn had to buy. And it is hot after all; a little nakedness didn't seem like a bad idea…" Klara's sentence trailed off and hung in the air.

"Are you sure?" he asked, eagerly.

Klara was not sure. But she had done it plenty of times before. And it always relieved the pressure in her abdomen that came in the middle of her cycle, a pressure she was feeling now. "I am sure of nothing," she replied and reached to take his hand.

Karn pulled her to him and kissed her gently. When they parted, he said, "At any point you can tell me to stop and I will."

Klara nodded.

Karn slowly unlaced her jerkin and pushed it off her shoulders. A flutter of excitement tingled through her limbs as his hands trailed across her clavicle. Pressing her body against his, he reached for her back and untied her skirt, letting it fall to the floor.

Klara wet her lips and gently bit her lip as she unfastened his belt and let it drop. Then she opened his tunic and pushed it back over his arms, revealing his well-muscled chest. Sighing audibly, she ran her fingers though his chest hair. They kissed again and as they did Karn reached down her sides, bunching her shift in his hands. He slid his hands up her sides taking the shift with them and pulling it over her head before letting it drop, so that she stood before him, wearing only her bandeau, stockings, and drawers.

Pushing her back, he looked her up and down, then said, "Are these the things you thought it a shame no one would see?"

Leaning in to him, Klara closed her eyes, drinking in the intoxicating mixture of his musky scent. "Aye," she whispered.

Karn held her close and asked, "Do you want me to stop now or keep going?"

"Keep going," she said.

Karn kissed her neck as he unlaced the bandeau, his hot breath and the tickle of his beard sending shivers of delight down her spine. Once she was free of it, he cupped her breast and lifting it, kissed the scars that stood red and angry against her skin. Then he led her to the bed in the corner of the room and kissed the length of her body as he rolled down her stockings. Her hips rose as he used his tongue to pleasure her, continuing until she climaxed, her body arching and quivering with desire. When he came to lie beside her, she pulled him on top of her, feeling the firmness of him through his trousers as their bodies rose and fell to meet the other.

She reached inside Karn's trousers, but he stopped her and whispered, "There isn't time. I have to go earn the rent for this room."

"Now?" Klara asked, breathless. She was eager. She was aroused. None of the men she serviced had ever seen to her pleasure. After experiencing this, how could he stop now?

"Soon," Karn said. "Ffearn will not thank me if I'm late. But, we can continue this later."

Laying her head on his shoulder, Klara ran her fingers through his chest hair. Once their breathing slowed and the heat of the moment was gone, Karn kissed her forehead and said in a playful tone, "I think Thorn got his money's worth—or rather, I got his money's worth. Will you be showing your underclothes to everyone in the company or is this privilege reserved exclusively for me?"

"You are truly terrible, you know that?" Klara said.

He rolled her off him, pinned her down, and kissed her. "I'm horrible," he agreed. "There is just one thing, though. If you take a notion to show Ffearn your undergarments, tell me first so I can be there to watch!" Then he got out of bed and, still grinning, found his tunic and put it on.

It was after midnight when Karn returned. Standing before the bed, he took off his tunic, his muscular body rippling in the moonlight. Sitting, he removed his boots and socks, and then stood again to drop his trousers. When they shared a room before Karn kept his breeches while they slept; she had never seen him without his trousers and enjoyed the sight.

Crawling into the bed beside her, Karn took her in his arms. "The game went well," he said. "And it's still going strong. I nearly tripled the money they sent me with. There were two young farmers, eighteen or nineteen. We cleaned them out early and didn't bother losing a little back for their benefit. The next two took longer because they were merchants and shrewd with their money. I left not long after them. The last four look rough, but Ffearn brought Ruis with him, so he should be alright if trouble comes. Three of them are already wasted anyway. The last feller, though, still has some of his wits."

As Karn recounted the evening, Klara sleepily ran her fingers through his chest hair. Karn looked down at her now. "You don't care a bit how the game went, do you?"

"No," she replied, flicking his nipple with the tip of her finger.

Karn kissed her and ran his hands down her body. Klara sensed his eagerness as he pressed against her. Her body arched to meet him of its own accord, but her needs had been satisfied earlier in the day, so she no longer felt the pressing urgency of before. In her mind, she struggled with the knowledge that this could not be.

Pushing him away, Klara said, "Karn, we can't."

He leaned down and kissed her before answering. "I know I am thicker than most, but I have learned to be gentle. I'd not hurt you."

"It's not that," Klara said, pushing him back once more. "I've had Keltoi before; I know what to expect. It's just I haven't any herbs. Without them, if we were to couple it might result in a child."

"I would not mind that, Klara. But I take it you would," Karn said.

"To be with child is the one thing I fear above all else," Klara said. "I took pennyroyal every day when I was working, sometimes twice just to be sure. I ran out quite a while ago. Since Thorn was adamant about there not being any sex, I haven't bothered to look for more."

"Then I will be content to just hold you," Karn said and wrapped in each other's arms, they fell asleep.

⤸

They slept late the next morning and Klara woke to Karn tugging a lock of her hair. "It's a grand day to be a Kelto," he said.

"You're headache-free this morning, I see," Klara said, reclaiming her hair.

"That I am," Karn replied. "Klara, I don't want to sound pushy, but these herbs you spoke of last night, if we had them would you have been willing?"

"Possibly," Klara mused, laying back and pulling the blanket up to her chest. "I've not done this without pay and I'm not sure how or even what I feel. I know that I like being in your company and waking in your arms, but I don't know a lot else right now. Until just a couple of days ago I didn't even know you were nobility."

What she did know was that a good orgasm alleviated the mid-cycle pressure she felt, but that was not something she wanted to discuss with Karn. For her, intimacy and sex were entirely separate, and she did not necessarily crave either. Still, she felt safe with Karn and found him trustworthy. In her experience that was a rarity among men. She was more accustomed to lecherous behavior and groping hands.

"I've no land or title, Klara. Those were stripped from me when Ffearn and I were banished," Karn said. He was propped on an elbow, his hand resting on her belly. "And since you bring up title, why me? You could have chosen to pursue Thorn. He has the potential to be King and I've seen how he looks at you. I'll never be more than a tradesman, vagabond, and gambler."

"I didn't know I chose you," Klara said. "I thought it was the other way 'round and you chose me."

For all the intensity of emotion there, the most Thorn had ever done was hold her hand. And he had never asked for the pleasure of her company. Surely, if he had been interested, he would have made his intentions known as Karn had.

"You could have run me off," he said. "But you didn't."

She could have. She probably should have. Klara chewed her bottom lip and thought for a moment before answering. "I guess it's the way you looked at me and how you make me laugh. You're quite clever, and honest, and loyal. And I like that you can hold me and do nothing else. It made me realize that in some ways I could trust you. But I think the biggest reason is Ffearn."

"What about Ffearn?" Karn asked, confused.

"You're devoted to him beyond reason. I've watched as the two of you have shared tender moments and it's clear you love each other. I guess, I hoped…" Words failed her. Unable to give voice to hope, she reached up and ran her fingers through his chest hair. "That and you're incredibly attractive."

Karn smiled, looking down at her as she petted his chest. "I've noticed, on more than one occasion, that you're fond of Kelto-flesh. Now, about this herb, where might we get some?"

"At home I collected pennyroyal myself most of the time," Klara said. "If I couldn't find any, I'd get some from a midwife. You can sometimes get the herb from an apothecary, but as I am unwed, it's a dead giveaway for the Disciples of Elah. Besides the herb is dear and in my trade I couldn't afford it in the quantities I need from a chemist."

"There's an apothecary in town and today you happen to be a happily married woman. We can stop there before we leave," Karn said. "Do you need to take the herb every day or only if we couple?"

"Only if we are joined. I took it every day before, because of my profession, and I wanted to be sure nothing would go amiss. But, Karn, even if the chemist has pennyroyal, I lack the funds," Klara said.

"Then I'll buy it," he said with a shrug. "After all, I'd be benefiting from the herb as well."

"Karn, the herb is dear," Klara began, but Karn stopped her by putting a finger to her lips.

"Well, if you'd rather chance a child," Karn said, mischief in his eye.

"No," Klara quickly cut him off, "the herb."

They took a late breakfast at the inn, made their purchase, and headed out of town without stopping to hear the gossip about last night's game. Klara was amazed by the line of boats along the riverbank. The wind caught her hair as she scrutinized them from the ferry, happy not to make another forced crossing at Waywyrd's hands. After that, the day was hot and the riding slow, so they did not catch up to the party of Keltoi until late in the evening.

"You should have been here hours ago," Ffearn said as he rose from his seat at the fire. A painfully swollen black eye covered most of his face and his lip was split.

Ruis reached for the front of Ffearn's tunic, displaying bruised knuckles, and pulled Ffearn back down. "Now is not the time, lad. You two can talk it over later." There was a gruffness in his voice that indicated he was not in the mood to be trifled with.

"Absent gods! Ffearn, what happened? Why are you bruised?" Karn asked as he dismounted and handed Bardus the reins.

"Little you care." Ffearn spat, fire flashing in his green eyes. He brushed aside Ruis's arm and stood to meet his brother. "You left early when there were still too many men at the table."

"It was after midnight," Karn said. "And half the men already left. I'd nearly tripled my money; there was no reason to stay."

Ffearn poked a finger in Karn's chest. "There were still four men at the table and only half drunk. We had to flee in the night while you bedded your whore!"

"Don't say that," Karn warned, knocking the offending finger aside.

"Oh, come on, Karn," Ffearn said. "I smelled her on you when you got to the table. And the whole night it was clear that you were eager to be back in bed with her. You would not believe what was said about you after you left."

"Klara has nothing to do with your black eye," Karn retorted. His voice was steady, but his anger was evident by the clenched fists at his sides.

"She has everything to do with it!" Ffearn shouted, now pointing at Klara. "If it weren't for her, you would have finished the game and been there when the fight broke out."

"I never finish the game," Karn said, coldly. "That's how we play. I double my money if I can, then I leave. How would it look if I stayed? In case you've forgotten, my new role in this scheme is that of a married man."

Ffearn was beside himself. His jaw was clenched, as were his fists, and the veins in his neck were rapidly pulsing. "Even married men stay out dicing and groping the serving wenches. Did you learn nothing of marriage from watching our fathers? Besides, doubling isn't good enough anymore. Do you have any idea how expensive she is to keep? A trip to the chemist because she isn't smart enough to bind herself properly, a dagger because she didn't come armed, new clothes so she isn't running through the countryside half bare, and in every town another room so you can bed her while we flee with what little money is left!"

"I would not be like my father for any amount of land or title!" Karn shouted, punching Ffearn squarely in the jaw. Then he lunged at his brother with uncharacteristic fury, knocking both of them to the ground.

Klara stared in disbelief as Karn and Ffearn rolled in the dust, beating each other. In the end, Ruis and Bardus pulled them apart. When the brawl was over, Ruis and Bardus stood them before Nuallan as they emptied their purses and the money was counted. Despite protests of there being little money, Ffearn nearly doubled his. When Karn's coins were counted, Ffearn challenged him again, "Where's the rest of it?"

"That's almost triple what I started the game with," Karn said, refusing to make eye contact.

"But it's not what you left the table with. Where's the rest?" Ffearn demanded, shoving Karn hard enough that he was forced to take a step back.

"A purchase was made," Karn said, returning the shove.

"An item for your whore, no doubt," Ffearn sneered. Karn balled his fists and took another swing at Ffearn, but Ruis caught his arm and held him back. Undeterred by Karn's aggression, Ffearn shouted, "Next time you buy something, do it with your own money." Bardus pulled Ffearn away and steered him across camp so that only Karn stood before Nuallan.

"You know that any purchases made with company money must be approved by Thorn. What did you buy?" Nuallan demanded. Klara felt her stomach tighten.

"It was a personal item," Karn said, staring at Nuallan and thankfully avoiding eye contact with her.

"Personal items are purchased with personal money," Nuallan said. "Get out your purse, you need to pay that back."

"I have no coins left," Karn said.

"You had no right to spend the company's money. We do not have money to be spending on personal items for you or anyone else," Nuallan said, gruffly.

"Show me the ledger," Karn demanded.

"What?" Nuallan replied, stunned to be given an order by the young Kelto.

"Show me the ledger," Karn repeated.

Nuallan consented and dug a worn piece of leather out of his saddle-bag. He handed it to Karn who scrutinized it carefully. Klara craned her neck to see the object which had symbols and tally marks scratched into it. Unfortunately, she was unable to discern their meanings from a distance. Without speaking, Karn handed the ledger back to Nuallan and walked off.

Klara stood, silent, stunned into disbelief. Had she really caused so much trouble? Nuallan had always disapproved of her, but now Ruis and Bardus were giving her the same judgmental stares. She felt unsure of herself or of where to sit: not at the bedroll, Ffearn was there; not at the fire among the elder Keltoi; not with Karn, she already caused him too much trouble. Out into the night perhaps? She had a bedroll now and could sleep alone.

From across the camp, Karn, laden with their gear, approached her. Taking her hand, he said, "Come with me." They walked away from where the other bedrolls were thrown. Once they were far enough away to talk without being overheard, Karn threw down the bedroll and said, "We'll sleep here."

"Karn, I'm so sorry," Klara began, but he hushed her.

"You have nothing to be sorry for. Let's bed down, and then we can talk," Karn said.

When they lay facing each other, Karn spoke, "I'm going to leave early in the morning, but I'll be back tomorrow night, probably late. Sleep well away from the camp so I'll know which is you. Uncle Thorn's is going to be angry; you best stay away from him and keep your own company. If you must ride out, stay with Waywyrd and no harm will come to you, but I don't think they will travel tomorrow."

"Karn, what will you do? Where will you go?" Klara asked. Her head was a muddle of questions and she felt just as unfocused as the stars twinkling overhead, disappearing and reappearing behind a thin layer of ever shifting clouds.

"I don't know, but I have to make things right with the company, Klara. Do you understand?" Karn asked.

Klara nodded, but she did not understand. She had been the cause of the trouble and had no idea how to make it right. Nor did she know what Karn thought he might be able to do to rectify the situation.

"Good," Karn said and kissed her forehead. "I need to sleep now. I have a long day ahead of me."

## CHAPTER 15

# A RIFT IN THE PARTY

KLARA WOKE FEELING chilled, eager to snuggle into Karn for warmth, only to discover he was already gone. The remainder of the party still slumbered, their snores a rude accompaniment to the birdsong filling the morning air. After rolling up her bedroll, she headed for the picket line intending to take Constant and Night down for water, but Night was gone, too. Wherever Karn went, he took the horse with him. After watering Constant, she picketed him near her bedroll, giving him access to fresh grass.

Not wanting to wait for breakfast, she dug through the panniers, colleting handfuls of dried fruit and nuts. Thorn was unlikely to arrive before midday. Hoping to avoid the rest of the company, she took her bow and headed up stream to hunt. The walk helped ease her troubled mind. After bagging a fat rabbit, she returned to camp and rummaged through the panniers until she found the flint and started a small fire near her bedroll. Cutting the rabbit into chunks, she skewered them on young willow shoots and laid the meat over the coals to roast.

The rabbit was still roasting when Thorn and Waywyrd rode into camp. Klara watched with interest but was unable to hear what was said among the party. Then Thorn shouted, "At least, they had the good sense not to draw attention to themselves!"

The horses jumped and became skittish at the sudden outburst. Bardus appeared to be attempting to calm Thorn as the conversation continued. Klara strained to hear but discerned nothing.

Thorn shouted again, his voice booming though the camp. "You chose a rough tavern for the game and invited rough company! Karn talked to the merchants and business men—those who do not make trouble. Did it never occur to you that I ask after all you do?" She had never seen Thorn so angry; Karn was right to warn her away from the camp.

There was silence in which Klara assumed someone was responding to Thorn's latest charge. The horses were pulling at their reins, white eyed, eager to get away from the threat of violence rolling off Thorn.

"Well, where in the blazes has he gone?" Thorn roared.

Klara involuntarily jumped. That was a question not even she could answer.

There was movement among the horses as Thorn and Waywyrd watered their mounts and added them to the picket like. Then, like a storm cloud, Thorn appeared on the horizon heading her way. Waywyrd followed at Thorn's heels, though from his demeanor Klara was unsure of whether he thought of himself as sheep or sheep dog.

"What did he buy and where in the blazes has he gone?" Thorn demanded the moment he reached her.

"I don't know where he is," Klara said, meeting his gaze. She refused to be cowed by this man.

"He must have told you something!" Thorn towered over her. "Or maybe you saw something? Which merchants did he visit before you left town? Did he decide to run a side game and lose?"

"He made a purchase. It was a personal item," Klara said, choosing to use the same words Karn had. "And he said to stay here, away from the camp, and I have."

Thorn did not look pleased with her answer. Anger and frustration radiated from him. "Why in the blazes would he tell you to stay away from camp?" he snapped.

Klara looked him in the eye when she responded. "He said you'd be angry and it seems he was right." She had dealt with plenty of belligerent drunks in her lifetime. Dealing with a man who was belligerent and sober was not all that much different.

Thorn thrust his thick finger in her face. "When you protect him, you defy me and I am your employer. I said there would be no sex; I could sever your contract and leave you here in the wild."

Thorn's words stung, but Klara held her chin up, defiantly. "We did not have sex."

"Don't lie to me," Thorn said. "Both Ffearn and Ruis said it was obvious when he was at the game."

"We did not have sex," Klara repeated. Well, not exactly. And, well, not yet. She was not particularly good at lying, so she looked away, hoping Thorn would not see the lie in her eyes.

"Then what? Something else?" Thorn said. "You brought him enough pleasure that he was eager to get back to your bed for more." He suddenly stopped, as if the answer to some question just came to him.

Thorn looked down at her, then knelt so they were eye to eye. Klara turned her head to avoid his gaze. He reached out and gently took her by the chin, drawing her gaze back to him. When he spoke, this time it was without anger. "How much did he pay you?"

Klara shook her head, giving him a confused look, so he quietly repeated the question. "For the sex, or whatever you did: how much did he pay you?"

Klara was shocked and hurt. After all this time, and despite earlier declarations, he still saw her as just a whore. "We did not ... he did not ...," She turned unable to look at Thorn, her hand involuntarily rising to her mouth as tears welled in her eyes.

"Where is the money?" Thorn asked, laying a hand on her shoulder. Klara sniffed and shrugged it off.

"I have no money," she said. "What little I had I gave—," but stopped herself before she finished the sentence.

"You gave to Karn?" Waywyrd asked gently.

Klara nodded, her back still toward him and Thorn.

"For a personal item," Waywyrd coaxed.

Klara nodded again.

"Come away, Thorn," Waywyrd said. "We've done enough damage here."

The rabbit was done, but she had lost her appetite. Instead, she lay back on her blankets and stared at the clouds. After finding out that she had been riding amongst noblemen, she should have left. Instead, this was the result of willfully deluding herself into thinking they were her friends. While chiding herself for refusing to acknowledge the situation for what it was, she dozed off and was eventually awoken by the smells of supper.

Klara sat up and sniffed. It was Nuallan's turn to cook and his food was generally fit to eat. But what place did the village whore have at the table of the King? Resolving not to partake of the meal, no matter how good it smelled, she contented herself with the rabbit. It was dry from having been on the fire overlong, but it filled her belly. As the Keltoi ate, she took Constant down for water again. At least he still enjoyed her company.

After supper, Waywyrd came and sat beside her, laying his staff across his lap. "Do you know when Karn will return?"

"No," Klara said. "He only said it would be late tonight."

"And did he give you any further instruction?" Waywyrd asked.

"He said if we rode out I should ride by you. But that didn't happen, so the point is moot," Klara replied.

They sat in silence for a long time, before Waywyrd asked, "And what do you intend to do if Karn does not return?"

"I suppose I will continue to ride with the company and trust that he will find us," Klara said. "Unless Thorn severs my contract, then I'll have to think of something else." At that, Waywyrd rose and returned to the fire with the Keltoi. Exhausted from her cry earlier, she lay down and was soon asleep.

In the dark of night Klara awoke to Karn crawling into the bedroll beside her, smelling of fresh cut pine. She drank in the scent as it mingled with the cool scents carried on the nocturnal breeze. He asked after her day and she reported what she knew. After the tumult of the afternoon it felt good to be with someone who seemed to care about her welfare.

"I need to be away again early," Karn said. "Ride with Waywyrd and I'll find you, wherever you camp."

Snuggling up beside him, Klara laid her head on his chest. Whatever he had been doing during the day had left him exhausted. He was asleep the moment he closed his eyes.

⌘

Klara woke to find Karn already gone, dew on the blanket where he had been. She fished dried fruit and a handful of nuts out of the panniers, intending to avoid Thorn and Ffearn at breakfast. Then she took Constant for water and re-picketed him so he could graze while she packed her belongings.

After dropping her gear by the horse, she began saddling Constant. The bridle still lacked a bit. Since Constant never gave her any trouble, she never bothered to reattach it. At least the horse was predictable, even if the rest of the company was not. When Thorn called for the party to mount up, she mounted and followed. Waywyrd fell in step beside her.

"Karn seems to come and go as a thief in the night. Is there any more you can tell me regarding his whereabouts?" Waywyrd asked.

"He smelled like trees," Klara said. She was not in the mood to talk, but not about to shun the only person still talking to her.

"Trees! Is that all you can tell me?" Waywyrd said, rattling his staff in irritation.

"Evergreen," Klara said, "pine or fir, but not cedar."

"You're not very helpful," Waywyrd said, exasperated by the situation. "If he is in trouble, we want to help."

"I don't think he's in trouble," Klara replied, keeping her eyes on the road. "Nor do I believe any in the company actually want to help."

Waywyrd sighed. "It's quite possible that you are the most stubborn person I've met."

Klara rolled her eyes but did not bother to reply.

It was still early in the day when she heard the ring of an ax in the distance. Before long they came to a farmstead. In the yard, Karn, shirtless, was splitting cordwood. Not far off, a farmer and his sons sawed rounds from a log they had dragged into the barnyard. The other Keltoi in the company did not even look his direction. When Klara smiled at him, Karn shook his head, indicating that she should say nothing, so she too continued on without speaking.

Once they were out of sight of the farmstead, Waywyrd turned to her and said, "Well at least that explains the smell of trees. Will you now tell me why he is laboring as a farmhand?"

"That is not for me to tell," Klara said. It was an impertinent answer. The truth was, she had no notions about what he was doing or why.

Waywyrd regarded at her for a long moment as if he were considering something, before saying, "You don't give up many secrets."

"Neither do wizards," Klara countered and patted Constant on the neck.

At midday Klara watered her horse well away from the others, who were clustered around Waywyrd standing in the shade of a large tree. All she saw was their backs, but she heard them arguing. The argument was about her.

"You can read minds; I've seen you do it before. Can you not read theirs and be done with it?" Ruis said.

"I could read his, if we could catch him, but I cannot read hers. Bugger me all, but I've tried," Waywyrd said.

Klara made a note of that, intending to tell Karn so he might avoid the wizard altogether—though, if Waywyrd could read minds, what prevented him from reading hers? An experiment was in order.

That afternoon as she and Waywyrd rode together in silence, Klara thought all kinds of nasty thoughts: "bootless prattling wizard," "hedge-born feeble dotard," and even "pestilent foolhardy charlatan." None of them made any impression on Waywyrd. Maybe she needed to be thinking, not to herself, but to Waywyrd in order for him to read her thoughts. She thought very loudly in Waywyrd's direction, *"Withered, toad-spotted want-wit."*

Waywyrd's head snapped up and he gave her a sharp look.

Still thinking very loudly, her eyes fixed on Waywyrd. Giving him a smug look, Klara asked, *"Did you read that thought?"*

"Yes," Waywyrd said aloud, with a startled look.

Then Klara closed her mind, thinking only to herself, "How about this one?" She waited a long time, but there was only silence from the wizard. Then she asked aloud, "How about this one?" With the same closed mind, she thought of Constant's ears.

After a long pause, Waywyrd said, "No."

They looked at each other then and Klara thought loudly, *"And what of this one, you fool-hardy dotard?"*

"Yes," Waywyrd replied nearly jumping out of his saddle. "Tell me, how did you know how to do that?"

"I didn't," Klara said. "I heard you arguing at midday and thought I'd give it a try."

"Klara, did you know that your words actually appeared in my head?" Waywyrd said, stunned.

"I thought that was the point," she said and patted Constant. "I heard them say that you can read minds, so I thought something loudly in your direction to see if you could read mine. Then I thought it quietly, when I didn't want you to know what I was thinking."

"When I read minds, I don't hear words in conversation as you have done," Waywyrd said, adjusting the grip on his staff. "I get impressions and can generally tell if someone is lying. Occasionally, I can get a vision or bit of stored memory, but that is rare and typically only from people with very weak minds. What you have done is extraordinary and very few people are capable of it. Tell me, what do you mean by thinking loudly or quietly?"

"Just that," she replied, confused, "it was a loud thought or a quiet one."

"Well, have you ever done this before?" Waywyrd asked.

Klara shook her head. "Not that I know of, but you're the first wizard I've met, so I've never had cause to try before." Waywyrd mused to himself for the rest of the afternoon and Klara thought no more thoughts in his direction.

When they made camp that night, Klara did as Karn instructed her and arranged a place for them to sleep away from the camp. She picketed Constant near her again, hoping that he would take the hint and bring Night to where they slept. She did not want him getting caught bringing his horse in and out of the picket line if Waywyrd intended to read his mind. She was of the impression that if Karn wanted them to know his mind, he would have told them.

When the beans were ready, Klara joined the group of Keltoi by the fire. She was given a chilly reception. Ffearn refused to speak to her. Bardus merely grunted when she sat beside him. After the fire died down, Klara stood watch over the camp grateful for the opportunity to see Karn ride in, thereby alleviating her worries about Waywyrd surreptitiously reading his mind. Before retiring, Thorn approached her and said, "Karn has second watch tonight."

"He'll be here," Klara said. They did not speak further and Thorn walked off to find his bedroll.

A chilly breeze raised goose pimples on Klara's flesh, carrying with it the scents of the night and the jingle of tack. She tensed, alert for signs of danger, but none came. It was just Karn riding into camp. Sighing, she relaxed the grip on her dagger, glad that he had taken notice and picketed Night near Constant. After seeing to his horse, he approached.

Owing to the coolness of the night, Klara had draped her blanket over her shoulders. Now she enveloped Karn in it, using it to muffle her words as she whispered, "Waywyrd intends to read your mind. You best avoid him."

Karn nodded but did not seem surprised by this revelation. Raising a hand to her shoulder, he said, "I'm beat. I'll need you to wake me for my turn at the watch. As tired as I am, I won't wake on my own."

Klara assured him she would. It was an assurance she had no intention of keeping. If he spent his days working as a hired man and still managed to ride twenty miles, then she figured she could stand watch all night and let him sleep. Then he slipped from the blanket and sought his bed.

When Thorn woke and saw Klara standing watch, he was furious. She had roused Karn at first light. Karn had scolded her for letting him sleep then had left again, promising to find the company late that night. That meant he was not in camp now. Rising from the tangle of his bedroll, Thorn stomped across the clearing like a storm carried on the wind.

"Has he been here?" Thorn demanded.

"He was here and left again already," Klara said, pulling the blanket tight across her shoulders in defense against the morning dew and as a paltry means of warding off Thorn's bluster. As a ward, the blanket failed miserably.

"It was his turn for the watch," Thorn said. "It's bad enough he's deserted the company and is derelict in his duties, but to leave you standing here all night is disgraceful!" Thorn's shouting woke the entire company.

"He was here, he stood watch. I relieved him so that he could travel on," Klara lied. As little as Thorn slept, it was entirely possible that he knew it was a lie. "But now that you've woken the entire camp, I'll leave my post and go find something to eat," she said and headed for the panniers.

After breaking camp, Klara and Waywyrd rode in silence all morning. Near midday the sounds of civilization reached them. Voices and the clatter of daily living were carried on the wind. Soon wood smoke and the savory scents of roasting meat reached their nostrils. Everyone's spirits rose as the smell of food intensified.

"What say we water the horses at the stable and take a meal at the inn?" Ruis asked. Though he was not looking her direction, Klara pictured the Kelto already salivating.

"Our time would be better spent buying some fresh produce and a bit of cheese, then eating them in the shade," Bardus said.

Ruis turned to Bardus, who was riding beside him. "You offer me greens and cheese when we could be having meat and bread?" His disdain for the notion was evident in his voice and Klara smiled to herself.

They soon discovered their imagined village was no more than a collection of three houses and a blacksmith shop. She spotted Karn manning the bellows. As before, they did no more to acknowledge each other's presence than to nod in the other's direction. Thorn did not permit the company to stop for water until they were a couple miles farther down the road. That evening, Klara, being exhausted from having stood watch the entire night, was asleep before supper was ready.

In the morning, Karn was wrapped around her. The sun was barely creeping above the horizon. Birds had just begun their morning songs, softly lulling her back to sleep. Nuzzling into Karn, she drank in his warm musky scent. Coming to her senses, her eyes popped open. She shook him urgently, saying, "Do you need to be on the road?"

"Are you that eager to be rid of me?" Karn teased, squeezing her tightly.

"No, I'd rather keep you here. But I have no notion of what you've been up to, or why, or if you need to be doing whatever it is now," Klara replied.

"I've been getting us out of debt," Karn said. He released his grip on her, yawned, and engaged in a joint popping stretch before rolling out of the blankets. "But today is my turn to cook, so I'll be passing my time here with you."

"What we used of the company's money was not three day's wages,"

Klara said, as she too, exited her blanket. Taking a corner, she shook it out in preparation of being stored away.

"No, but it's also nice to have cash on hand," he said.

They took the opportunity to water and re-picket their horses before the rest of the camp woke. Karn dug in his pack for the fleece edged tunic he wore when they went into towns. Putting it on, he said, "You best wear your skirt today."

The others were waking and making their way to the fire in search of breakfast, so she did not have time to question him. Riding in a skirt was a nuisance, so she hoped there was a good reason for it. As she changed out of her breeches, Karn lit the fire and started a cauldron of honeyed-water.

Joining Karn at the fire, Klara helped him cook. "How about making oatcakes this morning," she suggested. "We're up early and have plenty of time." She hoped a menu change might put the company of Keltoi in a better mood than they had been lately. And there would be fewer dishes to wash, too, since oatcakes could be drizzled with honey, folded in half, and eaten from their hands.

Karn agreed and the oatcakes had the desired effect. The camaraderie the company previously enjoyed was not fully restored, but the menu change had lightened the mood.

While everyone was busy licking honey from their fingers, Karn reached into his purse and withdrew a few coins. These he handed to Nuallan, saying, "This is what is owed the company. I hope you will hold me in better stead now that I've made good on my debt."

Honey glistened in Thorn's beard and there was a spark of flint in his eyes as he said, "You still haven't told us what you purchased."

"It was a personal item," Karn said trying to rid his sticky fingers of the wool fibers and lint which had attached themselves when he reached into his purse.

"So you've said before," Thorn said. As he did, he shot a glance at Waywyrd, who in turn fixed his eyes on Karn.

Klara stepped between Karn and Waywyrd hoping her body might shield him from the wizard's probe. "It was herbs," she said. "To ease the cramps that accompany my bleeding. Normally, I gather my own, but on the road that has not been possible."

Waywyrd turned a penetrating gaze on her, and his voice appeared in her head, *"I can see by his mind that you do not speak the whole truth."*

Klara returned the wizard's stare, hoping she looked both confident and convincing. *"I speak enough of the truth that you need look no farther into his mind."*

Thorn looked expectantly at Waywyrd and the wizard nodded. Then he returned his gaze to her and Karn. "Very well," Thorn said, "the debt is paid. But the pair of you are dressed as though you were heading into a village. Are you planning to leave the company?"

"No," Karn said, still rubbing his hands together, trying to ridding them of the lent. "The mood of the countryside is not favorable. For Klara's protection, we will ride as husband and wife, apart from the rest of the company, until there's no longer any threat." The others began to protest, but Karn refused to hear them out. He sent her to pack their things and saddle up while he cleaned and stored away the cooking supplies.

On the road, Waywyrd lagged behind the others until she and Karn overtook him. Despite his earlier pronouncement about riding apart, Karn seemed pleased with Waywyrd's unexpected company.

"It's good you're here, Waywyrd," Karn said. "There are things I need you to tell Uncle Thorn. There have been attacks and killings in the surrounding villages. Some say it is the work of the Disciples, others say demons. If the Disciples of Elah are in the area, it's best that Klara not appear as an unwed woman traveling in our company."

"That is troubling," Waywyrd agreed, adjusting the grip on his staff. "How came you by this information?"

Karn replied, "When I was working alongside the Mordvins, they talked. I took meals with them, too, and their women are fond of gossip. Given Klara's situation, I figured it might be best if I spoke little and listened much." Karn paused. "There's something I'd like to ask of you. Tomorrow I will ride ahead of the company again. In my absence I'd like you to ride with Klara and claim she is your niece, as you did in Yar Chally."

Klara had been listening patiently and now became indignant. "I'm not in danger or in need of protection. I've been out running the Disciples since I was twelve. Besides, what we took has been repaid. Why must you go again?"

"I wouldn't go if I felt I had any other choice," Karn said. "There is something I must do. Besides, it gives me a chance to know the locals' minds and that is my best chance of keeping you from harm. I may be riding ahead of the company for some days."

Klara fumed. What more must he do? And why must it remain a secret?

At midday, after watering their horses, Waywyrd left them and trotted ahead, bringing their news to Thorn and the rest of the company. Later that night at camp, Klara helped Karn with the beans as a way to avoid conversation with the others. After dinner, Karn tried speaking with Ffearn, but Ffearn sent him away. It was evident that the separation was hard on both of them, but Ffearn stubbornly insisted on holding his grudge.

# CHAPTER 16
# A DEBT IS PAID

S SHE RODE though the countryside, Klara spotted Karn mucking out stables. Her thoughts turned to the farmers who sought her out, claiming their wives had refused them. Karn would smell of sweat and manure when he returned this evening. She was not looking forward to bedding beside him and wrinkled her nose in sympathy with farmwives everywhere.

As Karn slipped between the blankets beside her that night, she was pleasantly surprised to find him bare, damp, and smelling fresh. He had washed before coming to bed. Running her fingers through his chest hair, Klara nuzzled into him, eager to explore his flesh.

Taking her hands in his, Karn pulled them to his mouth, kissed them, and whispered. "My uncle is standing watch and we'd best not anger him further." Then he rolled her over and pulled her to him, so he could spoon her as they slept.

When Thorn woke Klara for her turn at the watch, he stayed at their bedroll, talking with Karn briefly before retiring. At dawn, Klara roused Karn to send him on his way and asked, "What did Thorn want?"

"Uncle Thorn isn't mad anymore," Karn said, tentatively sniffing his manure-stained tunic. "Though, he said I should have spoken to him directly rather than pass information through Waywyrd. I'm glad Thorn's not angry with me anymore, but I wish Ffearn would talk to me. I know I've hurt him, but I can't apologize if he won't listen."

Thorn was the only other person awake so Klara joined him at the fire while Karn dressed and attached his gear to his saddle. It was her turn to cook. As she worked, Klara sensed Thorn watching her, though they did not speak. She noted with some sadness that the elder Keltoi had not caught her any fish to fry for breakfast, so she made oatcakes again. Pouring the batter in the oven, Klara looked across the fire at Thorn. His dark eyes smoldered with anger, sadness, and concern.

"You see why I am not King," he said, grabbing a piece of bark laying between his feet and tossing it into the fire. "I can't even manage these five Keltoi without them splitting into factions."

"But I hear the horses hold you in high esteem," Klara said and smiled as she wiped batter from the lip of the bowl. It did little to lighten his mood.

Thorn rose and gently laid a hand on her shoulder. "I do not think I am worthy of even the horses' good opinion." Then he wandered off to be alone.

That day as they rode, Klara spotted Karn sweeping grit out the door of a lonely roadside inn. She marveled at this Kelto who took any work that came his way. Clearly, he did not feel superior to anyone, despite his noble birth. It seemed that he worked eagerly at each task and she admired that quality in him.

Not far from the inn, Klara saw the silver fir rune carved into a tree near the road. When she and Constant neared the spot, concealed in the tall grass was another sapling trapped beneath a stag's antlers, tines down. The trapped sapling made Klara anxious. Protection. Did the demons need it or was it being offered?

Demons and the Disciples of Elah had long been enemies. Was this simply evidence of an age-old spat? Or was something else out there? If so, having Karn riding out alone was unwise, especially since she did not know the source of the threat.

Waywyrd's eyes darted to the rune. Klara knew he saw it too, but he never spoke of the matter and there was no way she was going to bring it up. If there was a second trapped sapling on the road tomorrow, she could be certain the demons were trying to communicate with them. There was no point in bringing it up before then.

That night Klara made beans and bread for supper and then did the washing up but grew anxious when it was time to extinguish the fire. Tonight Karn had first watch. His absence worried her. Sighing, she knew there was only one option. She took the post and began the watch as the others bedded down. It was no great hardship. Sleep would elude her until he was safely reunited with them anyway.

Thorn's long strides carried him across the clearing. In the dim light, it was impossible to read the emotions on his face until he was standing directly before her. Fortunately, he seemed more concerned than angry.

"What are you doing?" he asked. "It is not your turn. You were on watch this morning and did the cooking today. Karn should be here; tonight is his turn."

"We'll he's not here," Klara said. "And I will stand in his stead until he returns." She was not about to deepen the rift in the party by asking anyone else to stand in his absence.

"That is not your place," Thorn said. "You should be sleeping."

"If not my place, then whose?" Klara asked, refusing to let Thorn get the better of her. "Someone must stand watch and I'm willing to do it."

Shaking his head, Thorn said, "You are a wonder to me."

He turned to walk away, then paused, turning back to her. "The other day…I didn't mean to upset you. I'm sorry I made you cry. I was just worried." He walked away, shoulders hunched. Evidently, worry was still eating him.

It was nearly time to wake Ffearn for his turn and Klara did not relish the task. She contemplated standing all night, simply as a means of forgoing the trouble. As she stood weighing her options, she heard the soft thud of hooves on the road and the gentle blow of an exhausted animal.

When Karn arrived and slipped from the saddle, he was visibly pleased with himself. Pulling her to him, Karn kissed her passionately. Klara tasted ale on his breath.

Karn's lips moved to her ear and he whispered, "I'll be riding out no more. Let me wake Ffearn, then I'll take you to bed." They parted and headed in opposite directions, she to the bedroll and Karn to wake Ffearn for the watch. She was asleep before he made it to their bed.

❧

Klara and Karn slept through breakfast and woke to Thorn shaking them. It was time for the company to leave. Karn yawned then addressed his uncle, "Take the company and ride ahead. We'll catch you up."

It was not long before Klara and Karn were dressed, had tended their horses, packed their belongings, and were on the road. Once they were moving, Klara asked, "You were in high spirits last night. What brought about this change? And is it true that you'll not be riding out again?"

"It's true," Karn said, and patted Night's neck, mischief and morning light sparkling in his eyes. "But I'll not tell you the reason until tonight when the company is assembled." He did not wait for her to protest, but urged Night into a trot in order to hasten their return to the company.

Upon reaching the others, Karn called to Klara, "Follow me," and led her to the head of the column to ride with Thorn and Waywyrd. They slowed their horses to a walk as Karn fell in beside Thorn. Waywyrd fell back to ride alongside Klara.

"We'd best be a party of Skolts and Keltoi riding together for safety," Karn said, addressing his uncle.

"Why is that?" Thorn asked, looking less than pleased with his nephew.

"Because I can't figure out how to disguise Klara as a man; she refuses to grow facial hair," Karn said and grinned. Klara was glad to see that he was back to being his usual self but thought Thorn might not appreciate his nephew's playful banter.

"Have you any reason for traveling as a mixed party, other than Klara's unwillingness to grow a beard?" Waywyrd chided, shaking his staff at Karn.

"Oh, not a full beard," Karn teased, looking over his shoulder at Way-wyrd. "I don't think I could sleep beside a maid that was fully bearded. Some nice bushy side burns might be alright, though. But, to answer your question, it's known in these parts that there have been attacks by demons and Disciples of Elah both. It would be far too dangerous for me to travel with just my wife and her uncle. To reduce the risk, groups often travel together. If a well-armed party of Keltoi happens to be heading in the same direction, I see no reason not to throw in with them and possibly pay them a little to act as an escort."

"It certainly solves the problem of what to do with Klara and provides another reason for her being with us," Thorn said. "When we left Zlatoust, I never would have anticipated having a woman in our company would cause this much trouble. Did you learn anything else while you were away?"

"Nothing worthy of report," Karn said.

They fell into silence after that. Klara's ears had perked up at the mention of demons and Disciples, but she felt it was better not to ask questions. Something in Thorn's past left him fearful of demons. There was no reason to evoke that fear needlessly.

At midday, when they stopped to water the horses, Thorn informed the company of the plan so all of them could play along if they met other travelers on the road. After Thorn made the announcement, Klara saw Ffearn's hurt expression as he turned his back on the company and wandered off. Karn tried following him in an attempt to talk privately, but Ffearn sent him away. Some unfathomable schism had come between them and Klara worried what damage might be done if it were not mended soon.

Slow moving clouds gathered in the west during the afternoon and promised rain, hiding the afternoon sun and cooling the travel weary party. Klara was grateful; it had been over a fortnight since it last rained. In the Ural Mountains it was not uncommon to have summer storms. She was beginning to doubt that it ever rained elsewhere.

They had left the steppes and marshes behind and were traveling through forest again. Concealed in shadow under the forest's canopy, there was a definite chill in the air. Ever vigilant, Klara continued scanning the trees for sign of demons. Had she already missed a sign owing to their haste to return to the party this morning? She sighed. Even if there had been a sign, no harm was done because no response was given.

The wind picked up, blowing her hair wildly about her face. At the onset the breeze was refreshing, but the gusts steadily became stronger as the afternoon progressed. Trees bent and swayed. The other horses became skittish. Even though it was still early, the sky had become dark and heavy, the clouds pregnant with precipitation. Klara was grateful Constant remained true to his name, though he flared his nostrils on occasion. As the first clap of thunder rolled overhead and the rain began to fall, Thorn called the company to a halt.

Bardus strung a taut picket line between two trees and began attaching horses to it. Klara added Constant and Night to the line while Karn helped stretch and hang the tarp used to keep their gear from being damaged by the water. By the time all the tents were pitched and the gear stored under the tarp, the rain had become a deluge. It was too wet to start a fire or do any cooking. The Keltoi gathered near the tarp as Ruis handed out jerky, nuts, and dried fruit. Klara pushed her wet hair from her face, looked up at the sky, and began to laugh.

Ruis nodded in her direction and said to Karn rather gruffly, "What's wrong with your woman?"

Not waiting for Karn to respond, Klara shouted at Ruis, "The Goddess has delivered us from your cooking!" That garnered a laugh from Bardus and Karn.

Ruis stood, water dripping from his beard, food sack in hand, and said, "Them herbs you bought her, you sure they weren't cannabis or poppy?" This finally broke the tension and the rest of the group joined in the laughter.

"And on that merry note," Karn said, "I have something for Ffearn and Nuallan." This drew everyone's attention. Remembering that Karn had something to say this evening once everyone was assembled, Klara pushed closer, eager to hear what it was.

Pulling his purse from his belt, Karn said, "You said doubling my money wasn't good enough anymore and that it was too expensive to keep Klara in the company. I have solved that problem. Put out your hands."

Ffearn and Nuallan looked at him questioningly, but neither moved.

"Put out your hands," Karn said again and winked. "I'm not a task master here to rap your knuckles with a stick."

This time they obliged. Karn dumped the contents of his purse into their outstretched palms. Klara had never seen such an amount of money all in one place, not even at the alehouse, because Serik emptied the cashbox every night to keep from getting robbed.

"That," Karn said, "pays back every copper spent on her since the beginning of our journey. It covers the salve, the dagger, the clothes, even the extra rooms. If Klara needs anything from now on, I will take work and provide it out of those funds." Karn paused. When he spoke again, his tone was less jovial and more sincere. "This way, Ffearn, you needn't feel pressured to bring in more money at the dice tables."

"Six days wages could not possibly cover what was spent," Nuallan said, greed showing in his eyes.

Money-grubbing bastard, Klara thought. Karn just dumped a pile of coins into his grasping palm and he wanted more.

"It was six days wages and two nights' gambling," Karn replied, eyes flashing with the light of challenge. "And I've a few coins left to cover future expenses."

"What is the meaning of this?" Thorn said, forcing his way to the center of the group.

The jovial mood ended. Thorn stood grim, rivulets of rain running down his face and steaming off his beard as he scanned the faces of Nuallan and his nephews. None of them made any reply. Their silence was almost as deafening as the thunder rolling overhead.

Looking over the group, Thorn asked at large, "Can someone tell me why my nephew has worked like a slave to repay funds I authorized to be spent?" And turning to Nuallan he said, "And I want to know how he even knew how much was spent?"

The party remained silent with shock.

Klara stepped forward, laying a hand on Thorn's arm, hoping to soothe his anger. "Thorn," she spoke softly, waiting for him to turn toward her. Once he was facing her, she continued, "When we caught up with the company outside of Kazan', Karn and Ffearn had words."

"More like they had fists," Ruis said. Klara glared at him; Ruis stepped back and stood quietly.

"Karn asked to see the ledger, Nuallan obliged," she said. "I don't think this a matter that should trouble you greatly. It has been resolved now."

Thorn looked at the gentleness in her eyes and she looked back into the dark pools of his own. In a useless gesture, Thorn raised a hand to her cheek and brushed away the rain, saying, "But the amount for the clothes should not have been in the ledger. Those were purchased with my own funds."

Klara held his gaze, trying to decide how to respond. Around her, she felt the circle of Keltoi simultaneously suck in air and take a step back, waiting for the next blow to fall.

Thorn lowered his hand and turned to Nuallan. "Explain yourself."

"A king does not spend money on gifts for a harlot," Nuallan blustered, his face ruddy with anger and embarrassment.

Thorn poked Nuallan in the chest with a stout finger. "I am not a king, she is not a harlot, and I will spend my money any damned way I please. If you cannot do as you are told, I will manage the money myself," Thorn said. "Or better yet, I'll have Ffearn do it. He did it for me in Olbia and at least he is honest." Thorn stormed from the circle, the party parting before him as water parts for a rock. Then, slowly, the group dispersed, seeking the shelter of their tents.

Karn took Klara by the hand and led her to where he pitched their tent and crawled inside. Gratitude welled within her. Karn had eliminated any need for her to consider repaying Thorn or having to worry about what he might expect in return for purchasing her clothing. With luck, the frowns and disagreeable looks Nuallan cast her direction might cease, too. Now that she was no longer a financial burden on the company, Bardus and Ruis might start speaking to her again. But how to express her gratitude? She knew of one thing all men liked. She leaned forward and kissed him.

"What's that for?" Karn asked, taken by surprise.

"Because you're here and I can," Klara said, sliding her hands over his shoulders. "You put an awful lot of money down for me and I've never brought you pleasure."

She kissed him again and said, "If you'll let me help you out of your tunic, I'll show you my gratitude and we can put those herbs to use."

Karn pulled away, leaving her confused. "I'm glad you're happy," he said, gently pushing her back. "But do you remember the last time it rained? You shared a tent with me and Ffearn. Ffearn isn't in the tent with us right now. That means he's out there in the rain. And I'd not let him pass a night in the rain any more than I'd let you."

Karn sighed, worry creasing his brow. "Get out of those wet clothes while I go find him."

Klara peeked out the tent flap as Karn exited. The rain had let up, but from the look of the clouds on the horizon it was far from done. She wriggled out of her wet clothes and since there was no room to hang them out to dry, wadded them up in a ball. Then she fished in Karn's pack for the soap.

Poking her head out of the tent flap, she surveyed the camp. It appeared deserted. Assuming everyone was snug inside their tents and she would have the shower to herself, Klara left the tent, stood bare in the rain, and began to lather up.

Thorn exited a tent on the other side of the clearing. Fully coated with sudsy foam, and lacking a good place to hide, Klara quickly wrapped her arms across her chest in an attempted to cover herself. Thorn averted his eyes. Turning his head aside and looking down, he made his way to the edge of the clearing. Stopping under a large tree, he stood with his back to her.

The rain began in earnest again, bringing her focus back to the task of washing, and keeping her wet enough to complete the job. She cast furtive glances Thorn's direction the entire time. What was he doing, just standing there?

She was just finishing a rainwater rinse when Karn and Ffearn emerged from the same tent Thorn had exited. Perhaps Thorn was simply giving his nephews time and space for a private conversation. But what might they need to discuss out of ear-shot of Thorn? And why might he consent to stand in the rain while they did it, rather than make them wait for better weather?

Catching sight of her standing bare in the torrent, Karn rushed toward her, exclaiming, "Absent gods, have you gone mad?"

"Just bathing," Klara said, offering him the soap, which he seemed disinclined to accept. "I'm nearly finished now. I was beginning to wonder if it ever rained. I don't think I could live anywhere where water didn't fall from the sky of its own accord."

Karn was not impressed with her musing about the source of water. "In the tent with you before you catch your death."

Klara wrung out her hair then slipped through the flap and wrung it out again before climbing under the blankets. Karn and Ffearn stripped to their skin outside the tent and deposited their clothes in a heap at the flap as they crawled in. Once they were inside Klara asked, "You sure you don't want the soap? I don't think it's going to let up anytime soon; you'll have plenty of time to wash and rinse."

"No," Karn said, pulling her close so he could spoon her. "Now lie still and go to sleep."

❧

Klara woke early the next morning. Though his arm was around her, it was not her Karn held. Before her, Ffearn and Karn's hands were clasped as they slept. She knew immediately that today was a grand day to be a Kelto. Snuggling down under the blankets, she drifted back to sleep. A cool breeze roused her sometime later. When she woke the second time, Ffearn was holding the blanket aloft, admiring her naked body.

"With the blanket up, I can see just as much of you as you can of me," Klara said, reaching for the covers.

"Go ahead and feast your eyes," Ffearn said, relinquishing his hold on the blanket. "Karn already told me you were fond of Kelto-flesh."

"Have you no modesty?" Klara pulled the blanket tight around her. Although, he was right; the sight was pleasing to her; he was leaner than Karn, so the muscling of his body was more distinct and unlike Karn, his body hair was brown not black.

"Modesty? None," Ffearn scoffed, "and neither have you."

"Well, then I best wake Karn," Klara said. "He asked that if ever I took a notion to show you my undergarments to tell him first so he could watch."

"But you're not wearing any undergarments," Ffearn corrected, a grin playing across his face.

"Perhaps," Klara said, "my underwear is magic and cannot be seen until Karn awakes."

"Then you best not wake him, for I liked what I saw." Ffearn tugged playfully at the blanket, threatening to uncover her again, and admit the breeze.

Behind her, Klara felt movement as Karn woke. He propped himself on an elbow and said, "I see you two are getting reacquainted."

"I woke to find him looking at me as though he'd never seen a woman before," Klara said, snuggling against Karn for warmth.

"Oh, I've seen my share of women; it's just that you're so smartly built, as far as women go," Ffearn said. "Most Skoloti women tend to resemble Elb maids and I don't fancy them at all. You, though, are thick and thin in all the right places. I see why my brother fancies you."

"I've heard Karn say much the same thing," Klara said. "I thought Elb maids were supposed to be fair and beautiful."

"Fair aye, beautiful no," Karn replied, "The main problem is you can't tell the sexes apart. Neither gender has any facial hair, so you'd think they were all maids."

"And," Ffearn added, "The he-Elbs have no chest hair and the she-Elbs have no chest, just as flat as the men they are, so even without their clothes it's hard to tell the genders apart."

"That cannot be true," Klara said. Grand day to be a Kelto indeed. They were already up to their usual antics.

"It's true," Ffearn said, nodding earnestly. "I once spent an entire evening making advances toward an Elb maid. When I got her back to our room, I was shocked to discover it wasn't a maid but a lad."

Karn laughed. "That isn't how it happened. You knew it was a lad the entire time. The Elb was so taken with Ffearn's long locks and green eyes that he mistook Ffearn for a maid. It was the Elb who'd been making the advances. The lad was more than a little surprised when the trousers came off that night!"

"Poor, misguided lad," Ffearn said. "After setting eyes on a Kelto without his breeches, he'll be thinking himself inadequate for the rest of his life."

"Surely, you jest," Klara said. With his broad shoulders and well-muscled chest, there was no mistaking Ffearn for anything other than a man.

Ffearn winked at her and said, "Keltoi are well known for being much better endowed than other men. In your line of work, surely you knew that."

Nuzzling into her hair, Karn said, "You needn't believe us on any count; you shall see how alike the genders are when we pass through Lusatia."

Klara shook her head. Having caught them in their ruse, she fully intended to get them to fess-up. "That's not what I was talking about. I meant, I don't see how anyone could mistake Ffearn for a maid."

"Oh, well, he was prettier when he was younger," Karn said. "At the time his face had yet to see a razor."

"And I'm still prettier than you," Ffearn said, reaching across her to pat his brother's cheek. "Though, I don't get mistaken for a maid nearly as often now that I'm bearded."

Giving up on getting anything that might resemble truth out of either of them, Klara said, "Let me up, I have to pee."

The three of them emerged from the tent under the clear blue of what promised to be a bright, sunny day. Ffearn and Karn strode shamelessly to the tarp where the party stored their gear and began digging for their packs and dry clothes. Klara, at least, had the sense to wrap herself in one of their blankets while she dug for her saddlebag and the dry clothing it contained.

Once dressed, Klara tended the horses with Bardus while Ffearn and Karn hung their wet clothing out to dry. Since everything had been drenched and was now sodden, the party remained in camp while waiting for their things to dry. Having nothing else to do, Thorn gave Karn, Ffearn, and Klara permission to hunt. With all their clothing wet, the trio hunted in various states of undress. Klara had a dry shirt and breeches, Karn had a tunic, but no breeches, and Ffearn ended up hunting in just his undershirt and drawers.

Before midday Klara returned empty-handed, demons on her mind. What she saw in the forest weighed heavily on her and she was not eager to share the information with Thorn but knew she must. After putting her bow away, she headed for Thorn.

As was his habit, Thorn sat apart from the company. Klara joined him on a log overlooking the stream that ran along their camp. Deeply troubled by what she had seen, she sat in silence while trying to organize her thoughts.

Eventually, Thorn spoke, continuing his gaze over the water and avoiding eye contact. "Have you already grown so tired of my nephews that you now seek out the company of an old Kelto?"

"I don't think you're old," Klara said, softly. "At least, you're not much older than them. I'm certain the lines that crease your brow come from some burden you carry and not the passage of years."

"I see Waywyrd has told you much," Thorn said, still refusing to look at her.

"It wasn't Waywyrd who betrayed you but your eyes," Klara said. "You forget it was my business to know the hearts and minds of men. Though, you are harder to read than most."

Thorn looked at her then, and asked, "And what does my heart tell you?"

Klara's own heart skipped a beat. The intensity with which he looked at her often took her by surprise. A hunger radiated from him that was both unsettling and thrilling yet contained not a hint of lust. Well, okay, just a hint, but the man was also surrounded by sorrow and grief.

Finding her voice, Klara finally said, "I know that you suffered long ago and still have not had time to mend. Your eyes contain such sadness. I'm amazed that the others don't see it, too. It makes me apprehensive, because I don't want to burden an already troubled mind."

"I would gladly hear what you have to tell," Thorn said and reached for her hand. Despite the roughness of his callouses, his grip was always warm and gentle.

Taking a deep breath, Klara took a moment to steady herself before beginning. "While hunting I came across another camp in the forest. The camp was abandoned, but from the signs it appeared to be Ke'lets. It had been the site of butchery, though I cannot fathom why. Demons take work among men and come and go without giving much thought to anyone. When I lived among them, they never did me harm."

Thorn looked across the water and it was a long time before he spoke. "I too, lived among demons for a time. The Charun let me live, ignored me. But in my heart I knew they might just as easily have taken my life as spared it. You said yourself that they are as beasts and you can never fully predict the actions of either wolf, or bear, or boar."

"But why kill Ke'let in their own camp?" Klara asked. She knew many people feared demons, but Ke'lets were hunters who kept to the forest and, like their wolves, tended to avoid men.

"It was the demons who were butchered and not the ones doing the butchering?" Thorn asked, his brow furrowed.

"Aye," Klara said. "I have learned some of the demons' signs and saw one on the trail. It indicated a need for protection. But why would they need protection? Demons, like beasts, do not kill unless provoked."

"Or paid," Thorn said, fear and anger creeping into his eyes. "It is well known that they hire out as mercenaries."

Klara and Thorn sat in silence again for a long time. In her gut, she knew something was wrong. She also knew that Thorn's animosity toward the demons prevented him from seeing it. There was something out there to be feared, of that much she was sure.

The day turned hot, but under the shady trees along the stream the heat had not yet reached them. Hands entwined, they watched as Bardus watered the horses and were so lost in their own thoughts that neither moved to help. When Karn and Ffearn arrived, carrying a young deer on a pole between them, Klara rose. Before she left, Thorn pulled her back toward the log and gestured toward his nephews.

"As much as this development surprises me, it is now clear to me that my nephew loves you, even if he has not said as much," Thorn said. "Tell me, do you love him?"

Sighing, Klara shook her hand free of Thorn's. "I don't believe I'm capable of even knowing what love is." Then she left him and rejoined the party of Keltoi by the fire, but her mind was still with Thorn. In her line of work, love had never been necessary or expected. It was not something she had ever experienced and felt certain she never would.

That night they roasted the deer over the fire and ate meat fresh off the bone. The deer was last year's fawn so the company fed well. The Keltoi were jovial and merry, singing and laughing as they ate. Klara's mind, though, was still troubled by what she saw earlier that day. She did not join in the merriment and was grateful when it was time to put out the fire and head for their bedrolls.

# CHAPTER 17
# MIDSUMMER RITE

K LARA LIFTED HER spoon then let it drop back into the bowl, its contents uneaten. The monotony of beans had become just as tedious as the journey.

Over the past several days the company traveled deeper into the forest, the road narrowing as they went. Trees grew thickly all around them, hiding the Volga River from view and blanketing their camp in shadow. There had been no sign of demons or Disciples since she had found the camp of slaughtered Ke'lets. Consequently, she had relaxed, enjoying the closeness of the forest and delighting in the birdsong carried on the breeze. Travel weary and tired of eating beans, she now sought an excuse to change her routine and to hunt.

"Will we stop for Midsummer?" Klara raised her eyes to her companions seated around the fire and dumped another uneaten spoonful back into her bowl.

"We have no druid among us," Thorn said, abandoning his spoon to the gooey mass in his bowl, "so we have no way of knowing on which day to stop."

"You needn't a druid for that," Klara said. "It's the day after next."

Thorn looked at her, baffled, but it was Waywyrd who spoke. "She's right. Knowledge of the sun's movement isn't limited to druids. We wizards track it too."

"But," Bardus said, pointing his spoon at her from across the fire. "Klara isn't a wizard or a druid. How'd she figure it out?"

"I think you'd be better off asking Klara," Waywyrd said, winking and giving her a mildly amused look, as if they shared some secret knowledge of the heavens. She nearly laughed at the thought.

The entire company stared at her, spellbound, expecting an answer.

"All women's bodies track the moon," Klara said. "We are now enjoying the Oak Moon and Midsummer always occurs during the Oak Moon. If you know where you stand in the cycle of the nights, it's not hard to figure out the days. The sun still marches north, but it will turn soon." The answer seemed to satisfy them.

"We'd best see if we can buy a cask of ale tomorrow then," Karn said, nudging his brother, almost giddy with excitement. With her and Karn back among them, all had been forgiven and the pair of brothers had returned to their usual merriment on the road—merriment that seemed only to annoy Thorn.

"That's not necessary," Thorn said. "And you can do without it."

Whether as punishment for Karn and Ffearn because their last dice game resulted in fists being thrown or a means of keeping her and Karn from sharing a room, Thorn had begun refusing to stop at the inns. Apparently, he saw no reason to relent now.

"But it is necessary," Ffearn said. "The gods demand it and there is a birthday to toast."

"The lads are right," Nuallan said. "We should buy veg and give them time to hunt so we can have a proper feast." This was the only time Klara had seen Nuallan willingly want to part with the company's coin. Was this out of respect for the gods and impending holy day? Or was the birthday needing celebrated his?

Thorn did not look pleased at the suggestion, but the rest of the company was in agreement. Both Bardus and Ruis added their good opinions of ale and better fare. Despite his bristly outward appearance, Thorn consented to the purchase, provided they came across a farmer or innkeeper who would part with a cask at a reasonable price.

The area was sparsely populated, lacking any villages or towns, consisting only of widely spaced clusters of a few thatched-roof houses and an occasional roadside inn. They were just as likely to come across someone willing to sell as not. Perhaps Thorn was hedging his bets.

Klara looked around and asked, "But, whose birthday will it be?"

"Ours," Ffearn and Karn announced simultaneously.

The purchase was made the following day, thanks in large part to Ffearn and Karn's antics. Since they were still passing themselves off as a mixed company of Skolts and Keltoi, Klara waited near Waywyrd while Thorn and Nuallan haggled with the innkeeper in the dusty yard of a lonely inn. The innkeeper staunchly refused to part with either ale or vegetables. They were about to give up and move on when the lads walked over.

Karn looked the innkeeper up and down, then said, "You can sell us the ale and veg and see us on our way, or we can stay here and do the eating and drinking after you've served us. Either way, both will be in our bellies. The only difference being, if we do the eating and drinking here, you and your wife will have more work at hand, washing dishes and repairing furniture, since we are known to fight when drunk."

"I'll also have more coin in my purse," the innkeeper said, looking smug, "since a cooked meal is worth more than a raw one. Besides, there are no other guests here for you to fight with."

"We don't need other guests," Ffearn said and laughed. "The last fight we got into was with each other."

That decided the matter. Accepting the offered price, the innkeeper had the items quickly loaded onto one of the pack horses and seemed grateful to see the back of them.

That night they camped at the eastern edge of a stunning lake, waters as blue as the sky. A peninsula jutted out from the south, blocking the westerly view. It also blocked the westerly winds, keeping the waters of the bay still. Willow and cedar grew along the lake's edge, but farther back the forest gave way to silver firs. Much of the ground was rocky and over centuries some of those rocks had given way to create a sandy beach not quite as long as a tree is tall. Lush grass grew tall in the land between the hills surrounding the bay. Though the horses would like that, the ground was moist. No one fancied sleeping on damp earth, so they made camp on a bench part-way up the hill.

With everyone settling into camp, Klara turned to other domestic activities. She found some rope in one of the panniers and began fastening a taut line, head-high, between two trees.

"What're you up to?" Karn asked as he approached.

"I've just built a clothes line," Klara said. "I'm going to wash my clothes tonight since they'll have plenty of time to dry before we move on. You should come with me and do the same."

"And why would I do that?" Karn asked, looking affronted at the suggestion that he engage in woman's work.

In Skoloti, everything was woman's work, hunting and warmongering included. However, men were far less eager to assist women with the wash than they were to assist in battle. Klara sighed, regretting having left Skoloti behind. Still, she figured garnering his cooperation would be easily accomplished.

"Because," Klara said, "If I'm washing my clothes, I won't be wearing them."

"I'll get the soap!" Karn exclaimed and eagerly turned in the direction of his pack.

As the pair made their way down to the lake, Ffearn called to them from where he sat by the fire. "Where do you think you're off to?"

"To wash my clothes," Karn said. "Klara put forth a rather 'effective' argument in favor of it."

"Effective, as in 'her interrogation techniques are effective?'" Ffearn asked. Klara shook her head and kept walking.

"Something like that," Karn replied.

Ffearn jumped to his feet. "Then wait up, I'm coming too!"

Klara washed everything but her shift, preferring to have at least one dry piece of clothing to wear while they ate. Karn and Ffearn did a good deal more splashing and swimming than actual washing, but at least their clothes were wet and had seen soap. The trio was blissfully skinny dipping when Bardus shouted that supper was ready.

With their clothing hung out to dry, they sat down to a meal of beans with the other Keltoi. Nuallan did not seem overly happy to have them at the fire and chastened them, "You lads ought to be ashamed of yourselves coming to supper bare."

Klara thought she saw a flicker of anger in Ffearn's eyes as he said, "Our clothes have been washed and are now hanging up to dry and each of us has only got one set of breeches." The fact that Thorn carefully watched the exchange was not lost on Klara. Did he side with Nuallan or his nephews?

After supper they sang and talked around the campfire late into the night. Everyone was in high spirits and looking forward to the day of rest tomorrow. Eventually, the men drifted off to their bedrolls and Klara sprinkled water on the fire to quiet the coals. The best part of this night was they made merry around the fire for so long that her watch was nearly over before it had even begun.

The moon had moved less than a quarter of the way across the sky when she woke Karn to tell him it was his turn. Around them, camp was quiet except for the snores of their companions. As they stood together in the moonlight, Klara nodded toward a rocky outcropping at the edge of the bench. There, silhouetted in the moonlight, Thorn sat.

"It worries me that he sleeps so little," Klara said, leaning into Karn.

There was no need to define who he was. Karn was well aware of his uncle's habits: last to sleep, first to rise, always. Karn sighed and kissed the top of her head. "Ever has it been so."

"I think I'll go talk with him a while," Klara said. "Perhaps I can convince him to sleep."

"Will you be bringing him back to our bedroll then?" Karn teased. "It'll be getting quite crowded in there."

Klara smiled up at him, eyes filled with mirth. "Well, he hasn't seen my undergarments yet. Shouldn't he get a chance to see if he got his money's worth?"

"I have since covered the cost of your stockings and they were definitely worth the money," Karn said. "If you wish to be showing them off again, you can show them to me anytime."

"Go take up your post," Klara replied, playfully pushing him away. Then she walked over to Thorn.

The rocky outcrop was high enough to see over the trees on the peninsula and to the main body of the lake beyond. From here, the view of the lake was more magnificent than it had been by light of day. Moonlight appeared as a silver streak across the lake, the trees casting black shadows along the shoreline. Light wind ruffled the water, causing the lake to dance as the moon's light played across its surface. Caught by the breeze, Klara's shift joined the magic of the night, dancing about her as she admired the shadowy scene.

"With a sight such as this, one can clearly see that silver is precious to the Goddess. She has painted the entire landscape with her own silver light," Klara said as she surveyed the countryside.

Looking down at Thorn, she saw awe scrawled across his face. But he was not looking at the water or the moon. He was looking at her.

With a slight bend of his head, he replied, "In naught but your shift you appear as the Goddess herself, dressed in silver with hair of gold. At the city of Duirness there is a reflecting pool that catches the moonlight and casts it onto a statue of the Goddess Abnoba; you look just as she does in that statue. I have often been struck by the similarity in your features."

"You think too highly of me," Klara said, taking a seat on the rock next to him. "Now, what troubles are keeping you from sleep?"

Sighing, Thorn placed a hand on her thigh. Words tumbled out of him and into the night. "I fear the quest will be for naught and that I lead my nephews into danger. If we turn back now, you and Karn could have a passel of children and live in peace somewhere. He is a diligent worker and excellent farrier. Given your own skill with the horses, the pair of you might live quite comfortably. But if we continue down this road, I fear all our lives will be filled with sorrow, for that is all I found when I was King. My people are given to fighting among themselves. If Ffearn takes the throne, his head may end up in a basket, just as my father's did."

Klara's eyes widened in shock. She had never heard him speak so much at one time, and never of matters so grave. And she did not like being seen as the mother of a passel of children, either.

Taking her hands in his, Thorn said, "I'm sorry. I did not mean to upset you."

Taking a long slow breath, Klara chose to forgo chastising him for making presumptions about her reproductive future and addressed the more weighty issues. "I think everyone fears the future when it is uncertain," she said. "And our thoughts grow unnecessarily dark when surrounded by the night. Things often look brighter with the dawn. You spend too much time alone and I think you worry needlessly."

"Klara," Thorn asked, "do you believe it is possible to mourn the loss of a thing you've never had?" His words cut her to the quick.

"I think so," Klara said. As she spoke, tears welled in her eyes and rolled down her cheeks. "I'm sometimes overwhelmed by sorrow, not for the experiences I've endured or those things taken from me, but for the loss of things I've never had."

Brushing the tears from her face, Thorn asked, "Pray, tell me what absence causes such pain?"

"I don't think I can give voice to my grief because I know of no words to describe my longings," Klara said as tears continued to flow. Her desires were vague and elusive, comprising an ambiguous otherness: safety, permanence, contentment. Her inability to explain derived from the fear that daring to hope would only result in future pain.

Hastily wiping tears from her cheeks, she said, "But I didn't come here to burden you. I intended to ease your mind so you could sleep. Now I've been crying and I still don't know all your troubles. What is it you mourn?"

Thorn put his arm around her shoulders. "You needn't worry about me. I feel comforted whenever you are near, tears or no. Like you, I mourn for what will never be. When I left Kenetlon all I wanted was to work as a tradesman, find a wife who would love me, and raise a few children. Many men lust after money and power, but all I ever wanted was to find contentment. Now, I am old with no hope of taking a wife or fathering a child. I had a good business though, and once my nephews found me, I had kin enough. I was almost happy when that fool of a wizard showed up at my door saying to cart my nephews off to a place I've long been trying to forget. It is those thoughts that have kept me up so many nights."

Klara looked at Thorn, her cheeks still wet with tears. "Sleep now and let the Goddess shine her light on you; surely she will protect you and your kin."

"Thank you," Thorn said softly, and then he leaned forward and kissed her cheek. "You should do likewise. A bed awaits you with one or the other of my nephews to keep you warm. I know Nuallan disapproves, as do many, of unions with foreigners, but know that whether nobleman or pauper, you will always be welcome in my household." Then Thorn rose and headed in the direction of his bedroll.

Midsummer brought as lovely a day as one could hope for with sunny skies and a gentle breeze. It was Ffearn's turn to cook, but he gratefully conceded to Klara when she asked if she could help prepare the evening meal.

"Of course," Klara said, "if I'm going to cook, I'll need something to cook."

Ffearn and Karn exchanged glances. "Ffearn and I can go hunting," Karn said, nonchalantly poking a stick into the fire. Despite their attempts at casualness, it was obvious those two wanted out of camp.

"Good," Klara said. "Then I can use the time to gather berries and maybe some herbs for seasoning if I can find any. With luck, we won't be stuck eating another bland meal."

After breakfast, Ffearn and Karn prepared for the hunt, choosing to forgo clothing after finding it still damp from the washing last night. This put Nuallan in a bad mood again.

Standing before the fire with their hair smartly braided, the pair of Keltoi checked their gear. Karn wore his quiver across his back and carried his bow at his side. Ffearn had a game bag, which contained the strings for the snares, slung across his body and was holding his spear. They wore their boots and their daggers were belted at their waist, but they wore nothing else. It was an impressive sight. It was easy to see why their enemies found them terrifyingly barbarous when they met in battle.

Nuallan harrumphed. "Can you not show some decency when you are going out to hunt for a meal that will be offered to the Goddess tonight?"

Klara looked at Nuallan over the drinking horn and said, "Seeing as the ceremonial rites are completed bare, I think this seems quite appropriate." Klara saw the corners of Thorn's mouth turn up in a smile. Nuallan, however, harrumphed again and stormed off. Smiling to herself, Klara recalled Thorn's look from the prior night. So it was Nuallan, and not his nephews, who was trying his patience. If no one cared for Nuallan, why was he with the party?

As the lads headed out of camp, Klara passed off the drinking horn and turned to Ruis and Bardus, saying, "You two would do well to spend some time washing your clothes today. I'll be out of camp this morning so you'll have no excuses."

As she left, she patted Thorn's chest and added, "You, too."

Dressed in her riding boots and white shift, Klara headed into the summer sun. She had borrowed a bag from Bardus to hold whatever herbs or berries she might find. Hoping the others might bathe and wash their clothes, Klara left the lake behind, giving the men some privacy. By following the stream through the meadow and into the trees, she found strawberries and wild leeks growing in the shadows. She picked enough berries to make pastries and pulled half a peck of leeks, intending to use them in several meals to come. Farther on she found mushrooms, but passed them by. Not being familiar with the fungi in this country, she did not want to risk illness or even death by feeding everyone something potentially poisonous.

After a couple of hours, Klara left the stream and headed cross-country back to camp. This brought her in contact with several serviceberry bushes. Most of the berries were still green and she ate nearly as many as she put in the bag with the strawberries. Engrossed with the berries, she failed to notice a fallow doe enter a nearby patch of sun. Twin fawns bounded to their mother, finally drawing her attention away from the bush. The fawns' tails wiggled frantically as they each found a teat and latched on. Smiling at the sight, she decided to go around so as not to disturb them. It was a lucky coincidence, because her new path led her directly to some wild greens.

When Klara returned, she had a bundle of leeks under her arm and her bag was bursting with good things to eat. Bardus had all the horses picketed in the long grass. She patted Constant and nuzzled his neck, promising to brush him later. Then she headed for camp.

Bardus and Ruis sat at the fire, in only their drawers, sharpening their weapons. She spotted Thorn and Nuallan on the overlook, still in their clothes. Laying the food bag aside, Klara shook her head and turned her attention to cooking. The most pressing matter was making a cake for the rite tonight. She would deal with Thorn and Nuallan later.

While she was taking the greens out of the bag, Ruis asked, "You bring back anything fit to eat?"

Berries tumbled out of the bag as she upended it over the wrought iron oven.

"Oh, well them don't look too bad," Ruis said.

"Not too bad at all," Klara said and stuck out her berry-stained tongue as evidence. Using her fingers, she scooped some berries into a bowl and passed it to him. "You two can share these." Then she set about scooping more berries into another bowl to be saved for the others.

She kept a watchful eye on Thorn and Nuallan as she stemmed the strawberries, absent mindedly tossing them back into the oven with the serviceberries. Waywyrd was neck deep in the lake. She swore fish were jumping all around him, but maybe he was just splashing. Having never met a wizard before, she had no idea if this was normal behavior or not. Sighing, she took up the crock of honey and poured a good measure over the berries, and commenced to make the batter. Once the cake was set on to bake, she sought out Thorn.

Klara knew she was interrupting him and Nuallan but did not care. "I see you're still dressed," Klara said as she handed Thorn a bowl of berries.

"I see you're not," Thorn replied, popping a berry into his mouth.

Nuallan harrumphed.

Ignoring Nuallan, Klara sat beside Thorn. "Not yet. I've just put a cake on to bake and was planning to wash this shortly. Ffearn and Karn only washed one set of shirts yesterday, so I'll wash the other set at the same time. I would appreciate it if you would join me. Your clothes need washing just as much as ours do."

"Klara, I know this may seem odd," Thorn said, "But there is good reason for me not to join you at the lake. As leader of the company I need to set myself apart. It is inappropriate for me to stand around camp bare as my nephews do." This garnered appreciative noises from Nuallan.

Odd noises from Nuallan be damned, Klara thought. "As our leader it is your place to set the example for the men and to do that you must be clean."

"Nuallan, would you leave us?" Thorn asked.

Nuallan harrumphed but left as he was bid. Thorn took a deep breath and let it out slowly. When at last he was ready to speak, a pained expression painted his face. "Klara, none here have ever seen me without a shirt, not even my nephews. I have been lashed; these Keltoi do not know."

"I'm sorry, Thorn," Klara said, laying a hand on his shoulder, "though I doubt they would think less of you for it."

"I would prefer not finding out how they would react," Thorn said.

Immediately an idea came to her. "Wait here," she said, then scurried to the clothes line and returned with Karn's tunic. She handed it to Thorn, saying, "You're broader across the chest than Karn, so it may be a little small, but it should work, though I don't think his breeches will fit you. If you'll wear the tunic, I'll wash your clothes as well." This way Nuallan would be the only one left who stank. Rather than argue with the old curmudgeon, she resolved to simply stay upwind of him.

Thorn pulled her to him and kissed her forehead. "Thank you," he said. Then he hid behind a bush to change out of his clothes and into Karn's tunic. It did not take long before he returned and handed her the clothing, eyes full of gratitude.

The washing complete, Klara removed the clean, dry clothes from her make-shift clothes line and laid them by their packs. Then she began hanging the freshly laundered batch up to dry. She was standing bare, wet clothes in her hands, when Ffearn and Karn returned to camp, both of them carrying game. Depositing their kills by the fire, the pair quickly moved to join her.

"I see someone has been following our good example," Ffearn said. Then looking around he asked, "Camp is deserted, where is everyone?"

Klara smacked Ffearn with a wet shirt. "I just finished washing my shift and the rest of your things. I haven't had time to dress yet." Turning her attention back to the clothes line, she said, "Everyone except Thorn decided to go fishing rather than sit about camp while I was here bare. Ffearn, your dry things are by your pack. Karn, I'm afraid you've no dry clothes yet. Well, you did, but I lent them to Thorn, he's still on the bench up the hill."

"Absent gods, what for?" Karn asked, pulling the quiver over his head and discarding his hunting gear. "Why isn't he wearing his own clothes?"

"He had not bathed, nor washed his clothes, when I returned to camp. I offered to do his washing for him, so his clothes are still wet. He said none of you have seen him without his shirt and he did not want to start now.

He has good reason," Klara said, though she sincerely hoped Thorn would sneak off for a bath.

"So I'm supposed to just stand about bare so he doesn't have to," Karn protested. Having finished hanging out the wash, Klara slipped her arms around Karn and laughed as he shivered from the chill of her damp body.

"I rather like the sight of you bare," she said. "Besides, it won't be long before the rest of the clothes are dry." This seemed to pacify him and he returned her embrace.

"He has good reason, you say," Ffearn asked. "Care to tell us what that reason is?"

"If Thorn hasn't told you, then it's not my place," Klara said. "Now let me dress; the cake is done and I need to start the bread."

Karn let her go and went to dress the game while she and Ffearn put on clean clothes. Ffearn had snared a large fowl, which Karn put in the cauldron to keep it clean until Klara had time to brown it. Karn had shot a young fallow deer, which was slated to be their dinner tonight, roasted over the fire. Was it one of the pair she had watched earlier?

Choosing a reasonably clean, rounded rock, she began mashing garlic, salt, pepper, and the mustard greens into a paste. After rubbing the fawn with the paste, she set it aside, letting the flavors meld before putting the meat on to roast.

Inverting the cake onto a clean dish towel revealed a top covered in a gooey mass of berries. After scouring the oven clean, she made bread. With the loaves baking, there was little left to do at the fire, so Karn and Ffearn recounted their hunt for her benefit.

The land was overflowing with game and they enjoyed being out of camp. Since Karn had been playing the part of a married farmer, he and Ffearn were not able to spend the vast quantities of time together they usually did. Klara noticed they always seemed happier after having been off together and that was the case now. After their tale was told, the bread was done. She set it aside to cool. Then she gathered up Thorn's dry clothing and brought them to him.

"I hope you'll join us tonight," Klara said. "I've made a cake for the rite, though it may seem a little silly using a drinking horn full of ale rather than mead or something stronger."

"Wait here," Thorn said. "I'll dress, and then I have something for you."

When he returned fully dressed, Thorn led her to his bedroll and indicated that she should sit. After riffling through his pack, he withdrew an item wrapped in the same gray fabric as the tunic Ffearn wore with the King's crest embroidered on it. Unwrapping the item, Thorn handed it to her, saying, "This was to be used at my coronation, during the union of myself to the land. By that time there was no druidess in Duirndunum and none of the other clans would consent to lend one of theirs. You may use it tonight."

In her hands Klara held an ornately decorated silver chalice. "Thorn, this is magnificent," she said, gently running her finger around the lip of the cup.

As she admired the chalice, Thorn pulled another item from his pack, a small flask. Handing it to her as well, Thorn said, "We were to use this, but I've no use for it anymore. I think these Keltoi might enjoy a sip of this far more than another swig of ale."

"Thank you," Klara said and smiled up at him. "It's time I help Ffearn with supper." Klara rewrapped the chalice and carried it her bedroll, where she knelt and handed Karn his clothes.

Seeing the other items in her hands, Karn asked, "What's that?"

Klara showed him and Ffearn the chalice. Then she remember Thorn had not agreed to join them. She silently cursed herself for becoming distracted and not pressing for a promise.

"I think I should taste the flask's contents," Karn said grabbing it from her hands. "Just to make sure it's still fit to drink."

Ffearn swiped the flask from his brother. "You wouldn't know fine liquor from horse piss. As frequenter of many taverns, I should be the one to test the contents."

Klara reclaimed the flask and batted their hands away as both reached for it. "You two need to keep your lips off my liquor," she said. "If it needs tested, I'll do it beforehand." Then she turned to the task of making supper.

Turnips were quartered and put in a cauldron to boil and the meat was put over the coals to roast. Carrots and onions were chopped, seasoned with salt, pepper, and garlic, and then wrapped in cabbage leaves before being set on the coals to steam. The fowl was cut up and browned so it would keep in the heat. It was to be supper tomorrow, but the grease that remained from the browning was used to make gravy.

The smells emanating from the fire brought the company up to camp long before supper was ready. Nuallan, Bardus, and Ruis were pleased with themselves for having caught more than enough fish for Karn to fry for breakfast. Stooped over the campfire, Klara and Ffearn ladled out food, filling the men's bowls. With meat, vegetables, and bread, it was as tasty and filling a meal as they were likely to get at an inn and the company tucked into the meal with gusto.

Tapping the ale and passing the drinking horn around brought many hearty toasts to Ffearn and Karn's health and long years ahead. Toasts to the gods and goddesses, to Midsummer in general, and to the success of the journey soon followed.

Nuallan fished a pouch out of his pack. "I thought a little of this might be a nice, seeing as it's a holy day." After seating himself before the fire, he took a bit of herb from the pouch, placed it on a thin rock, and set it to smoldering.

Klara recognized it at once. "Cannabis. Whose tent will we use to collect the smoke?" Her opinion of Nuallan had greatly improved as did her hopes of passing a merry evening.

"No tent, lass," Nuallan said. "We'll just catch what we can by passing the rock around the fire."

"That won't have much of an effect," Ffearn said. "The best way is to fill a tent with the smoke, then go in to fill your lungs."

"Little effect is better than none," Nuallan snapped. "Besides, we are out in the wilds. Best to pass the night with at least some of our wits."

They intended to wait until sunset before starting the Midsummer rite, when the last rays of the sun and the first light of the moon sparkled across the water. That gave the company time to relax around the fire. Leaving the company of Keltoi to their drinking and smoking, Klara gathered the supplies she needed and took them down to the beach. After undressing, she waded into the water and washed every part of her body thrice. Then she sat in silence to prepare her heart and mind for the ceremony to come.

There were few worshipers of Abnoba in Skoloti, so holy days were often spent alone. These Keltoi were worshipers, she could tell. Ever since childhood she honored the quarter days and the cross-quarter days, but always did so alone. Now it was time to honor the Goddess in her mother aspect, thanking her for the blessings and abundance that came with the fullness of summer. Assuming the role of the Goddess was an important task, and she hoped one of the Keltoi might assume the role of consort. Smiling as she uncorked Thorn's flask, Klara took a sip. The liquid was sweet in her mouth and slid smoothly down her throat.

Deciding it was time to start, Klara waved at Karn and Ffearn to garner their attention. "It's time. Round everyone up and send them to the beach," she called.

Only Ruis and Bardus chose to join them, leaving Thorn and Nuallan in camp with Waywyrd. Klara sighed. She would have to fetch them from the fire.

Looking at her four devotees, she said, "Remember, you need to wash every part thrice before partaking in the rite." Leaving them to their washing, she trudged up the hill to collect Thorn and the remainder of the company.

Klara took Thorn's hands in hers and stood before him, clad in naught but the sky. "If you will not join us to be an example for your men, will you come for me?"

Nodding, Thorn said, "I will come for you."

Thorn rose, letting Klara lead him to the beach, leaving Nuallan and Waywyrd to sit by the fire. The other Keltoi were just finishing their ablutions when she and Thorn arrived. He hesitated. Klara touched his arm encouragingly. Slowly, Thorn reached for his belt and began to disrobe. Once bare, Klara took his hand and led him the water's edge, where the other Keltoi stood dripping. Noticing the scars, surprised whispers issued from the assembled company. Thorn paused again, but Klara led him farther into the water. When the water reached their waists, she wet the soap and stood behind him, tracing each of the lines that crossed his back.

Silently, she counted seventeen scars. A king must be free of blemish or defect. If someone knew of the scars, it would be enough to prevent him from claiming the title. Having finished washing his back, Klara handed him the soap, quietly saying, "Be sure to wash every part thrice." Then she waded back to the beach.

After washing, Thorn took a place at the end of the line of Keltoi. Klara began by inviting the spirits of the air, mountains, water, and groves to join them.

Facing east, Klara said, "From the eastern spirits we ask for knowledge and intuition true." Moving to the south, she intoned, "From the southern spirits, we ask for courage in all that we do." Walking around the company to face west she said, "From the spirits of the west, we ask you bless us with love." Continuing her path, she stopped to face north and said, "From the north we ask for the strength of the gods above." Then Klara completed the circle, standing where she first started in the east.

Seating herself cross-legged before them she asked, "Does anyone know the male portion of the offerings?"

Silent, the men sat before her.

Thorn looked up the row of Keltoi, then to Klara. "I know it," he said. "And I would prefer to use my own blade."

Moving to the pile of his clothes, Thorn collected his dagger. It was iron, with a double blade. The guard and pommel were decorated with silver and the grip was covered with fine black leather. It was entirely possible that Thorn had crafted it himself. It was a far finer blade than the kitchen knife she planned to use and for that she was grateful.

Klara held the cake on the inverted lid of the iron oven as an offering before him and Thorn lowered his dagger into the cake, saying, "The body of the God lowered into the body of the Goddess."

Then Thorn cut the first slice, took it in his hands, and held it out so she could take a bite. As she did, he offered the blessing, "May you never hunger."

Taking the same slice in her own hand, she offered it back to Thorn. As he took his bite, she returned the blessing, saying, "May you never hunger."

Once the pair of them had eaten, Thorn and Klara worked their way down the line of Keltoi, with Thorn cutting a slice for each member of the company and offering them the same blessing as he handed them the cake.

Having finished serving the cake, Klara uncorked the liquor and filled the chalice. Nodding to Thorn when she was ready, he held his dagger out, blade down.

Positioning the chalice below the dagger, Klara recited, "The body of the Goddess raised up to meet the body of the God." As she spoke, she raised the chalice so that it engulfed the lower portion of Thorn's blade. She held the chalice there for a moment and then lowered it so he could put aside his dagger. Once that was done, she offered him the chalice with the blessing, "May you never thirst."

Placing his hands over hers, he drank. Then still holding the cup, he returned the blessing, offering the chalice back to her, saying, "May you never thirst."

Klara drank deeply of the sweet liquid, then she walked down the line of Keltoi offering each the chalice and blessing as they drank from the communal cup. Afterward they offered their thanks to the Gods and Goddesses, and then the men began to dress. Klara gathered up the remainder of the cake, the chalice, the bottle of liquor, and headed toward Thorn.

"I want to thank you," she said, pausing briefly, "for everything. Will you take the cake back to camp so Nuallan and Waywyrd can have some?"

"Are you not returning to camp?" Thorn asked as he accepted the hodge-podge assortment of items.

"No," Klara said and smiled. "I want to swim out to meet the moon."

The night was cool, but the sun had been on the water all day. In the shallows of the bay, the water was warmer than the air. She loved the feeling of floating as the water engulfed her. Delighting in the Goddess's gifts seemed like the perfect way to end the rite.

"Go, enjoy the night," Thorn said and turned, heading back to the fire.

As she began to wade in, Karn called to her, "What are you doing?"

"Going swimming," she said. "Want to come?"

"Of course," Karn said, immediately reversing direction with his clothing, pulling his shirt back over his head.

Klara was in the water to her waist when she heard Karn and Ffearn talking on shore.

"Alas, I look on her and I lust. Press her to the earth beneath me, I desire," Karn said.

Ffearn answered him, "No, bend her over. Take her from behind, I would."

The pair had spoken in Kenetlon. Klara's head swiveled back and forth between them. It was clear this conversation was not meant for her ears, so she did not question them about it, but she understood every word. So far none of the Keltoi had spoken their native tongue around her. Perhaps they thought she did not know the language? If that was the case, she had no intention of enlightening them now.

Turning her back on them, she swam out into the trail of moonlight that sliced across the bay. Enjoying the feel of the water as it surrounded her body, Klara paused to float in the silver light and drink in the night. Goosepimples rose on her wet skin where it was exposed to the cool night air. Having her fill of the night and thanking the moon for its presence, she turned and using strong, sure strokes, returned to shore.

Sitting naked in the moonlight, Klara watched the pair of Keltoi enjoy their swim. It was not long before they too exited the water and joined her on the beach, flanking her as they sat. Klara felt the heat radiating off their warm bodies in the cool of the night.

"You know," Klara said, "the rite we just performed is meant to represent, and thank, the gods and goddesses for the creation of the blessed union. On this night the Goddess and her consort are joined and from this union she conceives. There are other offerings that can be made to honor the Goddess, the kinds of which I don't think Thorn would much approve."

Klara added playfully, "Though, I get the feeling the pair of you might like to make an offering, especially if it were done in tandem."

Being devoted to a goddess who fully approved of sex had served her well as a whore. Mostly, it helped ward off the pit of despair and self-loathing she felt when faced with her own economic vulnerability. Knowing Karn and Ffearn as she did, she doubted they would be bashful at sharing a pleasurable experience.

Karn leaned in, kissed her neck, and whispered loud enough for Ffearn to hear, "What kind of offering did you have in mind?"

Ffearn did the same, and replied, "Whatever it is brother, I'd be willing if you are."

Klara did not answer with words, but took each of them in a hand and began to stroke them. The Keltoi lay back in the sand, allowing her to bring them pleasure. In time the sounds of the night were eclipsed by their moans and grunts. Klara felt that it was taking an impossibly long time. Her arms began to tire and her grip to loosen. Each of them placed a hand over hers and aided her until they climaxed, issuing forth their ejaculations and final grunts of satisfaction.

Letting her arms fall to her side, and lying back between them, she said, "If I were to do that very often, my biceps would be as large as yours."

Ffearn propped himself on an elbow. "If it's muscle building you're after, we'd be happy to assist any time."

Karn, likewise, rolled to face her and encircled her waist with his arm. He had mischief in his eye as he spoke, "Perhaps you'd like to make an offering of your own?"

Klara smiled at him, arms still limp. "I don't think that's necessary."

"Not necessary," Karn said as his hand floated across her body, "but it would be fun. And seeing as you've brought us pleasure, I do believe we should return the favor. Is that not right, brother?"

Reaching across her and placing his hand on her hip, Ffearn said, "I do believe my brother makes a good point. You have only to lie back and relax as we did."

Together the pair of young Keltoi began. Their hands and mouths caressed her body with a tenderness she had not known possible. The pair moved both in unison and opposition as though they were one being, sharing one mind. They managed to communicate their intentions to each other through some language that Klara neither heard nor understand. Ffearn and Karn's arms reached for her and past her to each other. They brought her pleasure with both their hands and their tongues. The three of them were entwined as one cord that could not be separated. Klara climaxed and marveled that before now she had not known that her own release could be so sweet. Afterward they lay together in the sand, arms and legs intertwined, so it was impossible to tell where one body ended and another began.

When Klara's heart stopped racing, she returned to the water to wash the sweat and sand from her body. Again she chose to swim far out into the bay and reaching the center she turned to face the moon. Through the trees on the peninsula she saw the flicker of torchlight and her heart stopped.

# Chapter 18

# Demons in the Night

Torches flickered like fireflies in the night, their bearers rapidly approaching the Keltoi camp. The hills surrounding the bay made it impossible to see the flames from camp or even the shore, but here in the middle of the bay Klara was far enough out to see the glow between the trees. She quickly swam back to shore, where Ffearn and Karn had already managed to put on their boots and breeches.

Abandoning thoughts of her own clothing, she grabbed them by the arms, saying, "Hurry, a group bearing torches approaches camp at speed."

Ffearn and Karn ran for their swords, but Klara ran straight to the overlook where she knew Thorn would be sitting. She was panting when she reached him. Dropping to her knees between Nuallan and Waywyrd, Klara tried to catch her breath. Between gasps she said, "People with torches. Coming quickly. Will crest hill soon."

The three of them left her panting and rushed for camp to take up arms. Stumbling, Klara followed after them. No sooner had each Kelto assembled with sword in hand than the torch bearers crested the hill, wolves at their sides. It would be an uphill battle if it came to it, which gave their opponent the advantage. That was not the only advantage their opponents had, for swarming down the hill before them was a pack of Ke'let, who were accustomed to night raids and seeing in dimly lit places.

The wolves reached them first, circling the company, quivering with excitement. Yellow eyes flashed in the firelight as they paced, awaiting commands. Their masters soon followed. As the pack encircled them, Klara saw the gleam of red skin, made redder by the flickering glow of the torches, and counted twenty-three demons. She knew there were more in the shadows.

Gristly skin appeared as though it were dripping off many of the demons, giving them the appearance of soft wax set too near a flame. They were twisted and disfigured, but Klara knew anyone who thought them disadvantaged by the deformities was a fool. Demons fought as well as any man and many of them fought a good deal better.

When the company was fully surrounded, a demon whose face was badly misshaped stepped forward and said, "Give woman and quick your death be. Give not and die anyway, but longer it take."

Thankfully, the demon had spoken in Kenetlon. The demon's native tongue was indecipherable to the human ear and, though she lived among Ke'lets for many months, she never managed to learn any of it. Because demons often took work in Kenetlon mines, many spoke Kenetlon but for some reason scorned all other languages. It was out of a need to communicate with Asmodaios that Klara had learned Kenetlon, though she had not yet let her Keltoi companions in on this secret.

"Give battle we will, if death it be," Thorn said through gritted teeth, his sword already held aloft and ready to strike.

The entire company stood at the ready. Klara refused to let them die needlessly. Sill bare, she stepped forward and in as strong a voice she could muster, addressed the demon in Kenetlon. "I'm Klara, a pleasure woman, protected of Abnoba. We have no dispute with you."

A large demon pushed his way forward, parting the pack, and stepped into the circle of torchlight. His body was covered by the scars of many battles. A gray wolf, almost twice the size of the others, accompanied him, staying near his master's side. The spoke directly to her, as if the armed company at her back was no more than a trifling annoyance. "See you around, think good I do. You go with demons, protection we give."

Klara looked at him a moment and blinked, recognition slowly dawning on her face. "Asmodaios?"

Asmodaios smiled, showing mangled teeth and pulled her into a hug.

The unexpected action caused her companions to rush forward. Twirling her out of his arms, as though they were dancers, Asmodaios prepared to meet the challenge. The wolf artfully dodged between her and Asmodaios, eager to stay between his master and the threat.

"No," Klara shouted, lunging for the wolf. She wrapped her arms around its muscular frame, successfully knocking both of them to the ground. She came up panting, arms full of the beast's thick coat, hanging from his neck. Her actions had confused everyone, even the wolf. The impending battle was momentarily delayed.

Asmodaios held his hands out in a placating gesture. Regarding her as though she were deviant spawn who had hidden his favorite knife and refused to divulge the location, he addressed her. "Remember me you do, pleased I am. Protect you another time we did. Now, move, we slaughter everyone."

"Have mercy," Klara pleaded, her face and arms still buried in the wolf's ruff. The wolf, too, was treating her as an errant pup, trying to wiggle away without causing injury. Asmodaios had often treated her as a pet; surely he would grant her request. "Proclaim friends, I do."

In a ridiculously paternal gesture, Asmodaios pointed to Ffearn and Karn, who stood, still shirtless, swords in hand. "Smell of someone's penis you do. Desire you not the penis of men, I thought."

Sensing a decrease in tensions, the wolf had begun licking her face. Klara released him and crawled out from under the massive beast, then stood. Tossing a glance over her shoulder, she saw the Keltoi, still holding their weapons, arms sagging as confusion scrawled its way across their faces.

Klara shrugged and turned back to Asmodaios. "With Keltoi, remaining the night I allow."

Asmodaios took another step forward. His massive hand reached for her and raised her left breast. Would he see the scars and think they had injured her? To her relief, he dropped her breast and stepped back without anger.

"Increases your skin in beauty with new scars," Asmodaios said. "Yet many more cuts come soon. Seek you Elah does, safe you are not."

Tension fled Klara's body. Asmodaios had just proclaimed her scars beautiful.

Waywyrd placed a hand on her shoulder, causing her to jump. Motioning with his staff, as if its use might improve their understanding, he addressed Asmodaios. "Seek her Elah does. Safe we hold her," he said, though his Kenetlon was nowhere as good as the demon's. And if he knew Elah was seeking her, why had he neglected to impart that information beforehand.

Asmodaios snorted. "Safe she is not. Between you, betrayal. Take her to Belial we do, to hide from Messias."

Klara cocked her head as she processed the information. Betrayal? Was he referring to Thorn leaving the Kingship behind? Or was something more sinister brewing? She decided to stay with the company of Keltoi and take her chances.

"No," Klara said. "I will remain."

Standing toe to toe, Klara and Asmodaios sized each other up. Physically Asmodaios was taller, broader, and stronger, but she had always been more willful. If he attempted to cart her off, she would make him miserable and they both knew it. The only question now was, would he try? With half a dozen armed Keltoi at her back, she very much doubted it. The demons had the superior numbers, but she and Asmodaios knew each other well.

Asmodaios sighed. Klara had won. The demon stepped back and signaled to the pack that it was time to retreat into the night. Many of them had already slipped silently from sight.

"Wait," Waywyrd called, then checked himself and changed languages. "What of Messias? Seek you Klara?"

Pausing, Asmodaios turned back to Waywyrd. "When seek you omens, in the prophecies you find. Hold her safe or bring battle against you demons do." Then he turned and disappeared into the dark with the rest of his pack.

Prophecies? What bloody prophecies? And why did Asmodaios think Waywyrd might know something about them? Klara stood stunned, watching them go. The wizard had a lot of explaining to do.

When the last torch passed them by, Ffearn and Karn turned toward Klara and said in unison, "Why didn't you tell us you spoke Kenetlon?"

"You never asked," Klara said, allowing her gaze to linger on the backs of the retreating demons. She was still considering how best to approach Waywyrd and was not interested in their quibbles now.

Thorn stabbed his sword in the ground, the force of the action leaving it swaying slightly. Storming toward her, shaking his finger, reeking of fear and seething with anger, he shouted, "Put some clothes on! Your nakedness caused this trouble; they thought we used you ill."

Klara wheeled on him. "My nakedness saved your life. If I had bothered to dress, they would have slaughtered you before I made it back to camp. Try being grateful." Of all the senseless accusations, he chose nudity as being the cause of the trouble. There were far more pressing concerns than where she put her clothes, but since that was the easiest to solve, she headed toward the beach, leaving Thorn blustering behind her.

When Klara returned from the beach, wearing her shift and carrying the rest of her clothes, the Keltoi were sitting around the campfire questioning Waywyrd. She noted, with little surprise, that the fire had been built up larger than usual and much larger than necessary, though all of the men were huddled around it as if they were chilled.

"Why didn't they strike us?" Ruis asked, eyes intent on the wizard.

"Because I'm a whore," Klara snapped, interrupting the conversation and taking a seat on the log next to Karn. "Abnoba is the protector of prostitutes. As long as they know I am here willingly, you're safe."

"Blasphemy!" Nuallan shouted, raising to his feet. "How can you claim that our sacred Goddess, Mother of the Kenetlo, is a protector of whores?" The elder Kelto had gone red in the face and looked ready to start throwing punches.

"She says it because it's true," Waywyrd said, pushing Nuallan back down with his staff. "After Dur's death, Abnoba left the Kenetlo. As punishment for openly consorting with a mortal, she was not allowed to return to the Divine so she walked among the men of the Aegean instead. She was not as happy there, and finding them less satisfying, needed a multitude of lovers, so she offered herself as a prostitute. She had another child as well, one whose father was Odrysian."

Nuallan coughed and sputtered but eventually caught his breath and sat quietly. Waves of anger radiated from him, his face just as crimson as the demons. Obviously, there were things they did not know about their Goddess, or perhaps had chosen to forget.

"What about the prophecy they spoke of?" Bardus asked.

"Utter nonsense for the most part," Waywyrd said, though Klara noticed that he was not meeting their eyes. Was he hiding something? Probably. In the short time she had known him, the one thing she had learned was that he was not one to divulge secrets.

"The demons follow the *Oddly Accurate Prophecies of a Nutter*," Waywyrd said, "The woman was barking mad and none of what she wrote makes a lick of sense. The demons try to decipher her writing because as near as any can tell her prophecies have been quite accurate. The problem is, she was drunk most of the time, so her prophecies are written in such a jumble of nonsense that they are incomprehensible until after they have come to pass. There is no way to tell if the remaining prophecies were wrong, have not yet come to pass, or are simply the records of failed experiments for distilling spirits."

"But what does any of that have to do with Elah? And why is he looking for Klara?" Thorn asked.

Klara looked at Thorn, who was doing his best not to look at her. He seemed to have recovered from the fear and panic of before, but the façade might crumble at any moment. The fire crackled before them and Klara feared that one loud pop, or the sudden collapse of logs, might send him running for the hills.

"Elah has been looking for Klara for a long time," Waywyrd replied, stroking his staff. "There are a couple of theories on why, but nothing definite. Much to the dismay of my sister, Klara is particularly good at making herself hard to find, which also means she successfully manages to elude Elah, though the demons have no trouble finding her. As for the demon's involvement, a likely answer to that is found in the *Book of Woe*."

Waywyrd cleared his throat, then began to recite:

> "Elah turned his hand to creation, but failed at his task,
> He made a line of demons who would not do as he asked.
> Abominations, mutations, and deviations abound,
> For in the line of demons all of these can be found.
> Unsatisfied with his work, he cast the lot aside,
> Flinging them to Earth and there they do abide.

"Alone and unshepherded, they began to mate,
And lacking a creator's love, quickly learned to hate.
The demons abandoned Elah, as he had done to them,
And went in search of new masters in the lands of men.
The Divine came to Elah, saying evil you have done,
You cannot create more beings, for the Earth is overrun.

"But Elah wanted a being who would worship him alone,
And thought he found in Belial a way he could atone.
Angel, Elah called him, and said that he'd be blessed,
Of all his creation, Elah thought this one the best.
But Belial saw in Elah a God wrought with sin,
He left him for the Earth, to gather the demons in.

"After the abandoned ones, Belial looked with care,
Because when they needed him, Elah wasn't there.
They hailed him as master, and look to him as Lord,
And now Belial manages the vast and mighty hoard.
To bring about creation and abandon it is wrong,
And so to the Angel Belial the demons now belong."

"The demons hate Elah and will go out of their way to thwart his plans," Waywyrd said. "If Elah wishes to kill prostitutes, Belial and the demons will see they are protected. Now, I must sleep. I leave at first light. I, too, have many questions and they can only be answered by other wizards." With a wave of his staff, Waywyrd dispatched the group.

As Klara turned to walk away, Waywyrd's voice appeared in her head, *"You should practice with Constant while I am away. I believe your horse needs neither bridle nor saddle but would eagerly respond to your whim."* Klara only nodded in acknowledgement of Waywyrd's request.

*"And Klara,"* Waywyrd's voice came again, *"don't be too hard on Thorn. It was a demon who put his father's head in the basket."*

Knowing the only thing she needed protection from was the Disciples of Elah eased her mind a great deal. Klara had been avoiding them since childhood. Besides, it was easier to avoid the Disciples of Elah now that she was among a company of Keltoi who were happy to pass her off as a married woman when they traveled through villages.

Ffearn put out the fire and took his turn at the watch while Karn and Klara made their way to their bedrolls. Klara was not the least bit sleepy. She communicated this to Karn by running her hand under his shirt to caress his chest. Then she buried her face in his neck and began to nibble, working her way to his ear.

"Are you still not satisfied?" he asked playfully.

Klara simply shrugged her shoulders and made to free him of his breeches. The few times she had let Karn caress and fondle her had been incredible. Her patrons had only ever cared about their pleasure. Having someone solely focused on her was exhilarating, as were the climaxes.

"You know we can't," Karn said, pulling her fingers free of their purchase. "The others are too near." In response she slipped below the blanket and began a series of kisses that ran from his nipples to his navel. Karn pulled her back up to face him. "There is a pack of demons out there."

Klara kissed him before answering. "And they will not harm a whore with her patron. I'll protect you just as I protected Ruis from the rabbit. Though, I hope you won't be as quickly dispatched as a rabbit," she said and grinned.

"I give up," Karn said. He threw aside the blankets, scooped Klara up and held her over his shoulder like a sack of barley. Then taking her bedroll in his other arm, Karn headed for the trees. Klara giggled profusely and nipped at his tunic as they went.

"Where are you two off to?" Ffearn called from where he stood watch.

"Someone isn't sleepy," Karn called back as they headed away from camp and into the forest.

When Karn decided they were far enough away that they were unlikely to disturb the slumber of their companions, he put her down and spread out the bedroll. Klara undressed him and as they lay down together she addressed him in Kenetlon, "Alas, I look on you and I lust. Pressed to the earth beneath you I assent to be." Karn needed no other invitation.

Their love-making was loud and vigorous. Klara was extremely vocal which further excited Karn. Climaxing, she seized his back and held fast as successive tremors cascaded through her body. Holding him tighter, she said the only word she could: "more." Then she issued forth a great wetness.

Karn was not long after her in finishing and they both lay panting, bodies glistening with sweat, cocooned by the trees, under a blanket of stars. Below them the bedroll was soaked and, though she was wrapped in his arms, Klara shook as though she had caught a chill.

"Did I hurt you?" Karn asked.

"No, it was very good," Klara replied, still basking in the afterglow of her orgasm and dreamily running her fingers through his chest hair. "I didn't want you to stop. It's just that I've never done that before, made things wet."

"Just like the Goddess," Karn said and kissed her temple. "Can you stand?"

Klara's mind was willing to leave their woodland bed, but her body bade her stay. Attempting to rise, her legs buckled beneath her. Though he, too, was exhausted from their encounter, Karn had to carry her back to camp just as he carried her there. When they returned, it was not Ffearn but Nuallan who stood watch. Neither realized they had been gone so long.

As they reached the bedroll, Ffearn said, "The whole camp heard you, both of you." Noticing how Klara shook, a look of alarm crossed his face. "Have you injured her? Is that what the screaming was?"

"I'm fine," Klara said, slipping from Karn's shoulder, "just tired."

Karn deposited her in Ffearn's arms and said, "Keep her warm, nothing else. I've got to wash a bedroll; I'll be back soon."

Ffearn's strong arms wrapped warmly around her. "Absent gods," he exclaimed. "You have done her damage."

"Nay, Brother," Karn said, holding up the sodden bedroll for Ffearn to see. "She is as Danu. Keep her warm for me until I return." Then he walked toward the lake, dragging the soggy blanket.

Klara had never been held by Ffearn. Realizing she liked the scent of him, she nuzzled into his chest, using him as a pillow and burrowing into his warmth. Barely conscious and in a sleep addled voice she asked, "Who's Danu?"

Ffearn brushed a stray hair from her face before answering. "Danu is the goddess who brought the gift of water. The Danube River is named after her. Danu and Daghda were very much in love. They hid themselves on the earth to couple in private, away from the other gods. At that time all that covered the earth were soil, rock, and stone. The couple passionately embraced each other in a love-making session that lasted nine days. When Danu reached her climax, she issued forth a great wetness, which created the Danube and provided all the water for the Earth. It was from her loins that the sweet waters necessary for all life came."

Ffearn paused to yawn but continued to hold her. Klara was nearly asleep when he spoke again, this time in little more than a whisper. "Karn and I walked the river from its source to its mouth when we went in search of Thorn. The river and the water it contains are sacred. We honor her and give thanks with every drink we take. It seems you may honor her in other ways, too."

When Karn returned, Klara was vaguely aware of being passed from one set of strong arms to the other as the three of them settled into to sleep.

CHAPTER 19

# WORRIES LAID TO REST

UALLAN WOKE THE trio of slumbering companions as rudely as he might conceivable get away with. "Up you lot," he demanded, leaning over them with a look that was equal parts menace and glee.

"Go away," Ffearn said, pulling the blanket over his head.

Nuallan admonished them, "Just because you were up half the night doesn't mean you get to shirk your duties."

Karn pulled Klara close as he spoke to the aged Kelto. "We aren't riding out today. We get three days rest, the day before, day of, and day after; you know that. Let us sleep."

Nuallan was nearly in a fit as he directed sharp words to Karn, "Well, forgive me, Master Kelto; it may interest you to know that it's your turn to cook and the horses need watering whether we ride or not."

"Is anyone else even awake?" Karn asked.

As if in reply, from across the camp Ruis shouted, "Absent gods, Nuallan! Shut yer trap and let them sleep so we may do likewise."

Nuallan looked down at them. "Ruis is awake," he said.

Karn relented, "Fine, I'll start breakfast." Then he passed Klara off to Ffearn and went to rekindle the fire.

Klara, only partly roused from slumber, nuzzled into Ffearn's neck and ran her fingers up his chest. "I think you've got the wrong Kelto," he said with a chuckle, clasping her hands to prevent further exploration.

"I know which of you I've got," Klara said. She yawned and nuzzled into him, letting her eyes drift shut. Still in the fog between sleeping and waking, she asked, "If a rooster says cock-a-doodle-do, what does a hen say?"

"I've only ever heard them say cluck," Ffearn answered, bemused.

"They say," Klara said, "any-cock-will-do." And with that she settled back into sleep.

Klara did not know how long she slept, but when she woke again breakfast was ready and Bardus stood before her and Ffearn. "I heard there was a blanket that needed washing," Bardus said. "She's no virgin; if there was blood, she was damaged. I'll need to examine her."

"I wasn't hurt," Klara said. "It was the best sex I've ever had." She pulled the blanket snug around her, warding off the morning chill and Bardus's intrusion into her slumber.

"I can vouch for her health," Ffearn said. "This morning she had the presence of mind to discuss the vocal patterns of chickens." Bardus gave them a rather bewildered look, which invoked fits of laughter, at which point he consented to leave her where she lay and forgo any examination.

After breakfast, Klara joined Bardus and helped him with the horses. As she was letting Constant and Night drink, Bardus looked over at her and asked, "Vocal patterns of chickens?"

Klara smiled at him. "Bloody brilliant birds, though it's not true what they say; it appears only a Kelto will do." Leaving him to puzzle that out on his own, she headed for the picket line to get another pair of horses.

After all the horses were watered and picketed in the meadow, she went in search of the brush and curry comb. Bardus had informed her that Waywyrd was long gone, but she still wanted to try communicating with Constant as he suggested. Constant loved being brushed, so she knew he would not wander off if she held those in her hands. Returning to him, Klara unfastened his halter so he was completely free. Constant stood alert as she pressed her forehead to his and thought, *Don't run off and I'll brush you.*

There was no reply, but she began brushing the horse anyway. Every muscle in Constant's body relaxed and his eyes rolled up in his head. The horse was so engrossed in the grooming that she thought a stiff breeze might knock him over.

As Klara brushed Constant, Thorn approached. "You have the same effect on that horse as you have on my nephews."

When Constant relaxed under her touch, even the muscles that kept his penis sheathed relaxed. The horse now stood obviously pleased, the long, pendulous organ swaying beneath him. Klara glanced up at Thorn and noticed for the first time how much alike he and Karn looked when he smiled. Every remnant of terror from the night before was gone. Knowing how much he feared demons, she was glad of that.

"The smile suits you," Klara said. "And if brushing their hair has this effect on your nephews I wouldn't know, for whenever I've brushed their hair they wore their breeches."

Thorn laughed. It was a heart-warming jovial sound. He was in a better mood than she had ever seen him and was not sure how to respond.

"It wasn't the hair brushing I came to talk to you about," Thorn said. "You had them engaged in a number of other activities last night."

Klara felt instantly ashamed. She instinctively tried to clasp her hands behind her back but became flustered at finding she still held the brush. Not sure what to do with her hands, she stammered, "I'm sorry, Thorn. I know you said no sex. I just got carried away. It's my fault, please don't be mad at them."

Thorn raised his hand to her cheek. "I'm not mad—I was sick with worry. I just have a couple of favors to ask of you in the future. The first is that you try to contain yourself when there are demons about. I did not know whether the sounds I heard were of pleasure or torture. The second is that should the two of you choose to couple again, go further afield so we won't hear your sounds of pleasure at all."

"I'm sorry," Klara said, looking down at her hands and fidgeting with the brush. Guilt washed over her. Given the state of nervous agitation he was in last night, surely he saw visions of torture at the sounds she was making and imagined him sitting at the overlook, fists clenched in his hair.

"There is no need to be sorry, Klara," Thorn said, raising her chin so that she again looked him in the eyes. "I love them as if they were my own sons, and if a child were born of this union I would love it as a grandchild."

Klara's mind raced. This was the second time he had mentioned children. Did the whole world conspire against her to get her pregnant?

Thankfully, she had the herb, which she took right after breakfast. But how could she tell Thorn that she had no intention of bearing anyone's children when the thought of it brought him such happiness?

"And here come my nephews now," Thorn said, gesturing across the meadow.

Turning to look, Klara saw Karn and Ffearn approaching, absent the usual swagger in their step. When they left with their hunting equipment earlier she did not expect to see them until late in the afternoon. They carried no game and did not appear to be nearly as pleased with themselves as they usually were after having been off together. Klara searched Karn's eyes, but saw no hint of what they had been up to.

When the pair reached them, Ffearn knelt before Thorn, his eyes cast downward. "Uncle, I now understand why you desired me to stand for election. I'm sorry I refused you before. If it is still your wish, I will do as you have asked."

"What brings about this change of heart?" Thorn asked.

"It was last night at the lake," Ffearn said, raising his eyes to meet his uncle's. "You see, we didn't know of the lashing; at least we assume that's how you came by the scars. Karn and I talked this morning. Still, I am glad you didn't tell us sooner. If I had assented to the nomination as a child, we wouldn't have sought you out and gotten to know you as we do now. I swear to punish whoever did this to you."

Thorn looked kindly on his nephew. "You cannot punish a Kelto who is already dead." Raising Ffearn to his feet, Thorn embraced him, and then Karn. "You are good lads. I am proud of you both." Having been relieved of this burden, Thorn looked ten years younger.

Karn took Klara by the hand and asked, "Now that Ffearn has made his announcement, there are things I'd like to discuss with you. Will you walk with me?"

"I'd prefer it if we rode," Klara said. "Waywyrd wanted me to put some time in with Constant. Can you give me a leg up?"

The three of them looked at her dumbfounded.

"He's not been saddled," Karn said gesturing to the horse, who despite Klara's lack of attention, had not wandered off to graze.

"If he was saddled, I wouldn't need a leg up," Klara said, grasping a hank of mane at Constant's withers. "Waywyrd wanted me to try him without saddle or bridle."

"I'll help you on your mount, for the simple pleasure it will bring me to watch him unseat you," Ffearn said. Then he stood beside Constant and cupped his hands so she could place her foot in his palms. With his assistance, Klara quickly mounted Constant, who stood perfectly still the entire time.

"I'll walk Constant 'round the meadow while you saddle Night," Klara said. "It will give me a chance to see if he will behave." Karn shrugged and went to saddle his mount. Thorn and Ffearn watched as Klara wordlessly convinced Constant to walk.

By the time she and Constant returned to their starting position, Bardus had joined Thorn and Ffearn. Once the horse was stopped before them, he asked, "How are you commanding him?"

"As far as I know, I'm not," Klara said and patted the horse's neck. "Waywyrd said he believed Constant would respond to my whims without need for saddle or bridle. It seems the wizard knew what he was about, for I only thought, 'Let's walk around the meadow,' and around the meadow we went. I'm a little nervous about taking him out of camp like this, so it's good that Karn and Night will be along."

When Karn arrived on Night, Klara instinctively tapped her heels against Constant's side and followed them northward along the lake's edge. She chastised herself for having already forgotten she was supposed to be using her mind and endeavored to stay focused. The rocky point that marked the end of the bay had terrain too difficult for a horse to navigate, so they backtracked and crossed the ridge at a place with fewer rocks and a gentler slope. Returning to the water's edge, they were greeted by miles of shoreline filled with round stones worn smooth by the actions of the waves.

Several times during their ride Karn tried talking to her, but Klara shushed him each time saying she needed to concentrate. Karn reined in Night when they came to a section of beach where a large log, bleached white from the sun, lay near the water's edge. He dismounted and walked over to Klara and Constant. "If you'll not talk to me while we ride, then I'll not ride."

Slipping off Constant's back and into Karn's waiting arms, Klara said,

"I'm sorry. It's just that I have a good deal more to think about when I've got neither saddle nor bridle to hold on to." She did not tell him that she had been desperately trying to communicate with her horse and was more than a little irritated that the horse was not talking back. Nor did she tell him that she felt silly for trying and was beginning to think she had misunderstood Waywyrd.

Karn tied Night in the shade of a tree and Klara thought in Constant's direction, *"Stay close,"* though she was not sure it did any good. Then they sat with their backs against the log, watching the waves caress the shoreline and listening to the water burbling as it filtered through the rocks. Gulls squawked at their intrusion, destroying the serenity of the scene. While waiting for Karn to tell her what was on his mind, Klara watched the gulls land and bob on the waves, only to take wing and sail over the water before landing again.

After a moment of silence, Karn found his voice. "I've enjoyed the times I've got to play husband to you, both on the road and in towns, but I'd like it better if we were pretending no longer."

"Oh, good," Klara said, a wave of relief washing over her. "I'm tired of going about in a bloody skirt. It'll be nice to be able to ride in breeches again."

Karn let out a long sigh, letting his head fall back against the log. "No, Klara, you've missed my point. I don't want to pretend to be your husband. I want to be your husband, if you'll have me."

Klara was shocked. She was not expecting a proposal and it must have shown on her face because Karn continued, "I want to spend the rest of my life with you, Klara."

Words tumbled out of Klara, "Karn, I know you've wanted me in your bed since the day we met and I'll grant last night was very good, but I don't want to be your wife, or anyone's wife, for that matter. If it's sex you want you can have it, but I can't go and be your wife."

"It's not the sex I want," Karn said, straightening up to look her in the eyes, "it's you. When first we met I was taken by your beauty. I would have gladly bedded you that day and paid any price you asked. But since then I've gotten to know you. I admire your strength of will and determination. You have a tender heart and gentle soul that brings me comfort. I like that you are playful and are not ashamed to join in a bit of foolishness. And you get along so well with Ffearn and Thorn. I want you to be part of our family. I want to know that I will be able to wake each morning with you in my arms and I want you to know that I will do everything in my power to protect and provide for you."

Klara looked away. Since childhood she had been determined never to marry. Never to be bound to any man. The only person she ever relied on was herself. Why did Karn have to ruin a perfectly good arrangement with talk of marriage? After Thorn's good mood this morning, might he sever her contract and send her away if she refused?

She swallowed down the lump a rising in her throat and whispered, "I did not want this. Please, say no more."

Karn turned her to him and kissed her gently. When they parted he brushed a stray lock of hair from her face and whispered, "Tell me now you feel nothing for me."

"I don't know what I feel, Karn," Klara snapped. "I only know that I don't want to be a wife. The only thing I fear aside from motherhood is a cage. I need my freedom. If we married, I would be expected to stay home and bear heirs."

"Klara, I would never expect you to bear me children or deny you your freedom," Karn said, laying a hand on her shoulder. "Among my people Kelto and Kelta are equals. You will have as much right to land and industry as any Kelta. And you will always have your freedom."

"Just because you would never deny me freedom does not change the fact that every day my freedom would be a gift you could withhold," Klara said. "And should I become pregnant I would lose my freedom whether you would have it or not, for children saddle a woman with a responsibility that a man cannot know."

"Then I shall give myself to you anyway and you may take me however it pleases you, or not at all," Karn replied.

This was not something Klara had contemplated. She knew she could never be a wife, but then what, his whore? Clearly that was not what she wanted and she would never demand silver from him. Might she take him as a lover? And were they not lovers already? Klara leaned in to Karn and said, "If it be my choice, then I would very much like it if we could continue as we have been."

"Before or after last night?" Karn asked, the twist of smile just starting at the corner of his mouth.

"After," Klara said and leaned against him. Karn draped one of his strong arms around her shoulders, pulling her close and the two of them sat in companionable silence as they looked across the sun-dazzled water at the bobbing gulls.

Constant stayed close, but whether that had anything to do with her she did not know, and he behaved himself during the ride back to camp. Karn told her that he and Ffearn needed to check their snares and left her with her horse.

Seeing her and Karn return, Bardus came down to meet them. "I see that horse is still with you."

"Aye, I've not had any problems," Klara said, leaning forward and patting Constant appreciatively on the neck.

"Would you mind putting him through some paces while I watch," Bardus asked.

Klara agreed.

Bardus called out instructions which included backing, walking, turning right or left, and even a pattern that resembled the Oak Rune. Each time Klara thought her directions and Constant did more or less what she wanted. When they finished, she dismounted, and was confident that simply thinking "*stay close*" was enough to keep Constant nearby. The only part that left her stymied was that the horse never communicated anything back to her.

"That's very impressive," Bardus said. "How did you get him to do that?"

"I don't know," Klara said and shrugged. This left Bardus slightly confused, but Klara had no better explanation to offer. Leaving Constant to wander freely among the other horses, she headed toward her bedroll intent on taking a nap.

Klara woke to Ffearn's smiling face. He was lying opposite her, tickling her nose with the end of one of his braids. "Karn told me you have refused him. I guess that means there's still hope for me."

Klara laughed at him. "There's no hope for you."

"You are a hard woman," Ffearn teased, "and you will break both our hearts." Then jumping up he added, "Come, Karn says supper's ready."

Ffearn and Karn had managed to snare two fat fowl, which Karn had used to make a thick stew. As they were finishing supper, dark clouds rolled across the lake, bringing rain. Everyone scrambled to set-up the tents and store their gear under the tarp. Lightning flashed and thunder rolled across the sky as the winds picked up. Thankfully, neither she nor her tent mates had to stand watch, so they passed the night warm and dry.

⤐

The rain passed over them as quickly as it came. The tents and tarps were dry by the time breakfast was over and the company once again found themselves on the road. Over the next several days Klara and Karn argued multiple times. Karn insisted that Klara continue wearing the skirt. But with so few houses in the area, Klara thought the precaution was unnecessary and refused to ride in anything but breeches.

Klara was irritated, but more than irritated, she was worried. She often wondered about the trustworthiness of the chemist where they purchased the herbs. When gathering pennyroyal herself, she always increased the doses as an extra guard against pregnancy. The chemist who sold them the herbs had already dried it and divided it into dosages, each wrapped in their own packets.

Knowing that Thorn was eager for her to get pregnant only added another stressor. And while Karn was willing to let her take what precautions she thought necessary, she knew he also wanted children. This had more to do with their arguments than simply wanting to wear breeches, but she refused to discuss her concerns with Karn.

When it was once again Karn's turn to stand watch, Klara was grateful not to share a bed with him for at least part of the night. Instead, she found it easier to talk with Ffearn. Tonight another summer storm had left them huddling in their tent.

As they lay in bed together, Ffearn said, "I was counting on you and Karn to produce the required heir and a spare so I wouldn't have to. Now it seems you won't let him within a sword's length of you."

"Heir and a spare?" Klara asked, dismayed that one child was not enough and they were expecting her to bear more.

"Aye, it's not enough for a noble to produce an heir; there must be a second child in case tragedy befalls the first one," Ffearn explained, shifting on the rocky ground, trying to find a comfortable spot. "There is fear that the line of Duir is no longer intact because lordship wasn't properly passed from parent to child. Having an heir makes life a lot easier because you can pass land and title without having to involve the other clans. I mean to name Karn's children as my heirs."

"I don't intend to ever be a mother," Klara said, turning her back to him. "You'll have to produce your own heirs."

"That's not very likely," Ffearn said. "I'm not the type to take a wife. Thorn would if we could find a Kelta who would have him. I always assumed Karn was going to be the one to produce bastards. I'd be happy for him and gladly name them as my heirs. You might have been the mother of kings. Now you won't let him near you. Care to tell me what happened?"

"Nothing happened. Now, roll over so I can go to sleep." Klara sighed, realizing that was indeed the problem. Absolutely nothing had happened. There was no blood her cycle had not started. To keep from becoming emotional, she pulled the blanket tightly around her and bit her knuckle.

Ffearn obliged and rolled over so they could press their backs together as they slept.

The rain continued most of the night, stopping only a few hours before dawn. When Klara woke she had the tent to herself. Exiting the tent, she found camp deserted. Ffearn and Karn were nowhere in sight, though she figured that Thorn was awake somewhere if Ffearn was no longer standing watch.

Klara examined their tent, rubbing the fabric between her fingers. It was completely sodden and since the sky was still overcast, there was little hope of it drying anytime soon. They might be stuck in camp most of the day. Sighing, she headed for the trees, searching for a spot to empty her bladder. She squatted and relief welled inside her at the sight of blood, her bleeding had started. It was late, but better late than pregnant.

When she returned to camp Thorn and Bardus were sitting at the fire. Accepting the drinking horn from Thorn, Klara asked, "Where have Ffearn and Karn gone?"

"You're chipper this morning," Thorn said, ignoring her question and looking glum.

"Aye, I feel much better today. Did they go hunting?" Klara asked. "It looks like we'll be in camp awhile."

"If the sun doesn't show itself today we may have to camp here again tonight; the tents are quite wet," Thorn replied.

"Well, if we're stuck here all day I'd like to hunt and bathe," Klara said. "I'll grab my bow. Ffearn and Karn can't be very far ahead of me. Which way did they go?"

"You may hunt or bathe if you like," Thorn said. He was not looking her in the eye and his shoulders were slumped.

"Thorn," Klara asked, "have I upset you? Did Ffearn tell you of our conversation last night?"

Thorn spoke, but did not meet her eyes. "You have done nothing to upset me and I have not talked with Ffearn yet this morning." Then he walked back to his tent.

Klara turned to Bardus. "Have I done something wrong?"

"Nay, lass," Bardus said, "he just gets moody when the lads go off together."

"Why? And where have they gone?" Klara asked.

"When those two go off together it's best not to try finding them," Bardus said. "They'll want to be alone." Then Bardus left the fire and headed for the horses. Klara followed him and helped water and re-picket them.

Because Ruis was cooking today, Klara decided there was no point in hunting, as anything she killed would be ruined in his hands. Since no one was in the mood to talk, she went to talk with Constant. Constant never talked, but he listened. At least, she thought he listened. And she had no idea if he comprehended. But he did not walk away and today that would have to be enough. After brushing him she turned him loose to graze.

Shortly after midday, Ffearn and Karn returned to camp. It was evident they had bathed. Despite the fact that neither of them carried any game, they appeared to be in high spirits. Klara wrapped her arms around Karn and kissed him.

Karn was visibly surprised by Klara's change in disposition. Holding her at arm's length, he asked, "What's that for?"

"It's a grand day to be a Kelta," Klara said. "If you need more reason than that, I'll give you one later. What were you two doing? You've brought back no game."

"I couldn't bring myself to take a life knowing Ruis would ruin any meat we brought him," Ffearn replied, pulling the game bag over his head and taking a seat on a log near the fire.

"But if you weren't hunting, what have you been doing?" Klara asked. "I woke early and suspected you were either hunting or bathing and hoped to catch you up since you couldn't have been gone long."

Karn did not answer Klara immediately, but slipped his arm around her and walked toward their tent. Once they were away from the others Karn said, "You know Ffearn and I are close and have enjoyed each other's companionship since we were young. From time to time we will go off together because we wish for each other's company. Just as I would never deny your freedom, you must respect this." Then he added, "You said there was reason for your change in mood, care to share that reason now?"

"I have started my bleeding. I was worried before, but now my mind rests easy," Klara said. Why they needed to be alone to hunt and bathe was beyond her, but the request was not unreasonable. Although, the simple knowledge that she was not pregnant left her relieved enough that she might have granted any request.

"I'm glad you feel better, Klara," he said. "But you should know that even if you carried a child you have no reason to worry. I would care for you, as would Ffearn and Thorn."

"So I've been told," Klara replied, wrinkling her nose in disgust. "Ffearn seems to think I will bear the next king. I'm not fit to be the mother of nobility. I think Thorn may be right; it would be so much easier if you were just a farrier."

"As of this moment, I am just a farrier," Karn said, pulling her close. "You forget that I have been banished and have no land or title. There is no guarantee that Ffearn will be able to claim the title and Clan Duir lies in ruin; we may be tradesmen all our lives."

After they talked, the rest of the afternoon passed pleasantly. It wasn't until Ruis started the beans that the tents were deemed dry enough to fold up and pack away.

# Chapter 20
# Washing at the Widow's

Nder the bright summer sun, the Keltoi cheerfully sang as they rode. Having been chastised for not singing enough, Klara paid particular attention to the words, hoping to commit at least some of their songs to memory. None of the songs were fit for polite company. She could not imagine many Skolt women tolerating such verse in their presence and wondered if being a whore were a prerequisite for successfully living among Keltoi. Still the song had a catchy tune.

"To town we go a traveling,
with silver in our hand,
To find a tavern full of ale,
the finest in the land.

"A copper for the bard
to tell a merry tale,
Another for the beggar child,
who began to wail.

"THE REST FOR THE WENCH,

WHO BRINGS US PLEASURE SO,

WITH MONEY AND MANHOOD SPENT,

BACK TO HOME WE GO."


The vision of a horse's hoof with a stone wedged next to the frog appeared in Klara's mind, interrupting her concentration on the lyrics. Eventually, the word "*stone*" began to throb in her head.

Klara thought to Constant, *"Are you trying to talk to me?"*

Constant nodded his head in acknowledgement.

Encouraged by this, and feeling that she was finally making progress, Klara thought, *"Have you picked up a stone?"*

The horse shook his mane in a manner that she assumed meant no. Klara sighed, confused. It was progress, but not particularly useful progress.

After a short reprieve the vision returned along with the throbbing of the word "*stone.*"

Klara was irritated. *"Constant, if you haven't picked up a stone, then why put the vision in my head?"* In that instant another image appeared: Flax, Nuallan's gelding.

Klara turned to Karn and said, "We need to stop; Flax has picked up a stone." Then she directed her gaze at Constant and thought, *"Did I get that right?"*

Constant nodded his approval.

Karn called up the line, repeating what Klara said, but Nuallan insisted there was no change in the horse's gait. He added that there was no way that either Klara or Karn could tell if his horse had a stone from their position at the rear of the column and refused to stop for what he thought an unnecessary reason, so they continued.

"I tried," Klara said and patted Constant's neck. The horse blew with what she thought was frustration. "Well, it's not my fault they won't listen."

Karn gave her a worried look. "Are you talking to your horse?"

"Aye," Klara replied.

"And does he talk back to you?" Karn asked, a strange mix of bewilderment and concern evident on his face.

"Not generally," Klara said. "He's more of the strong silent type." Karn's brow furrowed in confusion, but he asked no more questions.

The company traveled well into the afternoon before coming across a stream where they could stop to water the horses. As soon as Constant heard the water, the word *"stone"* began pounding in Klara's head.

Looking at Karn, she asked, "Will you see to Nuallan's horse? I would feel better if you were to check each of Flax's hooves. It will do no harm and may do some good."

"If it will put your mind at ease, I will check them." Karn dismounted and passed her Night's reins, though he did not look entirely convinced.

Klara took the horses down for water while Karn sought out Nuallan and his mount. It was not long before Karn's voice rang out above the din of rushing water and the chatter of her companions. "Absent gods, Nuallan, how could you not feel a difference in the gait? The sole has been cut and the frog bruised. The animal's nearly lame!"

Klara raised an eyebrow at Constant. The horse gave her a look that plainly said, *"I told you so."*

When Karn returned for Night, he was clearly aggravated. "Put your skirt on. We're riding out to wherever the Goddess provides. Nuallan is determined to ruin his mount."

"I don't understand," Klara said.

Karn was already taking the braids out of his hair. "We have to ride ahead and hope for an inn because Nuallan will not consent to stop unless we can earn a little money and restock provisions at the same time. The horse needs to rest its hoof or it won't heal and we'll be down a mount. We should just stop now and not travel on hoping for lodging."

Klara reached for her saddlebag and headed for the privacy of the brush to change. A short time later she emerged looking very much like a farmwife. She and Karn mounted their horses, and taking a packhorse with them, rode ahead of the company. Soon they came to a small hamlet nestled along the banks of the Volga. Apart from the docks, the village consisted of a blacksmith shop, a mercantile, a few scattered houses, and one small inn.

"We won't all fit in that inn and I don't much fancy sleeping in the stables," Karn said.

Behind them shouting erupted as a merchant began beating a boy of about seven for pilfering a carrot. The boy's mother was hysterical, begging the merchant not to take the boy's hand, which, it seemed, was the punishment for thievery in this town.

Jumping from her saddle, Klara ran to the woman and wrapped her in a hug while crying out, "Cousin, we're here; so good to see you." The woman was startled enough to stop crying.

"Here, let my husband pay for the carrot," Klara said, waiving Karn over.

Hurrying the woman and child away from the merchant, Klara left Karn to pay for the produce. Walking them and the horses toward the edge of the hamlet, she quickly gathered as much information as she could. When Karn caught up to them, Klara whispered, "This woman's name is Vera, her son is Laszlo. She's a widow and I've just procured us a warm bed for the night. She lives some distance from town, but not too far."

The three of them talked out of earshot of the townsfolk while Laszlo looked from Klara to Karn with something akin to awe, since they had just saved him his hand. Continuing to pretend to be cousins, the pair of women headed to the widow's house. Needing to meet with Ffearn later and wanting to earn a little money, Karn remained in the village with hopes of picking up work. He kept Laszlo with him under the pretense of showing the boy how to behave like a man. Then, when he was ready to find Klara, he had Laszlo for a guide.

The walk gave Klara time to assess their host. Vera's woolen dress was worn but was still in better shape than most of the clothing she owned during her lifetime. Dark brown hair had come loose from Vera's bun and fell in wisps around her face. Stoutly built and lacking much in the way of curves, Vera was muscular from having done all the work around the farm since her husband had died.

About three miles from town they came upon the widow's cottage. Klara was grateful for the sight. The secluded home was surrounded by lush pasture. The fact that it was not visible from the road was an added bonus.

Vera's husband had been a farmer and left her better off than most. Gesturing toward the barn, Vera said, "I had to sell most of the livestock, so there's plenty of room to stable yer horses. All I've got now is a few goats and some chickens. You can use the pasture, too, if you'd rather turn them out."

"Thank you, Vera," Klara said. "I think they might enjoy some time in the pasture. I'll see to their tack, then join you inside."

After turning the horses loose to graze, Klara ducked through the doorway, letting her eyes adjust to the dim light. The main room of Vera's home contained the hearth, on which rested an iron spider, absent its pot. At first glance the house was tidy. Looking closer revealed evidence of neglect. Vera was unlikely to be able to afford to hire someone to make necessary repairs. The room was austere, with a row of nearly bare cupboards lining the wall. A churn and a table flanked by a pair of benches were the only pieces of furniture.

Looking up from her attempts at kindling a fire, Vera said, "Those curtains lead to rooms off the back. I've cleaned out Laszlo's. He'll sleep with me tonight so you and yer husband can take his room."

Vera cast her gaze over the empty cupboards. "Though, I ain't sure what I'm going to feed you."

Fortunately, Klara had brought the pack horse carrying the food with her. "You needn't worry about us consuming your stores," she said. "We have food enough for ourselves, and you, too. It's the least we can do to pay for the lodging and pasture."

Using her and Karn's supplies, Klara and Vera made a pot of beans and two loaves of butt bread. Vera had some goat cheese to contribute to the meal, a nice accompaniment for the bread. The women talked as they cooked.

"I'm worried about my boy," Vera said, kneading the bread. "Trouble will find him, if he don't find it first. I hate bringing him to town with me when I pick up and deliver the wash, but I can't leave him home either. I hope he don't cause any more trouble for yer man."

Klara stirred the beans. "I'm sure he'll be fine with Karn." However, she had no real notion of how well Karn and Laszlo would get on.

Sometime later, Karn arrived carrying Laszlo in his lap as he rode. In his arms the child cradled a cabbage and, beneath a mop of brown hair that matched his mother's, he wore a huge smile of satisfaction. Karn took the cabbage from Laszlo while his mother collected him from the saddle. Karn passed the cabbage back to the still grinning child before dismounting and putting his horse out to pasture with the others.

Supper was on the table when Karn entered the house. He handed Klara a handful of carrots and an onion, then took a seat on one of the benches, saying, "Smells good; I always prefer your cooking to mine."

Klara put the vegetables in the cupboard and joined them at the table.

"You do the cooking?" Vera asked amazed, as she dished up a bowl of beans for Laszlo and placed a hunk of bread on top.

"Only when I have to," Karn said between mouthfuls. "It's good you've got plenty of room here; the rest of the company will be along tomorrow."

"Rest of the company?" Vera asked, a tremor of fright in her voice.

"Why aren't they staying at the inn?" Klara asked.

"Nuallan refused to pay for more than one night and Thorn thought it best to get everyone out of town as quickly as possible after the game," Karn said, tearing off a hunk of bread. "That horse needs rest, so we'll have to stay somewhere until Bardus says it's on the mend. Thankfully, there's plenty of room in the barn. I've taken work at the blacksmith's. He thinks we're here to help your dear cousin with the farm for a few days before traveling on to visit your ailing mother. Tomorrow when I ride into town for work, I'll take Laszlo with me and pass him off to Ffearn. The boy will show them the way here. It's good this place is well off the road so we can keep the company hidden while the horse heals."

"How many more?" Vera asked, concerned. "I'm grateful for you saving my boy's hand, but we ain't got much. I can't feed you."

At the mention of him, Laszlo looked up from his meal for the first time. He had been using his bread to swipe every morsel of food from the bowl. It was a sad sight. Beans and bread was likely the best meal this child had eaten in a long while.

"Five others are coming," Karn said. "They will pay for the use of the barn and we're able to provide our own food."

"Otso's claws, five others!" Vera said, evoking the name of her god and clearly reconsidering having brought Klara home with her. "Why must you hide? You look to be decent folk, but are the others wanted by the law?"

"No, no," Karn assured her. "We needn't hide as such. If that were the case, they wouldn't be at the inn tonight. We just do our best not to attract attention to ourselves while we travel." This seemed to satisfy Vera.

After dinner, Karn saddled his horse and rode back into town for the game. Klara stood in the yard, watching until he was out of sight.

Vera walked up beside her and nodded toward Karn. "Where's he going?"

"To gamble," Klara said, "It's how we earn our money."

"Great Otso," Vera said, obviously confused and not at all inclined to trust her. "I thought he was a blacksmith."

"Ferrier," Klara replied, "though, his uncle is a smith. You'll meet him tomorrow. The money that comes from gambling goes into the company's coffers; the money he earns from other work he gets to keep for himself."

The two women went inside and washed the dishes. Laszlo was too excited to sleep so Klara told him about all the wondrous sights she had seen on their journey. She told him about the oak trees so tall she thought they touched the sky. Then she talked of the grasslands that stretched to horizon and how she feared getting lost among the grass if she strayed from the road. And she told him about the lake that shone silver in the moonlight and how she had never seen anything so lovely in all her life. Eventually, he nodded off and Vera put him to bed.

Unable to sleep, Klara intended to keep vigil by the fire. When Vera resumed her spot after putting Laszlo to bed, Klara said, "You should sleep. I expect Karn'll be late in coming home." But Vera remained in her chair, so the women sat in silence.

To Klara's surprise they heard horses' hooves on the road well before midnight. As a precaution, Klara drew her dagger before heading for the door. Vera armed herself with a long stick of firewood and followed.

The night was dark, with only the faintest sliver of a crescent moon for light. Though they could hear the horse, it was a long time before they were able to see it. Klara did not relax even after discerning Karn's outline among the shadows. There was no reason for him to return so soon unless there had been trouble in town.

Sick with worry, Klara went to meet him. "Was there a fight?"

"Nah," he said, "Kineshma isn't much of a town. There weren't enough people to support a game. I brought home little more than I started with, and I don't think Ffearn will fare much better. I figured I'd better not get greedy since my employer was at the table and I had a lovely wife to come home to."

"Will this result in another fight between you and Ffearn?" Klara asked.

"I don't think so," Karn said. "There really isn't a whole lot of money in the town. The game was nearly over when I left. Nuallan won't be happy, but then he never is."

Karn stabled his horse while the women returned to the house. When Karn made it into the house Vera, was already in her room. Klara led him to their room. As the curtain fell in place behind them, Karn took her in his arms and whispered, "I'm glad I'll be able to have you to myself tonight."

With a child in the next room, they did no more than hold each other, but for Klara and Karn that was enough.

In the morning, Karn asked Klara to trim his hair so he would be better able to pass for a Mordva, if the women were to be cousins, he needed to change his disguise to look less like a Skolt. While he shaved, Klara and Vera made breakfast: eggs, toast, and the remainder of the goat cheese. After breakfast Karn rode out with Laszlo again seated before him in the saddle.

Seeing that Vera was nervous about letting her child ride off with a stranger, Klara said, "You needn't worry, your boy will be back soon."

Vera sighed. "Well, I've got washing to do and at least this way he won't be under foot." Arms loaded with laundry, Vera headed into the pasture, which was bisected by a bubbling brook. Klara followed with her and Karn's extra clothing.

Poles had been erected near a pool that was just over knee deep. These served as the clothes lines. The pair of women were kneeing on the streambank, scrubbing the laundry and slapping it against the rocks when the rest of the company rode up the lane. Ffearn was at the head of the column, a wide-eyed Laszlo riding with him.

Vera raised her head, looking over party with mixture of consternation and apprehension. "Otso's tooth and claws!" she exclaimed. "You didn't tell me they were Kenetlo."

"I forgot," Klara said, "it happens sometimes."

Ringing out the garment she had been washing, Vera gave her a stern look. "How can you forget yer own husband is half Kenetlo?"

"Oh, he's not half Kenetlo, he's all Kenetlo," Klara said, standing and shaking out the tunic she had been scrubbing. "I forget I'm not a Kelta so I don't think to mention it to others." Vera looked at her as though she were mad and went to collect her child. Klara followed.

Ffearn dismounted and took Klara in his arms, spinning her around. "You look quite domestic here on a farm. I see why my brother was so chipper this morning."

Klara laughed. "I think it had less to do with me than the eggs he had for breakfast. Now let go of me so I can introduce you to our host."

Klara made the introductions to a rather standoffish Vera while Laszlo entwined himself in his mother's skirt. Then she showed them to the barn where they would be sleeping. After they turned the horses loose and the men were milling about the yard, Klara began assigning tasks.

"Ffearn, you should go hunting," Klara said. "It would be nice to have some meat for dinner." Not needing to be told twice, Ffearn collected his game bag and happily disappeared.

Turning to Ruis, Klara said, "You have an ax and that woodpile is woefully insufficient for all the cooking that needs done." Ruis gave her a stern look, so she added, "I know… The ax one uses to fell a man is kept apart from the axes one uses to fell a tree. There's got to be another ax or saw around here somewhere—find it and go cut firewood. And take Thorn and Nuallan with you."

Ruis stood his ground. "As much as I like a woman who can give orders, I prefer it when you've got yer breeches on and are wearing yer dagger while you do it." Klara did not dignify that with a response and waved him away.

Bardus was busy, hunched under Nuallan's chestnut gelding, soaking Flax's hoof. Since he was already occupied, he avoided being assigned any other tasks. With the Keltoi out from underfoot, Klara returned to helping Vera with the wash.

Vera seemed dismayed at the sight of so many men coming and going in her yard and after a brief pause asked, "Do all Skolt women command men so?"

Klara snorted out a laugh. "If I had any real power to command them, I wouldn't be the one rubbing my hands raw with the wash."

As loads of wood were brought to the yard and stacked against the house, Vera became accustomed to the sight of the Keltoi and relaxed a little. By the afternoon, Laszlo had gotten over his awkwardness, too, and was following the Keltoi around pestering them with all kinds of questions about their journey. The lad would not consent to stay at the house with his mother while she laundered the villagers' clothing. Much to the dismay of Nuallan, Laszlo crawled into the cart and begged to be allowed to ride out to get the next load of wood.

When Ffearn returned from his hunt with three quail and a satchel of raspberries, Laszlo began questioning him about how Ffearn could be a Kelto and his brother a Skolt. Klara laughed and left Ffearn to figure that out on his own.

With the majority of her traveling companions back at the farm, Klara stripped to her shift and gathered clothing from the others, leaving the men to sit about in their undershirts and drawers. By washing them herself, she could be certain the cloths were actually soaped and not just given a passing rinse. And, with Vera for company, it felt like less of a burden to wash everyone's clothing.

Since the only person left on the property fully clothed was his mother, Laszlo also stripped and ran about in his drawers. The lad handed Klara his clothes just as he saw the others do. When Klara accepted them, she pointed at Ffearn and said, "You see that Kelto? He can tell you far more stories about journeys and adventures than I can, because he's been to more places than I have."

When Ffearn was finally rid of the child, he came over to where Klara was busy washing and said, "You are devious and underhanded. The lad never stops talking or moving, but mostly he does both at once."

"Well, you were the one so keen on having heirs around. I thought you should know what it'd be like," Klara said.

"I hardly think Karn's young will be much like that," Ffearn said.

"No," Klara replied, pushing another tunic deep into the creek. "I expect they'd be worse."

"In that case, I will produce my own heirs," Ffearn said. Then winking he added, "Are you free tonight?"

Klara laughed at him. "I am never free and you cannot afford me. Now go on."

Once all the laundry was hung up to dry, Klara went inside and began supper.

Vera sat at the table mending. "That boy'll sleep tonight. I ain't seen him so happy in ages. Those Keltoi are quite good with him."

Klara was glad Vera's opinion of the Keltoi had improved because Bardus had told her the horse needed at least another day, and possibly two, to rest its hoof.

While Vera continued her work, Klara made bread. After setting the loaves aside to rise, she chopped the cabbage and seasoned it with vinegar, oil, salt, and pepper to make a slaw. Then she seasoned the quail and put them on to roast. Delighted at the simple pleasure of having access to a proper hearth for cooking, she used the raspberries Ffearn had picked to make pastries. The carrots and onion Karn brought from town the previous day she cut up and put in a cauldron to boil. Moving everything aside to stay warm, she headed outside, desperate to escape the fire's heat.

When Karn rode up he was greeted by the sight of the entire company in their drawers. Ruis and Ffearn were giving Laszlo lessons in hand to hand combat while everyone else sat in the grass watching.

"I see you cannot be trusted to be left on your own," Karn called to them, "for you will return to your uncivilized ways."

"Tell that to your woman," Ruis said, rebuffing Laszlo's charge with no more than the palm of his hand. "For it was she who sent us out to work like dogs all day then stole our clothing and told us to mind this young pup."

"Is that true?" Karn asked as he dismounted.

"Every word," Klara said. "They got in a cord of wood and made repairs to the house as partial payment for the use of the barn. Then I made them strip so I could wash their clothes, and I'll have your clothes before the night is out. Go wash up, I'll put supper on the table."

When the Keltoi filed into the little house to fill their bowls, Ffearn carried a cask of ale, which he tapped. The drinking horn was passed around and the company was merry while they ate and drank. After supper, Karn and Ffearn settled up with Nuallan. Neither had earned much gambling and the innkeeper paid with the ale, so they had not covered their expenses. Fortunately, they still had plenty of funds, though Nuallan did not see it that way.

The men sat outside quaffing ale and swatting mosquitos in the cool evening while Klara washed Karn's clothes. Stopping to wring them out, she noticed that Laszlo, who had been so shy of the Keltoi that morning, had found his way into Karn's lap and was asleep. Clearly all the excitement of the day had been too much for him and he was plumb tuckered out. The sight stirred maternal feelings in her that she had not known existed.

After hanging the clothes on the line, she walked over to where Karn sat and kissed him on the forehead. "Put the child in his bed," she said softly, "then join me in mine."

∽

Klara made porridge for breakfast and told the lot of them that they were to go without drawers or undershirts today, but could have the rest of their clothing back. She intended to wash whites that afternoon when she returned from the village.

To keep up the pretense that Klara was Vera's kin, she accompanied Vera into town to deliver the laundry. Before they left, every member of the company instructed Laszlo to mind his manners, keep his mouth shut, and not say one word about the Keltoi or do anything that might cause trouble in town. Karn put Laszlo on Night and led the horse, holding Klara's hand as they walked. Vera walked beside them carrying the laundry as they made their way into the village.

Most of Vera's customers were happy to have the laundry back so soon. They commented on how well behaved Laszlo was and attributed it to having a man in the house. Vera told them that extra hands made the work go faster and agreed that Karn had been a good example. Klara smiled to herself each time this was repeated, knowing it was not a man setting a good example but a heavily armed company of Keltoi, who put the fear of the gods into the lad.

The exchange did not go as well at the last house. It was two bachelors and Klara did not like the looks of them. She knew men and these two were trouble.

The taller of the two, a gangly ill-kempt man said, "Yer sure a pretty one. Don't look nothin' like yer cousin."

"You wash good," said the shorter, greasy-haired man, as he made a show of inspecting his garments, "but to please a husband you need to be right good at 'ther things. From the looks of you, I'd say y'er good at all kinds o' things."

"What say, you let cousin Vera go on an' you stay with us?" the tall man said. "Pretty thing like you needs a man 'round to protect her."

"I have a husband," Klara replied. "He's working for the smith. Now, if you'll excuse us, we need to be on our way." That bit of information got their attention and Klara was able to usher Vera and Laszlo away, but she knew Vera would always have trouble with them.

When the two women returned to the farmstead, another cord of wood had been stacked against the house. Klara sent the men out fishing and told them to pick any berries they came across. The brook that crossed Vera's pasture was too small for anything other than fry, but the river was not far off.

Letting Laszlo go with them, Vera seemed grateful for the reprieve. Milk from the last couple of days had been saved. Vera intended to make cheese while Laszlo was out of the house.

Klara was at the stream laundering the company's whites when the two troublemakers came lumbering up the lane. Reaching her, the taller of the two said, "We went to the blacksmith to see if'n you had a husband and sure 'nough there he was. What we can't figure is how a handsome woman like you ended up with a man ugly as 'im?"

The shorter man ran his fingers through his greasy hair and said, "We seen 'im at the dice game. Plays right well, he does. We reckon he must o' won you in a round o' dice. 'Cause there's no 'ther way to explain how the two o' you ended up together. I'm guessin' there's some Goth trader out there on the Volga who was mighty sorry to lose his favorite thrall."

The taller man gave her a malicious smile. "I bet yer man'll be right happy t' know we've taken it upon ourselves to show you a good time, for we doubt he could please you."

"Stay away from me," Klara said, backing away. "Go back the way you came before you do something you'll regret."

The tall man grabbed her by the arm. "The only one who'll have regrets is you. But if you'll be nice to us, we'll be nice to you an' that husband of yers. If you raise a fuss, that man of yers won't make it home tonight, you understand?"

"Where's Vera an' the boy?" the shorter man asked.

"Vera's inside. Laszlo went fishing," Klara said.

"Well, ain't that nice," the tall man said, smiling again. "The two of us can get t' know the two o' you real private like, without any interruptions." Then still holding her arm, he pushed her toward the house.

Klara went willingly, which surprised them. They were expecting a fight. This would work to her advantage. If they expected her to be meek and submissive, she might catch them off guard and be able to grab a knife.

"Great Otso!" Vera shrieked, the moment they were through the door.

Her frightened cry drew their attention long enough for Klara to seize the butcher knife. Pulling Vera behind her, Klara said, "Leave or I'll cut you through."

The tall man eyed her severely and said, "If we leave, you'll never see yer husband again, but you'll see us every washday an' we'll give you more than just our wash."

The shorter man smiled at her saying, "Put the knife down an' I'll be real friendly toward you."

Klara lowered the knife, but did not let go of it. The shorter man edged toward her. When he made a grab for her, Klara struck, quickly cutting him from sternum to navel. Pushing him aside, she turned on the taller man, who launched himself at her. All her practice with Ruis paid off; Klara ducked and took out the man's knees, sending him sprawling onto the floor. Redoubling the attack, she whirled, putting her knee in his back and grabbing his hair with her free hand, raising his head to expose his neck, which she cut without hesitation. Vera cowered in the corner, screaming as blood gushed from the man and pooled on the floor.

In the other corner of the room, the shorter man was struggling to his feet, his guts spilling down his front. Klara walked over to him and said, "I will ease your suffering, which is more than you deserve." Then she cut his throat, too. Searching their purses, Klara found a few loose coins. These she put in her own purse, but the men had nothing else of value.

All the while Vera had been rocking in the corner, screaming hysterically. Straightening, Klara walked over to Vera and slapped her hard. The next scream caught in her throat. Vera's eyes were as red and wild looking as the blood-smeared mark Klara had left on her cheek. She took a few huffing breaths, then quieted.

"Get the cart," Klara said as she surveyed the scene. "We need to move these bodies and clean up this mess."

Once the men were loaded, Klara hitched two of the pack horses to the cart and drove it into the woods far enough that it was not visible from the house. When she returned, she and Vera cleaned and scrubbed the house so there was no trace of blood left anywhere inside.

Stripping bare, Klara first washed Vera, who had stopped speaking altogether, and sent the woman inside to don clean clothing. Then she washed herself. Still bare, she remained outside to finish laundering the clothing. Now that the threat was gone and she was no longer acting on instinct, the magnitude of what just happened settled on her like a weight, leaving her numb.

Klara had hung out all the whites and was washing her and Vera's bloody things when the Keltoi returned from their fishing expedition. Ffearn whooped when he saw her. "Do you never wear clothes?"

Klara looked at him with blank eyes and said, "I need you to dig a hole."

"Absent gods, Klara, what's wrong?" Ffearn asked.

Klara pointed in the direction of the cart. "Go there; you'll find it, but don't bring the lad," she said. "Take shovels, as many as you can find."

Sending Laszlo inside to his mother, the men headed in the direction she indicated. She was scrubbing the blood from her dress when she heard Thorn roar. It was a primal sound filled with hatred and anguish. Of all of them, only he was capable of such a sound.

When they returned Klara was just hanging out the last of her and Vera's things. Thorn shook, looking as though he might break apart. Waves of tumultuous emotions filled his eyes. Placing a hand on each of her arms, he asked, "Did they—"

Klara interrupted him before he could finish. "No, I stopped them first."

"But you're bleeding," Bardus said.

Between Klara's legs her thighs showed crimson. "It is just the blood of my cycle. They never got close," she said in a subdued voice.

Pulling her to him, Thorn held Klara so tight he nearly crushed the air out of her. When he let her go, Klara just said, "I need to wash." She turned, took a rag off the line, and headed for the stream to wet it and clean between her legs before she dressed.

Afterward, the men gave her a wide berth. Bardus cooked supper without having been asked and the rest of them gathered their things off the line as they dried and either put them on or put them away. Seeing Ffearn in the barn, Klara headed his direction. He had just donned his freshly laundered drawers and was putting on his breeches. She stopped him before he managed to reach for his shirt. Standing before him, Klara absently mindedly ran her fingers through his chest hair. He gave a look that was both puzzled and concerned.

"It's not true what Ruis says, that the knives for butchering hens and the knives for butchering men should be kept separate. The butchery I did today, I did with a kitchen knife. I didn't have time to get to my dagger," she said, not looking him in the eye, but continuing to follow the path of her fingers as she traced the outline of his pecks.

Ffearn raised his hands to her arms and said, "I know it wasn't Karn's arrow that pierced the last man we saw dead and you were not so affected then. What has made this different?"

"It's my fault," she said. "They only wanted sex. If I'd given it to them, they would be alive and Vera wouldn't be sitting by the fire with that tortured stare. But I refused and now I have put all of you in danger. It's a small village; they'll be missed before long."

Ffearn held her to him. "You cannot think like that. They had no right to come here and demand that of you. You only did what you had to do, there is no wrong in that."

"I'm just a whore, Ffearn," Klara said. "If I'd done my job, everything would be fine."

Klara tried to push him away, but he refused to let her go. She shuddered and then added, "They said if I wouldn't have sex with them, they'd kill Karn on his way home tonight. I thought I was protecting him, but what I have done is so much worse because now the town folk will think he killed those men." This time Ffearn let her go when she pushed away.

After collecting her clothes from the line, Klara returned to the barn seeking Constant's company. Thorn sat alone in a pile of hay that had likely been his bedding.

Calling to Klara, he asked her to sit beside him. "Ffearn tells me you blame yourself," he said. Klara made no reply but laid her head in Thorn's lap and cried herself to sleep.

When she woke it was to the sound of Thorn and Karn talking.

"Klara is not well, we should leave immediately," Thorn said.

"No," Klara said, taking them by surprise as she sat up. "If we leave they will suspect our guilt and come after us. With Nuallan's horse lame, we cannot outpace them. We must stay and damper suspicion."

"The smith knows they were on their way here," Karn said. "They stopped by and made some rather vulgar comments before they left. When these men don't return, the villagers will suspect that either you or I killed them."

"They only know they were headed this way," Klara said. Then she looked at Thorn and asked, "Did you pick any berries?"

"Aye," Thorn said, "but I fail to see how that is relevant."

"It's relevant because those men never found us," Klara said. "Karn can tell the smith Vera and I weren't home this afternoon because we went berry picking after leaving town. He can say that as far as we know no one was at the house, or if they were, they left before we returned. Perhaps the smith will think that after finding no one here they went carousing elsewhere. I can make some pastries and send them with Karn tomorrow as evidence of our absence. It will buy us a little time, but that may be all we need for the horse to mend."

The trio agreed that Klara's idea was probably the best for casting aside suspicion. Anyone who had killed two men the night before was unlikely to return to work the following day.

## CHAPTER 21

# MURDERERS ON THE RUN

ERA SEEMED TO have recovered from the previous day's ordeal. Feeling somewhat better herself, Klara wanted to send everyone fishing again, but Thorn insisted that he and Ruis stay behind for protection. Freeing themselves of their tunics, the two Keltoi busied themselves making repairs to the barn.

Staying inside, the pair of women made bread and pies. Vera was amazed at how much and how well the company ate; she and Laszlo had been subsisting on little more than beans since the death of her husband. About midday, the rumble of a wagon garnered their attention. Rising from their places at the hearth, the women went outside to see what their visitors wanted.

A wagon containing four men pulled into the yard. Two more men followed on horseback. Klara recognized the driver as the merchant who wanted to take Laszlo's hand.

Setting the brake, the merchant stepped down from the wagon and addressed Klara. "Your husband doesn't seem the least concerned about the visitors you had yesterday and is at this very moment happily working with the smith. If it'd been my wife, I'd be bloody mad that the likes of those two paid her a call. And more, several of our wives noticed you didn't wear a ring when you delivered the wash yesterday. So we're guessing you're not his wife, but just a common whore. Since you insist on sinning, we figure you can do it in hell, and not here among decent folk."

Klara began to protest, but one of the men on horseback pushed back his hat and said, "We don't take to immoral behavior in Kineshma. Even if you ain't a whore, you're livin' in sin. Elah would not be pleased. Where's the boy? He needs punished for his sins, too."

Vera looked like a cornered mouse before a pride of prowling cats. She started to answer, but Klara cut her off.

"He's in the house," Klara lied. "I'll fetch him."

Heart racing as she abandoned Vera, Klara forced herself to walk calmly toward the house. Once inside, she darted for the room she and Karn shared, grabbed her bow, and pulled the quiver over her head. She did not trust Vera to remain calm for very long.

When Klara re-emerged in the doorway, her bow was drawn and an arrow nocked. Loosing the arrow, she knocked the man who had just addressed her from the saddle with a killing shot. Vera screamed and bolted for the trees. The merchant ran for cover. Klara pulled another arrow from her quiver, drew and let it fly, killing him, too. Ruis and Thorn, still shirtless, charged in from behind the house, swords in hand.

The remaining mounted man wheeled his horse, attempting to escape. Running from her position at the door, Klara sought a spot where she would have a better shot. Sounds of violence erupted behind her.

When she cleared the wagon, she took aim and released her arrow. It hit the fleeing rider in the back. He crumpled and fell from the saddle. Fortunately, the animal was well-trained and stopped running. The last thing they needed was a riderless horse running through the village alerting the town to trouble. Shouts from the men behind her made the horse skittish. By the time she caught the animal, Thorn and Ruis had dispatched the remaining three men.

Using the back of his arm, Thorn wiped blood from his face and asked, "Disciples of Elah?"

"I think so," Klara said. A quick inspection of the wagon proved she was right; it contained the beams to make the cross and the wood for the pyre.

Winded and leaning on his sword, Ruis said, "I believe we just killed every man in the village except the smith. You want to leave them for their women to find or are we going to bury them, too?"

"We're going to get that cross in the ground and build a pyre," Klara said.

"Are you mad?" Ruis shouted. "We light a pyre the smoke will bring Karn running! Then the whole village will know something happened out here."

"That's what I'm counting on," Klara said, and then she told them her plan.

Klara knew the villagers expected a column of smoke and that such a column meant the menfolk would be engaged for quite a while, so they would not be missed immediately. She intended to use that time to gather their belongings and flee. The stray horses were rounded up and put in the pasture with their own animals. After searching the men's bodies and taking their purses, Klara helped Ruis and Thorn put the three she killed on the pyre.

"Why three?" Ruis asked, huffing under the dead weight of the merchant. "Why not just two, for you and Vera?"

Klara dropped the man she was dragging and wiped sweat from her brow. "Because Karn is going to light out of town like the wind as soon as he sees the smoke and everyone will know that. Since the menfolk were supposedly burning me and Vera, they'll assume Karn ended up in the flames too. That's why we need three bodies. No one knows you lot are here and no one will suspect Karn or me of murder if our charred remains are lying in the yard."

The three Ruis and Thorn killed were left where they lay to show signs of a skirmish. Klara hoped the two already buried in the woods would be fingered for the killings.

The fishing party returned before Klara had time to light the pyre and was shocked to find the yard full of dead bodies. At Klara's direction, the pyre was lit and most of Vera's belongings were loaded in the wagon. There was no reasonable way to leave her behind since she was expected to be dead and burned. A hallmark of an Elah killing was that the house was left intact. But if this were also the sight of a botched robbery, having Vera's belongings turn up missing might not be out of place.

Karn arrived riding Night at a run, the horse thickly lathered. Pulling the horse up hard, he dismounted, grabbed Klara, and held her to him. "I worried when I saw the smoke; I came as quick as I could!"

"I'm alright, but we must hurry if we are to be well away from here by nightfall," Klara said. "Water your horse and rub him down while we finish packing."

The yard was a bustle of activity as belongings were fetched and gear was packed. It was decided that Nuallan ought to drive the wagon, since his horse still had not recovered and should not be ridden. The gray Kelto was quite put out by this.

"I should not have to drive," Nuallan protested as he crated a chicken. "There are other horses. I can ride one of those."

"Someone has to drive, and it might as well be you," Ffearn said, tying the head nanny goat to the rear of the wagon. "We could have avoided Kineshma altogether if you checked the hoof and removed the stone when first told of the problem."

Nuallan harrumphed and stuffed another chicken into the crate, then motioned to Ruis to tie the lid down. Neither Vera nor Laszlo knew how to ride, so they were loaded into the wagon alongside the crate of chickens. Klara led the three pack horses and Bardus led Nuallan's mount and the two saddle horses they just acquired. Thorn and Ruis rode at the head of the party, Ffearn and Karn rode aft, each pair alert for possible threat. When the party departed, it was a wagon, three goats, nine chickens, four horses, and two people larger than it had been.

Determined to travel as far as possible before the light gave out completely, the wagon rumbled on, accompanied by the rumbling of the party's stomachs. There was no more than a thin copper line on the horizon when they finally stopped for the night. Supper consisted of jerky, fresh bread, and the pies she and Vera made earlier. It was an unusual meal, but given the unusual nature of the day they were lucky to even have a meal. There was no singing or campfire that night. Eager for sleep, everyone headed for their bedrolls.

With Vera and Laszlo in camp, Klara and Karn maintained the pretense of being married, which meant they shared a bedroll and Ffearn slept alone. Wrapped snugly in their blankets, Klara asked, "Will this cause problems between you and Ffearn?"

"I don't believe so," Karn said. "This is an unavoidable situation." Then Karn looked at Klara, concern in his eyes. "A lot has happened these last couple days and you have not been yourself. Tell me what I can do to make things better."

"I feel that the entire situation is my fault," Klara said, feeling overwhelmed. "And there is no way to make it better. I shouldn't have gone to town with Vera because the women noticed I didn't wear a ring. And when those men showed up, I should have just had sex with them and sent them on their way. I've endangered all of you and forced Vera from her home."

"Klara, I would not have you give yourself to such men," Karn said. "The fault is mine, not yours, for I have not been the husband I should have been."

"But you are not my husband," Klara said.

"I told you that I would protect and provide for you and I failed to do that," Karn said, pulling her close. "As a result you've killed five men in the last two days. When we ride into a town or village and say we are married, then I need to be more aware of how a husband should act. The fault lies in my own shortcomings, not yours." Karn paused and buried his head in her hair. "You have no idea how worried I was when I saw the smoke. I was afraid I lost you."

Thorn woke everyone at first light and passed out handfuls of dried fruit and nuts. Klara doubted he slept at all. While Vera and Laszlo milked the goats, everyone else huddled around the empty fire ring discussing what to do with the woman and her child.

"Yesterday we left in haste," Thorn said. "Luckily, we encountered no other travelers and that is a good thing, because looking like the band of misfits that we were, we would have attracted attention."

Around her, Klara saw heads bobbing in agreement as Thorn paused for a handful of nuts.

"Karn," Thorn continued, "I want you to continue playing the role of a farmer, which means you'll drive the wagon. Klara, Vera, and Laszlo can walk and drive the goats. My goal is for it to look like Karn hired the rest of us as guards while he moved his household."

"I'd rather ride," Klara interjected. "All Skolt women ride."

"But Mordva women don't," Vera said, arriving at their circle with a full milk pail. "You might as well drink this now. The way that wagon bumps, it'll slosh all out the sides before we stop for the night."

"Vera's right," Karn said. "If we're pretending you are cousins, then Mordva you must be."

"But what are we supposed to do with Nuallan?" Bardus asked. "Flax still isn't fit to ride."

"I'll not walk with the women," Nuallan grumbled, rubbing his backside. "My bones are too old for such abuse and riding in the wagon is worse for all the bumps and jolts."

"You can ride one of the newly acquired saddle horses," Thorn said. "Now it's time we were on our way."

Thorn and Ffearn rode at the head of the column, Ruis and Bardus rode aft. The wagon, the goats, and Nuallan, leading a long string of horses, were in the middle. Laszlo soon tired of walking. Since Constant was the best behaved, Klara allowed Laszlo to ride him, provided he did not annoy or abuse the horse.

As she and Vera drove the goats, Klara asked, "Do you have any kinfolk nearby?" She doubted Vera wanted to stay with the company indefinitely. Besides, the wagon, chickens, and goats slowed their progress tremendously and they needed to move quickly if they were going to outrun rumors of murder.

"My family lives to the south," Vera said. "But going there would require traveling back through Kineshma." She shook her head at the thought and considered for a moment. "My aunt married a man from a western town called Timerevo, but I have no idea where it's located."

Klara instructed Laszlo to ride ahead and ask Ffearn to come back and talk with her. The lad quickly did as he was told.

When Ffearn followed Laszlo back, Klara said, "Unless you know a town by the name of Timerevo, we'll need to make inquiries. Vera has family there and that's where we can leave her." Ffearn had never heard of the town, so he returned to his place and conferred with Thorn.

The party stopped at the next village. Karn set the brake and hopped down. He took Laszlo off Constant and, before handing him to Vera, ran through a list of rules, which mostly consisted of not getting more than a swords-length away from his mother or the wagon and not speaking unless spoken to. The lad had seen far too much over the last few days, and they did not want to risk him giving anything away by chatting with the locals. Then he went to ask after the whereabouts of Timerevo.

Klara watched as Thorn, Ffearn, and Karn each entered a different building. Thorn chose the mercantile, Ffearn the tavern, Karn the smith. Then Nuallan caught her eye. He was supposed to be tending the horses, but he just disappeared through the doors of the apothecary. Even stranger, Nuallan was the last one to reemerge, and when he did he was carrying a parcel which he placed in his saddlebag.

"Timerevo is three days from here," Karn said, swatting a nanny who had jumped into the driver's seat. "We travel two days by this road, then turn off and take a smaller road. The town's about a day's ride from the crossroads. It's much larger than Kineshma, Vera. I think that bodes well for you." The nanny bleated at the offense but hopped down.

"How is going to a larger village good for me?" Vera asked.

"Large towns usually have more money flowing through them. Since you're a rich widow, your relations will be more likely to take you in and the townsfolk less curious about your wealth," Karn said. Then he put Laszlo back on Constant and took his seat in the wagon.

Vera waited until they were out of town before questioning Klara. "Karn said I was a rich widow, but I have so very little. What makes him think my relations will take me?"

"You're richer than you know," Klara said, swatting a goat on its rump to discourage it from stopping to nibble the brush. "Most widows don't have a team and wagon, plus you've got the chickens, goats, and what we've managed to pack in the wagon besides. The Keltoi intended to work off part of our room and board. Unfortunately, someone else will be enjoying the mended barn and all that cordwood. This morning Thorn said you'll be getting some coins when we stop tonight."

"By Otso's claws," Vera exclaimed, suddenly looking like being forced from her home was a banner change of luck. "You cannot mean to give me coin and the team as well."

"The wagon slows us down," Klara said. "We'll take the two saddle-horses, though. If we gave you all the horses you'd look too rich. That might cause people to ask questions. If we keep the saddle-horses, it'll seem less suspicious all around."

Thorn did not stop at midday but kept the company moving until they came across a reasonable place to camp for the night. Lighting a fire, Thorn got supper started as Klara and Bardus looked after the horses. Ruis and Nuallan went fishing while Ffearn and Karn disappeared into the woods. Vera was left to look after her goats and chickens. By the time Klara finished with the horses, Ffearn and Karn returned, each carrying large armfuls of firewood.

Sitting near the blaze, Klara was joined by a sheepish looking Vera who asked, "These Keltoi don't let you do much by way of work, and at the house they readily took orders from you. Are you a noble woman?"

Klara laughed. "No, I am simply one of the company; we all share the work. Tonight I'll stand watch and tomorrow is my turn to cook. The day after that is Ruis's turn. I expect he'll try getting you to do the cooking, though. He pawned his turn off on me the day we met."

Their conversation was cut short by Laszlo, who excitedly asked his mother to come down to the creek and see the fish he caught. Klara smiled to herself and worried for Vera. After spending so much time among Keltoi, there was little hope of the lad growing up to be a respectable man. At least the somber mood of late kept the men from singing on the road. Who knows what the lad would pick up and later repeat?

While they were eating supper, three young men rode into view. The Keltoi were instantly alert, watching them approach. The riders showed no sign of fight but showed no sign of passing the camp by either. When they were near enough, one of the young men shouted their helloes and asked permission to join them.

Thorn warily waved them in and asked, "Why do you wish to camp near our company?"

The oldest of the three, a tall man with sandy brown hair said, "Yesterday we passed through a village where every man except the smith had either been killed or vanished. Some say it was witchcraft, others said it was demons. Either way, we'd feel safer sleeping where there are more folk about."

Thorn asked them a few more questions. Once he was satisfied they were not a threat and no one from Vera's village was looking for their company, Thorn said their party could share the clearing. Not wanting to encourage the young men to join them at the fire, the company ate, washed the dishes, and retired early.

Snuggled beneath their bedroll, Karn asked, "Can I hold you tonight?"

Surprised by his question, Klara said, "Of course, you always do."

Karn pulled her to him. She thought he would spoon her as he often did, instead he slipped the collar of her shift down and cupped her breast. The scruff of his beard trailed along her skin sending shivers down her spine. She met his lips and tasted a hunger in the kiss.

When they parted, Karn said, "I've purchased something for you." Then he withdrew two thin silver rings from his purse. "I wanted to save up and get you a finer ring, but it seems you need one now." Taking the smaller of the two rings he placed it on her finger. "Will you do me the honor of wearing this?"

Klara admired the ring, and noticing the other still in his palm, asked, "And what of that one?"

"This one I will wear if ever you decide you'll have me," he said.

Would she have him? He was offering protection, comfort, and security, all things she had never had before and desperately wanted right now. Over the course of their journey he had repeatedly sought to keep her from harm. Of course she would have him.

Klara kissed him and slipped the ring over his finger. There was no ceremony or announcement, but Klara needed none. She knew that from this moment forward Karn would be her husband and she his wife.

When Thorn woke Klara for her turn at the watch, Karn refused to let her go. "I'll stand," he said. "You've stood for me before and I'll feel better knowing you're safe in bed."

"You don't need to," Klara said. "It's no bother."

Karn raised his hand to her cheek, his ring flashing silver in the moonlight. "Aye, I do. I'll not have you stand watch while there are strange men in camp." Then he kissed her forehead and walked off.

# CHAPTER 22

# DEMONS ON THE ROAD

KLARA WAS FRYING fish for breakfast when Vera arrived at the fire carrying nine eggs in her apron.

"There's one for each of us," Vera said, "and the milk besides."

Having Vera in their party meant the company no longer needed to heat a cauldron of honey-water to drink since the goats provided fresh milk morning and night. Klara pointed Vera in the direction of the panniers. The woman returned with the smaller of the copper cauldrons, filled it with water and hung it over the fire so the eggs could boil.

While they sat round the fire eating, the three men who camped near them rode out. The fact that they left without eating breakfast was not lost on Laszlo, who said, "When I grow up, I'm going to be a Kelto."

The company was amused and Ruis asked, "Why's that, lad?"

"Keltoi never go hungry. Those men didn't eat this morning, but Keltoi eat a lot every day. Also, you get to go fishing and ride horses, plus you don't have to wear your clothes on wash days," he said enthusiastically. "And no one gets mad when you burp and fart."

Laughter rose from the circle of Keltoi.

"Well, lad," Ruis said, "then you best marry a Kelta while you're at it. Most women don't care for such behavior. Our Klara seems to be the exception."

The day passed with the company making slow but steady progress.

Thorn again chose to forgo stopping at midday in favor of stopping earlier that night. As Klara made bread, she watched Ruis walk over to where Vera and Laszlo were tending the goats. The pair conferred for a while before Ruis reached for his purse and handed Vera something. Then Ruis took Laszlo by the hand and headed for the stream.

Klara raised her eyebrows. If she was right, Ruis had just pawned off his cooking duties. Looking at Karn across the fire, she said, "Get your bow and go shoot something for supper tomorrow."

Karn said, "Not on your life. It's Ruis's turn to cook."

"Ruis won't be cooking tomorrow, Vera will," Klara said. "Ruis has just gone fishing and that isn't something he'd do if he thought he'd have to fry them in the morning. Now, hurry or it'll be beans again." Wasting no time Karn followed her orders, taking Ffearn with him.

The rest of the company had eaten and Klara was washing up when the pair of Keltoi returned bearing a roe buck on a pole between them. Excited, Laszlo raced off to examine their kill. The tenderloin and one of the legs were cut off and handed to Laszlo.

Delivering the meat to Klara, Laszlo said, "They asked if you'd cook this for their supper."

No Keltoi alive ever turned down such fine fare as that, even if they were full to begin with. Around the fire, the men used their daggers to cut off pieces of meat as it cooked, occasionally burning their fingers in the process. After they finished the meat, Nuallan put a cauldron of water on to heat and added some herbs. Now, what was he up to? As Klara watched the elder Kelto, the rest of the company sang around the fire.

"At dawn they ride out for the hunt,
Anticipation quivering through the land.
At dusk they ride back again,
No game in their hand.

"Daghda wasn't with them,
Lugh had passed them by,
Because they'd made no offing;
So game was swift and shy.

"If you wish to thrill to the hunt,
Give the gods their due.
the stag is not so fleet of foot,
When the gods hunt with you."


Klara was sitting next to Karn enjoying the camaraderie around the fire when Nuallan handed her a steaming drink. "You've not been yourself," he said. "This will settle your nerves."

"What is it?" Klara asked, sniffing the horn warily.

"Just a draught to relax you," Nuallan said. Then nodding to Thorn added, "And maybe put him to sleep. I don't think he sleeps enough."

Nuallan would get no argument from her; she had not been herself. The fact that she had forced Vera and Laszlo out of their home weighed heavily on her, as did the knowledge that the results of her actions likely meant all of them may still be hunted as murderers. She did not trust Nuallan, but figured it was safe to drink since he was unlikely to attempt poisoning Thorn, too.

Taking the horn with her, she went to sit beside Thorn. He also gave the contents a suspicious sniff but willingly shared the communal horn. At first the contents tasted harsh and bitter, but the taste improved as the pair drank.

Klara dozed off, then woke to Karn shaking her. Yawning, she asked, "Is it time for bed?"

"It's time for breakfast," Karn said and laughed. "You've slept the night through. Whatever Nuallan put in that draught worked. Both you and Thorn fell asleep by the fire. I carried you off to bed, but Thorn they only dragged away from the flames and threw his bedroll over him. Ffearn is trying to wake him now."

Vera earned her place among the Keltoi by producing a breakfast of steak, eggs, fried fish, and fresh milk. Gratefully accepting a bowl of food, Klara said, "I see Ruis talked you into cooking."

"He did more than talk," Vera replied, forking over a steak and dropping it in Klara's bowl. "By Otso's honeyed tongue, he paid me. Just a small copper, but better than nothing, and we have to eat anyhow. I didn't even have to fetch the wood and water, Ruis and Bardus did it for me. These Keltoi don't behave like Mordvins at all."

"I expect they were just happy not to be eating Ruis's cooking," Klara said, savoring the steak.

By the end of the day, they had passed through the crossroads and were camped as far off the track as they could get. Vera made stew and bread for supper. After supper, Nuallan again hung a cauldron of water over the fire.

Ffearn called to the gray Kelto, "You're not planning on drugging them again are you?"

"I'll admit the draught I made yesterday was a bit strong, but there's no denying they did sleep," Nuallan said as he sprinkled herbs in the pot. "I'll cut the dosage and see how they fair tonight."

"I do prefer having Klara awake when I take her off to bed," Karn teased. "She's not as much fun when she's sleeping." In the end, Klara and Thorn were able to make it to their bedrolls under their own volition.

❧

Klara woke and nuzzled into Karn, sliding her fingers under his shirt, seeking his warm flesh. Roused from slumber Karn said, "I see you're feeling friendly this morning."

"It's a grand day to be Kenetlo," Klara said, nibbling his ear.

"But," Karn said, "you are not Kenetlo."

"Aye, but you are," Klara replied. "And if you give me but a little time I can make it a grand day for both of us."

Klara was busy undressing Karn, who was half-heartedly protesting, when Ffearn walked up. "It's a good thing you're here," she said to Ffearn. "He's being uncooperative. Tell him he should not refuse a lady."

Ffearn laughed. "You're no lady. No lady I've ever met kills men as readily as you. Besides, Thorn has called a meeting and I think he would prefer if the pair of you attended fully clothed."

"Absent gods," Klara said. "When I was working at the alehouse I had sex nearly every day, some days more than once. Now that I am freed from the burden of having to perform and can choose to indulge when it suits me, you expect me to go without coupling for a whole moon or longer. I do believe that amounts to cruel and unusual punishment."

"Shall I pass those sentiments on to Thorn?" Ffearn asked, with a chuckle. "Or would you prefer to tell him yourself? He is expecting the pair of you directly." Then he walked off.

Karn kissed her and said, "Well, Wife, if you will consent to dress, I will promise to carry you off tonight, provided chance allows."

Klara and Karn dressed and joined the others around the campfire. Bowls of porridge were passed out, and the company ate while Thorn spoke, "Today we should reach Timerevo. I'd like to depart quickly after delivering Vera to her kin. That means you need to ride today, Klara. Karn will still drive the wagon." Then turning to Karn, Thorn added, "You will do the talking. If her kin asks after our company, say only that you and your wife are traveling to visit distant relations and have thrown in with us for added protection as we did before."

The company traveled through the day, arriving at Timerevo early in the evening. Karn inquired at the inn and learned that Vera's relations lived a considerable distance from the village. Not expecting additional travel time, the company continued on, hoping a joyous reunion might result in being granted a place to sleep and stable their horses for the night.

It was well after dark when they arrived in the yard of a small and shabby house that likely contained no more than two rooms. The pungent odor of manure hung thickly in the air, wafting from a barn that showed noticeable signs of disrepair and neglect. It was immediately obvious that Vera would have been better off living on her own.

Wrinkling her nose against the offensive odors, Klara watched as Karn set the brake and helped Vera and Laszlo subdue the goats, which had begun tasting the corral fence. The situation unnerved her. A team and wagon, along with a dozen other horses, a crate full of squawking chickens, and a bunch of bleating nanny goats just entered the yard and no one had opened the door. Surely, they heard the commotion outside.

Karn knocked on the door and a male voice shouted from within, "Whoever you are, you've no business here. Be on your way."

Karn called back, "Your wife's niece has been widowed. I deliver her and her possessions to you."

"I'll not take a poor beggar into my house; I've enough mouths to feed. And you may be lying just to get me to unlatch the door," called the voice. "Those who come after dark do not come for honest purposes."

"Then we will camp in your yard and you can see for yourself that she isn't poor in the morning," Karn said. "Shall we stable her horses and other stock or have them stand here until dawn?"

The door slid open and a male head poked out. "How much stock?"

The firelight flickering in the house was behind him, obscuring his features, but he seemed just as ill-kempt as the barn. Klara listened while Karn ran down a list of Vera's possessions. The man nodded greedily each time an item of value was mentioned.

When Karn finished the inventory, the man called for his wife, who appeared and ushered Vera and Laszlo into the house. Then the greedy man directed Karn and the other Keltoi to stable the stock and bring Vera's belongings inside. After everything was put either in the house or barn, Karn asked if they could pass the night there.

The greedy man eyed Klara and asked, "Who's the other woman? Another widow you're off to deliver?"

Klara shifted in her saddle, uncomfortable under the man's gaze.

"Nay," Karn said. "She's my wife."

"Well, you and your wife may stay but the Keltoi must go," said the man. "I wouldn't mind sharing my bed with the likes of her."

"We have our own bedrolls," Karn said. "There is no need to share your bed. We can sleep quite comfortably on the floor."

The man was undeterred. "You and my wife and even that other wench you brought can have the floor. I'll have her in my bed. That's the price for having a roof over your head."

"I do not share my wife," Karn said. "We will see ourselves back to the inn." Then he mounted Night and the company traveled the back the way they came.

When they reached the inn, the fire was out and the place dark. Karn and Thorn rapped on the door until the innkeeper shouted for them to stop. Karn requested a bed for him and Klara, and Thorn asked for a room for the remainder of the company. Being a large trading village, the innkeeper had rooms available and was happy to let them for the night. As they stabled their horses, Nuallan passed out jerky, nuts, and dried fruit, to be eaten in their rooms.

Behind the thin wall, Klara heard the Keltoi settling down for the night. Karn reached for his belt, but Klara stopped him, saying, "Let me do that." Then she leaned in and kissed him as she unbuckled his belt and let it drop.

"Still feeling friendly, I see," Karn said as he began to unlace her jerkin.

"You said you would carry me off tonight, if chance allowed," she said.

Karn chuckled. "We'd wake them and the innkeeper. You know that."

"I'll be quiet," Klara promised as she slipped her hands into Karn's tunic. Sighing audibly, she closed her eyes and ran her fingers though his chest hair, drinking in his scent.

"If you can be quiet, I shall pleasure you," Karn said. "But I cannot be quiet so you must be content with that."

Klara was quieter, but despite her best efforts, the rustling from the next room indicated at least some of the Keltoi woke when she climaxed. Having finished, Klara ran her fingers across Karn's chest, sighing deeply. "It doesn't seem fair that you have brought me pleasure and I have not done likewise. After all, they're already awake over there."

"Thorn wants to leave early, so you must sleep," Karn said. "But if it is what you desire, I'll secret you away as often as I can." Then he kissed her forehead and rolled her over so he could spoon her as they slept.

The innkeeper's wife was every bit as good a cook as Klara and she put out an impressive spread. The entire company ate hungrily of eggs, sausage, oatcakes, bread, cheese, and fresh raspberries. Since there were no other guests, and they did not need to pretend they were traveling separately, Ffearn sat with Karn and Klara as they dined.

Between mouthfuls Ffearn said, "It seems you keep Klara well pleased, brother, even if it means waking the lot of us."

"Did I wake all of you?" Klara asked, grabbing another sausage from the platter.

"Nah, just Thorn, Ruis, and myself," he said. "I think Nuallan is partly deaf and Bardus can sleep through anything."

"Is Thorn angry?" Karn asked, slathering butter on an oatcake.

Ffearn speared a sausage and took a bite before replying. "As surprised as I am to say it, no, he seemed amused. I think those rings have something to do with it, and I think he's hoping for an heir." He took another bite and winked at Karn before adding, "Though, I know there wasn't near enough noise coming from that room last night to have resulted in an heir."

The day was bright and beautiful and the morning air fresh with dew. With their bellies full, the company set out cross-country. This served two purposes, by staying off the road, they were less likely to encounter other travelers, and it might make up for the time they lost delivering Vera to her kin. Not everyone was happy to leave her behind, though.

"We should ride back there and get her," Ruis said, fiddling with the lead of the pack horses. "She'll not be treated well in that household."

"We are not her kin and can make no claim on her," Thorn said. "Besides, the wagon, goats, and everything else slows us down. We cannot take her and still make it to Duirndunum before it snows."

"We don't need the wagon or the goats," Ruis said. "The lad can ride and Vera can be taught. Klara rides as well as the rest of us."

Klara felt insulted by the remark. She rode a good deal better than the rest of them but let the comment pass. Like Ruis, she believed Vera was destined for poor treatment in her uncle's household. However, she knew Ruis's arguments were futile. Thorn was unlikely to change his mind.

"Ruis is right," Bardus agreed, leaning forward in his saddle. "She'll likely be abused and ill-treated. She and the lad would be better off with us."

"We have a hard enough time inventing reasons why Klara should be with us," Nuallan said. "We could never explain the presence of another woman."

"We can claim she's Klara's kin," Ruis persisted.

Thorn raised his hand, silencing them. "We cannot take the woman and her son. They are with kin and will have to fare as well as they can. I'll speak no more on this matter."

Aside from Nuallan, no one was happy about leaving Vera in her uncle's care. But it was equally clear there was nothing they could do about it.

After midday, the forest became darker, the trees growing thickly all around them, blocking the afternoon sun. Constant began to flare his nostrils. Unease crept through Klara.

They were being watched, though she could not say from where or by whom. The darkness persisted and grew heavier. It reminded her of a brewing storm, save there was no wind bearing either thunder or rain. Soon it was so dark that it was difficult to see and the horses began to stumble.

There was a crash, followed by Thorn shouting, "Damnable rank-scented clod!"

"You alright?" Ruis called.

"My tardy-gaited mount has stumbled and unseated me," Thorn said. "Might as well stop and light a fire. I can barely see my hand before my face."

Klara slipped off Constant's back and approached Thorn. "I think we are being watched," she said, nearly whispering. "I've felt it most of the afternoon but have seen no sign of man or beast to give reason for it."

"Your intuition is generally good," Thorn said, turning his eyes to the trees. "Are we not safe?"

"I can't say," Klara replied. "I have first watch and will let you know if I see anything."

"Since Bardus and I did not stand watch last night, I'll have him stand with you and I'll stand with Karn," Thorn said. "No harm in having a second set of eyes on guard for this black night."

Well into the watch, long after the men bedded down, the horses began to snort. Some pulled at the picket-line, others stood trembling in their slot. Something was near enough to bother them but concealed in shadow well enough that neither she nor Bardus could catch a glimpse of it.

Klara reached her mind out to Constant, *"What is it?"*

The horse was a jumble of confusion and blackness filled her mind. Whatever was out there was beyond the horse's knowledge. That frightened her. The horse knew men, wolves, and demons. Did he know the scent of a bear? Yet, if it were a bear, she should have seen some sign of it. If not scat, then rolled over logs where it dug for grubs or hair where it scratched itself on the trees.

When it was time to wake Thorn, Klara told him of her unease. "I don't know what's out there, but I don't like it. Whatever it is has the horses spooked, too." She looked up, staring into the night and shivered. The darkness was oppressive, making her fearful.

Trusting Constant's keen ears and sense of smell to detect a threat long before Karn or Thorn, she took the horse off the picket line and brought him to her bedroll. *"Stay close,"* Klara thought. *"And let me know if you sense a change."*

Klara had not slept long before Constant began nuzzling her. The horse gave her a vision of demons and wolves. With Constant feeding her all the information his senses gathered, Klara saw that Ke'let were surrounding the camp. She rose and patted Constant's neck to reassure him, then she slipped through the camp to where Thorn and Karn stood watch.

"We are surrounded by Ke'let," she whispered. "You two stay on watch, I'll wake the others."

With everyone awake, Klara returned to Constant's side. Ke'let encircled the camp, though they were still invisible behind the wall of shadows. With the demons standing sentinel, the oppressive darkness began to dissipate. Soon stars were visible overhead and the terror the horses felt was replaced by normal fear.

Through the darkness a single being appeared, walking toward the camp. The being was tall and fair, dressed in a long white robe, belted with a golden cord. Hair so blond it appeared white fluttered in the breeze about its youthful face. Was it an Elb? Klara saw no sign of gender and Karn had said that was common among the Elbs.

The being stopped when it was still some distance from them and spoke, "I am Belial, and I proclaim my friendship." As he spoke, he unfurled his wings so they could see he was the angel who abandoned Elah. Then he added, "Asmodaios told me you were traveling this way. I offer protection. Sleep this night and leave fresh in the morning."

"You proclaim friendship, yet you cause mortal fear," Thorn said, his trembling hand as he fought back his own fear of demons. "You brought an abhorrent darkness. Not even the horses trust you."

Demons are horse-eaters, so the horses had good reason not to trust them. Having never encountered an angel before, she had no idea if they ate horse, too. But whatever the darkness was, the horses feared it more than they feared demons.

"The darkness you perceived is Elah. The council of the Divine disembodied him years ago. Without a body, Elah cannot harm you. He greatly desires Klara, so has sent many men against you," Belial said, softly fluttering his wings. "We are working to prevent Elah's advance and will strengthen your position tonight to keep her safe. Flee in the morning. Travel as swiftly as you are able and you will outrun his disciples."

"What does Elah want with Klara?" Thorn asked.

"The same thing you want," Belial said, "an heir." Then Belial flapped his wings and rose into the night.

Belial's proclamation left them greatly puzzled. Taking Klara in his arms in a protective gesture, Karn held her to him.

"Why would Elah want me to produce an heir?" Klara asked at large. "He has Messias and is fond of virgins." Although if he took a virgin for himself, maybe he wanted a whore for his son. It was not uncommon for men to bring their sons to a prostitute for breaking in. Did gods do the same for their offspring?

Ffearn walked over to her and placed a hand on his brother's shoulder, saying, "If they will let us sleep, we should take the opportunity."

"And have them slaughter us in our beds?" Thorn spat. "Karn and I will remain on watch. We leave at first light."

Looking at his brother, Karn said, "Keep her safe." Then he let go of Klara and turned to follow Thorn.

Settling in their bedrolls, Ffearn started to spoon Klara as they slept. "Roll over," she said. "This isn't how we sleep."

"If Karn comes to wake us and finds that I haven't got you in my arms, he'll likely have my head," Ffearn said.

"Ffearn," Klara asked, "Why would Elah seek me? If he has no body he couldn't produce an heir, could he?" She had plenty of knowledge regarding sex, but that knowledge was limited to the functioning of mortals. Still, it was supposed that the gods coupled in much the same way.

"I think those are questions for a wizard," Ffearn replied. "And our wizard happens to be absent just now. Maybe he doesn't seek a wife for himself, but for his son. You said the son was dead but has been made undead. Either way there is naught we can do about it tonight. We best sleep while we can."

❧

"Absent gods, Klara, even your horse is friendly in the morning."

Klara was jolted from sleep by Ffearn's excited exclamation. Rolling over, she saw Constant nuzzling Ffearn in the faint gray light of dawn.

"I've never been kissed by a horse before," Ffearn said, pushing Constant away.

Despite the tension of the night, Karn and Bardus were attempting to suppress their laughter as they watched the scene unfold. "It seems they come as a set, brother," Karn said. "I shall bed the woman and you can have the horse, though, seeing as the horse is a gelding, you've got no chance for heirs."

Glowering at his brother, Ffearn got to his feet. "You're not funny," he said and then stormed off to saddle Thunder and dig out the supplies for breakfast.

Klara scratched Constant's forehead while saying, "Never mind the grumpy Kelto. I don't think he got enough sleep last night. I'm sure you and Ffearn would've made beautiful babies if given the chance." This garnered snickers from Karn and Bardus, but Constant gave her a look that said he was about as pleased with the notion as Ffearn was. So contemptuous was the glance that she wondered if the beast would let her saddle him later.

Ffearn passed out dried fruit and nuts as they mounted up. When they encountered the circle of demons surrounding the camp, the creatures parted and let them pass. Poor light under the forest canopy made the brush difficult to navigate, hindering their progress. Once they returned to the road, traveling was easier. Thorn set a pace where they galloped the horses for an hour, followed by an hour of walking, and kept them moving swiftly through the afternoon. When they stopped for the night, both men and horses were exhausted.

Ffearn made a pot of beans while the others tended to their horses. After supper Nuallan again gave Klara and Thorn the brew of herbs stating, "Thorn'll not sleep tonight unless drugged and if I'm making some for him, I may as well give some to you."

Since Vera was no longer with them, Ffearn joined Karn and Klara in their bedrolls. Nuallan did not approve and made his displeasure known each night when he passed Thorn and Klara his brew of herbs. If giving Klara the draught before bed was an attempt at preventing her from enticing Karn, it failed. The concoction put her to sleep, but she slept so soundly and woke so refreshed that she greatly desired Karn upon waking. Her ardor waned as the day progressed but was renewed each morning. The pair was often caught kissing or fondling each other while watering horses or as they cooked breakfast. This amused the rest of the company who often whistled or let out catcalls. Thorn too was sleeping more and was happier in the mornings, growing more introspective as the day waned.

Coming across Karn and Klara locked in a passionate embrace behind the picket line, Nuallan harrumphed to indicate his displeasure.

Karn looked over at him and said, "If you'll not drug her tonight, I can take her out in the woods and give her what she wants. Once she's been satisfied, I'm sure our mornings will run smoother."

Klara laughed, but Nuallan only harrumphed again and walked off.

## CHAPTER 23

# SHE'S BEEN DRUGGED

FTER SEVERAL DAYS of hard riding, Thorn slowed the pace, allowing them to travel at a walk. Klara knew the horses appreciated the change, especially since the days had been hot and dry. That evening, as they were unsaddling the horses Thorn asked her and Karn to join him. The pair exchanged glances as they followed him to the edge of the clearing.

Thorn stopped under a large tree, out of earshot of the rest of the company who were busy making camp. "I think you two ought to be sleeping apart," he said. "Klara's had her own bedroll for a while and it's time she started using it."

"Are you mad?" Karn said. "We've pledged ourselves to each other."

Klara was shocked. Thorn had been delighted with their union at Midsummer and had displayed nothing but happiness since. Why the sudden change?

"I know you have," Thorn said. "And I can see that you've exchanged rings, but there has been no formal ceremony. If a child is produced, it would be deemed an illegitimate heir and have no rights to hereditary title. You must also consider what effects your sleeping arrangements have on Ffearn."

Legitimacy, or lack thereof, had not bothered Thorn before. Klara studied his face, trying to decipher what else was going through his mind. It was clear the topic troubled him, more so than it was troubling Karn with his outbursts.

"Ffearn doesn't mind," Karn said. "And I can name any child I choose as my heir, just as my father has done with his bastards."

Thorn sighed and leaned against the tree. "I know Ffearn doesn't mind, but it's not Ffearn I'm worried about. Do you honestly think any of the clans will approve his kingship if they learn he's been sharing a bed with his cousin and his cousin's whore?"

Karn bristled, preparing to challenge Thorn, but Thorn raised his hands and said, "I know you do not think of her that way, nor do I, or anyone else in the company. We've lived on our own for years, you, Ffearn, and I, away from the prying eyes of nobles. What we did while living in Olbia was our own business and mattered little to anyone. As we approach Kenetlon, word will travel before us. If Ffearn is to have any chance at claiming the kingship, all the rumors that reach the nobles' ears must be favorable. You may name any child an heir and pass on your own property, but an illegitimate child could never claim the right of Lordship and Ffearn is unlikely to produce heirs of his own."

Politics. Klara shook her head. Nuallan must be behind this. He had been riding alongside Thorn all day. Nuallan was quite blatant in showing his disdain for her. What other ideas might the gray Kelto be trying to plant?

"You can't expect us to wait until we reach the waters of the Danube just to wed after we've already given ourselves to each other," Karn said.

"No," Thorn agreed. "I think it might be easier if you were wed before we reach Kenetlon because the nobles will not look kindly toward your marrying Klara at all. We will reach Gnyozdovo in another ten days or so. It's only a quarter moon ride from there before we reach Lusatia. I think we might be able to find a priest or priestess who would wed you there, because I cannot fathom your union being allowed here in Mordovia."

"So, really, you're only asking us to sleep apart for little more than a fortnight," Klara said. Thorn's request was reasonable and his reasoning sound. Though if Nuallan was behind this, he was bound to be disappointed. Karn was just as headstrong as his uncle and just as unlikely to change his mind.

"Aye," Thorn said, nodding. "But even after you are wed and the ceremony recorded, you cannot bring Ffearn back into your bed."

Karn appeared crestfallen and his shoulders slumped. "Ffearn and I have always shared a bed. The only times we've slept apart is when situations or circumstances required it, and even then it was only for a short time."

Thorn put a hand on Karn's shoulder. "This would be one of those times when it is required. When you were lads, there was grumbling about you sharing a bed, but it was allowed because your mothers raised you as siblings. You are adults now and if you add Klara to the mix, no one will approve."

"I know," Karn said and sighed. "Grandfather wasn't at all pleased when he learned about the serving girls. Ffearn and I were always discreet, but we ended up banished anyway."

Serving girls? Klara was certain Thorn told her their banishment likely had nothing to do with serving girls. She would have to ask Karn about it later. As it happened, later never came. After breaking the news to Ffearn, the brothers wandered off to be alone.

When they returned, bearing armloads of firewood, it was obvious that Ffearn was equally unhappy with Thorn's edict. After supper, the pair of young Keltoi still bedded down near each other. While sharing blankets was forbidden, they clearly had no intention of spending their time apart.

An owl hooted in the distance as Klara finished her turn at the watch and headed for the twin lumps that were Ffearn and Karn. Though each Kelto was wrapped in his own blanket, each had outstretched an arm to clasp the other's hand. Even when enveloped in sleep, they the insisted on being within an arm's reach. She shook Karn to wake him for his turn, then slipped into the bedroll he had just exited.

Despite not being able to spend their nights together, the trio saw no reason to spend their waking hours apart. The pair of brothers still rode together and any time one of them was assigned to cook the other often helped. Owing to the effectiveness of Nuallan's brew, Klara and Thorn were spared from having to drink it on nights when either of them had to stand watch.

As the days passed, Klara noticed that she felt more like herself when she was permitted to forgo the drink. What was Nuallan putting in it? If his intent was simply to ensure she slept the night through and eliminate the possibility of her sneaking into Karn's bed after everyone else fell asleep, his venture was successful. But why give it to Thorn, too?

∽

It was Ruis's turn to cook. While unsaddling horses and preparing to make camp, Nuallan said, "I'll eat no more ruined beans and will do the cooking myself if I have to." Ruis, and everyone else, happily let Nuallan take over responsibility for the meal.

After filling a bucket with water from the stream, Klara lugged it up to the fire where Nuallan was busy cooking. Setting down the bucket, she asked, "What's in that brew you keep giving Thorn and me?"

"Just a bit of herbs," Nuallan said as he scrounged through the panniers in search of cooking utensils.

"Which herbs?" Klara asked. She was clever enough to know many herbs aided women in getting pregnant, as well as prevented it—not to mention all the other medicinal properties from pain relief to curing stomach upset, and a good many herbs were poisonous. These particular herbs made her sleep and left her feeling a bit hazy.

"Oregano to settle your nerves, poppy to help you to sleep, and mint to help with the flavor. I'll be using some of the oregano in the beans tonight. I'm getting tired of the same old fare," Nuallan said, extracting the cauldron and sack of beans from the panniers.

The herbs were harmless enough. The depth to which she slept and the fuzziness of her mind must be owing to the exhaustion of travel. She became more convinced of this when the rest of the company retired directly after supper.

Stretching, Karn said, "I'm done in." Then he leaned over and kissed Klara. "I'm going to find my bedroll before I fall asleep here at the fire."

Ffearn also kissed her cheek saying, "I'll see that Kelto of yours safely to his bed and return him to you in the morning."

Feeling drowsy herself, Klara passed the dirty bowl to Nuallan. Abandoning thoughts of her bedroll, she lay down near the fire figuring she might as well sleep here. Sleep consumed her the moment her head touched the ground.

Someone was shaking her. "Come on, up you get," called a voice.

It was Nuallan. "You need to drink this," he said as he handed her the horn. "Thorn already had his; you drink the rest."

"Absent gods, Nuallan," Klara groaned. "I was asleep. Why do I have to drink a brew to put me to sleep if I was already sleeping?"

"It'll settle your nerves," Nuallan said, pressing the horn to her lips.

"They were settled," Klara said, pushing the horn away. "I was sleeping."

Undeterred, Nuallan pushed the horn to her lips again. Klara pulled the horn away and glared at him. "If it'll make you go away, I'll drink it." Then tipping up the horn, she quaffed the contents.

The morning brought a raging headache, like the ones she had after a night of excessive drinking. As she came to her senses, the headache was eclipsed by a more pleasurable sensation. Karn had joined her in her bedroll and was spooning her now, warmth radiating from him. Eyes still closed, she rolled toward him, sighed, and buried her head in his chest.

With clumsy movements, Klara slipped under the blanket, pulling his tunic open and running her fingers through his chest hair. His hands were awkward and uncertain as they reached for her. Slipping a hand in his trousers, she felt him already firm. Embracing him she felt the ridges of scars across his back.

Her heart stopped. It was not Karn she held. It was Thorn.

Pushing herself away, Klara pulled back the blanket and looked into Thorn's startled face. He wore a bewildered expression and it was clear that he was just as groggy she was. They both spoke at once.

"What are you doing?" Thorn demanded.

"Why are in you my bed?" Klara said.

They answered each other simultaneously.

"I'm not in you're bed, you're in mine," Thorn said.

"I… I thought you were Karn," Klara stammered.

Confused, Klara looked around. She was in Thorn's bed. His bedroll was gray and black whereas hers was plain gray and lying empty across the clearing. She recalled falling asleep at the fire. She had never made it to her bed.

"How did I get here?" Klara asked.

"I… I don't know," Thorn said, pulling his tunic closed. "I was alone when I finished the drink. You must have come after I fell asleep."

Klara was shocked. "I would not have come…I could not have; the drink makes me sleep."

Having come to their senses they looked around the camp and saw the rest of the company awake and assembled at the fire eating breakfast. They did not sit in a circle as they usually did but sat with their backs to Klara and Thorn. An oppressive silence hung over the group. Scrambling to her feet, Klara stumbled across camp in the direction of her bedroll.

Collapsing into her blanket, Klara wrapped it tightly around her. Her head hurt and she was shaking violently. Something was horribly wrong. She pushed herself to her knees and began to retch. When she finished, she wiped the vomit from her mouth and fell back onto the grass. Her stomach hurt. Though she knew she should see to the horses, rising from where she had fallen seemed like an insurmountable task.

When Klara opened her eyes again, Bardus was kneeling beside her. "Are you with child?"

"Goddess, help me, no!" Klara exclaimed and began to shake again.

"Are you sure?" Bardus asked. "Is it possible?"

Stricken, tears welled in her eyes. "I cannot be sure. I last had my usual bleeding when we were at Vera's. Then I bled again about a fortnight later. It was not much, but there was some. Even if I were with child it would be too soon to be ill in the mornings. Still, I cannot be sure because I can't remember some nights." Then her tears gave way to sobs.

Bardus took her in his lap as if she were a child. "Tell me what you remember of last night."

Klara tried to puzzle the evening together and managed to get the story out, but, for the life of her, she had no notion of how she ended up in bed with Thorn.

"Are you sure it was Nuallan who woke you and no one else?" Bardus asked. "And that he only gave you the drink and left you to sleep at the fire?"

Klara nodded her assent.

"Do you know which herbs he's using?" Bardus asked.

"Mint, oregano, and poppy," Klara said through sniffles.

"Absent gods! I think he's poisoned you," Bardus said. "Poppy will make you sleep and settle your nerves so you feel better, but it also causes confusion, memory loss, convulsions, and vomiting when you've had too much. It can also cause a person to do something they otherwise would not."

Bardus patted her shoulder. "Wait here, I'll fetch you some breakfast."

When Bardus returned with a bowl of porridge, Klara said, "You said that poppy can cause a person to do things they otherwise would not. Does that mean…" Klara choked on the words, and then tried again, "Does that mean I'm to blame?"

"Nay, lass," Bardus said kindly. "If anything, it means you're not to blame. And you must remember that Thorn has been consuming the same drink."

Klara thought of the packets of pennyroyal hidden in her gear. Should she take the herb? She had no memory of how she ended up in Thorn's bed or even memories of much else that had transpired since leaving Vera's. Then a thought occurred to her. "Bardus, we set a watch every night. Someone knows how I ended up in Thorn's bed. Someone knows if I've done anything I might regret."

Bardus looked at her, realizing for the first time that this must be so. "Ruis was on watch this morning," he said. Then he called the Kelto over and asked him what he saw.

"There was no movement while I was on watch," Ruis replied. "Camp was quiet and all slept. Whatever happened, happened during Nuallan's watch." Bardus had Ruis carry Klara over to the fire so she might benefit from its warmth.

"Why isn't she dressed?" Thorn demanded. "We need to be on our way."

"She's not dressed because she's ill; Nuallan's poisoned her," Bardus said. "And I have questions for him." Karn's and Ffearn's heads swiveled Bardus's direction.

"What do you mean he poisoned her?" Thorn's bluster evaporated, replaced by concern.

Bardus related to them the uses of poppy as well as the effect of an overdose. When he finished, Bardus added, "And since Klara ended up in your bed on Nuallan's watch, not long after he drugged her, I'd like to know exactly what he saw. Klara is understandably concerned about the possibility of a pregnancy and I get the feeling that she might wish to seek the aid of herbs as a preventative if it becomes necessary."

All eyes turned to Nuallan, expecting an answer. The Kelto was clearly uncomfortable under their gaze.

"The King's business is his own," Nuallan blustered. "It's not for us to question if he takes a mistress."

Thorn was visibly shocked by what he heard. Notes of anger and self-loathing seeped through as he asked, "Do you mean to tell us I brought her into my bed?"

Nuallan cowered before the fire. "No, you'd do no such thing. But if she found her way into your bed, none would blame you."

"Did I couple with her?" Thorn demanded, pointing an angry finger at Nuallan.

"No," Nuallan squawked. "You only slept while on my watch."

Thorn turned and walked away. Karn and Ffearn turned their backs to her. Relieved to know she did not need to worry about pregnancy, Klara still had trouble comprehending Nuallan's assertion that it was she who made her way to Thorn's bed. At present, she was unsure of her ability to make it to the brush for a piss.

"I know you aren't feeling well, but do you think you can sit a horse, lass?" Bardus asked.

"I think so," Klara said. "Karn, would you—"

Ffearn and Karn stood and walked off without so much as a glance her direction.

"—help me gather up my things," Klara said, staring open mouthed at his retreating back. As the gravity of the situation donned on her, she imagined the magnitude of hurt Karn must feel. He would come around. Surely, he understood the fault could not possibly be hers.

While Klara tried to choke down her breakfast, Bardus gathered up her belongings. After saddling Constant, he helped her tie her gear down, and then cupped his hands to give her a leg up. Surprising them both, Constant knelt, allowing her to mount.

Tears rolled down her cheeks while she rode, alone, at the rear of the column. Confusion reigned in her hazy mind as she tried to make sense of what happened. The last memory she had was of sitting by the fire. She drank the liquid Nuallan gave her, and then he walked off with it. The next thing she remembered was thinking Karn joined her in bed. She was certain that was it: he joined her, not that she joined him.

When they stopped at midday, Klara tried talking to Karn, but he avoided her, turning to walk off whenever she approached. She felt like an outcast or leper; the entire company shunned her. In the evening it was no better. While Karn was unsaddling Night, Klara tried talking to him again. He refused to even look her direction.

"Karn, please," Klara said, hurrying to get in front of him as he carried the saddle away from the picket line. "You must know I would never—"

Ffearn pulled her away. "Stay away from him. You've done enough damage already."

"But Ffearn," she protested. "I just—"

Ffearn shoved her. "Just go."

Klara stumbled back into the line of horses, who sidestepped her, swishing their tails in irritation. Unable to look her companions in the eye, owing to the embarrassment she felt, Klara found a spot away from camp to throw her bedroll, leaving the horses in Bardus's care.

The following morning, Bardus refused to speak to her or even meet her gaze as they watered the horses. Despite his silence, he, at least, was able to tolerate her company. Everyone else avoided her altogether. Confused and filled with grief, Klara grabbed Bardus by the shoulders and forced him to look at her.

"Tell me what has happened," she said. Something was different, more so than having just woken up in the wrong spot.

"I don't know what it's like where you're from, or maybe it's because of the work you've done before, but among our people oaths are taken seriously. You pledged yourself by wearing that ring," Bardus said, grabbing her hand and raising it to eye level. He paused as her eyes settled on the thin silver band. "You broke your oath and by rights Karn can have your head or both of your heads if he chooses."

"I don't understand," Klara said, tears rolling down her cheeks. "You said it was an accident, that it was because of the poppy. If I don't drink Nuallan's brew, it won't happen again."

"By our laws when someone is unfaithful the aggrieved spouse has three days in which they may take the life of the unfaithful spouse, the lover, or both of them. And we are not to speak to you until that decision is made. If Karn chooses death for either or both of you, your heads will be severed and put on a spike to serve as a warning to others."

Klara sank to the ground. "I didn't… I didn't. I have no memories of that night or how I got there."

"Well, it seemed to Karn that you were there and willing enough in the morning," Bardus said.

"I thought it was Karn, I thought he had joined me. I stopped as soon as I realized—" her words trailed off. Karn might kill her. Or Thorn. Should she flee? She was resourceful and had lived on her own in the wilds before.

A sudden realization came to her. This was Nuallan's plan all along. He had never wanted her in the company, disapproved of her bedding arrangements and her relationship with Karn, so he had devised a plan to get them to send her away. That was why he convinced Thorn to separate her, Ffearn, and Karn. There was no way he could have dragged her out of her bed without accidentally waking one of them.

By the time Klara had processed that information, Bardus had left her at the stream and re-picketed the horses. She looked from Bardus to the other Keltoi at the fire. Would any of them believe her if she accused Nuallan? They refused to even speak to her. Three days. Bardus said Karn had three days to make a decision and during that time no one was to talk to her.

Klara sat apart, slept apart, and felt apart from the company as she bided her time. She did not speak because no one would speak to her. She did not eat because eating required her to join the others at the fire. The uncomfortable stares Ruis and Bardus sent her were tolerable, but she could not bear the hurt-filled angry mask Karn wore or the disappoint looks that crossed Thorn's face whenever he set eyes on her.

She knew Karn would not kill her, but would he take her back? And because he was so quick to doubt, did she even want him too? The separateness she felt, not just from Karn, but from all of them, cut deep and left her feeling wounded.

<br>

Three days after waking with Thorn, Klara woke to the sight of Ffearn's boots. The Kelto looked down at her and said, "He has decided he will not kill you, but he hasn't decided if he'll keep you."

Ffearn turned to leave, but Klara called to him, "Ffearn, please wait."

"There is no message I can give him that will ease the pain you've caused," Ffearn said.

"If you will not give him a message, at least just hear me out," Klara pleaded, pushing herself into a sitting position. "I have no memories of that night. The last thing I remember was drinking Nuallan's brew. I wouldn't have gone to Thorn's bed on my own and Thorn wouldn't take me after I slept, either. You know Karn has carted me off to bed without me rousing after drinking that damnable brew. And you saw how Nuallan reacted when he was questioned. He knows what really happened."

"You say you did not go willingly?" Ffearn asked, disbelief evident in his eyes.

Klara thought of all the times she and Thorn had held hands. They had never done it openly and never on purpose. Did Ffearn know? And Thorn had kissed her cheek at the lake. Karn had witnessed that. Everything seemed so innocent when it happened. Was there reason to doubt?

"You know I wouldn't have," Klara said. "When I roused I thought Karn had joined me in my own bed, because Thorn was spooning me as Karn does."

"I will tell him," Ffearn said. Then he turned and left.

Klara sighed. Had she planted the seed of Nuallan's guilt? And if Karn refused her, then what? Sighing, she packed her things and took them down to the picket line. After having not eaten for three days she felt just as weak and shaken physically as she was emotionally. When it was time for breakfast, Klara buried her face in Constant's mane and cried for both the heartache she felt and the hunger gnawing at her insides.

Bardus arrived carrying a bowl of porridge and handed it to her saying, "Karn says he won't kill you, but I didn't think you'd join us at the fire since it's his turn to cook."

Klara greedily took the bowl and began spooning the thick bunches of oats into her mouth. Bardus looked at her gravely and asked, "When was the last time you ate?"

"Three days ago," Klara said between mouthfuls. "It was when you last brought me porridge."

"Three days ago!" Bardus said.

Klara did not answer but nodded and kept eating.

"You need to eat every day, Klara," he said.

Klara handed the empty bowl back. "Every day isn't possible when you're an outcast."

The next two days passed much as the last two had, with Klara spending her time alone. Karn still refused to talk to her. The closest she came to another being was standing with Bardus as they watered the horses. She had not eaten since Bardus brought her breakfast because Thorn followed Karn in the cooking rotation. Her desire to avoid Thorn far outweighed the desire for food. And though she had been spared from drinking the brew again, the hunger gnawing at her left her just as dizzy and confused as if she had been drinking it.

When Thorn woke her to take over the watch, he did not speak. He only shook her until her eyes opened, then walked away. Even he blamed her for what happened. But since it was her in his bed, what alternative was there? He was too close to Nuallan to lay blame where it belonged.

At the conclusion of her watch, Klara started breakfast. She made oatcakes, stacked them in a clean cauldron, and set the jug of honey nearby. Taking one off the top, she folded it in half and stuffed it in her mouth. Being able to eat was the only good she found in the day. Taking the dirty dishes to the creek, she washed them well away from the rest of the company.

For supper she made beans and ate them mutely. An oppressive silence hung over the company as she cooked and ate. Was the silence because she was present? Or had it been that way since the morning she woke in Thorn's bed? Her work complete, Klara went to bed with a heavy heart.

In the morning Ruis handed her dried apples and nuts for breakfast. It was the closest he had gotten to her in the last seven days. He did not smile or speak, just handed her the food and walked off.

That evening Bardus insisted on cooking. "The lot of you may not have noticed, but she's been skipping meals and Ruis's cooking only gives her another excuse. I'll not have her starve to death here on the road."

Because starving to death in a village was more convenient? Holding her tongue, she sat on her bedroll in silence.

When it was time to eat, Bardus brought her a bowl of beans. Handing them to her, he said, "I told you to eat every day." Then he turned and walked back to the fire.

CHAPTER 24

# KING DOVSK'S HALL

KLARA AND BARDUS rode in silence, bringing up the rear of the column. At midday, all save Bardus avoided her and it was not until they were back on the road that Bardus finally spoke. "We'll reach the fortified city of Gnyozdovo today. Tonight you'll have a bed at King Dovsk's hall. As you are unmarried, it'll likely be well away from the lot of us and that's probably for the best."

"Has it been that long already? The days have all blended together in my mind," Klara said, feeling confused and a little disoriented. Then she thought to ask, "How can we take lodgings at a king's hall? Why won't we be staying at an inn?"

"You forget that you are in the company of a king," Bardus said. "Kings provide each other lodgings when they visit one another's estates. As I understand it, Thorn wants to use this as an opportunity to make it known that he is returning to Duirness and the city will again be under kingly rule. Otherwise, I expect he might avoid the other rulers altogether."

"I've never been inside a fortress," Klara said. "Or even a great house."

"Nor have I, lass," Bardus said, "nor have I."

The sun was setting behind the city as they approached. Fields, orchards, and stockyards surrounded the settlement. The timber palisades cast long pointed shadows, which seemed just as menacing as the palisades' spear-like tips. As they passed through the gates, red-shirted Mordva warriors stared at her. She stared back. The scalps of their enemies dangled from the warriors' shoulders and a bear paw was emblazed across each of their chests. Klara shuddered at the thought of keeping such gruesome trophies.

A sprawling market, overflowing with trade goods, lay just inside the city gate. The Skoloti and Moksha languages filled her ears as scents of savory foreign dishes spilled from the inns, taverns, and food vendors that lined the main thoroughfare. Side streets and alleys provided glimpses of the ramshackle homes of the city's inhabitants. Containing more people than Klara had ever seen together in one place, the town was a bustle of activity.

King Dovsk's hall dominated the scene, sitting atop a hill where it overlooked both the city and the Dnieper River. It was easily the largest building she had ever seen. A lime wash applied the hall's exterior protected it from the elements. Because it turned the walls white, the hall very much appeared to be a beacon on the hill.

Upon reaching the hall, most of the party happily passed their mounts to the stable boys. However, Klara insisted on remaining with Bardus and looking after Constant herself. As she brushed Constant, the stable hands made a show of being busy feeding, watering, and brushing the other animals, all while casting glances her direction.

Klara was used to garnering the attention of every man for miles around. But she was not accustomed to them hanging back and whispering rather than boldly stepping forward to introduce themselves and proposition her. Their behavior made her nervous.

Leaning over the stall's rail, Klara said, "Bardus, they're looking at me."

Bardus laughed. "I expect word of you has passed all through the city by now, and if not, it will have by morning."

"Why me?" Klara asked, feeling self-conscious.

"Well, let's see," Bardus said, ticking items off on his fingers. "You are the only woman in a party of men. You just rode into town in the company of a foreign king. You had a bow slung across your back, a dagger belted to your waist while you did it, and you're wearing breeches. Then you insisted on caring for your own horse. That's not something visitors to a king's hall generally do."

"You're here with me," Klara said, passing Bardus the brush. "Why don't they look at you the same way?"

"Because it is a squire's job to care for his master's horses," Bardus said. "Now let's get you inside. I expect you'll be wanting a bite to eat and a bed before long."

A girl of about fourteen burst from the hall, nearly colliding with Klara and Bardus. "Beg pardon, my lady," the girl said, balancing a tray of food in her arms. "I was sent to bring you supper, but you weren't the in cottage and I didn't know where to find you. Follow me and I'll show you to your lodgings."

Klara raised an eyebrow at Bardus and shrugged. She had never been referred to as a lady before. Eager for a meal and a bed, she left Bardus and followed the girl across the yard to a two-room cottage near King Dovsk's hall. The stables were visible from the doorway. Klara felt comforted knowing she was housed near her horse. Then she followed the girl inside.

Despite the scorching summer heat, a fire was burning on the hearth in the middle of the room, the smoke collecting beneath the thatch. A bench was pushed back against the wall and a small table flanked by a pair of benches was set in the corner. An ox hide curtain hung in a doorway, partitioning off another room which contained two pallets, each piled deeply with fleeces.

As Klara stored her belongings in one of the wardrobes in the bedchamber, the girl, who could only be described as a plain brown spot, placed the platter of food on the table. Lingering awkwardly, the maid finally asked, "Will you be needing anything else, my lady?"

"I am no lady and the food is fine, thank you," Klara said, as she returned to the main room. She had never been waited on before and was unsure of how to respond.

"Are you not the wizard woman then?" the girl asked. "We was told a wizard woman was to arrive and we'd know her for she'd be wearing breeches."

"I am no wizard, though I have met one," Klara said, looking over the offerings on the tray. "I cannot say that I am nearly as impressed with wizards as many seem to think I ought to be." Was the girl disappointed or relieved?

In an attempt to be friendly, Klara asked, "What's your name, girl?"

"Hanja, miss," the girl said and dropped into a curtsy. "I'll be your servant as long as you're here. I was told to look after the needs of the wizard and her guest."

"Well, Hanja, have you been given any indication as to how long I'll be a guest here? My companions haven't told me," Klara said. She was not entirely sure she wanted to be the guest of a wizard or anyone else for that matter.

"I was told you'd be here through Pyhä Äkräs Festival," Hanja replied, "and will see the blessing of the crops."

Klara nodded. To her it was Lughnasad; everyone, it seemed, had an agricultural celebration and associated deity.

There was another knock, this time admitting several servants carrying a round cedar tub and pails of water. Backing up, Klara made room for the newcomers, who placed the tub and water before the fire.

A tall servant handed Hanja a bucket containing the soap and laid a blanket across her arms. Turning to Klara, he said, "The Kenetlo King said you'd be wanting a bath, miss." Then he exited the cottage, taking the other servants with him.

Klara stood in the middle of the room feeling somewhat bewildered. After all the trouble she had caused him, and all the disappointed stares, Thorn had ordered her a bath?

Hanja laid the blanket on the bench, then filled a kettle with water and hung it over the fire to heat. "Will you need help undressing, miss?"

"No, Hanja, I can manage that on my own," Klara said, tearing her gaze from the tub.

"Do you have clothes that need washing?" Hanja asked, wiping her hands on her apron. Clearly the girl was well trained and knew her business. Klara was about to send her away when she realized that everything she owned needed a proper laundering.

"Aye," Klara said and hastily collected her garments from the wardrobe. Then she took off all her clothes and handed them to the Hanja as well. As she did, she held up the bandeau she had altered. "This bandeau is not to be mended, altered, or changed in any way. It is to come back to me exactly as I have given it to you. It is the only thing that will hold me in when we need the horses to move swiftly."

The girl nodded her understanding, curtseyed, and left with the arm load of laundry.

Leaving the water before the fire to heat, Klara sat naked on one of the benches as she ate a supper that consisted of cold meats, bread, cheese, and fresh apricots. When she finished eating, she filled the tub and gratefully sank into it. She had finished washing and was enjoying her soak when there was another knock at the door. Was there any peace to be had in this settlement?

Unwilling to entertain visitors, Klara shouted, "Go away, I'm naked."

"Just me, miss," Hanja shouted through the door. "I've come to collect your tray."

"Very well," Klara said. The girl entered and walked directly up to Klara, bent over her and peered at her scalp. "What are you doing?" Klara asked.

"Judging how much soap and scrubbing you'll need," Hanja said, poking through Klara's hair.

"I've already washed," Klara said, batting Hanja's hands away.

Hanja screwed up her face in disbelief. "Could use another soaping, then." At which point she soaped her hands and began working at Klara's scalp.

After she finished, Hanja wrapped her in the blanket and said, "I'll take down your tray and send some servants to empty the water and remove the tub. You can breakfast in the hall with the other guests in the morning."

Klara was glad of the blanket, since it was all she had to cover herself with when the servants returned for the tub. She had given all her clothing to Hanja. Then, she sank in the fleeces that comprised her bed and enjoyed the most comfortable night of sleep she ever had.

It was midmorning when Klara was awakened by a knock at the door. It was Hanja bearing freshly laundered clothing. Klara rubbed the sleep from her eyes and donned the dress she wore when in town, while Hanja lingered near the door.

"Have you seen the wizard yet, miss?" Hanja asked.

"No, is she here?" Klara asked, feeling uncomfortable at the thought that the wizard may have passed the night in the bed beside her without her knowing.

Disappointment settled in Hanja's shoulders. "If she is, no one's seen her yet. Will you be needing anything else?" Klara did not and sent Hanja away.

Having been in the company of Keltoi for so long, Klara was unaccustomed to being alone. She wondered how, or even if, they would send her word of their whereabouts. Eventually, she abandoned the hut in favor of making her way to the stable to see Constant. There she found Bardus.

"I see you've survived the night," he said as he exited Flax's stall. "You weren't at breakfast this morning. Have you eaten?"

"Not yet, I slept through breakfast," Klara said, reaching out to scratch Constant's forehead. "I'll eat supper tonight, though."

"We are not on the road where food is packed away," Bardus said. "You are in a hall overflowing with food because they are in the midst of preparing for a harvest festival. The kitchen will be happy to provide you with food. Provided, of course, that we can find the kitchen." Then he offered her his arm, which Klara gratefully accepted.

They found the kitchen easily enough, having only to follow the scent of roasting meats to a smoke-filled shack not far from Dovsk's hall. One of the maids put some bread and cheese in a sack for them. Then she gave them directions to a brier where they could help themselves to fresh blackberries.

As they left, Bardus asked, "Have you seen the back of this place yet?"

"No," Klara said. "All I've seen is the stable and the cottage where I slept."

"Then we need to walk around back before heading to the brier," Bardus said. "But you must keep your eyes closed as we do."

Klara felt awkward being led by the arm with her eyes shut and tried to peek. Bardus caught her in the act and admonished her for it. When at last Bardus permitted her to open her eyes, the sight took her breath away.

Before her was a spectacular view. To the south the Dnieper River dominated the scene, winding its way westward. Between them and the river, fields and pasture were dotted with stock. And beyond the fields was a forest of evergreens that stretched westward into the misty, blue horizon.

"This place must have been chosen as much for its beauty as the hill top location," Klara said.

"It's beautiful no matter which way you look," Bardus replied. "I was out here last night and the light of the setting sun turns the hall's walls red. It won't be nearly as impressive tonight, though, with all these tents going up on the lawn to block the view."

Standing at the edge of the yard, Klara turned to take in the hall and the lawn full of tents which housed guests who came for the festival. The hall's steep roof was heavily thatched and tall enough that the smoke collected well above the heads of its inhabitants before seeping through the thatch or escaping under the eaves. The building was more impressive from this side than from the stable. In the center of the hall, a large porch had benches for those who wished to sit and enjoy the view. The main porch was flanked by two small ones. Having been in few buildings that contained more than two rooms, she could not imagine living in such a place. How many rooms were there? Six? Eight?

After Klara had her fill of the view, she and Bardus picnicked at the blackberry patch. Fingers stained purple from berry picking, they sat in a shady patch of grass, avoiding the sweltering heat.

"This afternoon I'll see if there is any pennyroyal to be had in town, in case it becomes necessary," Bardus said, almost casually. "I know you've used it before. I recognized it as one of the herbs you've added to the drinking horn on occasion."

Klara looked at him surprised. "The time for pennyroyal is since past, it's to be drunk as a tea the morning after intercourse." Bardus gave her an inquisitive look, so she added, "Such knowledge was necessary given my occupation."

"It's best to take it the morning after, then even a small dose will suffice," Bardus said. "In larger doses it can be used to re-start a woman's cycle and an extremely large dose can end an unwanted pregnancy. If it is any consolation to you, I don't believe you made it to Thorn's bedroll on your own. I've seen Karn carry you off to bed without you rousing after having Nuallan's drink. That morning you were as wobbly as a new colt and that was well after much of its effect had worn off. I'd wager someone put you in Thorn's bed, but I've yet to work out who or why."

"There was only the six of you in camp," Klara said, wondering why

Bardus still has not figured out who the culprit was. "The only one in camp devious enough to dump me in Thorn's bed is Nuallan."

Bardus sprawled in the grass, propped on an elbow. "I'm not entirely sure of that. Thorn was under the influence of Nuallan's brew as well. He weighs quite a bit more than you, so it would not have affected him to the same extent it did you. He might have put you there himself. Nuallan said what the King does is none of our business. And as I said, the poppy sometimes causes a person to do things they otherwise would not."

Klara had not considered that. Might Thorn be to blame?

"But," Bardus continued, "I don't think it was Thorn. He's not had a woman since his died and if any harm were to come to you, lass, I think it would break him."

Klara looked at him confused. "I thought Thorn was a bachelor, not a widower." Thorn had never spoken of a wife and, as awkward as he was around her, she could not imagine him having much experience with women. But then, he neglected to tell her he was a king and there was no denying that was pertinent information about his past.

"Thorn's woman was an Odrysian that he received as payment for a debt; they weren't married," Bardus explained. "But I think he treated her well. She took ill when they first came to Olbia and by the time he found me, there was nothing I could do. It was a vaginal infection. That was a dozen years ago now. Anyway, he was badly shaken and blamed himself when she died. Over the years Ruis and I tried getting him to visit Moanin' Mona, but he always refused. That's why I don't think it was him."

"Who's Mona?" Klara asked, tearing off a hunk of bread.

Bardus popped a handful of berries in his mouth before answering. "She's a whore in Olbia. I think the prospect of intercourse frightens him, so I don't see him carrying you off to bed. He sent me to examine you at Midsummer. And he nearly came apart when he thought those men might have violated you at Vera's. If he put you in his bed, it was only because he was drugged. A more reasonable option is Ffearn or Nuallan put you there to cause trouble between you and Karn."

Klara had been slicing the cheese with her dagger and nearly cut herself when her head popped up to meet Bardus's eyes. "Ffearn would not."

"Aye, he might," Bardus said, taking a slice of cheese from her. "I've known the lads a long time. He and Karn are closer than most and Ffearn's been keeping Karn away from you. Jealously causes people to do strange things. But I'm putting my money on Nuallan. It's no secret Nuallan doesn't approve of your union, and this business with the drink didn't start until after you and Karn exchanged rings."

"So why put me in Thorn's bed and not yours or Ruis's?" Klara asked pushing aside the food and flopping down on her side.

"Lass, had you ended up in either of our beds, Karn would not have thought twice about taking our heads," Bardus said. "Karn would not take Thorn's head, and that is evidenced by the fact that Thorn still has his head."

"Do you really think Nuallan wants to be rid of me so badly that he would arrange for my death?" Klara asked, plucking at the grass.

"I don't know, but death was a possibility for you. Karn must care for you a great deal because he let you live and keep the ring," Bardus said. "When Waywyrd gets here, I'm sure he'll sort it out. The wizard will know whether Nuallan lies or speaks true."

Klara perked up at that. "Will Waywyrd will be joining us or another wizard? The girl who brings me food said a wizard woman was coming."

"It's only a rumor I heard, but both Waywyrd and his sister, Pendrwyrd, are expected," Bardus replied. "Now, shall I take you back to your quarters or would you like to see part of the city?"

For the remainder of the afternoon, the pair of them wandered through the markets, admiring the wares of the street vendors. She saw no sign of the other Keltoi, but Bardus told her that Thorn, Ffearn, and Karn were probably stuck at court and that Ruis likely made his way to the garrison. Neither of them cared where Nuallan had gone off to. Afterward Bardus walked Klara to her quarters and told her that he would return to escort her to supper.

Supper was not as bad as she imagined it might be. Since it was summer, the fires normally burning on the hearth in the center of the room were out. The doors were flung open, allowing light and the evening breeze to freely enter the hall.

As visiting royalty, Thorn was seated with their host, King Dovsk, so she did not have to interact with him. Ffearn and Karn were seated with the other nobility, which left her, Bardus and Ruis to sit among the other commoners. If Nuallan was there, they did not see him. A sideboard was laden with rich meats, cheeses, breads, thick bowls of beans and lentils, and roasted vegetables. As commoners they were free to help themselves. The nobility must wait to be served, even though they dined on the same fare. As the dishes were emptied, the servants replaced them with bowls of fresh fruit in syrup, quick breads, and pies.

Pushing her bowl away, Klara looked at Bardus and Ruis, who were still busy filling their mouths. "I cannot recall when I have ever eaten so much," she said.

"It's not that you ate much," Bardus said. "It's just that over the last few days you have eaten so little that your stomach isn't accustomed to a full meal." Klara brushed his concerns aside. She had known hunger as a child and still managed to survive.

On the road most of her time was spent the Ffearn and Karn, so she knew little of her other companions. Seeking conversation now that her belly was full, she asked, "How did you come by your medical training?"

"I've no formal training," Bardus said, using bread to sop up meat juices. "When the city of Duirness fell, I was only a lad. My parents stayed to fight, but they insisted that my younger sister and I flee before the demons arrived. We ended up orphaned and managed on our own for a while, but my sister had a cut that got infected. Had I known the littlest bit about dressing wounds, it would not have. Ultimately, the wound turned septic and she died. After that I learned all I could about doctoring. I was too old to be apprenticed, so I hired myself out as a farmhand to houses that had healers. Since I was more eager to learn than their apprentices, they let me sit in on the lessons if my other work was done."

"And all of you knew each other in Olbia?" Klara asked. Her conversation was directed at her dining companions, but her eyes were focused on Karn. If Ffearn was actively keeping them apart, then Karn might listen to her pleas if she got him alone. But how would she get him alone?

"All except Nuallan," Ruis replied, sawing through a hefty hunk of roast beef. "He showed up with the wizard last fall. Bardus and I lived in Olbia near on twenty years and Thorn's been there about a dozen. We didn't know he was our King until the lads showed up three or four years ago. He and the lads were happy enough to live as tradesmen and be treated as equals. When Nuallan arrived, he got everyone worked up about returning to Kenetlon and even tried getting us to address Thorn as 'Your Majesty.' Well, Thorn would have none of that."

Cutting short their conversation, Hanja appeared, curtseyed, and said, "Several of the ladies have asked you to join them this evening, miss."

"Seems you're a celebrity," Ruis said with a chuckle.

"All thanks to you," Bardus said, scowling at Ruis. Turning to Klara he said, "Be on your best behavior. You will be among Mordva ladies, not Skolts, and certainly not men."

Hanja led Klara from the main hall and deposited her in an adjacent room. Finely dressed women surrounded her, while she was in plaid fitting only for a farmwife. Klara immediately felt self-conscious.

"Please sit," said a woman in a red dress, patting the seat beside her. Then she waved at a servant who brought Klara a goblet of wine. When Klara was seated and sipping the wine, the woman in red introduced herself as Lady Rozsa and quickly ticked off the names of all the other women in the room. Klara easily missed half the names.

Leaning in and smiling, Rozsa said, "Now, tell us all about your adventures."

At first Klara left out anything remotely dangerous. Instead, she focused on telling them about the different scenery she encountered along the way, just as she had done with Laszlo. Unfortunately, these accounts did not satisfy them.

Lady Rozsa clucked her tongue, leaned in conspiratorially and said, "I heard you were the first member of the party to kill a man? And that you've killed them with both bow and dagger."

"Where did you hear that?" Klara asked. Were the rumors of murder already catching up to them? Did they need to flee?

"It's been all the talk among the warriors," Lady Rozsa said, fluttering her hand. "Apparently, someone down at the garrison noticed you wore a dagger when you rode into town and remarked that it was a useless thing for a woman to have. It seems your weapons master set him straight."

Ah, Ruis, Klara thought, now I know why I'm a celebrity. The women were eager for gossip and she was expected to provide the required entertainment. Not all that different from working in the alehouse.

Rozsa took her hand and patted it, her eyes glinting with anticipation. "There is no need to be bashful here. Tell us everything."

Not sure of the proper etiquette for discussing murder, Klara decided to only confirm what Ruis had already said. Yes, she was the first kill and that man was taken with her bow. She killed men with her dagger but omitted telling them under what circumstances—or anything else that transpired at Vera's. Soon she was assailed by questions from all sides, as all the women in the room had something they wanted to ask.

"I heard you've trained with the young princes, to improve your fighting skills," said a blue-clad woman in back. Klara tried to recall the woman's name. Boroka? Yes, that was it.

"Aye," Klara said. "Ruis has me train with them quite regularly, to improve my skill with a dagger." That last bit set the room atwitter. Clearly it was more amazing to participate in weapons training alongside noblemen than it was to actually kill someone. When they finally had their fill of her, Klara gratefully sought her bed, wondering where or how she might contrive to run into Karn. Since he and Ffearn were always together, it seemed like an impossible mission.

# CHAPTER 25

# AN APOLOGY

LARA AND BARDUS were in the stables feeding the company's horses when a gangly stable boy caught her in Constant's stall and asked, "Is it true that you single-handedly faced down a whole hoard of demons and you were naked when you did it?"

From where he stood tossing hay in the manger for the pack horses, Bardus snorted out a laugh. Klara shook her head. She would give Ruis a good tongue-lashing later.

Looking at the lad, she said, "It wasn't a hoard, just a pack. I politely asked them to leave, and they did."

The lad looked disappointed, then brightened. "But you were naked!"

"Only because I'd just gone swimming," Klara said. "Which I hardly think is relevant."

The lad darted off to relay the information to his friends, who she saw poking their heads around the barn door. After he left, she said, "It might be easier for everyone concerned if I spend the rest of the morning in the cottage, out of sight, and away from gossip."

"Aye, that might be best, lass," Bardus agreed, leaning a pitchfork against the stable wall. "I don't think anyone in this town has had the pleasure of knowing any Skoloti women. Besides, a bit of rest won't hurt you."

Walking back to the cottage, Klara noticed that the villagers stared as she passed. It was the same the world over. When she was working at the alehouse, she had garnered just as much attention. In Skoloti they shunned her for not becoming a warrior; here she was too much like a warrior. Since there was nothing else for her to do, Klara stripped to her shift and indulged in the luxury of a nap.

During the heat of the afternoon she was awakened by Hanja knocking at her door. The girl slipped inside and said, "King Thorn wishes to see you, miss."

Klara sat up and rubbed her eyes. "Where is he?"

"He's here, miss," Hanja said. "Shall I help you dress, or will you give me a message for him?"

"I'll dress," Klara said, rising from the fleeces. "Tell him I'll see him."

When Klara emerged in the outer room, Thorn stood holding a bundle of red fabric in his arms. "I've come to apologize."

"For what?" Klara asked. She had some pretty good ideas, but wanted to hear from his lips exactly what he was apologizing for.

"We could speak more openly if your servant were not present," Thorn replied. Hanja excused herself without waiting for Klara to ask her.

Once the girl was gone, Thorn continued, "I've talked with Bardus. He's made some good points. I don't know how you ended up where you did. Like you, I have no memories of the night. Ruis agrees that it's unlikely you managed the distance on your own. I am willing to concede that it might not have been of your doing. If I have been the cause of this trouble, I am greatly sorry. I told Nuallan that we'll drink no more of his elixirs."

Klara sat on the bench and took in his words. Then she turned pleading eyes on him. "Has Bardus talked to Karn? Or will you? Do you think he'll ever forgive me?"

For the first time in a long while, hope glimmered in her chest. It was not just Karn she missed. She missed the comradery that came with being a welcomed member of the company.

"Karn has not spoken to me since—" Thorn paused awkwardly before continuing. "Since the morning you were found ill. If he would see me, I would apologize to him as well and take responsibility for what happened. Seeing as things stand ill between you and you cannot spend the evening with him, will you consent to join me at the head table?"

"I have no fine clothes, I would be out of place," Klara said, remembering how self-conscious she felt among the ladies.

Thorn held the bundle of fabric out to her. "I am told by one of the ladies that this might fit. She was quite impressed with you last night and was willing to loan you a gown for the evening."

Klara rose, accepted the fabric, and shook it out, revealing the dress Lady Rozsa had worn the prior evening. "But if I wear her dress what will she wear?"

"Noble women generally own more than one dress," Thorn said. "I am told this particular lady will be wearing yellow this evening and she was eager to have you join us at the head table."

Laying the dress across her arm, Klara said, "I would be happy to join you, though I fear my manners may make me an unwelcome guest."

"Follow my lead and watch the other ladies. Do as they do and I'm sure you'll be most welcome," Thorn said, offering her a sad smile. Then he turned and left.

Thorn had no more than shut the door when Hanja knocked and entered. He must have suspected the girl had not gone far, because he apologized without ever indicating what actually transpired. Clearly, he was more skilled at managing household servants than he let on.

Klara held the dress up for Hanja to see. "It's Lady Rozsa's dress. Thorn wants me to wear it tonight." Then she slumped onto the bench, rumpling the dress in her lap. "But I was born into poverty, so I can't even begin to imagine all the things I need to wear with this."

Hanja was grateful to finally have a task. The pair of them went through Klara's wardrobe. The stockings and what Hanja called the 'proper' bandeau were deemed acceptable. However, the sleeves of Klara's shift were too long for it to be usable; borrowing another one was necessary as were a pair of underskirts. Since she lacked hair combs, they decided to put baby's breath and red hollyhocks in her hair. And she needed ornamentation: the only jewelry Klara owned was her ring.

"Ladies that haven't got necklaces sometimes pin a broach or other bobble to a length of ribbon and tie that around their neck," Hanja said. "We might do something like that for you."

Klara rummaged in her purse and produced some coppers. "Take these for the purchase of the ribbon. It'll be faster if you go since I don't know the locations of seamstresses or tailors where such a purchase might be made." That solved the problem of the necklace, but nothing could be done about the fact that there was no broach to attach to it.

Taking the coppers, Hanja ducked through the door. She reappeared a short time later bearing a bundle of borrowed clothing: a short-sleeved shift, two underskirts, and Lady Rozsa's own red slippers. The slippers pinched, but were usable.

"My sister has gone to fetch the ribbon and flowers," Hanja said, explaining their absence.

Laying everything aside, Hanja stripped Klara to her skin and then began dressing her all over again. Though Klara did not think it possible, Hanja cinched her bandeau tighter than Ffearn, Karn, or Bardus ever managed, and talked without ceasing all the while she worked.

"You must greet all the ladies with a compliment," Hanja said. "Lady Rozsa is very fond of loaning dresses but expects all praise for whoever wears gowns be directed back to her. If you forget, there'll be a spat and she'll not lend you another."

By the time Hanja's sister, a girl of nine, arrived with the ribbon, Klara sat sweltering in under three layers of undergarments.

Handing Klara the length of crimson ribbon and wad of matching lace, the girl said, "Mama said that all the fine ladies wear sashes and lace, so we bought this also." Then the girl dug into her pocket, producing rouge and a vial of scented oil. "Mama says you'll need to borrow these too, but that I wasn't to get the flowers 'til the last 'cause they'll wilt in the heat."

"Thank you, but I meant for you to keep the other copper." Klara collected her purse and dug out another copper for the child, who quickly disappeared again in search of flowers.

When the girl reappeared with the flowers, Klara's hair had been braided, plaited, pinned, tucked, twisted, and a crown of golden locks artfully adorned her head. They carefully eased her into the dress. Hanja slipped the lace around her waist, gathering and tucking the excess, turning it as she pinned it in place. The result looked like an overly large rose, centered at her navel. After tying the ribbon around her neck and putting the flowers in her hair, there was a single large, red, rose blossom left.

Picking up the blossom and a straight pin, Hanja turned to Klara and said, "Hold still."

Hanja put the pin in her mouth and slipped two fingers under the ribbon at Klara's neck. Klara gulped, realizing what the girl intended to do. In the end, the rose was affixed to the ribbon and she was only poked twice in the process.

Klara looked down, swishing her skirt and trying to imagine how she looked. "I don't know, it seems tight across the bosom. Shouldn't we use the lace to cover that?"

Hanja stepped back, put her hands on her hips, and appraised Klara. "If we pinned the lace across your chest instead of using it on your waist, it would only draw attention to the fact that the dress barely contains you and I can't cinch that bandeau any tighter."

Someone rapped on the door just as the girls finished anointing Klara with the scented oil. Opening it, Hanja admitted Thorn. Reaching to take her hand, he said, "You look lovely."

"It is all thanks to Lady Rozsa, who lent me the dress," Klara replied, remembering Hanja's instructions. Out of the corner of her eye, she caught Hanja nodding approval.

Klara dismissed the girls and once the door was shut, reached out, laying a hand on Thorn's chest. He was wearing the gray tunic embroidered with the King's Crest. The one Ffearn sometimes wore when he played the part of the wealthy gambler. She had always been mesmerized by the crest.

"You've talked with Ffearn?" she asked.

"Aye," Thorn said, "though Karn still will not see me. I told Ffearn the same thing I told you. He will relay the message."

"Thank you," Klara said and hugged him.

When she let him go, Thorn held her at the waist and looked her over. "You truly look magnificent. Every man in the hall will be taken by your beauty. Come, I would like to show you off and we can talk on the way." As they walked, Thorn gave her even more instructions on how to behave than Hanja had.

As they stepped across the threshold to the hall, a warrior standing in the entry way announced, "King Thorn and Miss Klara." All heads turned and watched as they entered together.

Not being keen on the idea of socializing, she had not been in the hall, save for meals. Now the hall was devoid of commoners. The sea of well-dressed nobles before her left Klara feeling more anxious and intimidated than she had in the face of any foe. Beside her, she felt Thorn feigning confidence as they mingled with the others before dinner. That gave her courage because it meant he was just as uncomfortable as she was.

A fair, clean-shaven man in a green tunic hailed them. Thorn headed his direction. Like the Keltoi, he was shorter than the other nobles in the hall. A silver fir crest was embroidered across the chest of his tunic. Standing beside him was a woman who was just as fair; both of them had blue eyes and wore their blond hair long, free of braids or other adornment. Was he another king? Or just a high ranking lord? Whatever he was, he was not Mordva.

"Tell us, who is this beauty on your arm?" the man asked.

"I'd like you to meet Klara; she is the seventh member of our company and a most welcome addition." Then turning to Klara, Thorn said, "This is Lord Kiel and Lady Lis'ana. We'll be traveling through their lands during the coming moon. They happen to be the only Elben here."

"I'm pleased to make your acquaintance," Klara said. Knowing that she was now looking at a pair of Elbs, she eyed them more critically. The woman wore a cream-colored gown, which seemed only to blanch the color from her skin. The effect was not flattering. And Ffearn and Karn were right, she did not have much of a chest. Still, Klara was certain she would be able to tell the genders apart, with or without their clothing.

Remembering the required compliment, Klara added, "You have a very lovely dress, Lady Lis'ana, it suits you very well."

Lady Lis'ana dismissed the empty compliment and did not return one in kind, but asked, "Have you been enjoying your time here?"

"I have," Klara said, wondering if she had done something wrong. "Yesterday Bardus took me to see the river and then we walked down to the orchards and picnicked by a blackberry bramble. We don't get much time for leisure on the road. It's nice not to be constantly moving. We even spent some time wandering through the markets. I've not been in many large towns and have never seen so many trade goods all in one place."

Lord Kiel laughed. "Thorn, why have you hidden this delightful creature away and not brought her to court?" Klara thought he might be mocking her. "I would much prefer discussions of produce and trade goods than gossip about dresses and marriage prospects. If we're going to delay negotiations, we might as well discuss something useful."

As the cluster talked, Lady Rozsa joined them, clearly fishing for a compliment. "How do you find the dress, dear?"

"It is magnificent. You have been most generous to loan it to me for the evening," said Klara, "though, I don't think I do justice, it was lovelier on you last night."

The woman beamed and took Klara by the arm. "Come with me, I'll introduce you to the other nobles."

Klara looked at Thorn, who nodded his approval, so she allowed Lady Rozsa to lead her around the room. Thanks to Hanja's instructions, Klara was well received and everyone found her charming, especially Lady Rozsa, who introduced Klara as "The Lady Killer."

If someone complimented her dress, Klara told them it was on loan from Rozsa. If someone complimented her figure, Klara said it was only because Rozsa's dress was so well cut that she appeared to have a finer figure than she truly did. If someone complimented the lace, she said it was not as fine as the sash Rozsa wore last night. And in turn Klara complimented something about every lady she met. The empty conversations and shallow compliments dragged on and she found the whole business tedious. No wonder Thorn avoided nobles whenever possible.

While she was still surrounded by a gaggle of gossips, the warrior at the door announced, "Prince Ffearn and Prince Karn."

Klara's heart stopped. They appeared so jovial and handsome together in new tunics, both of which were gray. Ffearn had put the silver beads back in his moustache. Karn was sporting a closely cropped and neatly trimmed beard, and his silver clip held back his braids. A wave of sadness washed over her, realizing how long it had been since she last set eyes upon him. But as Karn raised a hand to scratch his beard, silver light glinted off his ring, giving her hope.

Klara was drawn back into the conversation when someone next to her said, "I believe this one has her eye set on one of those Keltoi." Klara did not know the expressions on her face were so easily read and was shocked by the comment.

Lady Rozsa giggled. "Don't worry, dear, I believe with your looks and manners you'll be able to marry well above your station without having to take a Kelto for a husband."

"But I like Keltoi," Klara said, forgetting herself. "I've traveled among them so long that I often forget that I'm not a Kelta myself." This garnered laughter from the circle that had gathered around her.

"How can that possibly be the case?" Lady Rozsa asked. "You are nothing like a Kelta. They're all labor and industry. Couldn't catch a husband if one landed in her lap. They're nearly as bad as Elb maids." The women surrounding Rozsa tittered and giggled.

"I just feel like I belong with them," Klara said and paused a moment trying to figure out how best to explain. "On the road we sometimes went days without seeing other travelers and there are places that won't permit a woman to ride with a company of men. In those areas Karn and I rode ahead, pretending we were married so I could safely pass through the village. I generally wear breeches when we ride, but must wear a dress in town. Once I changed into my dress and wondered if I would pass for a Skolt only to laugh at myself when I realized, I am a Skolt."

"Well," Lady Rozsa said, "I can certainly see why someone would want to forget they were a Skolt, but tonight we'll get your mind off Keltoi and on Mordvins." This proclamation brought giggles from the assembled ladies.

Klara shook her head and offered them a good natured smile. "I don't think that will be possible. I'll be sitting with Thorn most of the night."

"It's a wonder they keep you around at all," said Lady Boroka. She was wearing the same blue dress as when they first met and still wore the same haughty expression. "You've not used their titles once during this whole conversation. I think their cook should show more respect."

"I'm not their cook," Klara said, her temper flaring and feeling that she somehow needed to prove herself. "I am an equal in the party. As for not using titles, I'd been traveling with them for more than a moon before they bothered to tell me they had titles. Even then, Thorn does not want me to address him as King and Karn has told me not to consider his title either."

Leaving the other ladies dumbstruck, Lady Rozsa led Klara around the room again. Once they were away from the group, Rozsa said, "Don't mind Lady Boroka. She has no prospects and no money. She is the last of seven daughters and the six before her used up all her father's goodwill. She'll have to marry beneath her if she is to take a husband. That, or run off with a foreigner, frowned upon, certainly, but it does happen."

"And what of marrying because you enjoy each other's company and want to spend your lives together?" Klara asked. "Surely that is more important than money and titles." If all Karn had offered her was a title, she would have left him standing alone at the lake. Now the roles were reversed and it was him rejecting her.

"My, but you are quaint," Rozsa replied. "Only commoners marry for love. The rest of us have lands and connections to consider. We are our fathers' highest and best bargaining chips."

Lady Rozsa led her from one group to another, seeking compliments for her generosity and good taste in dresses. All the while Klara tracked Karn with her eyes. Her heart fell when he offered his arm to Lady Boroka. Was this how Karn felt when he woke to find her asleep beside Thorn? No, that would have been so much worse; Thorn was his uncle, whereas she had just met this woman.

As Klara watched Karn and Lady Boroka laugh together, Ffearn approached and took her by the elbow. "Excuse me, Lady Rozsa, I've not had a chance to chat with Klara this evening." Leading her outside, away from the crowds, Ffearn said, "You must stop looking at him."

"Will he forgive me?" Klara asked, pleading really.

"Klara, now is not the time or place for this discussion," Ffearn said, leaning in close, his words little more than a whisper. "And I don't see how he can forgive you, when you're here with Thorn."

"Thorn came to apologize. He said he talked to you," Klara said, searching his eyes. "I'll leave now if it'll help."

Ffearn's breath was hot on her cheek as he spoke. "You can't leave, it would only cause a scandal. The problem is you shouldn't have come in the first place. You must stop looking at Karn. It's awkward for him and makes it difficult to navigate the room."

"Awkward for him?" Klara said, incredulous. She pushed Ffearn back.

"You accuse me when I've done nothing wrong. Then you tell me it's awkward for him when I must watch him flirt with other women before my eyes. He hasn't spoken to me in days."

"He let you live," Ffearn said, his voice cold as stone.

"Then perhaps he should have taken my life because it doesn't seem to be worth much," Klara said and turned to leave.

Ffearn caught her elbow. "Don't trust Thorn."

"Why not?" Klara asked. "He was under the influence of Nuallan's drink just as I was and he's told Nuallan we'll drink no more of his brews."

"It is better to be safe," Ffearn said. "We've all seen how he looks at you." Then he turned and left her.

When Klara returned to the room, Karn was deep in conversation with Lady Boroka. Klara drummed her fingers against her thigh. She may only be a whore, but she was fast learner. She had watched the ladies gossip and knew she could put an end to Karn's and Boroka's conversation without setting another eye on him. Immediately she sought out Lady Rozsa, allowing herself to be paraded around the room once again.

It was not long before Rozsa introduced her to a crusty old lord with a jewel-covered wife covered at his side. "You see, my dear, one can be beautiful while not wearing a single piece of jewelry."

Klara flashed a smile at him. "I am afraid that on that count you are mistaken. I wear the ring Prince Karn gave me."

Lady Rozsa jumped at the bait. "The Kenetlo Prince has given you a ring?"

"Aye." This was the moment she had been waiting for. Holding up her hand, Klara fluttered her fingers and allowed them to admire the ring. Pausing to make sure she had their full attention, she said, "He wears its mate."

Rozsa excused herself and headed straight for a gaggle of unwed women. Klara knew this fresh gossip was sure to make the rounds of the hall and word would reach Lady Boroka before the night was out. Smiling to herself, she returned to Thorn's side, where she intended to stay for the remainder of the evening.

At dinner, Klara remembered Thorn had told her to only take half the serving he did. The first course was a clear beef broth that had no substance to it at all and the second course was fresh greens sprinkled with oil and vinegar. Thorn hardly took any of each course and her stomach rumbled at the lack of sustenance. During the third course, salmon cooked in butter, Thorn sought her hand under the table. Taking her hand in his, he gently pulled it toward him, before releasing it.

"The salmon runs on the Rhine and Elbe were poor this spring," Lord Kiel said. "Without fish, there may be a rise in prices for salt pork and other meats."

"Has anyone heard the prospects for the fall run?" Thorn asked. He had not looked at her or even paused in his conversation. Since Thorn had not included her, she returned to listening to the conversation on her other side.

The next course was roasted hen with bread dressing and cranberry relish. After that was roasted pork with mashed turnips dyed red with beet juice. That was followed by beef with roasted vegetables. Klara finally understand why Thorn instructed her to take no more than a bite or two of each dish.

Two more times Thorn sought her hand under the table, each time gently pulling it toward him, then releasing it. The last time, though, he was discussing trade on the Danube. Klara recognized the name of the river. Thorn was trying to get her to pay attention to conversations about his homeland. After that, Klara listened carefully to what those around them had to say.

"This whole business with the tin and copper is a mess," said a hearty, carrot-topped man sporting a boar crest. "I can get copper from Kiel, but have to go clear down the Dnieper to Olbia to get tin. And if I'm in Olbia, I'd rather get iron, though it costs more."

"Is there a problem with Bevin's mines?" Thorn asked, picking at his food.

"The problem isn't Bevin's mines, it's Bevin's leadership," Kiel said, waving for more wine. "We could smelt the tin, mix it with our own copper, and make fine brass products, but Bevin refuses to trade."

"Then why not get iron from Gaul?" Thorn asked. "You said earlier his mines are producing well."

"Because Gaul dedicates all his iron to making implements of war," Kiel replied. "I greatly fear he and Bevin will come to a head and then there'll be open war right on our border."

"I don't think anyone wants to see open war," Thorn said. "Does anyone know Brawn's mind? Surely Norikum would intervene."

"The salt mines in Hallstatt are extremely profitable," Kiel said. "As a result, Brawn has turned his back on the north, trading to the south or running trade lines down the Danube to Olbia and Byzantium. You'll find no assistance there unless Ffearn is able to make a strong showing."

By the time the breads, cheeses and fruits were passed through, Klara was more than full. She had also learned that the men supported Ffearn as heir. Further, they did not like the idea of the area remaining without a king's rule since the trade agreements were coming apart at the seams.

King Dovsk rose and announced, "Our evening's entertainment continues on the lawn."

Klara lingered to watch Karn. He offered his arm to Lady Boroka, which she accepted. Klara's heart sank.

Offering her his arm, Thorn led Klara outside. There were jugglers, jesters, and minstrels, but none of it amused her.

As they wove their way across the lawn, navigating the crowd, a servant approached. "King Thorn, I have been informed that an apology gift from Master Nuallan for Miss Klara has been placed in your room."

Thorn dismissed the man.

"Why would Nuallan put a gift for me in your room and not give it to me himself?" Klara asked, sidestepping children racing willy-nilly though the crowd.

"I expect it's because if he gets within a swords-length of you, Bardus or Ruis will have his skin," Thorn said, patting her arm. "You don't seem to be enjoying the entertainment. Shall we go see what Nuallan's gotten you?"

Klara nodded and Thorn led her to one of the smaller porches off the back of the hall and into his room. She was shocked to find that his room was the size of her entire cottage. On the table was a beaker of wine.

Klara picked up the wine. "Why would he give me such a gift as this; wine is quite dear?"

"I expect," Thorn said, "that he knows more than he's told us and for that he feels guilty."

"So you think he put me in your bed?" Klara asked, setting the wine back on the table.

"No." Thorn shook his head, seeming distressed by her accusation, but managed to collect himself. "He is a loyal companion. He would not have done such a thing."

Gesturing toward the wine, he asked, "Would you like to partake of your gift?"

Klara shrugged. "Might as well. Do you have flagons or goblets? Otherwise we'll be drinking straight from the beaker."

Thorn smiled at her. "A king's quarters come better provisioned than most." He rifled through a cupboard and emerged with two goblets. Once each of them had wine in hand, Thorn said, "You can see all the festivities on the lawn from the porch."

On the porch in the middle of the hall, King Dovsk sat with his entourage. One of the small decks was Thorn's. Klara was unable to see who sat on the other end. The festival unfolded before them. The jugglers finished and the minstrels and bards were just tuning up to prepare for songs and dancing. It was a merry scene, but Klara found no joy in it knowing that Karn and Ffearn were out there among the crush of bodies and she was not with them.

She and Thorn drank in silence for a while before he said, "You don't seem happy."

"I've been doing a lot of thinking of late," Klara said, wanting to press Thorn about his comment earlier. "What could Nuallan know that he's not saying?"

Rising, Thorn gestured toward the door. "This conversation is best had inside."

Once they were seated in his room, Thorn said, "Given the strength of the drink and the degree to which it affects you, Bardus and Ruis insist there is no way you made it to my bed on your own. The only other explanation is that I put you there myself. Nuallan was my father's advisor and petitioned to be my regent. He would never say anything that would cast Clan Duir in an ill light. The only reason to deflect blame onto you is to protect me. Bardus said poppy might cause a person to do things they otherwise would not." Thorn paused before continuing, "I am only glad that you do not hate me for what I've done."

"I could not hate you. I know how the drink affects me as well," Klara said. For all the longings she had felt rippling off him over the course of their journey, he had never behaved inappropriately. And, if what Bardus said was true, was unlikely, too.

Looking about the room, Klara changed the subject by asking, "Are all visitors to the hall given quarters so large?"

Thorn laughed. "Goodness no, I have been given this room because of my status. Would you like to look around?" Klara nodded and Thorn refilled their goblets before giving her a tour.

The room contained a table flanked by a pair of benches. It was large enough to seat eight. As Klara's fingers felt the smoothness of the wood, Thorn said, "This serves as a place for visiting nobility to meet privately with their advisors. I can have dinners brought in here for the company, too, but I did not want to burden the kitchen. And after what happened, I thought it might be best if we all dined on our own."

"What's behind this?" Klara asked. Pushing aside a heavy curtain on one side of the room, revealed a massive bed, the likes of which she had never seen before. "You could get lost in that bed!"

"I believe it's meant to be shared with a queen, or possibly an entire harem." Thorn was smiling again, something he seldom did.

"You have a beautiful smile," Klara said, letting the curtain drop. "You should wear it more often."

"If it will bring you pleasure, I shall," he said.

Moving to a wicker screen in the corner of the room, Thorn said, "Wait until you see this. I thought of you as soon as I saw it. I considered having you brought here to enjoy it the night we arrived but knew it would scandalize the hall, so I just ordered you a bath instead."

"And I wanted to thank you for the bath, it was wonderful to soak in the warm water before the fire," Klara said as she crossed the room.

"I can arrange for you to have a bath every night if you like. If you want, you can even use mine." As he spoke, Thorn pushed aside the wicker privacy screen, behind which was a large cedar tub. Klara ran her fingers over the smooth wood. "You bathe here?" she asked, amazed. The tub was large enough to completely recline. It would be nothing like folding oneself into a tub before a fire.

"Aye, more like swimming than washing. That's why I thought of you;

it reminded me of all the time you spent in the water at the lake." Thorn turned her to him and took a stray curl in his hand. "I thought of how you swam out to meet the moonlight and of the kindness you showed me there."

While they were talking, the moon had crested the hall and now was shining its silver light through the door to the porch. "You are so very beautiful in the moonlight," Thorn said. "If I didn't know better I would swear you were the goddess herself. May I hold you?"

Klara nodded. Her mind was fuzzy with confusion and her body ached with longing. She had felt so alone and neglected over the past fortnight that at that moment she wanted to be held more than anything else.

Slipping his arms around her waist, Thorn pulled her to him. They stood in silence a moment before he led her to the bench at the side of the room. Thorn wrapped his arms around her as Klara laid her head on his chest. Time passed and she began to doze.

Shaking the sleep from her mind, Klara tried to sit up, but Thorn raised his hand to her head and bid her stay. "My nephew is a fool not to keep you. I saw you and Ffearn leave the room together; have you had word from him?"

Tears fell from Klara's eyes. "Ffearn said I shouldn't look at Karn because it makes him feel awkward."

Thorn raised her chin and his lips sought hers. Their kiss was slow and tender. There was a tug at the edge of her mind as if she could feel what Thorn felt: hope, belonging, worship.

When they parted, Thorn whispered, "If he will not have you then I shall. I will not deny that this is something my heart has greatly desired."

"Do you think he has refused me then?" Klara asked, brushing aside her tears.

"By his silence and by Ffearn's words, I think he has," Thorn said.

They kissed again and again she felt the tug at her mind. He was worshiping… worshiping her. Kisses with Karn had never been like this. Kisses with anyone had never been like this. A feeling of rightness bloomed in her chest and radiated to the tips of her fingers.

When they parted, Thorn whispered in her ear, "Will you have me, Klara?"

Klara felt her response more than she thought it. The only thing she had ever wanted was to be loved. The answer reverberated through her until it found her voice. "Aye," she whispered.

Their hands sought each other in slow and gentle embrace. Even now that she had offered her consent he was not pawing at her or trying to get under her skirt. What she felt, what he felt, was contentment at simply being together.

They were still engaged in tender kisses when a knock came at the door. "What is it?" Thorn called.

A servant answered, "The wizard, Waywyrd, has arrived and wishes to meet with you."

Thorn kissed her again. "Will you wait here for me?" he whispered.

"Aye," Klara replied.

"I'm coming," Thorn called to the servant. Then stood and straightened his tunic before heading out the door.

CHAPTER 26

# UNACCOUNTED-FOR INJURIES

KLARA WAS RIVETED from sleep by Ffearn shouting beside her. "Absent gods, Waywyrd, don't you knock!"

Cognizance sluggishly forced its way through the haze in her mind. She was naked, lying between Karn and Ffearn, their arms clasped over her abdomen. Every part of her body cried for attention: dull aches, sharp pains, stiff joints, and a pounding headache. When her eyes finally focused, she saw Waywyrd and Ruis standing at the foot of the bed, both of them looking grim.

Waywyrd ignored Ffearn's outburst. "How do you feel, Klara?"

"I hurt," Klara replied. Her voice was dull and raspy. And what was she doing between Ffearn and Karn? She should feel happy to be back among them, but all she felt was pain.

"Where do you hurt?" Waywyrd asked, using his staff to gesture across her body.

"Everywhere," Klara said, testing the stiffness in her limbs.

"Now tell me honestly," Waywyrd asked, "do you have any desire for sex?"

"Absent gods, no!" Klara exclaimed. "What kind of question is that?"

"Well, that's encouraging," Waywyrd said, leaning on his staff. "I need you to think now. Do you know how you came to be in this room? What can you remember of last night?"

"Thorn invited me to sit with him at dinner." Klara paused and bit her lip, remembering. "I did something I shouldn't have."

Waywyrd nodded encouragingly. Beside her, Ffearn and Karn were sitting up, eyes intent on her. Klara told them how she made sure Lady Rozsa knew that she wore the mate to Karn's ring because she was jealous of Lady Boroka. And she told them of her and Thorn's kisses, but she was unable to recall anything that transpired after the servant said Waywyrd had arrived.

She had no clothing save the shreds used to bind her wounds, so Karn wrapped her in the fleece-edged tunic he wore when guised as a Skolt farmer. Then he wrapped her in a blanket and carried her to the building that served as the infirmary. The loss of her memory and the extent of her injuries frightened her.

"Karn, please don't leave me again," she begged. "I'm so sorry for everything I've done."

Karn laid her in a pile of fleeces that served as a bed, pulled a blanket to her chin and kissed her forehead.

"I know," he said. "I promise to return as soon as I'm able."

When he left, the physician had her disrobe and examined every part of her, including parts she never had examined before. As the physician cleaned and dressed her cuts he asked, "Do you have any idea how you came by these wounds?"

"No," Klara said. "I can't remember anything."

Her arms and legs bore multiple slashes from knife wounds. Under her left breast was a cut that, had the assailant been successful, would have killed her. It was placed between her ribs and a well-timed thrust would have pierced her heart. Nor did she know how she sustained the bruises or the lump on her head which ached so terribly. And she had no idea how she went from being fully clothed alone in Thorn's room to being naked and bloody in Karn and Ffearn's bed. But what concerned her most was that nobody was willing to tell her how it happened.

"Drink this," the physician said, holding a beaker toward her. "It will ease the pain."

Klara drank it and lay back, intending to nap until Karn returned.

When she awoke a woman sat at her bedside. The woman's anxious face was surrounded by black hair that fell loose about her shoulders. She wore the same blue tunic as Waywyrd and, like him, had a silver streak in her hair and matching scar that ran along the side of her face. Klara assumed she was dreaming.

At seeing her awake, the woman spoke, "How do you feel?"

"Thirsty and hungry," Klara said. "Where's Karn? And who are you?"

The woman poured Klara some water and handed it to her, then asked the physician's attendant to bring food before answering Klara's question. "Karn was delayed, but I have been asked to stay with you until you can be reunited. I'm Pendrwyrd, Waywyrd's sister."

"Are you the wizard woman who wears breeches?" Klara asked. "The girl assigned to me said one was coming and seemed disappointed that I wasn't her."

"Wizardess." Pendrwyrd smiled. "Yes, I am that woman. Do you know how you came by your injuries?"

Klara thought for a while, then said, "No, but I get the feeling other people do and aren't telling me."

"And they will not," Pendrwyrd replied. "You may be the only witness to a crime and someone's life depends upon what you know. None are permitted to bias you by what they know or suspect."

The assistant returned with the same clear beef broth that was served at dinner and Klara drank it down hungrily. Afterward, Pendrwyrd helped her up and steadied her as she used the chamber pot, then aided her in returning to bed. The physician appeared with the pain-relieving drink, which Klara gratefully accepted. She still ached all over. Then she took another mug of water from Pendrwyrd and went back to sleep.

When Klara next woke, Pendrwyrd was standing near the door, looking out, exhaustion evident in her shoulders as she leaned heavily on her staff.

"Did you pass the night here with me?" Klara asked.

"I did," Pendrwyrd said without turning around. "Would you like breakfast?"

"I'd like to know where Karn is and I'd like to get out of this place," Klara said pushing back the blanket.

Pendrwyrd sighed. "Neither of those things is possible right now, but breakfast is."

Pendrwyrd helped her to the chamber pot and back again, though this morning Klara felt steadier on her feet. She was given more water and the physician's assistant brought her a thin porridge. After she ate, the physician came and examined every part of her again.

"Are you sure that's necessary?" Klara snapped as he used a finger to probe her vagina.

"I wouldn't do it if it weren't necessary," the physician shot back. "But you do seem to be healing everywhere. Do you know how you came by your injuries?"

"No," Klara said. "And I don't expect I ever will because no one will tell me. There are whole portions of days I can't remember."

*"Stop, say no more!"* Pendrwyrd's voice resonated in her head and felt as if it were bouncing off her skull.

"Ouch!" Klara bent, taking her head in her hands.

The doctor looked concerned. "I'll bring you something for the pain, but if becoming excitable has this effect on you, I may have to keep you sedated."

Then softer, Pendrwyrd's voice came in her head again, *"Be careful what you say and to whom; lives depend on what you know."*

When the physician left, Pendrwyrd sat on the edge of Klara's bed, staff at her side. "You must rest and you must try to remember." Then inside Klara's head Pendrwyrd said, *"When you remember, tell me first. Together we can decide how much to tell King Dovsk."*

"I can rest no more," Klara said. "I've been in this bed since yesterday with no sign of my friends. I intend to get out of bed and go find them and I don't understand why they haven't been to see me."

"No, Klara," Pendrwyrd said, "You've been in this bed four days. You slept three days straight and woke yesterday only long enough to take food. The first day Karn remained at your side. Ffearn had to bring him meals because he refused to leave you. But you cannot see them now."

Four days. Klara swallowed hard, realizing that she may, in fact, need to remain abed. Had the bump on her head really done her that much damage?

"When can I see them?" Klara asked a little petulantly, kicking at the blanket.

"You can see them when you remember," Pendrwyrd said. "It's clear you'll not rest here. I'll talk to the physician about moving you to our hut. Now try to sleep; memories are often unlocked by our dreams."

How did Pendrwyrd expect her to sleep after telling her she had been in bed for four days? After an hour of determined effort, Klara had added no more to her memories, so she tried another tactic. If not memory, then use of logic might lead to a conclusion about what happened. The knot on her head meant she had been bludgeoned, which likely accounted for the memory loss. As for the rest of her body, it looked like she had been on the losing end of a knife fight and had grappled with someone in hand-to-hand combat as well. That at least explained the what, now the question was who and why?

Klara knew she started out in Thorn's room and had been alone. Had someone thought the room was empty and snuck in with malicious intent? If they had, they would have been startled to find her there. That certainly made sense.

All she had to do was figure out who entered the room. It must have been someone who wished Thorn ill, either because they were benefiting from the chaos in Kenetlon or because they did not approve of the intended line of succession. Klara tried recalling if she heard anything in the great hall that indicated who might wish Thorn ill, but all she remembered was gossip about dresses and jewels. She cursed herself for not paying more attention to Thorn's conversations about trade.

Frustrated at turning up no suspects and exhausted from the mental stimulation, she fell into a fitful sleep. When she woke, Pendrwyrd was at her side, holding her staff. It was similar to Waywyrd's, though his staff was hemlock and Pendrwyrd's was made of birch.

"If I cannot see my companions, may I at least have word of them?" Klara asked.

"That depends on what information you seek," Pendrwyrd said, stroking her staff.

"When I woke with Ffearn and Karn, Waywyrd and Ruis were there. I know they are well, or were when last I saw them," Klara said. "Bardus wasn't and I find that unusual. If he knew I was injured, he would have been there to treat me. Nor have I seen Thorn and I worry for him. Was he involved in the same fight I was and injured, too? Is Bardus busy tending Thorn? Is that why they haven't been to see me?"

"I cannot answer those questions," Pendrwyrd replied.

Klara was stricken. Not answering was as good as an answer.

Seeing her fright, Pendrwyrd added, "I can tell you that the entire company is alive and they were happy to hear that you are awake." That was little by way of comfort.

Supper consisted of the same broth and a bit of bread. While Klara ate, Pendrwyrd conferred with the physician.

When the pair finished talking, Pendrwyrd returned to Klara's bedside and said, "He has consented to have you moved. Now that you're awake and talking, the entire city will be abuzz with gossip regarding anything you've said. In the privacy of our hut, there'll be fewer opportunities for your words to be overheard and whisked about the village. I've sent Hanja to bring you something to wear."

Hanja arrived carrying a bundle of clothing and set it on the bed, saying, "There wasn't enough to make an outfit out of anything, so I brought it all."

Klara dug through the pile. Her shift was missing. That made no sense; she was wearing a borrowed shift the night of accident. That potential theft needed to be addressed later. In the end, she wore the skirt without the shift and used the shirt she wore when riding in breeches.

The walk from the infirmary to Pendrwyrd's hut was onerous. Klara collapsed onto the bench as soon as they were through the door. Then she tried to puzzle out when her shift went missing. She had been wearing the red dress and borrowed shift that night. Given the extent of the injuries she sustained, had she fought with an intruder to Thorn's room in those, they were likely ruined. Afterward she needed to be covered in something, so it was likely they sent for her shift.

But if she started out in Karn and Ffearn's bed with her shift on, she certainly was not wearing it when she woke. Of course, the three of them has slept together bare before, so she may not have been wearing the shift when she arrived in their room. If that was the case, where was the missing shift?

Then Klara remembered Waywyrd asked her if she desired sex and the doctor said the examination of her vagina was necessary. Bardus also wanted to examine her after she and Karn coupled. Did this mean that she coupled with Karn or Ffearn or both of them? Panic gripped her. If they had been joined, then she needed to take pennyroyal the following morning.

But, she reasoned, Bardus said it still worked later, if the dose was larger. How much larger? And did she have enough?

Still thinking, Klara realized Waywyrd would not have cared if she bedded Karn, or Ffearn, for that matter. If he cared, it must have been someone else. Klara's stomach lurched. If not them, then who? Had the intruder to Thorn's room overpowered and forced her? It was a possibility but made no sense in the context of Waywyrd's words; it was her desire he spoke of. Sleep overtook her as she sat trying to piece together the past few days of her life.

# CHAPTER 27
# AN ELABORATE BETRAYAL

KLARA REMEMBERED EVERYTHING. She had slept on the bench and roused as the first rays of morning sun filtered through the cracks around the door. She let the memories unfold in her mind as a play unfolds before the audience's eyes.

After Thorn left with the servant, Klara had explored his room by moonlight. A saddlebag that looked like hers lay on a shelf in the cupboard. She picked up the bag and underneath lay a dagger that looked like hers as well. Holding the dagger in one hand and the saddlebag in the other, she stood, not liking the conclusion she was drawing. Eventually, she put the dagger down and opened the bag. It was not like hers, it was hers; all of her belongings were neatly packed inside.

Klara dropped to her knees, unable to breathe. She recalled Ffearn's words. "Don't trust Thorn." She had been a fool. She thought he was showing her kindness, but he must have intended for her to remain the night all along because all of her belongings now sat, not where she left them, but packed in the saddlebag before her.

She felt panicked and short of breath. The bloody bandeau constricted her. Frantically, she worked at the laces of the dress and let it fall to the floor.

Untying the underskirts, she cast them aside, and then pulled the borrowed shift over her head. She pulled at the bandeau, wanting only to be free of everything Thorn had ever provided her. Once bare, she breathed easier, but there was nothing she owned that was not in some way connected to Thorn.

Klara pulled her shift out of the saddlebag and slipped it over her head. Then she took up her dagger. She was not going to be here when he returned. There was no way for her to stop Thorn. He knew how she fought and he was stronger; he would quickly overpower her. Fleeing was her only option, but where? Not back to her quarters, he might find her there. Had Bardus and the others been given a cottage? Or were they bedding in the tents outside? There was no way to find them.

From the shadows she peeked out the door. On the lawn the festivities had ended. Only a few revelers were left in the yard wandering drunkenly between the tents. Clutching her dagger, she darted though the door and ran barefooted to the only place she knew how to find—the stables.

Burying her face in Constant's mane, Klara cried. She cried because Karn had refused her. She cried because Thorn had betrayed her trust. She cried because she had been a fool. Grief, sadness, anger, and confusion welled in her until she could contain the hurt no longer. Slumping into the straw, she looked at the dagger she still held. How was it possible to feel so much pain and not have a physical wound?

Then she realized that was the answer. A cut. A hole. A way for the pain to escape the confines of her body.

First she cut her legs, watching as the blood welled to the surface. The pain cleared her mind, but not enough to maintain focus. She needed to banish the fuzziness overtaking her. Pulling up the sleeves of her shift, she cut her arms, but still it was not enough.

She had been a fool for allowing herself to hope. Now all those hopes were dashed. Everyone had betrayed her. Her life was worthless. She was just a whore. Taking the dagger, she placed the tip between her ribs just where Ruis had shown her. It was the spot to kill a man. Slowly she began to push, feeling the hot sting of metal as the blade separated her skin.

Bardus materialized before her, grabbing the dagger and throwing it aside. "Absent gods, lass! What're you doing?"

Klara lacked the mental ability to even contemplate where he had come from. Hanging her head, she slurred, "Karn refused me an' Thorn betrayed me."

"Blessed Goddess," he said and pulled her to him, "You've cut yourself to ribbons. We need to bind these wounds."

Bardus took her shift from her and ripped it into strips for bandages. He dunked one of the strips in a bucket of water and began to wash and bandage the cuts. When he finished, he took off his own green tunic and slipped it over her head.

Kindness, that was really all she wanted. Bardus's scent wafted up from his tunic, swirling around her. He was the only one who ensured that she ate, the only one to talk to her when the others refused.

Raising her head to meet his eyes, she slurred, "You 'ave always shown me kindness." Then Klara leaned in and kissed him.

Bardus pushed her back. "I don't think you're in your right mind. What you need now is a bed."

Klara nuzzled into him and sat astride his lap. "You're the only one lef' who'll even talk t' me," she whispered, then nibbled his neck while her fingers caressed his chest.

"You are in no fit state for any of this," Bardus said. "You need to get off my lap and let me take you to your cottage and put you to bed. Alone, in your own bed."

Klara started rhythmically rocking in his lap. She had not known she could be filled with such desire. "I need you." Klara wanted to say more, to communicate her desire, but her tongue was uncooperative and haziness prevented her from finding the words.

"Don't make me force you off me," Bardus said. "I don't want to do any more damage to you than you've already done."

By this time Klara had freed him of his trousers and kissed him again. "Please," she whispered.

"It's been a long time since I've been with a maid. I beg you not to tempt me, lass," Bardus said. Klara ignored his words and slid down over him.

"Blessed goddess, but you feel good!" he exclaimed, clutching her hips, drawing her down and seating her firmly against him.

Klara and Bardus were locked in the throes of passion when Thorn grabbed her by the hair and pulled her off him. "Are you such a harlot that you would bed every member of the company?"

Then Thorn turned on Bardus. "And you accused me of wrong doing, then I find you here engaged in the very acts you accuse me of." Thorn launched himself at Bardus, who was unprepared for the assault, and sent him sprawling. Blow after blow Thorn leveled at Bardus. Thorn was bigger and years of smithing left him with massive muscles in his chest and arms. Bardus had little chance of defending himself once Thorn had him down.

"Stop it!" Klara cried. "Stop it, Thorn; you'll kill him!" Dizzy and confused, she pushed to her feet and rushed at Thorn, hitting him in the side with her shoulder. It was enough to knock him off Bardus.

"Run, Bardus!" Klara screamed as she grappled with Thorn.

Both her mind and limbs were sluggish. It was hard to defend herself. All she had to act on were the instincts her practices with Ruis had developed. She had no chance of winning this fight. And once Thorn had her pinned, her mind slowly realized that it was not a fight he wanted. She had never felt an erection so hard in all her life and she had felt a lot of erections.

She kneed him hard and clumsily scrambled to her feet. Thorn caught her before she made it to the stable door. "Klara, no," he shouted, wrapping his arms around her waist and pulling her back. "I'm sorry. Let me explain."

Holding her tight as she struggled against him, Thorn pulled her to the back of the stable, away from the horses. Her body trembled with exhaustion.

"They told me I might have taken you in the night and not remembered it," Thorn said. She felt his rapid heartbeat though his chest as he held her to him. "They convinced me it was my fault, even though it was you with your hands in my trousers that morning. And I believed them, so I swallowed my pride and apologized. All I want is to serve you. Why do you insist on tormenting me the way you do?"

"I didn't," Klara cried, shaking her head. "I... I don't."

"You did," Thorn said. "You do. Your touch does something to me. I don't want to hurt you. I don't. But I long for even a fleeting moment of caress." His hands were all over her. No longer the careful and controlled man she knew, he resembled a rutting beast.

"If I am to be charged as guilty, then I will earn my guilt," Thorn said, nuzzling into her neck, his breath hot on her ear. Grabbing each of her thighs he lifted her, pressing her against the wall, forcing himself inside her. Her cuts screamed from the new abuse.

Frail and shattered, she lacked both the will and words to protest. She was tired, sore, and just wanted it to be over. There was no fight left in her. Muddy tears tricked down her cheeks. But somewhere deep inside, through the muddle of her mind, she still felt desire. There was still longing there. Why? It was more than she was able to comprehend. She should fight. She should scream. Her mind and body were uncooperative. The knife wounds and the fight left her exhausted. She began to shake.

Thorn was forceful, but not particularly violent, not beating her. Within a few strokes he slowed, gentled, and began kissing her. "Klara, I've wanted you for so long," he whispered, his hot breath scorching her skin.

Was that meant to be a comfort? It did nothing to soothe her.

Too weary to hold her head aloft, she let it slump forward. And then it happened; she was inside Thorn's mind. Thorn wanted her. And he wanted her to bear him a son, multiple sons. Not just an heir and spare, but an entire line of sons. Her overwhelming fear of pregnancy prevailed against the fogginess clouding her conscious thought.

Screaming, Klara bucked against the wall. They fell. Hitting her head on something hard, she slipped into blackness.

When she regained consciousness, Thorn was issuing his final grunts of completion. He rolled off her and curled into the fetal position. His back was to her, fists clenched in his hair, wailing, "What have I done?"

Through sobs, he issued the question over and over again.

Though their minds were no longer connected, Klara felt grief rolling off him. Forcing herself to her feet, she stumbled out of the stable and into Karn. Ruis was with him. Ruis passed her at a run heading Thorn's direction. Sweeping her into his arms, Karn carried her to a small cottage not far from the hall, leaving Ruis to deal with Thorn.

Once in his rooms, Karn cried as he held her. "I'm so sorry."

"Don' leave me, Karn," Klara pleaded. "Please, don' leave me."

"I'll not leave you," Karn said and kissed her forehead. "Bardus said you were injured. Let me look at you."

Karn helped her out of Bardus's tunic and unwrapped the bandages. Thankfully, the wounds did not require stitches. He re-bandaged the cuts on her arms and legs with clean linen. The cut on her ribs he left for last. Bending, he kissed the gash and said, "I didn't know my silence hurt you so badly."

"You refuse' me," Klara stammered, shaking with fatigue and chill. "Thorn asked me t' take 'im instead."

"I've not refused you. I never took off my ring nor asked for yours in return," Karn said. "I didn't understand what happened or how to go forward. Nuallan said those were not your first encounters with Thorn. He claimed he saw you holding each other on nights when you stood watch together and that you slipped away together on the steppes. Ffearn said to stay away from you until Waywyrd determined who was lying. Can you forgive me?"

Sliding onto his lap, Klara kissed him. His scent was intoxicating. She needed him to hold her. "Stay the nigh' with me."

"I'll stay with you," Karn replied and laid her gently in the fleeces that made his bed.

Desire still burned within her. She needed Karn. The disorder reigning in her mind was no longer a thing she needed to fight. Here she was safe, so she let it overtake her. It took little coaxing to prompt Karn and their love making was soft and gentle.

As she lay wrapped in his arms, there was a knock and Ruis entered. "Karn, Waywyrd wants to see you and Ffearn right away."

"I've no idea where Ffearn is, but I'll come as soon as I'm dressed," Karn said. When Ruis had left, Karn kissed her forehead and said, "Sleep; I'll return soon." She was already drifting off.

The door slammed, startling Klara to wakefulness as Ffearn entered the room. She watched bleary eyed as he began to disrobe, unable to focus on him.

"The little twit spent the entire night enticing me and leading me on, only to refuse once I had my trousers off. I'm hornier than a stag in rut," he said as he crawled into bed. She reached for him with clumsy fingers and caressed his chest.

"You're not Karn," he said, surprised.

"Un-uh," Klara mumbled as she nuzzled into him.

"I see he's brought you back into our bed," Ffearn said, sounding disappointed. "Where is he?"

"You 'ere wan'ed," Klara slurred as she pressed herself against him.

"You're drunk—and just as horny as I am," Ffearn said.

Klara nodded.

"How come you're bandaged?" Ffearn asked alarmed.

"In stable, got cut…not bad," she mumbled, her hands still occupied with his flesh.

"And Karn's out looking for me, you say?" Ffearn asked. "So, is my dear brother in a sharing mood tonight?"

Words were too much for her to master. Klara responded by nibbling his ear.

Ffearn laughed. "Don't you think we should wait for him?"

"Now," Klara said.

"If that's how it is, bend over and I'll give you want you want," Ffearn said.

Ffearn took her slowly at first but became more vigorous each time she begged for more. By the time they finished she was grasping the fleeces with both hands and each of them were grunting loudly.

"More," Klara begged. It was the only word she was capable of.

"That's all I've got," Ffearn grunted.

They climaxed together. Still breathing heavily from the exertion, he pulled himself from her, he scooped her up and laid her the proper direction in the bed again.

Pushing a stray hair from her sweaty brow, Ffearn said, "Blessed Goddess, but my brother is one lucky Kelto. You keep that up and we'll have no idea which of us your bairns belong to."

Klara was just about asleep when Karn appeared with Waywyrd and Ruis. Waywyrd sighed as his brow furrowed into a disapproving frown.

"Absent gods! Waywyrd said. "Don't tell me you've bedded her too?"

"She was quite persuasive," Ffearn said defensively.

"Sit her up," Waywyrd demanded and Ffearn complied. Then he waved a candle back and forth in front of her eyes. The light was too bright. She tried backing away and blocking it with her hands. Ruis grabbed her head and pried her eyelids open while Waywyrd came at her with the candle again.

"Did Thorn give you anything to drink?" Waywyrd asked. "Did he give you wine?"

The words were fuzzy in her head. She struggled to avoid the light.

"Can you speak at all?" Waywyrd asked. But Klara just clung to Ffearn.

"She was speaking earlier," Ffearn said.

"Did any of it make sense?" Waywyrd snapped.

"She was only using one-word commands," Ffearn said sheepishly, "but they made sense to me."

Waywyrd seemed satisfied. "Keep her here and see to it that the list of people she's bedded tonight doesn't get any longer." Then he took Ruis and left.

As Karn undressed, Ffearn asked, "You mind telling what that was all about?"

Karn climbed into bed and reached for Klara. She knew his smell. It was the smell of safety and comfort. She tried crawling on top of him, but her limbs no longer functioned properly. She looked at him with pleading eyes.

Karn kissed her forehead. "I think you've had enough."

"You've not answered me," Ffearn said.

Karn sighed. His concern replaced with rage. "Thorn drugged her. As you can see, he reduced her to being no more than a bitch in heat. He raped her in the stable and beat Bardus badly enough to send him to the infirmary with broken ribs and broken nose. Near as we can figure, the cuts she did herself, but that might not be the case since she was already cut when Bardus found her. Thorn is chained in the hostage pit."

"Absent gods!" Ffearn exclaimed, tumbling from the mound of fleeces and reaching for his clothes. "We need to get him out."

"No," Karn said, squeezing her hard enough that bolts of pain shot through her body. "It's the safest place for him. You get him out and I'll kill him."

Ffearn sighed and dropped his clothes. "If this night results in a bairn, we'll never be able to tell if it's one of ours or Thorn's."

"Or Bardus's," Karn said. "Fortunately, she has herbs she can take in the morning to prevent her from becoming with child."

"Brother, I can't believe Bardus too," Ffearn said.

"It's my fault," Karn said, loosening his grip on her. "I shouldn't have let Thorn separate us. She should have been sitting with me tonight, not Thorn."

❦

Thorn had drugged and raped her. Nuallan had acted as an accomplice. Those were the lives that depended on the return of her memory. She was still sitting on the bench, tears streaming down her cheeks when Pendrwyrd woke and entered their outer room.

"I can remember," Klara said. "I'll need a new shift if I am to address the court, unless you believe they'll let me wear breeches."

"I think breeches might make the better impression for what needs to be done," Pendrwyrd said and knelt before her. "Now, tell me what you know."

After Klara recounted the tale, Pendrwyrd said, "That is not the only crime committed. There is one you must answer to as well." Klara looked at her confused, so Pendrwyrd added, "Unions between foreigners are forbidden in Mordovia. If you are with child your life may be forfeited as well."

"It won't come to that," Klara said. As soon as they finished meeting with King Dovsk, she had every intention of consuming all her remaining pennyroyal, looking for more, and taking that, too. Then the women dressed and prepared for an unpleasant morning.

Before they left the cottage, Pendrwyrd directed Klara to take a seat at the table. "Klara, before we are received at court you should know that the entire company, not just Thorn, has been placed in the hostage pit," Pendrwyrd said. "Waywyrd said you were quick and we can communicate in our minds if we need to, but you must be careful what you say. King Dovsk will not hesitate to take a life, and he enjoys a bloody spectacle."

Pendrwyrd paused to make sure she had Klara's attention before continuing, "And Klara, it would be best if all lives can be spared."

Why should she spare Thorn's life? Or Nuallan's? She had been running from such men all her life. If this was her only chance at justice, she was going to see justice done. And if the spectacle were bloody, all the better.

The two women caused a stir upon arriving at court. Pendrwyrd was dressed in her blue tunic, breeches, and carrying her birch staff. Klara wore her breeches, shirt, and jerkin. Since Pendrwyrd carried her staff, Klara decided to complete her ensemble by wearing her dagger. Court was held in the same room in which they dined, only now the tables had been pushed aside. The pair of women joined Waywyrd on a bench near the back of the room and waited to be called on by King Dovsk. They did not have to wait long.

King Dovsk sat on a raised platform, stuffing rich meats and fine cheeses into his mouth, dark locks framing his jowls. There was some discussion on the dais, during which he rested his hands on his enormous girth. Then he addressed the crowd, "Miss Klara, come and stand before the court."

Klara rose, shakily, and stood before the King. She felt the empty space of the room around her. Spectators lined the walls eager to see this new drama unfold.

When she was in the center of the room, Dovsk said, "The wizardess, Pendrwyrd, was instructed to bring you to court as soon as you were able to remember certain events that occurred on Pyhä Äkräs Eve. I presume that your presence here means that you have remembered?"

"I have, Your Majesty," Klara said, clasping her hands behind her back to keep them from shaking.

"Then tell the court everything that occurred after you left my dining hall with King Thorn," Dovsk said.

It was as clear as the nose on his face that Dovsk was itching for a spectacle. If it might save her companions' lives she would give him one. "I will not speak until I have seen the members of my company and know that they are safe."

"Very well," Dovsk said, with a wave of his hand, "bring up the prisoners."

The wait seemed interminable. Eventually, the company of dirty and bedraggled Keltoi was lined up in the room before her. It was clear that their time in the hostage pit had done them no permanent damage.

"Now," Dovsk said, "you can see they are fine and I'll have your tale."

Klara wanted to go to Karn, to feel the safety and comfort of his arms, but held her place. Each of Keltoi watched her intently as she spoke. "Let the company first be divided into those who are innocent of any wrong doing and those whom I deem guilty."

King Dovsk was salivating like a half-starved hound from the simple knowledge that she intended to name someone guilty of something. Even if she had not been a whore, this man was easy to read.

"By all means," Dovsk said leaning forward, "we wouldn't want the guilty mixed with the innocent." A buzz of chatter and muffled laughter went through the crowd.

*"What are you doing?"* Pendrwyrd's voice reverberated through her mind. *"You're going to get them all killed."*

Klara ignored her and proceeded, pressing her heels to the ground to steady herself. "The Battle Master Ruis, the Squire Bardus, Prince Karn, and Prince Ffearn are innocent of any charge and have done no wrong. King Thorn and the King's Counselor Nuallan shall stand as the accused."

Gasps went through the crowd. Clearly they had not expected her to name the King. It was customary to foist blame onto an underling.

*"I said to spare their lives!"* Pendrwyrd's voice rang through her skull. Klara tried to block her out.

Once they were separated into two groups, one on each side of the room Klara recounted what happened in the barest detail, willfully omitting a number of incidents and softening the realities of others.

"When I saw my belongings in Thorn's room," Klara said, "I suspected foul play. Unfortunately, the drug had already started to act, driving me mad. I undressed myself and, in my madness, cut myself. Bardus found me cutting in the stable, saved my life, and bandaged my wounds. Thorn found us there, beat Bardus and forced himself on me." The rest of the night she figured was none of the King's business.

King Dovsk smiled and leaned back in his chair. "You've left out a number of details my dear. I have it on good authority that King Thorn was not the only one to enjoy you that night. The squire took you in the stable and the Princes had you in their hut."

Well then, they would have it. Looking King Dovsk in the eye, she said, "Bardus didn't know I'd been drugged and perceived only that I was willing. I hold that he is innocent of wrong doing. As for Karn and Ffearn; that was not my first encounter with them and I would have been willing even if I had not been drugged. Therefore, they too are innocent."

Chatter again rolled through the crowd.

Dovsk drew his palms together, tapping his fingers as if contemplating something. Dropping his hands back to his protruding girth, he said, "Now I'd like to hear about the guilty."

Klara began to speak, but Waywyrd's voice appeared in her head, *"You've said quite enough!"*

Loudly clearing his throat, Waywyrd drew King Dovsk's attention. "I wish to speak on behalf of King Thorn, Your Majesty."

King Dovsk gave his assent.

Waywyrd stepped forward and addressed the court, using his staff to punctuate his points. "King Thorn is innocent. He was drugged just as Klara was and we heard from her own testimony that he too drank the wine. The King's Counselor, Nuallan, was secretly drugging King Thorn and Miss Klara for the past fortnight, or more. This event is the culmination of a moon's planning on his part. Discussions with servants revealed that it was Nuallan who procured the wine and had it placed in Thorn's chambers and that it was Nuallan, not King Thorn, who ordered Klara's belongings be moved to Thorn's rooms. King Thorn knew nothing of these activities and therefore is a victim of the night's events just as Klara was."

King Dovsk laughed. "I have a hard time believing that a king doesn't know the movements of his own counselor. It is easy enough to see why any man, even a king, might want to drug the woman and have her brought to his bed. However, I see no reason for the counselor to also drug the King; it seems the effects of the drug would lessen the experience for him. Or," mused Dovsk, "were the drugs such that they would enhance the experience?"

"Your Majesty," Waywyrd continued, banging his staff against the floor in irritation, "This plot is more sinister than simply wanting a beautiful woman in your bed. Prince Karn and Miss Klara have pledged themselves to each other. Since the union is not permitted here, they were to be wed once the company reached Lusatia. King Thorn has approved of, and supports, the betrothal. Nuallan disapproves strongly. It is my belief that he was drugging Thorn and Klara as a means of inciting enough scandal that the young Prince would refuse her and call off the nuptials."

"If the intent was to break off the betrothal, then it seems to me the Counselor was the only one with any sense," King Dovsk said. Waywyrd started to protest, but Dovsk cut him off. "I'll hear no more excuses. Wrong has been done in my house. It is an embarrassment to me and my court. Someone must pay with their life, and since Miss Klara is the aggrieved party, she shall choose which life it be."

Waywyrd's voice rang inside her head. *"Do not choose."*

Klara ignored him, giving in to the anger she felt.

With Thorn standing before her, the images she had seen inside his mind played over again. He wanted her pregnant and for that she hated him. Nuallan may have secretly drugged them both, but that mattered little because Thorn desired her to produce an heir, even if he might not have acted on those desires alone.

Directing all of her attention and focus on Thorn, Klara sought his mind and into it said, *"I hate you and I will have your head."*

Thorn fell to his knees, clutching his skull. She wanted to hurt him, to cause him pain, to make him suffer as she suffered. His mind was full of agony and remorse. He sobbed and she saw that he would willingly give his life in payment for the offense.

*"Good,"* she thought, *"because I will have it."*

Waves of guilt and self-loathing interfered with the steady stream of hatred she was pouring into him. Not all of the anger she felt was hers. Thorn was angry, angry at Nuallan. Klara diverted her attention, following the threads of anger in Thorn's mind and saw truth.

Nuallan was not simply attempting to put a wedge between her and Karn; he had asked Thorn to get her pregnant. Thorn had refused his aged counselor's request. Why in the Goddess's name did Nuallan want her pregnant?

Klara tried reading Nuallan's mind, but it did no good. She was unable to delve into his mind as she did Thorn. He was as unreadable as Karn or Waywyrd. All she sensed was a jumble of fear.

Pulling her dagger, Klara leapt for Nuallan, pinning him to the floor before the Dovsk's guards had time to react. She pressed the blade to his throat as guards raced from their posts, quickly encircling her.

"Wait," Dovsk shouted. He was standing now. "Is this the life you intend to take?"

"I don't know, Your Majesty," Klara said, forcing her knee deeper into Nuallan's chest. "I'd like a few answers first."

Dovsk chuckled. "By all means, question your witness."

"Get up," Waywyrd said, grabbing her by the shoulder.

Klara shrugged him off. "Restrain the wizard."

Dovsk nodded and the guards encircled Waywyrd, leaving her to question Nuallan.

Driving her knee hard into his chest, she said, "If you are going to die, you should take the opportunity to die an honest man; it's the only chance you'll get."

Nuallan trembled. "Miss Klara, I don't know what you're talking about."

"Start with your brew of herbs," she said. "Tell me what was in it and why. And you should remember that the Goddess won't take liars in the afterlife." To make her point, Klara flicked her wrist and a trickle of blood ran down his neck.

"They weren't nothing harmful," Nuallan squawked. "First I dosed you good with pennyroyal to make sure you didn't already have a bairn in your belly. When Thorn separated you and the lads I added red clover, yarrow, and shepherd's purse to encourage you to conceive. The poppy kept you happy and relaxed. I put mandrake in the beans so no one would hear me dragging you across camp the night I put you in bed with Thorn. As friendly as you were with Karn in the mornings, I figured that nature would run its course. You never did couple and just ended up mad at each other, each thinking the other had done them wrong."

"Why do you want me pregnant?" Klara demanded. Of all the reason to drug a person and stir up trouble, that one made the least sense.

"The prophecy," Nuallan croaked. "Waywyrd mentioned it at the lake and then the demons mentioned another one. I tried convincing Thorn to discourage his nephew and take you for himself. He refused, saying he was happy for young master Karn and wouldn't interfere."

"Waywyrd said the demons' prophecy was nonsense," Klara said, raising him by his tunic, only to thump him soundly against the floor.

"Nonsense that's been completely accurate through the ages," Nuallan shouted, his legs flailing behind her. "There are other prophecies too; they all say you will bear the next heir. If you produced a bairn by either of the lads, Clan Duir ends and Nuin reigns in its place. Only an heir produced by Thorn keeps the line intact. That's why I needed the wine. I laced it with poppy and fertility enhancing herbs. And I used safed musli to increase Thorn's potency; it increases libido, too, and… and removes inhibitions. Thorn didn't know."

Klara had heard enough. Nuallan's confession filled her with a boiling rage. Calling to the King's guards, she said, "I need two of you to hold him."

Eager for more drama, King Dovsk waved two of them over. Klara had them hold Nuallan's arms while she cut open his tunic. On his chest she carved the holly and spindle runes, justice and fulfillment, watching as her lines reddened with blood. Then she had the guards pull him to his feet for the court to see.

"I am tired of hearing about bairns and heirs," Klara said to the assembled crowd. "And I don't give a damn about prophecies. The only one who has any say over my womb is me."

With one quick movement she cut Nuallan's throat. A gasp went through the crowd. Blood gurgled from the wound and pooled on the floor. Nuallan's body slackened and hung limp between the guards. Bloody spectacle complete.

Wiping the blade on her breeches, she turned to King Dovsk. "Your Majesty, I would have that head on a spike if it would not trouble you greatly."

"It would not trouble me in the least," Dovsk replied, rubbing his hands together. "Usually when I ask someone to choose who will die, my guards handle killing. This was much more satisfying."

Turning to Waywyrd, Dovsk said, "However, I want to know more about this prophecy. What makes Miss Klara special? Why her and not, say, any of the other ladies here at court or a Kelta? Surely, one of their own kind would be better suited for the task."

"There isn't much to it," Waywyrd said. "You are aware of the unpleasantness surrounding Thorn's kingship and since the Princes have been banished none of the noble houses will consent to marrying off their daughters. But Keltoi have long been known to take foreign wives. Klara is among the few women who would happily accept a Kelto husband. I had merely to put Klara in their presence and as Nuallan said, let nature run its course."

Waywyrd was lying. Klara was not sure how she knew, but she was certain he was hiding something from Dovsk. But what was it? And why? She tried looking into his mind as she had done with Thorn, but his mind was closed to her.

"This whole issue of heirs brings up the next matter for the court," Dovsk said. "The mixing of bloodlines is forbidden in this land. We do not take foreign wives, nor do we permit foreigners to take our own women to wife. If a woman is found to be with child from a mixed union, her life and that of the father is forfeited."

"None of the parties to this unpleasant incident are Mordvin," Waywyrd said, approaching the dais. "Klara is a Skolt and the rest are Keltoi. Both cultures openly allow marriages among whomever the parties choose."

"But you are not in Skoloti or Kenetlon," Dovsk said. "You are in Mordovia and must adhere to our laws. Before me I have a woman suspected of being with child and she bedded four Keltoi over the course of a single evening. I have no way to determine who the father is. Does that mean I am to kill all of them? Or should I just kill one? Perhaps the one who dares to wear a ring as a symbol of a pledge he made to this same woman? A pledge forbidden in my lands."

Klara's heart stopped. Mustering her courage she stepped forward. "Your Majesty, if I may. I am not with child. I have pennyroyal in my room. The herb was purchased some time ago and I know it's effective because I've used it before. No one's life need be forfeited."

Dovsk sent a servant to Klara's quarters to fetch her bag and sent another for the physician. When they returned Dovsk asked his servant, "Did you find anything?"

"Four packets of herbs, Your Majesty," the servant said, holding them up for the court to see.

Klara saw Karn shake, realizing her lie. They only purchased five packets of the herb and used one at Midsummer. Before him was evidence that she had not taken the herb as she claimed, which meant she might be with child.

The packets were handed to the physician for verification. "This is pennyroyal, but these are doses to be taken the morning after. I'm positive she didn't take any then. If this is the dose she used, she might still be with child."

"I took four doses when I got to my room yesterday. One dose for each day I slept," Klara lied, hoping that dosage might be large enough and wishing she had asked Bardus more questions about the herb. "I wanted to be sure nothing would run amiss."

"Well, that would do it," the physician admitted.

The packets were handed to the King, who passed them off to a guard. "Destroy these, and make sure she doesn't have access to more." Then Dovsk turned to Klara and said, "I want Miss Klara and Prince Karn before me."

Guards ushered the pair to the dais. Dovsk stood directly in front of them as he addressed the court. "These two have caused me a bit of a problem. It's too early to know whether she is or isn't with child. Miss Klara will remain imprisoned in Gnyozdovo for an entire moon's cycle. If her bleeding commences before the end of that time, she will be freed. If she does not bleed, her head will be placed on a pike alongside the counselor's."

Karn pulled her to him and held her tight when he heard the sentence. She took comfort in the gesture, but was not worried. The King might have destroyed this batch of pennyroyal, but she had no need of an apothecary. She was able to identify the herb and had been gathering it nearly all her life. She intended to collect more the first chance she got.

The King continued, "Prince Karn, I want you and the rest of the Keltoi out of the city and heading away from my lands before the sun rises tomorrow. Before you go, you are to take off that ring and publicly renounce my prisoner."

Karn held her tight, shaking his head in defiance of the King.

Seeing this King Dovsk added, "If you refuse to remove the ring, you will be lashed."

"Then I will be lashed," Karn said. Dovsk nodded and a group of guards descended on them, pulling them apart and dragging Karn away.

On the lawn, a pair of guards held Klara between them. Pendrwyrd stood in front of her and said, "It's best you don't look, and pray he gives in soon."

Klara pushed Pendrwyrd aside and watched anyway.

The sun beat down from a cloudless blue sky. Karn was stripped of his shirt and tied, kneeling, to a post as a crowd of nobles gathered. Commoners left their work and joined the throng.

King Dovsk gave instructions to the guard. "He is to receive five lashes, then ask him if he will renounce her. If not, give him five more and ask again. The lashings are to continue until he relents."

The whip cracked in the air and sliced through Karn's skin, opening his back. Though he clenched his jaw at the outset, he still cried out each time the whip separated his skin. His cries tore at Klara's heart. The first five lashes did no good. After the second five, blood poured from stripes on his back.

Despair filled her as the warrior commenced with the third set. He should relent. She was not worth the pain.

When the set was complete, the guard stood before Karn. "Will ya give her up?"

Karn did not answer. The warrior reached for his hand, trying to take the ring by force. Karn clenched his fist, hindering the guard's attempt.

"I'll show you," the guard said and walked behind Karn to begin the fourth set.

As the whip was raised, Ffearn ran onto the field, shouting, "Let me speak with my cousin. Perhaps I can convince him to end this madness?" The guard nodded his assent.

Klara watched as Ffearn bent low and whispered into Karn's ear. Slowly, Karn unclenched his fist and allowed Ffearn to gently remove the ring. Then Ffearn stood and walked across the lawn to stand before Klara and her guards. She saw her own pain reflected in his eyes. Ffearn took her hand and placed Karn's ring in her palm, closing her fingers tightly around it.

Tears streamed down Klara's face. "Take care of him."

"I will," Ffearn said. Then he turned and went to be reunited with his brother, whom the Keltoi had just untied from the post and were helping off the field. Flanked by guards, Klara, numb, watched them go. King Dovsk had decreed that she had a moon's cycle left to live. Karn was destined to leave before dawn. Would she ever see him again?

# Appendix

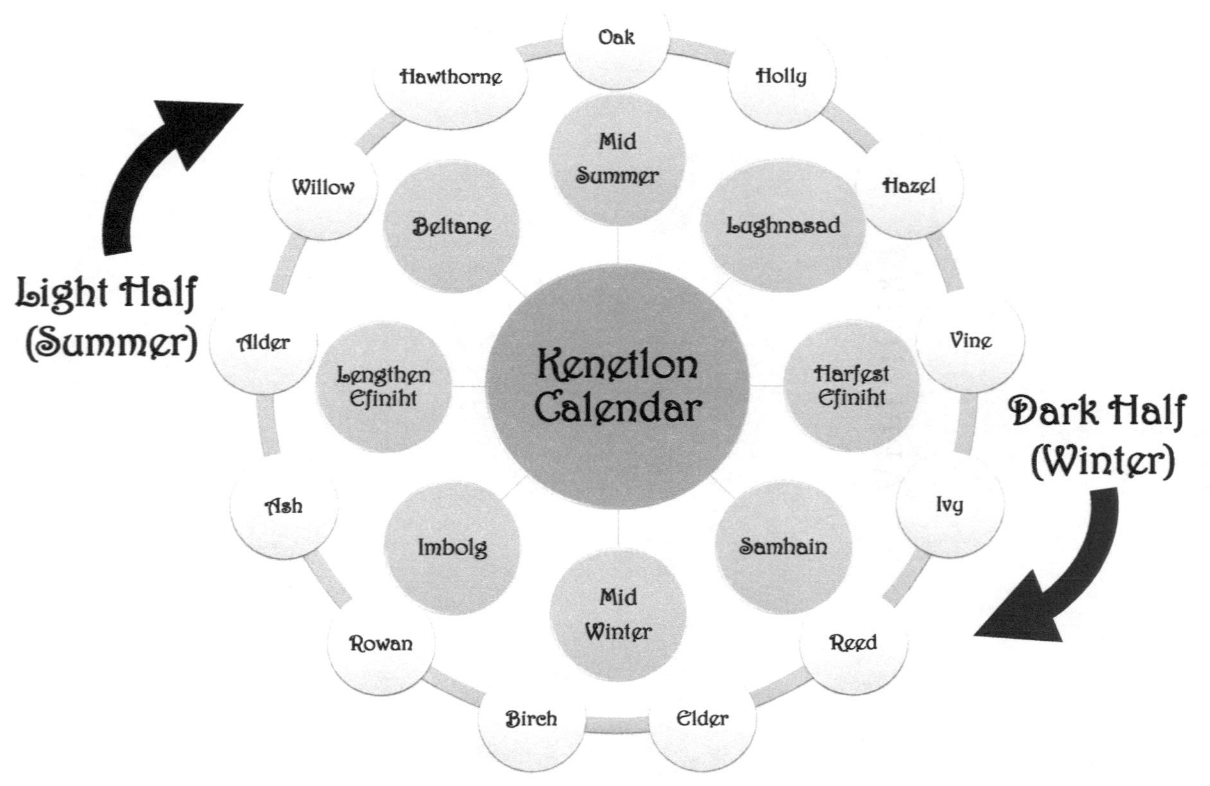

Light Half
(Summer)
Dark Half
(Winter)
Kenetlon Calendar
Oak
Hawthorne
Holly
Willow
Hazel
Beltane
Mid Summer
Lughnasad
Alder
Vine
Lengthen Efiniht
Harfest Efiniht
Ash
Ivy
Imbolg
Samhain
Rowan
Mid Winter
Reed
Birch
Elder

# LIST OF ETHNICITIES

## Human Ethnicities

| Singular | Plural | Collective | Language | Homeland |
| --- | --- | --- | --- | --- |
| Elb | Elbs | Elben | Lusatian | Lusatia |
| Goth | Goths | Goths | Gothic | Götaland |
| Kelto/Kelta | Keltoi | Kenetlo | Kenetlon | Kenetlon |
| Mordva | Mordvins | Mordvin | Moksha | Mordovia |
| Odrysian | Odrysians | Odysae | Thracian | Odryssa |
| Parthian | Parthians | Parthian | Aramaic | Parthia |
| Skolt | Skolts | Skoloti | Skoloti | Skoloti |

## Supernatural Beings

| Singular | Plural | Collective |
| --- | --- | --- |
| God/Goddess | Gods/Goddesses | Divine |
| Charu | Charun | Charontes |
| Ke'le | Ke'let | Ke'lets |

## Clan Divisions

| Clan | Leader | People | Territory |
| --- | --- | --- | --- |
| Duir | Thorn | Duirn | Duirndunum |
| Volk | Gaul | Volkai | Volkmer |
| Nuin | Brawn | Nori | Norikum |
| Bo | Bevin | Boii | Bohmer |

GÖTALAND
North Sea
JUTLAND
Baltic Sea
Western Dvina River
Gnyozdovo
LUSATIA
Polotsk
Elbe
KENETLON
Vistula River
Bug River
Brest
Brodno
Rhine
BÖHMER
River
Dnieper Lowlands
Dnieper
DUIRNDUNUM
Ore
Mountains
Budorigum
Pripyat River
Bohmer
Wood
Kłodzko
Pinsk
Swamps
Suabaha
Erlkönig's
Spring
Abnoba
Mountains
VOLKHMER
Degndorf
Radasbona
Carpathian Mountains
Hulma
Duirness
NORIKUM
Hallstatt
Olbia
Alps
ETRUSCANS
Danube
River
ODRYSSA
Mediterranean Sea

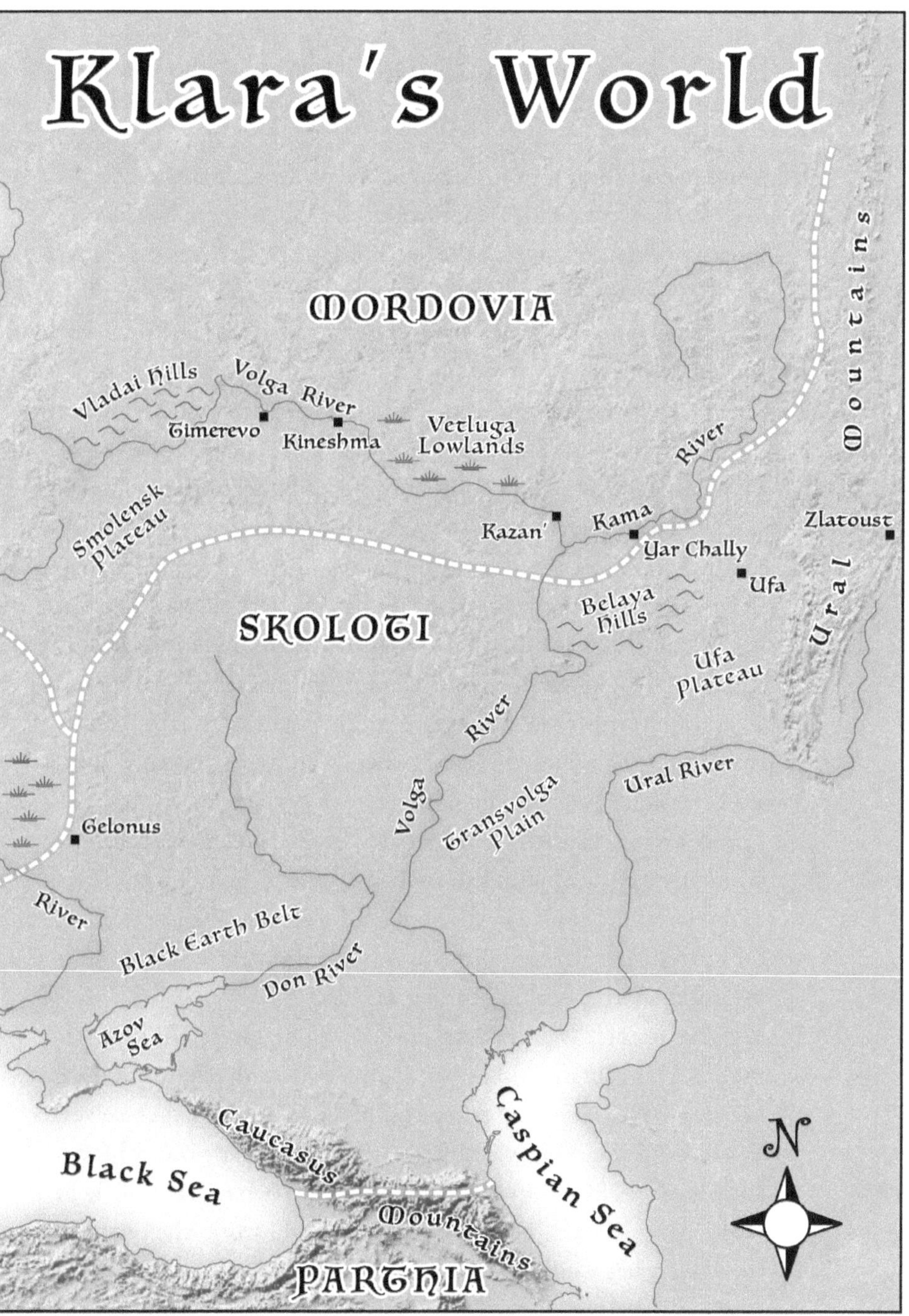

Klara's World
MORDOVIA
Vladai Hills
Volga River
Timerevo
Kineshma
Vetluga Lowlands
Smolensk Plateau
Kazan'
Kama
River
Yar Chally
Ufa
Zlatoust
Belaya Hills
Ural Mountains
SKOLOTI
Ufa Plateau
Volga River
Transvolga Plain
Ural River
Gelonus
River
Black Earth Belt
Don River
Azov Sea
Caucasus
Caspian Sea
Black Sea
Mountains
PARTHIA
N

# READING GROUP GUIDE

1. *Klara's Journey* begins by introducing the reader to an unlikely hero-
   ine who has experienced significant childhood trauma. How do
   those prior traumas impact the decisions she makes over the course
   of the book? What do you think of her choice of occupation? How
   does her occupation affect how others treat her? Is this treatment
   warranted or unwarranted?

2. The traditional high fantasy form often involves a quest. The stated
   purpose of the quest in *Klara's Journey* is for the characters to return
   to their homelands. What hints are given to indicate that more is at
   stake than simply returning home? What hints are given to reveal
   that Klara is more than just a common whore?

3. Over the course of the book, Klara has sex with several different
   men, each instance resulting in highly different emotional out-
   comes. Why might she have different emotional reactions to sex as
   a vocation versus sex as an avocation? How does the author handle
   consent? Do you think the scenes where affirmative consent is given
   are believable? Why or why not?

4. *Klara's Journey* introduces readers to different religions/cultures/
   ethnicities, each adhering to their own moral framework. What
   moral forces are at play in the book? Who are the villains and what
   motivates them? How do these cultural differences affect views
   regarding marriage, childbearing, and sex?

5. The love triangle is a reoccurring theme in literature. Throughout
   the book Thorn states that his nephews are unlikely to produce
   heirs and they need no other companionship than themselves.
   What is he implying with these statements? How does Ffearn
   and Karn's relationship with each other affect how each of them
   responds to Klara? Does the love triangle still work when each of
   the players has a different sexual orientation?

6.  Klara uses pennyroyal to prevent pregnancy. How does access to birth control affect her life and the decisions she makes?

7.  Toward the end of the book, Klara is sexually assaulted by a sympathetic character. What role did drugs and alcohol play in the assault? Does it matter than her assailant later felt remorse? What accounts for the very different reactions Ffearn and Karn have regarding the assault? How might have the events played out differently if the setting was during the #MeToo era, rather than the Iron Age?

8.  At the end of the book, Klara is alone, imprisoned, and possibly pregnant. How do you hope this situation is resolved in book two?

# Author's Note

Language is a fluid and ever-changing creature. As a result, many spellings for deities and holy days have emerged over the centuries. For example, you may have noticed Beltene vs Beltane in chapter one of *Klara's Journey*, along with many other differences scattered throughout the trilogy. To keep names consistent, I use the spellings attested to in the *Dictionary of Celtic Myth and Legend* by Miranda J. Green, augmented by the *Etymological Dictionary of Proto-Celtic* by Ranko Marscovic and the *English-Proto-Celtic Word List, Celtic Lexicon* from the Centre for Advanced Welsh & Celtic Studies, University of Wales. However, Volkmer, Bohmer, and probably some others, are partially made-up words and Norikum (Noricum) has succumbed to my irrational dislike of the letter C. The letter C is a Latinization. Proto-Celtic only uses the letter K, hence Kelto/Kelta/Keltoi/etc as well as the substitution of ka for ce in Karnunnos.

# Excerpt from The Upbreeder

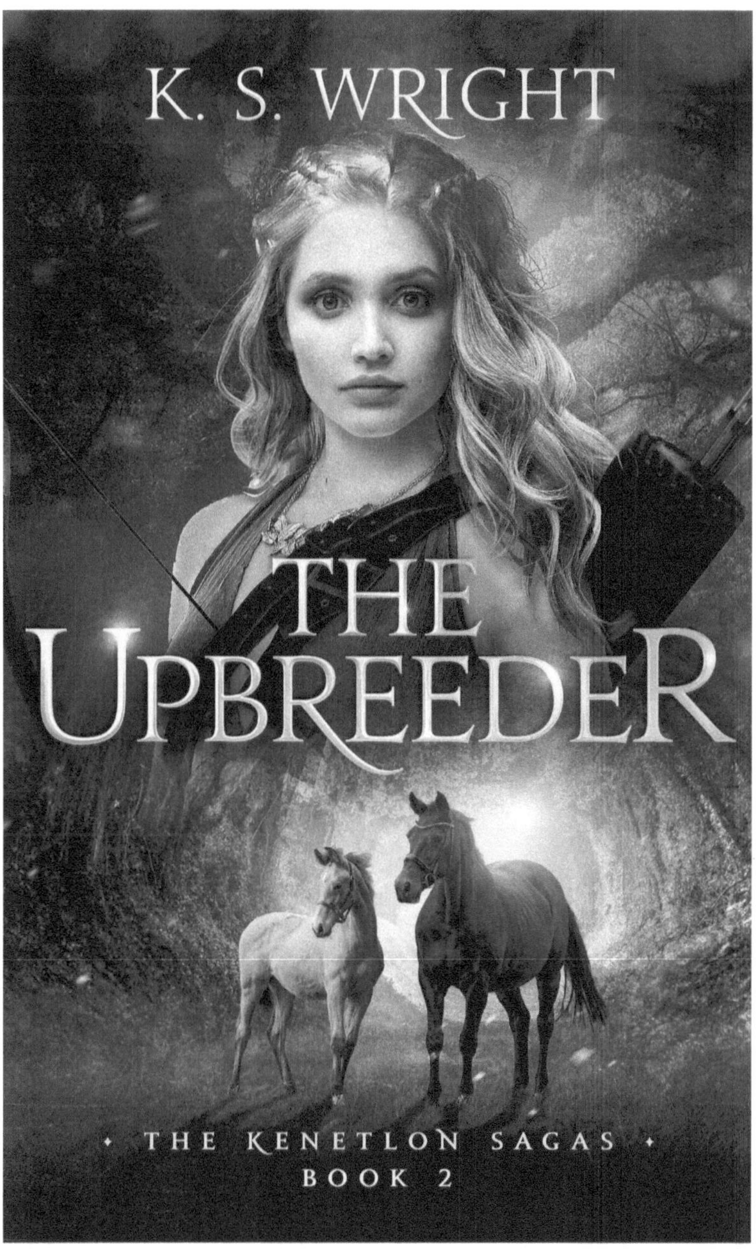


Available June 2024

# CHAPTER 1
# NO GOODBYES

KLARA STOOD, BLEARY-EYED, staring out the door of the two-room wattle and daub cottage where she had been staying. Under the faint light of the waxing crescent moon, the thatch-roofed houses of the village below were no more than dark blurry masses. Hot tears escaped her brown eyes, making it difficult to see. As she leaned against the wooden frame, a sweltering breeze dried the tears on her cheeks.

Purple bruises circled her wrists, which still ached from being man-handled by the guards flanking the cottage door. Their red tunics bore King Dovsk's crest, the bear paw. It was a symbol of the Mordvins' ferocity. Scalps of their enemies dangled from the warriors' shoulders, further evidence of their willingness to shed blood. She carefully contemplated each of her guards. Even the most barbarous men have weaknesses.

Earlier in the day, when the guards had forced her back to her quarters, she had fought them. They would have tied her in bed if the wizardess, Pendrwyrd, had not intervened and insisted she would take responsibility if anything that went amiss. It was Klara's status as Pendrwyrd's guest that had stayed the guards' hands. Being disinclined to argue with a sorcerer, the guards had turned her loose.

Klara rubbed her tender wrists, feeling broken and fragile. Exhaustion hung like a rope from her neck. In the cottage behind her, the piles of fleeces used for bedding sat empty. Neither she nor Pendrwyrd had any intention of sleeping this night. Under her bandages, her arms and legs ached from the cuts she had sustained. Brushing a hand across her ribs, she felt a tender spot just under her breast. Her dagger lay at her bedside. Should she take the opportunity to finish the job she started on Lughnasad? One well-timed thrust would end the pain forever.

The harvest celebration known to her as Lughnasad was called Pyhä Äkräs here in Mordovia. All she had reaped that night was sorrow. She had been beaten, violated, and abandoned in the infirmary where she had lain for days recovering. And by the King's decree, all that she had loved had been stripped from her.

The stable yard, full of red-shirted bodies, bustled with activity. The party of Keltoi would depart before dawn. It seemed that King Dovsk kept half his warriors awake to discourage—what? A fight? An attempted rescue? Or an escape?

Leaving her spot by the door, Klara retreated to the bedchamber. Collecting Karn's tunic from the cupboard that served as her wardrobe, she held it to her face hoping to catch some of her lover's scent. It was faint, but it was still there. Returning to the outer room she sat on a bench that lined the wall, waiting for the sounds of imminent departure. She needed to see Karn before he left; the tunic was her excuse.

Pendrwyrd reclined on a bench near the hearth, her features obscured by shadow. The pottage bowl containing Klara's supper sat untouched on a small table in the corner. A scuffle in the yard brought Klara to her feet. Pendrwyrd stood, catching her by the arm.

Klara jerked her arm free. "I have Karn's tunic. I need to return it."

Shadow and moonlight played ghastly tricks with the scar that ran from Pendrwyrd's temple to her chin. "You cannot speak to them."

"How dare you stop me," Klara said. She had never been impressed with meddlesome wizards. In her view, they were worthy of less than half the respect they were given. The argument drew the attention of the guards stationed outside the door, who grunted and entered the room.

"Is there a problem?" a sandy-haired young warrior asked.

"I want to say goodbye," Klara said. She and Karn had been apart for so long, and over the past couple moons she had been drugged most of the time they were together. What memories she had were muddled. The thought that things stood ill between them was unbearable. Had he really refused her…again?

The guard shook his head. Klara bolted for the door. She was caught by his companion, a guard with nut-brown hair, who threw her over his shoulder and carried her back to the bedchamber as if she were spoils of war.

Dumping her on the fleeces the guard said, "Otso's claws, I'll tie you yet!"

Eyeing her dagger, Klara contemplated stabbing him.

Pendrwyrd's voice was quick in her mind, *"Don't."*

Klara grabbed her skull with her free hand and curled into the fetal position, still clutching Karn's tunic. She was not fully recovered. The mental communication the wizards sometimes used was torturous when combined with an already existing headache.

Turning to the guards, Pendrwyrd said, "Let me take her to see them. She may be easier to manage if she's permitted to say goodbye."

The guards grabbed Klara by her arms, hoisted her to her feet, and marched her into the night. Her injuries screamed at the abuse, a torment she willingly endured so long as it meant being able see Karn one last time. Pendrwyrd hurried before them, hastening to Dovsk's hall to seek an audience with the King. Standing outside the door to the great hall, flanked by her guards, Klara waited for what seemed like an interminable length of time, but what in reality was likely only a matter or moments.

Pendrwyrd emerged from the hall and shook her head. "I wasn't able to change Dovsk's mind. He's adamant that you are not to speak with the company before they depart."

Cradling Karn's tunic against her chest, Klara watched from afar as those she loved mounted their horses and rode into the night. Morning was fast approaching. Even after the Keltoi had ridden out of the city gate, like a sentinel she stood, hoping to catch one last glimpse of them. The guards assigned to her were irritable and she suspected they longed to be back in their beds. They could wait. She would stand until the sun rose, maybe longer.

Muggy air surrounded her, making it impossible to sleep anyway. The nights of the Hazel Moon were just as hot and uncomfortable as the days, leaving Gnyozdovo's inhabitants with no reprieve from the heat. Slowly the sky began to lighten, illuminating the farmland surrounding the city and casting long shadows behind anything that dared stand in its way. Her eyes followed the road and settled on the spot where it was engulfed by the forest, but it did no good. Her companions were gone.

Would she live long enough to see them again? Or would King Dovsk have her beheaded before the moon's cycle was out? It was a strange thing, to know the appointed time of her death.

In Skoloti, her homeland, the penalty for rape was for a man to lose part of his manhood. The sentiments against rape were so strong that the law required all women to kill a man in battle before they could wed. It was unthinkable to sentence a woman to death if an act of violence committed against her resulted in a child. And if the act were consensual, no one cared if she issued a bastard. Here in Mordovia, her attacker had gone free, her lover had been lashed, and she was left to wait out a death sentence.

The tresses in her honey-colored braids shone like ropes of gold in the dawn light. Soon the sounds of the King's household filled the morning air. Dogs barked. Roosters crowed. Stable boys bustled about now that the warriors had retreated. Smoke and the cook's shrill voice rose from the shack that served as the kitchen.

When it was time for breakfast, Pendrwyrd approached and slipped an arm around Klara. The two women had met just three days before; Klara had woken in the infirmary to find Pendrwyrd sitting at her bedside. The wizardess had been granted lodgings in a cottage near King Dovsk's hall. When Klara arrived in Gnyozdovo, she had been assigned to share the woman's hut.

As the pair stood, staring into the distance, Pendrwyrd spoke. "Let's go into the hall and eat. You've had a long day. You need food and rest."

"I need neither," Klara said, still clutching Karn's tunic tightly to her bosom.

Pendrwyrd sighed, shrugged her shoulders, and removed her arm from Klara's waist. Her black hair caught the morning light, making it impossible to tell if the gray streak was really there or if it were just a trick of the light. The lightning-like scar that ran from Pendrwyrd's hairline to her chin was clearly visible, though. Her blue tunic and breeches appeared fresh, but the woman leaned heavily on her birch staff, exhaustion evident in her shoulders. Exhaustion was the only characteristic the pair of women shared; Pendrwyrd was just as dark as Klara was fair.

Only when the King's household started to emerge did Klara consent to leave her post. She had no desire to be a plaything of the noblewomen today. The guards escorted her back to the wizard's cottage. Once there, she sought her bed, where, still clutching Karn's tunic, she cried herself to sleep.

When Klara woke that afternoon, her head was clearer. If things went poorly, she would need a way to escape. To do that she needed to make friends with her guards. Now, though, all she wanted was to say goodbye to her horse.

During the past three moons, Constant had borne her safely across nations. The horse had been provided for her when she joined the company of Keltoi, leaving her home in the Ural Mountains behind. When the Keltoi rode out this morning the horse was not with them. Since extra stock would slow them down, she suspected Thorn had sold him to the stable.

Dressed in her blue and green plaid jerkin and wearing her breeches, Klara opened the door and found herself standing eye-level with a goiter. Forcing her gaze upward, she addressed the tall warrior. "I'd like to go to the stables. Is that permitted?"

The guard was near to her own age, with walnut-brown hair and gold-flecked hazel eyes that danced with mischief the afternoon light. With a broad chest and massive biceps, he was beefy enough to wield his two-handed sword with ease. The warrior gave her a disapproving look. Not only was she a murderer and harlot, but she was wearing breeches, an article of clothing Mordvin women were forbidden to wear.

"The King's orders state you're free to move about the hall and grounds so long as you've got a guard with you," he said. "My job's to see you don't escape."

Klara shrugged her shoulders. "Fair enough." She had no intention of escaping today anyway. To be successful she needed a plan and reasonable assurance of getting away. An ill-timed or hasty attempt would only result in a stint in the hostage pit, where she would have no chance of escape.

As they crossed the lawn, Klara tried engaging the warrior in conversation. "If we're to be spending a great deal of time together, I think I should know your name. I suspect you already know mine."

"I'm Durt," he replied without breaking stride, though he had cast a lingering glance her direction.

"Well Durt, is guarding me an enjoyable task or an onerous one?" Klara asked, hurrying to keep pace with the guard's long gait.

"I've not decided yet," he said. "Spendin' all day standin' outside your door like Zsolt did this morning sounds terribly boring. Walking you to the stables is easier, provided you don't try mounting a horse."

Winking, Durt smiled at her. Klara shook her head. Mischief still sparkled in his eyes, but there was no malice in the smile. Just a good-natured dolt, who simply thought he was being witty.

"I promise not to run off," Klara said, returning the smile. "Still, your time spent outside my door might be put to good use. I imagine you could use it to sharpen your blades."

"I'd not thought of that," he conceded, scratching his stubbly jaw.

Upon reaching the stable, Klara let out a sigh of relief. Constant was just where she had left him. Pressing her forehead into the horse, she drank in his earthy scent and patted his neck. The buckskin gelding leaned into her, nearly knocking her over. She and the horse had developed a special bond on the road. It was evident that he missed her attention and affection while she was recovering in the infirmary.

She was still petting Constant when Geza, the stable master, walked up. He was a friendly middle-aged man with salt and pepper hair and a soothing, gravelly voice.

"They said you'd be down to look after him, soon as you was well," Geza said, nodding toward the horse. "Them Keltoi must think highly of you; they've left you very well off."

"What do you mean?" Klara asked. So far as she knew, she was a pauper, and one sentenced to death at that.

"Few women own four horses," Geza said, patting Constant. "I thought they'd sell the extras, but they wouldn't hear of it. They were adamant that all the horses belonged to you. Left some tack and other items here as well. I was told nothing was to be sold unless... well, nothing is to be sold."

"Unless I'm put to death?" Klara asked. Leaving Constant behind was understandable if they hoped she might be freed or find means of escape, but to leave other horses made no sense. If Dovsk killed her, they not only lost the mounts but the money that might have come from their sale.

"Yes, miss," Geza said. "The sale is dependent upon yer death. But let's hope it don't come to that. Are you fetching yer belongings back to yer quarters or do you want me to keep them here?"

"As far as I know, I have all my belongings," Klara said. "I can't fathom what they left or where the extra horse comes from. When we arrived we had twelve horses. This morning all five of them rode their own mounts and they were leading four pack horses, so there should only be three horses here."

"Didn't you know the bay mare foaled?" Geza asked, his voice filled with an affection for the beasts he worked with. "The little colt was born Pyhä Äkräs Day. Looks like he might have come a bit early, too. With his dam on the road and all the unpleasantness in the stable that night, it's no wonder he came before he was due. Still, he's got the look of a fighter. I reckon he'll live."

"The extra bay?" Klara asked. "Show me."

Geza led her and Durt to a stall where a bay mare stood nursing a red foal. The little colt was sorrel and, covered in his fine baby hair, he actually appeared red. Klara entered the stall and made friends with the mare.

"He's not been named yet," Geza said, leaning over the stall's rail to admire the colt. "They said you were to name him."

"The mare hasn't a name either," Klara said, scratching the mare's forehead. "Or if she did, it's lost. We didn't learn it when we acquired her." She stroked the mare's neck while the little colt nuzzled under its mother's belly searching for a teat. The possibility of her own pregnancy terrified her. The sight of mother and child, even if they were horses, brought tears to her eyes.

Sighing heavily, Klara said, "The mare I'll name Despair and the colt I'll name Fury, since that's all that consumes me now."

Leaving the stall, Klara saw the Keltoi had also left her Flax, a chestnut gelding who owed his name to his flaxen mane and tail. The horse had been Nuallan's mount. Nuallan's bearded head was supposed to be on a spike somewhere on the King's grounds. Believing it might quell the anger welling up inside her, she longed to see it now.

Addressing Geza, Klara said, "The tack can remain in the stables. If anything else was left, send it to Pendrwyrd's hut." Then addressing Durt, she said, "Will you take me to see Nuallan's head?"

"Gladly," Durt said. "It's at the fortress gate, with the rest of his body, too!" He seemed entirely too eager to view the carnage. Klara shrugged. Killing was his business.

The city's inhabitants stared as Durt led Klara across the grounds. When she first rode into Gnyozdovo, she drew stares for being armed, wearing breeches, and riding in the company of Thorn, the Kenetlo King. Worse, the company's weapons expert had bragged of her skill among the warriors. That gossip made its way to the noble women, prompting Lady Rozsa to introduce Klara to everyone she met as "The Lady Killer." The reputation was not helped when, in a fit of rage, she killed Nuallan before an audience that included King Dovsk and those who attended court yesterday. The city's inhabitants were giving her a wide berth now.

The putrid odor of decay reached Klara's nostrils long before she spotted Nuallan. King Dovsk had added his own gruesome touch by propping Nuallan's body up beside his head. The heat caused the carcass to swell. Flies gathered. Her guard hung back, looking green.

Klara stood rigid, viewing the elder Kelto's lifeless frame. The sight was not nearly as satisfying as she had expected it to be. Nuallan was King Thorn's advisor. And a traitor. All who passed through the gate were able to see that she had carved the holly and spindle runes on his chest with her dagger before killing him. The runes indicated that justice had been fulfilled, but had it?

On the spike, Nuallan's stiff gray hair rustled in the wind. The braid of his beard had soaked up a good deal of blood and was crusty now. Well, Nuallan, she thought, you nearly cost me my head. Now, I have taken yours. His treachery had driven a wedge between her and her lover, Karn, and he was responsible for drugging her the night she was raped. Death felt like an inadequate punishment for the Kelto. Rage boiled within her. Were it possible to kill him twice, she would have.

Red-shirted warriors stared at her from the earthen ramparts, the pointed ends of the timber palisades just as menacing as their spears. From the lane below, commoners cast her furtive glances as they came and went, visiting the sprawling market just inside the city gate. Moksha filled her ears as the locals bartered in their native tongue and gossiped about her.

Klara's mother tongue was Skoloti, but she had grown accustomed to speaking the common tongue as she plied her trade in taverns and ale-houses. The trade language was a mixture of Skoloti, Moksha, and Gothic. She understood most of what was said. None of it was favorable.

Tired of viewing the body, Klara said, "I'm done here. Let's head for the garrison so you can stop at your barracks."

"Why'd you want to see the barracks?" Durt asked.

"I don't particularly want to see the barracks," Klara said. "I've just attracted a number of onlookers and figured that if I'm going back to the wizard's hut to get away from them, you may as well stop by the garrison and get your whetstone."

Klara drew just as many stares at the barracks as she did at the gate. The only difference was, these men did not pretend they were not looking.

When they reached his quarters, Durt seemed not to know what to do with her. Clearly, he did not want to let her out of his sight but could not bring her into his quarters. By now the whole township must know that she had bedded the squire before King Thorn raped her. Then, of course, there was the tryst with her lover and his cousin. If she accompanied Durt into his quarters, gossip would spread that she was bedding her guards, too. Klara was certain King Dovsk would not take kindly to hearing that rumored about the hall.

Red-shirted warriors lingered in the yard, waiting to see what would transpire, obviously eager for a show. The sun was hot overhead. Sweat trickled down her back. She had no intention of standing in the heat all day while waiting for Durt to make up his mind.

Placing a hand on Durt's arm, Klara addressed a group of warriors lounging near the door. "Gentlemen, it appears Durt has a bit of a dilemma. I cannot accompany him into his quarters in order for him to collect his whetstone and he cannot leave me here as he does it. Will you consent to watch me until he reemerges?"

One of the older warriors nodded to him, "You go ahead, we'll see she don't run off."

Durt collected his whetstone without incident. Then he took her arm and, as he led her away, leaned in to whisper, "Thank you kindly for that. I couldn't take another reprimand."

A warrior shouted across the parade grounds, "I thought you were supposed to be standing guard outside a hut. This don't look like punishment to me."

Durt turned crimson.

"If watching me is punishment, I'd like to know the offense?" Klara asked, looking up at him.

"Public drunkenness, in uniform, on Pyhä Äkräs Eve," Durt replied.

"Seems it was a bad night for both of us," Klara said and Durt cracked a smile. "Are you assigned to me for the whole moon or will you be rotating?"

"The whole moon," Durt said. "But for your sake I hope it won't be that long."

"It won't be," Klara assured him. Durt's revelation heartened her. She now knew escape was possible and whether he knew it or not, Durt was going to help her. The King's first mistake was assigning a young man, fond of drink, to guard a whore. With luck, King Dovsk might make other mistakes along the way.

Entering the wizard's hut, Klara saw Hanja, the serving girl, holding an odd assortment of items. The poor girl was clearly fearful of Durt, who had taken up his post outside the door. Mordvin women rarely interacted with foreigners, seldom strayed from their homes, and had a bad habit of doing whatever they were bid. Counting just fourteen years of age, and every bit as docile as her countrywomen, Hanja could only be described as a plain brown spot.

"They sent yer things up from the stable, miss," Hanja said, laying the pile on the table.

Klara was delighted to see that the items the Keltoi left behind were all of Nuallan's belongings. Like her, Nuallan had admitted to possessing pennyroyal. Pennyroyal not only prevented pregnancy, but in large doses was capable of ending one. Since the death sentence was dependent on pregnancy, pennyroyal meant freedom. All she needed now was a little bit of privacy.

Hanja was pleasant and diligent in her work. And easily duped. Since Pendrwyrd was not in the room, Klara invented an errand for Hanja.

Opening Nuallan's pack, Klara slipped her hand in, searching for his purse. She withdrew her hand, clutching her prize. The purse was nearly empty. He must have spent a good deal to purchase the herbs he had used to drug her and Thorn. Well, some money was better than none.

Passing Hanja some coins, Klara said, "I can't walk through the village with guards always trailing after me. Since my shift was destroyed, I need you to get me another. And I'd like a length of black ribbon, too." Klara's shift had been torn into strips and used to bind her wounds on Pyhä Äkräs Eve. If she was ever to wear a skirt again, it needed replacing.

Hanja curtseyed. "Yes, miss. I'll be quick as you please. It'll be nice to see you out of breeches and dressin' like a lady again." Then she spun on her heels and slipped through the door, intent on her errand.

Because trousers were an article of clothing most women were forbidden to wear, when Klara had first arrived Hanja had mistaken her for a wizard. Recalling the disapproving look her guard had given her, the skirt might aid her cause when it came to befriending her captors. Who knew? The skirt might prove useful in other situations, too.

Once she had the room to herself, Klara upended Nuallan's pack searching for his stash of herbs. Disappointment washed over her as angry tears welled in her eyes. All she found was poppy, clover, and shepherd's purse. The latter two herbs she had absolutely no use for, but the poppy might come in handy. At the very least she might drug her guards. Nuallan's other belongings consisted of a bedroll, two changes of clothing, a pouch of cannabis, a leather map, his sword and dagger.

Klara put the map, herbs, and cannabis among her own items then pondered what to do with the rest of the booty. She had no training with a sword, but it might be turned into ready coin. She was still sitting there when Hanja returned.

In addition to the shift and ribbon, Hanja carried a tray laden with fresh blackberries, cold meat, bread, and cheese. "You've not eaten today, miss, so I brought food as well."

"Thank you, Hanja," Klara said. "Put the tray on the table."

Klara put Nuallan's belongings in her wardrobe. Then she changed out of her clothing and donned the new shift. Sitting on her bed, she took Karn's ring from her purse and threaded it on the black ribbon. Then she tied the ribbon around her neck. The ring hung above her collar, visible to all she met. As she caressed the ring, her own ring softly clinked against its mate. If she were sentenced to death, she wanted everyone to remember the reason why.

# About the Author

Khaliela Wright is a freelance writer whose work has appeared in *IDAHO Magazine*, the *Latah Legacy*, and other outlets. Originally from Sandpoint, Idaho, Khaliela now lives in Potlatch where she currently works for the U.S. Census Bureau gathering information on income, employment, and housing trends in the Idaho panhandle. Refusing to be divided by state-line loyalties, she is a graduate of both the University of Idaho and Washington State University. Her free time is devoted to outdoor pursuits and, yes, finishing the trilogy. *Klara's Journey* is her first novel.

# Authors Need Reader Support

Support your favorite authors. If you enjoyed this book, please tell your friends and leave a review on Amazon and Goodreads. A review can be as simple as, "I liked it."

Know any high school students who are new adult readers? If they would enjoy this book, request that it be added to the Accelerated Reader Catalog by visiting https://www.renaissance.com/suggest-ar-quizzes-us/

CONNECT ONLINE
**Khalielawright.com**

LIKE ON FACEBOOK
**facebook.com/khalielawright.author**

FOLLOW ON TWITTER
**@KhalielaWright**

www.ingramcontent.com/pod-product-compliance
Lightning Source LLC
Chambersburg PA
CBHW061618210726

48287CB00001B/179